A

Linda Fai~
most le
childrer        ..~ades, she s                              ew
York County District Attorney, where sh~ .... ....~ of the Sex
Crimes Prosecution Unit. In 2010 she was the recipien~ of the
Silver Bullet Award from the International Thriller Writers association. Her Alexandra Cooper novels have been translated into
more than a dozen languages and have debuted on the *The Sunday
Times* and *The New York Times* bestseller lists, among others. She
lives in Manhattan and on Martha's Vineyard.

## ALSO BY LINDA FAIRSTEIN

The Alexandra Cooper Novels

*Final Jeopardy*

*Likely to Die*

*Cold Hit*

*The Deadhouse*

*The Bone Vault*

*The Kills*

*Entombed*

*Death Dance*

*Bad Blood*

*Killer Heat*

*Lethal Legacy*

*Hell Gate*

*Silent Mercy*

*Night Watch*

*Death Angel*

*Terminal City*

*Devil's Bridge*

*Killer Look*

Non-Fiction

*Sexual Violence: Our War Against Rape*

# LINDA
# FAIRSTEIN
# Deadfall

640 5275

Little, Brown

LITTLE, BROWN

First published in the United States in 2017 by Dutton, an imprint of
Penguin Random House LLC
First published in Great Britain in 2017 by Little, Brown

1 3 5 7 9 10 8 6 4 2

Map by David Cain

A CIP catalogue record for this book
is available from the British Library.

Hardback ISBN 978-1-4087-1028-9
Trade Paperback ISBN 978-1-4087-1027-2

Printed and bound in Great Britain by Clays Ltd, St Ives plc

Papers used by Little, Brown are from well-managed forests
and other responsible sources.

Little, Brown
An imprint of
Little, Brown Book Group
Carmelite House
50 Victoria Embankment
London EC4Y 0DZ

An Hachette UK Company
www.hachette.co.uk

www.littlebrown.co.uk

To the women who were

CAROLYN KEENE

You set my course

*Every man's life ends the same way. It is only the details of how he lived and how he died that distinguish one man from another.*

Ernest Hemingway

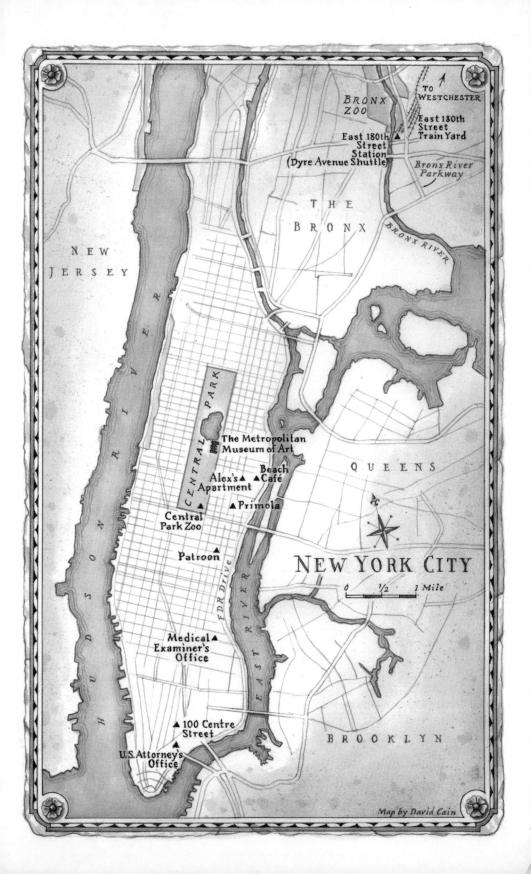

NEW
JERSEY

BRONX
ZOO

TO
WESTCHESTER

East 180th
Street
Train Yard

East 180th
Street
Station
(Dyre Avenue Shuttle)

Bronx River
Parkway

THE
BRONX

BRONX RIVER

QUEENS

CENTRAL PARK

The Metropolitan
Museum of Art

Beach
Café

Alex's
Apartment

▲Primola

Central
Park Zoo

Patroon ▲

FDR DRIVE

NEW YORK CITY

0      ½      1 Mile

HUDSON RIVER

EAST RIVER

Medical ▲
Examiner's
Office

▲ 100 Centre
Street

U.S. Attorney's ▲
Office

BROOKLYN

Map by David Cain

# ONE

I had stared at death before. I was way too familiar with the vagaries of murder.

I had seen it flex its muscles on the cracked pavement of New York City sidewalks and behind grimy stairwells in housing projects. I knew that doormen in the most expensive properties lining Central Park were often as powerless to stop it from entering the dwellings they guarded as the less fortunate who encountered it in random exchanges with strangers on the street.

I had comforted many of the shattered lives that murder left in its wake, and tried to do justice for them in a court of law for more than a dozen years.

But I had never held death in my arms until tonight. I had never cradled a killer's prey against my body—a life extinguished in an instant—while the blood dripped out onto my chest and pooled in my lap until the police arrived to release me from death's grip.

"You don't have to stay in here, Ms. Cooper," the older of the two uniformed cops said to me. "The medical examiner says you can wait in her office."

"I'm good for now," I said. "Thank you."

"It's not healthy," he said. "What you're doing, that is. Staring at a dead man."

I was standing in the autopsy room at the morgue, about ten feet away from the body of the district attorney, less than an hour after he taken two bullets to the head.

"I'm just— I'm just thinking, Officer. This is where I need to be at the moment."

The younger cop was at the far end of the metal gurney, facing me, as expressionless and erect as a soldier of the Queen's Guard at Buckingham Palace.

"Dr. Palmer's got a change of clothes for you, ma'am. She thought you'd be more comfortable if you got out of those bloody things, after the Crime Scene guys take pictures of you."

There wasn't much left of Paul Battaglia's skull. I didn't have the best angle of vision to see it, leaning against the counter where some of the tools were laid out, but that fact was pretty clear to me.

I lifted the glass of Scotch to my face and ran it back and forth under my nose. Jeremy Mayers, counsel to the chief medical examiner, was a snob about his single malts. That trait, at a bar after hours, usually irked me. I was fine with a few shots of Dewar's on the rocks. But in this cheerless space, reeking of formalin, the stronger concentration of my favorite amber liquid—without ice—helped me deal with the pervasive odor of death. Jeremy had poured me a snootful from his private stash.

"Did you hear me, Ms. Cooper?" the older cop said. "We can go down the hall and wait for the homicide team there."

"Sorry," I said, inhaling the peat-soaked flavor of Jeremy's Lagavulin before I lowered the glass to my mouth and took a sip. "I did hear you. I'm not ready to go."

"Just so you know we can, soon as you're ready."

"We? Aren't you here to stand watch over the DA's body?"

Paul Battaglia wasn't a candidate to lie in state anywhere, but it would be tradition for an NYPD honor guard to be with the body until his burial.

"No, ma'am," the officer said, pointing to his silent young comrade. "The kid's got Battaglia tonight. I've got you."

"*Me?*" That line got my attention. "What are you talking about?"

"I've got orders to stay with you, Ms. Cooper."

I bridled at the suggestion. "I'm in the morgue. I'm a prosecutor who works with these docs and technicians every day. The dead man is my boss. I've got Detective Chapman here and a posse of detectives on the way," I said. "I'm not in any danger."

"Nobody said you were."

"Then what did they tell you, Officer? Why have they got you glued to me? I'm not the suspect in this tragedy either."

He shrugged off my comment and looked away from me.

"The district attorney fell into my arms when he was shot, do you understand that?" I had started to gesture with my hands, quickly catching myself so no Scotch would slosh over the rim of the drinking glass and be lost to me. "I didn't kill him. I caught him."

"Whatever you say, ma'am. Orders is orders."

"Look, can you please go find Chapman and ask him to come here?" I said.

"Manhattan North Homicide? That Chapman?" the officer asked.

"Yeah. Mike. Tell Mike I need him, please."

The officer looked at the rookie, who made eye contact with him and nodded.

"Don't worry about leaving us," I said to my anxious captor. "If I run, just send an APB to the nearest Laundromat. That's about as far as I can get without being collared."

The older man turned and left the room.

I took another sip to steel my nerves and walked closer to the gurney.

Paul Battaglia had hired me out of law school at the University of Virginia. He was a legendary figure in national prosecutorial circles, Manhattan's elected district attorney for more than three decades. As one of the kids on his great legal staff—five hundred lawyers in all—I had idolized him.

Paul had been good to me from the outset, and I had risen quickly when he tapped me to lead the country's pioneering Special Victims Unit at an unusually early stage in my career. With his complete backing, the lawyers in my unit had created innovative techniques to get more victims access to the courtroom and had fought vigorously for legislative reform.

When I reached the side of the district attorney, I put my hand on his outstretched palm. It was cold now, of course, and it didn't respond to my touch, as I knew it wouldn't. But I did it to make myself feel better—putting my fingers around his, offering some sign of affection in this steel-structured room, which was the most lifeless place I'd ever known.

"You can't touch the body, ma'am," the young cop said. "You shouldn't do that."

I nodded. "You're right, Officer."

My feelings about the district attorney had been less than generous throughout this past year, but despite my discomfort level about his integrity, I found myself welling up with tears. I gently patted the sleeve of Battaglia's dark suit. "Good night, Paul," I whispered. "Rest in peace."

There would be no answers to the flood of questions that had overwhelmed me from the moment I had heard him call out my name in the late-night semidarkness and walk toward me—quite unexpectedly—up the steps of the Metropolitan Museum of Art.

I braced myself now to look at his face, or what was left of it, one more time. One of the bullets—the one that penetrated Battaglia's skull and landed behind me, taking along bits of his brain—had blown an eye out as it exited. The other piece of lead presumably lodged in the bony cartilage of his cranium, maybe blocked by the base of the classic Roman nose that accented his patrician appearance.

I walked slowly, circling the gurney, which caused the rookie cop to begin to fidget.

"Don't worry. I won't touch him again," I said to the kid. "I've worked for the man for a long time. I can't believe this has happened to him."

I couldn't believe it had happened to me, either, but that was a rather self-serving observation, of no importance to anyone else.

Paul Battaglia's body was part of the crime scene, which stretched from Fifth Avenue, where the shooter had leaned out a car window to fire at—well, presumably at the district attorney—to the museum entrance, several yards from where I had been standing.

The blasts had been so powerful that when Battaglia was struck and fell forward, he was lifted out of one of his shoes. The black-laced wing tip was still on his right foot, but his left foot, covered in a dark gray sock with black dots, rested on the gurney as though he had started the process of undressing for the night.

The strong odor of formalin in the room—already coating my hair and clothing, as it always did—made me cough. I finished my circumnavigation of the body and returned to my post against the counter, sticking my nose into the glass of Scotch to steady myself.

I kept thinking of things I wanted to know, but I wouldn't get any answers from the man on the table.

"Officer," I said, walking back over to the gurney and leaning against the left side of it. "I wonder if you can tell me—has anyone else from my office been here to see Mr. Battaglia yet? I mean before I came in."

"Don't know, Ms. Cooper. I got pulled off scooter patrol in the precinct to be here, like half an hour ago. I relieved the cops who rode with the morgue van to bring the DA down."

One of the city's great columnists—often quoted to us by Battaglia—once said, "Never kill anyone in a landmark location." First, because you make yourself instantly notorious for media purposes, and second, because the site itself was always compromised by a crush of onlookers.

I had never seen a body removed from a crime scene faster than Paul Battaglia was carted off from in front of the Met. The Costume Institute gala had ended a short time before—with hundreds of well-dressed fashion industry elites filling the sidewalks to find black cars and Ubers—and in a city that never sleeps, the museum's Fifth Avenue venue on the eastern perimeter of Central Park was always a magnet for rubberneckers, day or night.

Mike Chapman had pulled me back into the museum—security made a path for us—and out through a basement door for the ride down here to the morgue. The corpse made better time than we did.

"Ms. Cooper, ma'am," the rookie said. "You're leaning against the gurney."

"It's just my hand on the metal rim, Officer." I couldn't stop looking at the still figure that had been so very alive two hours earlier.

"There's blood all over your outfit, Ms. Cooper. You don't want to be contaminating the DA's clothing, do you?"

"It's dry, Officer. I promise you that," I said, looking down at the stained front of my borrowed sweatshirt and leggings.

"Still, it could fleck off and—"

"You're right," I said, taking two steps back, clasping my glass with both hands.

"I don't mean to put you off, ma'am," the officer said, eyes face forward again. "You mind my asking what he was like?"

"Paul Battaglia? Most people would say he was the best in the business."

For me, his character was much more complicated. He had been district attorney longer than most New Yorkers could remember. His campaign slogan—from his first run through eight terms—had been YOU CAN'T PLAY POLITICS WITH PEOPLE'S LIVES. But he had lost sight of that sentiment somewhere along the way and was more adept at using people for political purposes than Machiavelli had been.

"This must be so difficult for you," the cop said.

"It is." But not for the reasons he or anyone who wasn't close to me would think. I had once been so devoted to Battaglia that I never looked for flaws, or I had been blind enough that I hadn't seen them. Much more recently, I had become disillusioned with the man. I distrusted some of his alliances with corrupt figures among the city's satellite players, just as he had taken to undermining and second-guessing many of my investigative tactics.

It was difficult for me because Paul Battaglia and I had unfinished business, and now there were things that we could never resolve.

I bowed my head and looked again. There was just a slight indentation in the skin on the fourth finger of his left hand where Battaglia had once worn a wedding ring. For reasons unknown to me, he had taken it off months ago.

I lifted the drinking glass and placed it against my forehead. Had it been my usual cocktail, with ice, it would have refreshed me and anesthetized my pounding headache. But this motion was just a senseless habit that was no help to me at all.

The door opened and closed behind me. I didn't look up.

"How's the old man doing, Coop?" Mike said. "You making sure he's still dead?"

The comment took the rookie by surprise. His eyebrows rose and his expression changed. It was obvious he'd never met Mike Chapman before.

"Actually, I'm making sure that if Battaglia has a glimmer of life in him and has anything left to say, he says it to me."

"Unanswered questions," Mike said. "I know you don't like 'em, Coop, but very few people check out leaving a tidy package behind for their heirs, professional or personal—especially when the Grim Reaper shows up out of the blue like this."

"Why the hell was he rushing up the museum steps, after midnight, saying he had to talk to me?" I asked.

"To rip you a new one."

"Now, what makes you think that?" I said, turning to face Mike. "That's stooping lower than I would go."

"Really? I'll have to reset the bar a little higher. I thought you were as low as you could possibly get," Mike said. "'Cause all Battaglia's done lately is criticize you. Here you are, on a leave of absence, and you disobey all his orders to stay out of a case. Instead, you bring it to a head in front of an audience—"

"I didn't do anything to make the case break last night."

"Don't whine, Coop. It doesn't become you," he said. "Break it you did, with the police commissioner doing an instant presser at the museum, without waiting for the district attorney, and crediting you for your involvement too. Maybe Battaglia was charging up to butt heads with you again."

"What happened to the days when he and I trusted each other implicitly?"

"You—his fair-haired golden girl? Long gone, those days," Mike said, taking the glass of Scotch from my hand. "And drinking too much of this embalming fluid won't help, either."

I grabbed his wrist to hold the glass in place and breathed in one more shot of Scotch. "I wasn't drinking, Mike. I was sipping. Sniffing and sipping."

"No games, girl. This is all unfolding live, in prime time."

"Take me home, then," I said, glancing back over my shoulder at Battaglia. "Just take me home."

"That's a trick not even Houdini could pull off," Mike said. "No disappearing acts, according to Commissioner Scully."

I stepped forward to press myself against Mike's chest and feel his arms around me. He pulled back faster than I could get to him. "But—"

"Let's have you photographed in this getup before we hand over your clothing to the detectives."

"You saw everything I did, Mike," I said. "You talk to the guys tonight. They can interview me tomorrow."

"Any witness ever said that to you, Madame Prosecutor, and you'd start waterboarding her on the spot."

"I'm so tired, Mike. I'm so sick to my gut and frightened and confused," I said. Then I swiveled in place to take another look at the late Paul Battaglia. "And there's a part of me that feels really guilty about this."

The rookie cop turned to look at me.

"You didn't hear that, kid," Mike said, shaking his finger at the young officer. "She's not talking guilt as a matter of law."

"I feel—"

"No more running off at the mouth, Coop. You didn't fire the gun, okay, did you? That's guilt with a capital *G*. We don't know what the fuck was going on with the district attorney."

"Nothing good, Mike. You know that for sure. Whatever it is, it got him killed."

"C'mon. Crime Scene needs photos of you in your Halloween costume. Then you've got to answer some questions."

"Who's handling the investigation?" I asked, walking slowly toward the door.

"The mayor's putting a task force together with Scully," Mike said. "A new guy from Brooklyn South Homicide—"

"New? He's cutting his teeth on the murder of the Manhattan DA?"

"New because it can't be anyone who knows either one of us, Coop. Also, some broad just assigned to Major Case a couple of weeks back. And a task force designation because they have to throw in a few feds for the white-collar cases Battaglia was working with the US attorney."

"That means I've got to relive my tortured history with the man," I said, thinking about the details that would be gathered in the detective division reports, known as DD5s. "Every DD5 and interview will be public record when his killer goes to trial."

"You're always looking at the dark clouds, Alexandra Cooper," Mike said, holding the door open for me.

"I'm in a morgue, Mike, in the middle of the night, next to the body of the man who trained me to be what I am today."

"He sniped at you pretty good too. He had you in his sights these last few months and he nipped at your heels whenever he could," Mike said. "*Mortui non mordant.*"

"Save your parochial school Latin for the funeral mass. It's lost on me."

"That's not from the nuns, Coop. Think Robert Louis Stevenson. *Treasure Island*," Mike said. He cocked his finger and thumb and fired an imaginary bullet at the corpse. "It's your chance to get back on your feet."

I repeated the three Latin words. "*Mortui non mordant?*"

"Could be your lucky day, Coop," Mike said. "It means 'Dead men don't bite.'"

# TWO

I stood against a plain white wall in one of the conference rooms while Hal Sherman took a set of photographs for the case detectives. The first few were full frontal of me in the bloody sweatshirt and leggings. Then I was directed to hold both arms out at shoulder height, so the full pattern of spatter and stains was visible. Next there were close-ups of my face from every angle, which must have resembled mug shots of a felonious homeless woman. I turned to each side, as Hal asked me to do, before I posed with my back to the camera.

"Good to go, Alex," Hal said, leaning over the long table to make notes. "Give me a scrip of the items, please. Manufacturer and size."

"I don't know," I said. "They're not mine."

"Whose, then?" he asked.

"Mike and I were at the Met. I was dressed up for that fashion show at the start of the evening," I said, "till I got into a bit of a wrestling match."

"Oh, yeah. Our other team covered that mess," Hal said. "You lose your ball gown there, Cinderella?"

"Traded it in for a hairdresser's sweatshirt and these leggings from a model. I think there's blood on my sandals, too, Hal."

"We'll take it all, Alex. Dr. Palmer left some of her jogging clothes in the bathroom for you. I'll bag what you're wearing and you can get on with the business at hand."

I headed for the door—the restroom was between Palmer's

office and the conference room—then turned back to Hal. "This guy from Brooklyn South who's the lead dog, do you know him?" I asked.

"Jaxon Stern? Fresh out of Internal Affairs," Hal said. "Yeah, I know him. Homicide is his reward for squealing on cops for three years in IAB."

"What's he like, other than that? I mean, is he up to a case as big as this?"

"Smart enough. Good detail man, which sometimes causes him to lose the larger picture," Hal said. "Dogged. Bit of an attitude. Humorless."

"That won't last long around Mike," I said. "We'll be okay in this, I guess. I'm so used to working with teams of guys I know and trust."

"You'll get to know him pretty fast, Coop," Hal said. "He's a full-on prick. Don't let anything come out of your mouth that you'll regret saying later on."

I closed the restroom door behind me. What had I done to draw a full-on prick when I found myself dead center in an NYPD investigation?

I took off the sweatshirt and leggings, careful to keep them separate from each other so there was no cross-contamination of evidence. Palmer had been thoughtful enough to give me a new pair of underwear—the kind kept in emergency rooms so that rape victims who had to give up their clothing for testing could go home with clean panties. I folded my own so that Crime Scene could voucher them, in case any blood had seeped through the outer garments.

When I stepped over to the sink and checked myself out in the mirror, I saw that my face was worse than an image from a horror movie.

My skin was ghostly pale, smudged with dirt and blood and in all likelihood a bit of Battaglia's gray matter. My hair was so disheveled it looked like a circus clown's fright wig. It was matted and snarled, and some kind of foreign residue had nested there.

My eyes were bloodshot, and although I had teared up in the autopsy room, I didn't remember until now that I had cried all the way downtown in Mike's car. My thoughts were running out of sequence, and I knew too well how trauma could make that happen.

I squeezed the container and filled my hands with liquid soap, running the water to get it hot at the same time. Then I dipped my head down and scrubbed my face for at least two minutes.

I looked up, noted a slight improvement, but didn't feel any cleaner than when I started.

Of course Emma Palmer had a shower. How else to get the day's distinctive odor and debris off? It was behind another door in the bathroom. I went inside and turned it on, opening cabinets and drawers to find a clean towel and shampoo.

I waited for steam to form in the shower, then stepped in. I lathered my hair and held my face up to the showerhead, rubbing my skin so hard that I thought the top layer might come off in my hands.

After I toweled off and combed out my hair, I put on the one-size-fits-all underpants, courtesy of the Bellevue ER. There was room for at least one more woman inside the cheap, stretchy panties with me. Palmer hadn't thought of giving me a bra, but no one would even notice that since I didn't do much to come close to filling a B-cup.

I was thirty-eight years old and five feet ten inches tall. Dr. Palmer was in her midfifties, also tall and lean. Her zippered jogging jacket fit me fine, and the pants were a size six too, so I was all set to meet my interrogators.

I padded out of the bathroom in crime scene booties, which Palmer had also left for me.

When I reached her office, the door was open. Mike was inside, talking to Mercer Wallace. They were alone together.

Mercer dwarfed both of us in sheer physical size. He didn't say a word to me, but grabbed me by my shoulders and pulled me close to him.

He was a Special Victims detective—with as much empathy and warmth as he had intelligence and skill. Like me, he appreciated the need to handhold his victims and get them through the cold criminal justice system intact. Mike, on the other hand, worked homicide as much because it spared him dealing with living victims as because he did the job so well.

"What's going on?" I said to him. "Wake me up from this nightmare, will you?"

"No need to talk, Alex," Mercer said. "Plenty of time for that. You need to take a few minutes to gather your thoughts and get yourself together. Just hold tight."

I took a few deep breaths, cushioned against Mercer's powerful chest.

"Just get through the next few hours," Mercer said. "This will be over before you know it."

"Did you see anything, Mercer?" I asked, twisting my head around to look up at him.

"I was still inside the museum," he said. "But it wouldn't matter if I did. They need to talk to you first."

"Will you wait for me?"

"Of course we will," Mike said. "You're going to like Kate Tinsley."

"Major Case?" Mercer asked.

"Yeah. I worked a serial killer with her two years ago. A couple of years older than you, Coop. Totally stand-up broad."

"I hear the homicide cop is—" I started to repeat Hal Sherman's description, but stopped in my tracks when Mike held his hand up in my face.

"All depends who you heard it from," the man in the doorway said. "I'm Stern. Detective Jaxon Stern. Brooklyn South."

Mike held out a hand to shake, taking the detective's business card with his left hand. "Mike Chapman. Manhattan North."

"Mercer Wallace," my friend said, letting go of me to make the proper introduction. "Manhattan Special Victims Unit."

"Wallace? I'm Stern," the detective said.

He was shorter than all three of us—a stocky five foot eight, and lighter-skinned than Mercer. If he owned a smile, we hadn't seen it yet.

"I'm Alexandra Cooper," I said.

"Somebody give you permission to shower?" Stern asked.

"I—I—uh . . . I had to get myself—I—I—I had to clean myself up," I said.

"The medical examiner went over her from head to toe when we got here," Mike said. "She swabbed some samples from stuff that landed on Coop's skin and in her hair, and Hal Sherman has a complete set of photographs."

"I expect that will be the last question you answer for her, Chapman," Stern said. "She'll get over her stammering, I promise you."

Mike was biting the inside of his cheek as he stared at the detective's card. "Jaxon. J-A-X-O-N?" Mike asked, a bit too snidely. "Your mother didn't have spell-check on her laptop when she went into labor?"

"Spare me the 'yo mama' jokes, Chapman. It's an old family name."

"Okay, Jaxon," Mike said, "what's your plan?"

"I said it's Stern, man. Detective Stern. No need to get so cozy on our first date."

"Break it up, both of you. This sounds like kindergarten, guys," Mercer said. "It's been a long night for the three of us, Stern. You want Ms. Cooper?"

"Yeah, I do."

"Here?"

"Dr. Palmer said we could use her office," Stern said, looking around and eyeing the chair behind Palmer's desk. "This is good. Tinsley's just signing in at the front door. You know about her, Ms. Cooper—she's the officer you're going to like."

"Okay if I get her a Diet Coke from the machine before you start talking to her?" Mike asked Stern.

"If it helps sober her up."

"Who the hell do you think you are, Detective?" I said, too loud for my own good, slamming my hand down on the desk. "Where's the lieutenant? Where's the commissioner? I don't have to take any flak from you."

"See that, Chapman? She's got no stutter at all," Stern said. He threw his memo book on Palmer's desk and walked around it to stand behind her high-backed chair. "Word on the street says you've got yourself a bit of an alcohol problem, Ms. Cooper."

"The only problem I have at the moment is you, Detective Stern."

I had done the surname thing myself, more times than I could count. The formality kept the witness at arm's length and made her—in this case, me—doubly aware that we weren't buddies while in this hunt, even if I thought we were working for the same purpose.

"Have you been drinking tonight, Ms. Cooper?" Stern asked.

The physical dynamic in the room was disconcerting. No question Stern had put himself in the driver's seat, behind Palmer's enormous metal desk. Mike had moved toward the door to go to the vending machine, and now the only thing keeping him from taking a jab at Stern was Mercer's long left arm, holding him back.

"What do you mean?" I asked.

"Alcohol. I think you know exactly what I mean."

"I was kidnapped a month ago, Detective. I—I've been struggling with some PTSD issues for a few weeks, but I'm beating it now, okay?"

"Dewar's. Rocks. No twist," Stern said to me. "Have a familiar ring?"

"You're a quick study, Detective," Mike said. "I hope you know half as much about the cases she's tried and the assholes she's sent up the river and the pedophiles she's put away and the team of prosecutors she leads and—"

"Get the soda for her, Chapman," Stern said. "I asked you if you've been drinking tonight, Ms. Cooper."

I looked at Mercer, but he was stone-faced. I knew Stern was giving me the most basic test questions, as irrelevant as they were to Battaglia's murder. He would later ask Mercer and Mike the same things about me, trying to assess the credibility of each one of us—checking to see if any of us would lie for the other.

"I—uh—I was at a party at the museum. At least it started as a party," I said. "I might have had a glass of champagne before all the trouble broke out."

I knew my own rules for witnesses who'd been partying or barhopping. For each drink they admitted to me, I usually multiplied the number by three. Most people tried to make themselves look better in the eyes of the person who was judging the factual recall, and one way to do that was to minimize the amount of liquor consumed.

"Oh," I said, "I just remembered that at the very end of the night, the three of us were in the Temple of Dendur and—"

"Don't speak for these guys," Stern said. "Just tell me about your own actions."

"Well, Mercer brought me a glass of Scotch, but I wanted to

get out of there and go home. I really didn't drink much." No more than half the large glass, anyway, and a homicide at point-blank range has a sobering effect.

"How about here, at the morgue?" Stern asked.

"Here?" I said. I was stalling for time, as witnesses always did when they repeated a simple question before answering it. "You mean tonight?"

I was doing a double stall, breaking it down into two questions, two repeats.

"Jeremy Mayers's private stock. You have any of that?"

Great. Even Jeremy was a snitch.

"She wasn't drinking, Stern," Mike said. "She was sniffing. I'm the one who told her to sniff a glassful to keep that wretched odor of death out of her nose. The glass is still in the room with the dead body. If Coop was into drinking, it would have been an empty vessel."

"You're out of here, Chapman," Stern said. "Stick around down the hall, 'cause you'll be next."

"Mike," I said, reaching out to him, "Can I just—?"

"You'll be fine, Coop. Answer the man's questions," Mike said. "Don't waste any time trying to charm him. He clearly got his merit badge in policing from the Gestapo."

"Hey, Mike," a woman said, turning the corner and entering the room just as Mike was backing out. "Bad night in Black Rock. Back off my partner, okay? We've got work to do."

"Kate. Go on in," Mike said, patting her on the shoulder. "Meet Detective Stern."

Kate Tinsley stepped in the doorway and raised her hand to greet all of us. "Kate Tinsley, Major Case."

I nodded in her direction.

"Sorry to be running late, Stern," she said. It was obvious that she already knew him or had met him once she'd arrived here at

Palmer's office. Whether they had just been teamed up or had worked cases earlier on, she was smart to present a united front with him to the three of us.

"You must be Alexandra Cooper."

"I am," I said, pushing against the arms of the chair to stand up.

"No need," Tinsley said. "Just be as comfortable as you can. What a rough night you've had."

I nodded again, taking in the woman I guessed to be five or six years older than me, heavyset, with a round face ringed with curly black hair.

"I'm Mercer Wallace," Mercer said, reaching out his hand.

"I figured that," she said, smiling at him before looking down at me. "How are you feeling, Ms. Cooper? Ready to get this done?"

I was in no mood to be played against the good cop/bad cop bullshit setup. I had a very short story to tell and I was anxious to put it in their hands.

"Sure."

"Are you and Mike going to wait for us to finish with Ms. Cooper?" Tinsley asked Mercer. Mike was already out of sight.

"Yes. We'll be down the hall," Mercer said.

"I've got separate rooms set up for you, Detective," Stern said. "We'd appreciate it if you each keep to yourself."

"Understood."

"And best to stay off the phone with your wife," Stern said to Mercer, "if you don't mind."

"Actually, that's one thing I do mind," Mercer said. "I owe her a call, Stern. My kid has a fever and I'm checking in regularly. I won't dish about your case."

Mercer's wife, Vickee Eaton, was also a first-grade detective, with a senior post reporting to the Deputy Commissioner of Public Information. She virtually ran the department's press office. Their four-year old son, Logan, had spiked a fever a few hours ago, and Vickee had raced home from headquarters to take charge from the babysitter while the three of us were still unraveling facts on the fashion runway at Dendur.

"You waiting for the feds?" Mercer asked, on his way out the door.

"Not for this," Stern said. "Cooper and you guys are our piece of the case. They've got Battaglia's other jurisdictional assets."

"Stay chill, Alex. They're just doing what you do every day." Mercer pressed two fingers to his lips, then held them up and closed the door behind him.

I wriggled in my chair opposite Detective Stern as he opened his memo pad and got ready to write. I couldn't settle into a comfortable position, so I kept shifting my weight from side to side.

Kate Tinsley positioned her chair at an angle, next to mine, so that she could see both of our faces.

Jaxon Stern looked me directly in the eye and began to speak to me, slowly and purposefully. "First, Ms. Cooper, I need to tell you that you have the right to remain silent."

# THREE

"I have *what*?" I yelled back at him, grasping the arms of the old wooden chair.

Stern rested both arms on the desk in front of him. "The commissioner thinks it best to proceed with every caution in this case, treat you like any other ordinary witness who had a very conflicted relationship with the deceased—till we know where we're going, that is."

I was on my feet. There was nothing that would wake the dead in this place, but I was pretty sure my voice could shatter glass.

"I didn't shoot Paul Battaglia, Detective. For all you know, the killer could have been taking aim at *me* when he nailed the district attorney."

Kate Tinsley was leaning forward, trying to calm me down, urging me to sit and to lower my voice.

"You got a bad temper, Ms. Cooper?" Stern asked. "See, that's part of what makes this investigation so complicated. I come into this without a clue whose side you're on."

"Let me talk to Mike Chapman," I said, feeling like a caged animal, pressed against the wall of Palmer's office.

"Not an option, Ms. Cooper," Stern said, standing up, his hands on his hips. "Are you telling me you want to stop and bring in a lawyer, just because I give you the courtesy of informing you of your rights?"

"Of course I don't want a lawyer," I said, just like every other arrogant witness who should have seized the opportunity as soon as the moment presented itself. "I'm not in custody, am I?"

"No," Stern said. "I'm just reading your rights as a precaution. It's not just what the commissioner asked for. I do it every time I question—"

"I want Chapman and Wallace in here. I want to see Commissioner Scully. What you do 'every time,' Detective Stern," I said, making exaggerated air quotes around his words, "is of no more interest to me—no more an indication of your professional bona fides—than watching Charlie Chan solve murder cases."

He smirked and tried to interrupt me.

"You're just an amateur dick out of a cheap movie trying to play like the big boys," I said to him. "Pretending you're a grown-up who knows what he's doing in a homicide case. And you, Detective Tinsley, must be trying to put on a good front and let this horse's ass think he can bully me. You're better than that, and I don't believe for a minute that your cheesy smile is meant to disarm me."

"Stop it," she said to me.

"I've been bullied by real thugs, and you two don't begin to scare me."

"Sit down, why don't you," Tinsley said, "and let's just get this over with."

She had lost her smile in the process of walking me off my tantrum. I took my seat and threw back my head, staring at a chip in the paint on the ceiling to refocus myself.

"Give it your best shot, Detective Stern," I said. "Skip the rights and move on."

He played with his pen while he watched me blow off steam.

"Concentrate on the real victim here," Stern said. "Paul Battaglia. Stop feeling so sorry for yourself. Word on the street suggests your head is so swollen, Ms. Cooper, that if you had indeed been the target of the shooter, you would have been hard to miss."

"If there are as many words on the street as you seem to credit, you should have a short story under your belt by this hour," I said. "You'd hardly need me."

There was a sharp rap on the door before it opened. Mike stuck his head in and I covered my eyes with my hand so he couldn't see how fired up I'd become.

"Here's some caffeine," he said to me, passing the soda can to Tinsley. "And some dinner."

He threw me two packages of red licorice Twizzlers.

"So you all know, if you hear any wailing," Mike said, "Battaglia's wife just arrived. Dr. Palmer and some brass from headquarters are talking to her, before they bring her in to see the body."

I looked across the desk at Jaxon Stern. "Would you mind if we take five minutes so I can speak with Mrs. Battaglia? I'd like to offer my condolences while I have the chance for a private moment with her."

Mike Chapman spoke before Detective Stern could state his objection. "Keep on keeping on, you guys. You, Alexandra Cooper, are the last person in the world that Amy Battaglia wants to see right now."

"Why *me*?" The entire scenario continued to spin out of control. Nothing I said or did seemed to be right.

"At the moment, Coop, Mrs. B is blaming *you* for the death of the district attorney."

# FOUR

"What did you see, exactly, when you stepped out of the museum and stood on the top of the steps?" Stern asked me.

Stern had raced through the events of the evening before, including the famed Costume Institute's gala tribute to a designer named Wolf Savage. He had moved too quickly to get a thorough overview of the investigation into Wolf's death that had had its finale on the runway. He was not as good a detail man as Sherman had pitched him to be.

"There wasn't actually much to see at that hour of the night," I said, rubbing my eyes with my thumb and forefinger, as though it would help me see that scene repeated more clearly. "Mike and I waited inside the lobby—in the Great Hall—so that I was out of sight of the reporters and photographers while the commissioner spoke to them from the front steps."

"For how long did he talk?"

"Less than five minutes," I said. "Maybe just three. Scully didn't have a full picture of everything that had gone down. He just wanted to get the message out via the media that a big case had been solved, and one suspect was still on the loose."

"Then you walked outside?" Stern asked.

"I remember waiting until the camera crews had dismantled everything and packed up the gear in their vans. In fact, security was in and out of the door, letting us know the group was thinning and encouraging us to wait until people were gone."

"And the commissioner? You got him in your pocket too, Ms. Cooper? Didn't he get some face time with you?"

"I've known Keith Scully for a decade, Detective Stern. He's in nobody's pocket," I said. "He left me in good hands at that point, with Mike and Mercer. He's well aware of what I went through last month."

"Yeah, that's right. I almost forgot. You were a kidnapping vic," Stern said, flipping back through his notes. "Big news at the time. Full-court press by the department. Want to tell us about that now?"

"Another time, if it's a yes-or-no question."

I knew exactly what his interviewing technique was. I'd used it often with skittish witnesses who might be on their way to a breaking point.

Stern had jumped off questioning me about the confrontation on the museum steps at the moment of maximum impact in order to rattle me, to bring up an event that was even more personal, more stressful to me than Battaglia's death: my own abduction and days of captivity by depraved monsters.

He would count on unsettling me with flashbacks to my kidnapping, and then bounce over to the shooting again, hoping the cutaway would upset any narrative I'd put together in advance of his arrival.

"Stay on the kidnapping, Ms. Cooper," Stern said, ignoring the plaintive look on Kate Tinsley's face. "You didn't know the men who abducted you? It had nothing to do with one of your old cases, am I right?"

"Nothing."

"Something to do with Mike Chapman?" he asked.

"Indirectly."

"But you were already lovers by then, weren't you?"

I looked over at Kate Tinsley and threw up my hands. "You

know, in my own job," I said, "I could say 'objection' and we'd all just move on to something relevant."

"Yeah, but I could say 'overruled,'" Stern said, "and put the ball right back in your court."

"Yes, Mike and I were lovers—are lovers now. Asked and answered, Detective. Why don't you take your next shot?"

"Paul Battaglia put you on leave after the kidnappers released you, right?" he said, more than a dozen questions later.

"My shrink recommended the leave of absence," I said. "I was in no condition to work on cases when I was discharged from the hospital."

Stern hadn't known about the shrink. He gave himself away by raising his eyebrows when I made the remark, and stopping to scribble a note in his pad.

"How long have you been seeing a psychiatrist, Ms. Cooper?"

"Not quite as long as I've been sleeping with Mike Chapman," I said. "And his repressed sexual drive isn't what brought me to therapy, if that's what you're thinking."

Kate Tinsley bit her lip. Even Stern almost smiled.

"So, you've known Chapman since your first year in the DA's office," Stern said. "And you became intimate when?"

"Two months ago, Detective."

"That could hold a record for foreplay, Ms. Cooper."

"I'll answer your questions, Stern, but filter out your nasty commentary," I said.

"Why don't you eat something, Ms. Cooper?" Kate said. "I can send out to the bodega on First for food that's more nourishing than Twizzlers."

"No, thank you," I said.

"You must be starving," she said, continuing to play good cop as the tension between Stern and me mounted.

"Not even hungry." I was growing more and more nauseated on an empty stomach, but not hungry.

"So the museum security guards gave you the all clear, is that right?" Stern asked.

"They did."

"That's when you and Wallace and Chapman walked out the door?"

I had to think. "It was just Chapman and me," I said. "I don't remember seeing Wallace at that point."

"What did you do before leaving the museum?"

"Do? I didn't do anything," I said. "Chapman took off his jacket and put it over my shoulders. I remember double-checking with him about whether anyone was outside."

Jaxon Stern leaned in toward me. "What did he say to you?"

"'New York at night,'" I said, smiling despite myself and quoting Mike. "'Only pigeons and perps on the street.'"

"You think that line is funny, Ms. Cooper? Is that why you're smiling?"

"At the time, I did, Detective. In hindsight, nothing's the least bit humorous."

"Why did you ask Chapman that question?" Stern said. "About whether anyone was waiting on the street."

I shrugged. "I didn't want to be sandbagged. I didn't want to be photographed by some lone paparazzo, waiting for a gala guest who had lingered behind the others," I said. "Maybe waiting for the suspect that Scully just announced had escaped from the museum, hoping to get the money shot."

"You've been a poster girl for the tabloids before. Tell me the real reason for your concern."

"That was my only reason, Detective."

Jaxon Stern tapped the tip of his forefinger on the desktop. He did it four or five times, with force. A pause, and then four more again. It was annoying and disconcerting.

"You *knew* Paul Battaglia was on his way to talk to you," Stern said, lifting his finger to point it at my face. "That's why you had Chapman on the lookout, wasn't it?"

I had walked right into that one. That thought had not occurred to me at all.

"That's ridiculous, Detective," I said, throwing back my head and exhaling to blow off steam. "I had no idea that Battaglia was on his way to the museum. I still have no idea what he was doing there."

Kate Tinsley stood up and started to pace, walking behind me and facing Stern. His eyes shifted up and down in her direction. They were trying to box me in, thinking they had me on the ropes now that my concentration was slipping.

"Well, I sure don't have any idea why the district attorney was making his way up those steps in such a hurry," Stern said, "but I'm willing to bet my entire paycheck that you do."

"That would be a losing proposition for you, Detective," I said.

"When's the last time you talked to Battaglia before you saw him coming at you?"

"I was on a leave of absence, or did you forget that?"

"Now, why would that stop him from talking to you, Ms. Cooper?"

Damn. There was Battaglia's bodyguard, who would eventually let out that the DA had dropped by to see me earlier in the week.

"A few days ago is when I spoke with him," I said. "Saw him, actually."

"Saw him, did you?" Stern said, picking up his pen to make a note. "Tell us about that. Did you drop by the office?"

I shook my head in the negative. "Not the whole time I've been on leave," I said. "He was in his car. He stopped me as I was walking down the street to my apartment."

"House calls," Stern said. "Who knew the DA made house calls? Was he worried about your health, Ms. Cooper? Your mental health, that is?"

"He'd heard I was being drawn into a murder investigation," I said, admitting the fact because it would be readily available to Stern and Tinsley. "And he wanted to remind me to keep my nose out of it."

"We'll come back to that, Ms. Cooper," Stern said.

I had no doubt he would.

"Did you speak with him after that day?"

"No," I snapped.

"You can take your time, Ms. Cooper," Stern said. "Think before you blurt out a reply."

"Nothing to think about, Detective. That was the last time we spoke." It had been such an unpleasant conversation that I wasn't clear how a follow-up would have gone.

"And he didn't call you tonight," Stern asked, "telling you he wanted to talk to you? Tell you he was on his way to the Met? Text you to wait for him?"

"No."

"No point telling you that cell records and texts—well, they'll all be subpoenaed in a homicide investigation like this," Stern said. "Sometimes that reminder just jogs the memory a bit. Makes people remember a phone conversation that seemed so unimportant at the time."

"I'm familiar with your technique, Detective," I said. "I've used it with my fair share of witnesses. The ones I expect are lying to me, though. Not the honest ones."

"You never know, Ms. Cooper, do you? I've been fooled by the best of them."

"Don't you hate when that happens?" I said, fumbling with a package of Twizzlers, bending the wrapped licorice sticks in half and then bending them back in the other direction.

"Did you see him again, after that drive-by?"

"No," I said, just as quickly as I'd answered the question about the phone call. "Not until he came charging up the steps of the museum."

Jaxon Stern made another note. "Like I said, take your time."

"I didn't see him again. No," I said, firm and fast, holding my ground.

"You're certain?"

"I'm sure," I said, tired and angry at being challenged on every fact.

And then I remembered. Shit. I *had* spoken too fast.

"What's troubling you, Ms. Cooper?" Stern asked. "You've got a funny look on your face."

"That's just my face, Detective, like it or not."

I *had* seen Paul Battaglia after the day he had chewed me out in front of my building. Mike Chapman and I were together. I had seen Paul Battaglia but he hadn't seen me.

"Tell us what you're thinking, Ms. Cooper," the detective said.

"About how much I want to go home. Can we get this over with soon?"

"Did you see the district attorney between the afternoon—was it afternoon?—when he dropped by to talk with you, and this past evening, just to be clear?"

"No, Detective," I said. "I did not."

I had looked Detective Jaxon Stern in the eye and lied. I had a clear choice to tell the truth, about sitting with Mike Chapman in his unmarked car and spotting Paul Battaglia coming out of a town house on the Upper East Side, but I deliberately chose not to tell the truth.

My heart started racing again. I knew why I didn't tell Stern about the sighting. Mike was the only other person who'd witnessed it, and at the time, both of us had been puzzled about why

Battaglia was at the location where we'd seen him. I didn't know whether that moment had any significance in this investigation, but I wanted the chance to talk to Mike about that before I gave it up to Jaxon Stern.

Stern was asking more questions, but I was stuck in my lie as if I were up to my knees in quicksand and was unable to focus.

"Sorry," I said. "Could you please repeat what you just said?"

"You seem to be in the twilight zone, Ms. Cooper," Stern said. "Come on back to us."

I was trying to calm myself down. Mike wouldn't be the reason I got caught in the lie, because there was no point for Stern to question him about having seen Battaglia.

"I was just spacing out, Detective. My apologies. What did you ask?"

"I'm back with you at the top of the steps at the Met, this evening."

Of course you are, I thought. I was getting dizzier than a Mexican jumping bean, which was always the likeliest time for a witness to be tripped up.

"Oh," I said. "There."

"What happened from the time you walked outside?"

I closed my eyes for a second. "We used the revolving door," I said. "Mike went through first; then I followed. He reached for my hand and held on to me."

Stern looked over my head at Tinsley and smirked again.

"What did you see?" he asked me.

"Nothing. I was looking down. I had my eyes on the steps because it was kind of dark, and I was so exhausted."

"There came a point when you saw Paul Battaglia, right?"

"I heard him before I saw him," I said. "I heard footsteps, that is. I didn't know whose they were. I was halfway down to the sidewalk when I heard footsteps."

"Then?"

"I looked up because of the sound. I saw a man, but I couldn't make out who it was at first."

"Wait a minute," Stern said. "You've worked with this guy for at least a decade, and you couldn't figure out who he was?"

"I told you it was dark at that point, and he was wearing a dark suit," I said. "It was Chapman who told me the man approaching us was Battaglia."

"You're telling me that Chapman made him before you did?"

"Yes. He recognized the DA and told me that's who it was."

Stern looked back at Tinsley again. I was supposed to be rattled by all his smirking and sneering. But it was just rude, not unnerving.

"Like a warning?" Stern asked.

"No, Detective. I didn't need to be warned about Paul Battaglia. Chapman was just reassuring me that it wasn't a stranger."

"What did you say to him?"

"Nothing."

"Cat had your tongue, Ms. Cooper? I understand that's not usually the case."

"Battaglia spoke first," I said. "He called out my name and told me he needed to talk with me. Five minutes with me, is what he said."

Stern started tapping his forefinger on the desk again. Four times. Five. Six. "Now, about what?"

"What?"

"The five minutes, Ms. Cooper. You know what I mean. What was it that he wanted to talk with you about?"

"I don't know."

"C'mon, now."

I paused. I remembered a car pulling up on Fifth Avenue. I

remembered movement from the street—which must have been an arm coming out of the car window.

"I don't know," I said. "I didn't know then. I told him I wouldn't talk to him there."

I stopped again, biting my lip, as the image in my mind's eye seemed magnified.

"And I certainly don't know now," I said. "There wasn't another word spoken between us."

It was the image of Battaglia's face—his eyes opened wide and his mouth forming a word as he reached the step below me.

"Wild guess, Ms. Cooper. Take a wild guess."

"Bad form, Detective. I don't prosecute cases based on guesswork."

"Sometimes we get lucky this way, don't we, Tinsley?" Stern said. "Wild guesses sometimes hit the mark."

"Sure we do," she said. "We do get lucky. You must be wracking your brain, Alex, to think what drove the man to seek you out when someone was chasing after him. Maybe Battaglia knew his life was in danger, and he was coming to you for—well, you must have an idea for what."

"And all this time," I said to her, without turning my head, "I thought you were Stern's *silent* partner."

"Taking it all in, Alex. Taking it all in," Tinsley said.

A smart cop never did an interview like this without another cop to witness it. That way I couldn't deny something I'd said to them later on. I couldn't change my facts without two of them to swear to what I'd told them tonight.

"Wracking my brain," I said, "but I'm coming up empty. There must be word on the street, Detective Stern—to borrow a phrase."

I left out the sentence that had run through my mind at that moment—the last few seconds of Paul Battaglia's life—but then I hadn't said it out loud to Battaglia either. That I wouldn't talk to him then and there. That I wouldn't talk without a lawyer present. I didn't know if he was running up the steps to fire me for insubordination—for disobeying his orders to back off a murder case—or coming to me, as he had so many times over the years, because he wanted my help. It was the wrong time and place for either conversation.

"So what happened next?" Stern asked.

"I don't know, exactly."

"What do you mean, you don't know?"

I slumped down in the chair. The next minute of the evening's rerun was a jumble of sound and sight.

"I'm not sure what came first," I said. "Whether I actually heard the gunshots or I saw the DA fall forward, against me."

The fact of it didn't really matter, but it was the kind of detail that Stern and Tinsley would push me on over and over again.

"Being sure would help us," Stern said.

I raised my eyes to meet his.

"Two shots—one right after the other," I said. "I must have heard the shots."

They had split the quiet of the late city night.

"You're saying you heard them first?" Stern asked, looking down to make a note.

"I'm not sure," I said, shaking my head. "It seemed like it was all at once."

"What was all at once?"

"The loud noises, and then Battaglia almost lunging into my arms, against my body."

I thought the DA's brain had exploded in my face.

"I collapsed beneath him, on my back against the steps of the Met," I said. "We were a tangle of arms and legs. I tried to pull up and free myself from him."

I wanted the dead man off my body.

"But I couldn't move, Detective," I said, meeting his eyes with mine.

"Why not? Why couldn't you move?"

"Like I just said. The impact of the shots thrust Battaglia forward. His arms flew upward and somehow wrapped around my own as I crashed down too."

The DA and I were completely intertwined with each other when he died, just as we had often been in life.

"It was a deadfall, Detective."

"What does that mean, Ms. Cooper?" Stern asked. "No need to show off your vocabulary now. Just tell it straight."

"It's nothing but nature, Stern. You ought to get yourself off the street more and commune with the spirits," I said. "When you're deep in the woods, it's what you call a messy tangle of trees and limbs and underbrush."

I stood to stretch my legs. "That's exactly how Paul Battaglia and I wound up in the end—in a deadfall."

# FIVE

"Rise and shine, blondie," Mike said, rolling up the blinds on my bedroom window. "Four hours' sleep ought to hold you."

I put a pillow over my head and ignored him.

"Places to go, people to see, murder to solve."

I lifted the edge of the pillow and opened one eye. "It really happened, didn't it?"

"Yeah, babe. The district attorney is dead. Still dead."

"I didn't do it, did I?"

"Depends who you ask," Mike said. He was dressed only in a pair of light blue boxers, holding a coffee mug.

"Newspapers?" I said.

"Shooting was after midnight. Too late for the early editions on your doorstep."

"Have you looked online?"

"Ask me that again in a few hours, if you really want to know," Mike said. "Right now it's a sloppy mix of gossip and leaks and conspiracy theories. And right now, you're just part of the gossip, not anyone's coconspirator."

"What gossip?"

"Not good for you on an empty stomach."

"What time is it now?" I asked, rolling over and pulling back the covers, hoping to entice Mike to lie down beside me again. "Come back to bed and just hold me for a while, okay?"

"Can't say it's not tempting, but no can do, Coop. The *federales* want your ass," Mike said. "It's already eleven o'clock."

Detectives Stern and Tinsley had finished questioning me at about five A.M. They spent an hour with Mike before letting him bring me home, and were still talking to Mercer when we left the morgue.

I closed my eyes again. My head was pounding. The Tylenol I'd taken before I'd climbed into bed had long ago worn off. It was only Tuesday morning. "The feds are taking this over? What's the jurisdictional basis?"

"That you'd need an independent prosecutor to oversee this anyway," Mike said. "And Battaglia had a hand in some federal cases, too, as he always did."

"They really want me today?" I asked.

"They're putting together a team," Mike said. "Don't take it personally, Coop. The feds will have to interview Battaglia's entire senior staff and dig into all the big cases, open and closed, to see if this could have been revenge for someone he sent up the river."

I crushed the pillow against my forehead like it was a cold compress. "Why did that Jaxon Stern bastard have such a hard-on for me?"

"I don't have the answer yet, but I'm on it."

"Have you showered?" I asked.

"Next stop," Mike said, leaving his mug on my dresser. "Leave it on for you?"

"Please," I said, sitting up and swinging my legs over the side of the bed. "Mike, did you tell Stern and Tinsley about the last time we saw Battaglia?"

"What the hell did you think they were talking to me about?" he said, stepping out of his shorts and dropping them in the hamper.

"Not the shooting," I said. "I mean, last week, when we spotted him coming out of the town house."

"That didn't come up," Mike said. "Why? Did they know about it? Did they ask you?"

I hesitated. "Not exactly."

He backed up a few paces and turned to look at me. "'Not exactly,'" Mike said, mimicking me. "I want to know what questions Stern asked you."

"When had I seen the DA last, before the shooting."

"So you told them about when he stopped you on the street, near the apartment the other day."

"Of course I did," I said. He was with his driver then. I'd have been screwed if I'd covered that one up.

"Then you mentioned the bit about being in my car and seeing him when we least expected it?"

"That's what I mean, Mike," I said. "I left that one out."

"So you forgot it," he said. "No big deal. You can just remember it next time you sit down with the team."

I reached for the Tylenol bottle and the water glass next to my bed. "It wasn't a mistake, Mike. I lied about it," I said. "I lied to Jaxon Stern."

He leaned one arm on the doorframe in my bedroom. "Now, why the hell did you do that?"

"I was getting confused by the questions, Mike."

"You're not that easily confused. Trust me on that."

"All right, then. I was trying to second-guess what would be important in this investigation and what wouldn't be."

"Jesus, that is so damn like you to be second-guessing someone else's MO, Coop. And to do it with a guy like Stern, who'll be totally unforgiving if he figures it out," Mike said, slapping the wall and turning to walk out again.

"He can only figure it out if you tell him about it," I shouted after him.

Mike rotated back to face me and pursed his lips. He was mad at me. "You don't go to a doctor when you're really sick and leave out some of the symptoms to see how smart the guy is, to see if he can make a diagnosis with only some of the facts that you've chosen to tell him."

"No, but—"

"But people do it to cops all the time, right? See if us dumb schmucks can put the puzzle together with some of the facts missing."

"What difference does it make, Mike?" I asked. "The DA was coming out of George Kwan's town house the afternoon we saw him. And George Kwan was sitting in the museum last night, watching the events at the gala. He was one of the last guys to leave. His alibi is as solid as yours or mine."

"Give it up, Coop," Mike said. "You're a witness in this case. A very critical witness. You're not driving the investigation, are you? This team isn't going to let you anywhere near the wheelhouse, okay? The sooner you understand that, the better."

"Yeah," I said, standing up and wrapping my robe around me. "I'm beginning to get it."

"So the minute you walk in the door of that office in another hour—all clean and shiny-bright and eager to work your way back off the ice floe you found yourself on after the kidnapping and into respectability again—you get ready to regurgitate every last secret you think you and Paul Battaglia had on each other."

"I've got so many questions to ask them, Mike," I said, taking a sip from his coffee mug as I followed him into the bathroom. "They must have caught a license plate on one of the traffic cameras, didn't they?"

"You got it wrong, Coop. They've got a million questions to ask *you*. They're going to want to dig into what the hell was going on between you and Battaglia and the Reverend Hal Shipley."

"Oh, God," I said, running a washcloth under the cold water faucet and placing it over my eyes. "Talk about a man with a motive."

Shipley was a minister of sorts—a former backup dancer for a sixties R and B band and failed television commentator who scammed his Harlem flock with scheme after fraudulent scheme.

"There's a paper trail in that contretemps with Shipley that Battaglia tried to tamp down," I said. "And he really turned on me for getting in the middle of it."

"Those days of tamping down are over, kid. All that paper comes out of your desk drawer and into the sunlight," Mike said. "Not to mention one of the coconspirators in the Savage murder escaped not long before Battaglia came looking for you."

"I haven't forgotten," I said.

"We'd better let them know about any other dirtbags you're sitting on."

"That would be my entire caseload," I said. "I specialize in dirtbags. Can't think of a single one that has any respect for the DA, nor for me, for that matter."

Mike had stepped into the shower and the room was filling up with steam, which actually felt quite good.

"Who's got it for the feds?" I asked.

"I don't know who the agents are yet, but for the moment, the US attorney for the Southern District of New York is handling the investigation himself," Mike said. "The Honorable James Prescott."

"Skeeter? Damn it."

"Skeeter, really?" Mike asked, pulling back the shower curtain. "Grown man and that's the best he can do? Did he get bit by a bug or something?"

"Do you have a problem with names? First Jaxon and now this one," I said. "It's a southern thing, Prescott's name. A kid's nickname that took."

"You ever do him?"

"Why is that always your first question?" I said. "No, but thanks for asking. I went to law school with Skeeter's wife. His ex, actually. I just don't need him knowing all my business."

"Once the *New York Post* gets through with this, what Skeeter or anyone else knows will take a backseat to the tabs," Mike said, wiping his face and chest with a towel, then changing places with me. "Then there's the DA's fight with the mayor."

"They hate each other."

"Hated," Mike said. "Once you've got a dead man, the story gets rewritten. The mayor's a complete horse's ass, but I don't think anyone's going to go with a hired-killer theory."

"Then there's all the office politics," I said. "So much infighting."

"Yeah. A real hornet's nest."

"Five hundred lawyers. Most of them are loyal and collegial, but there's a handful or two who care about nothing except their own careers," I said. "All led by an elected official who was so vain he refused to deal with the idea that someone would eventually succeed him."

I'd gotten in the shower and was washing myself vigorously again, even harder than at the morgue. "Who would have thought the old man had so much blood in him?"

"Let it go, Coop," Mike said. "You still got blood washing off?"

"No, that's Shakespeare I'm quoting," I said. "Lady Macbeth, imagining forever that she couldn't get the bloodstains out. Just that crazy feeling that no matter what I do, I'll still be wearing a bit of Paul Battaglia for the rest of my life."

"Knowing the way you think, you probably will."

When I stepped out, Mike wrapped me in a bath towel and gave me the hug—long and close—that I had been waiting for. Then he patted me on my butt and told me to get dressed.

I had lots of lady lawyer clothes. A pin-striped navy-blue skirt suit with a white blouse would be appropriate, I thought as I took the pieces out of my closet. No makeup, no jewelry, no stilettos.

"Did they find the car the shooters used?" I asked.

"I know as much as you do."

"That's so hard to believe," I said, sitting down to pull on my panty hose.

"Nobody's telling me anything. I'm every bit as much a witness as you are."

Mike was adjusting his navy blazer—as much of a uniform as he owned—and went back into the bathroom to brush his dark hair into place.

I reached for my iPad, logged in, and hit the Google app. I typed in Battaglia's name.

"What are you doing?" Mike asked, walking back into my bedroom. "Turn that thing off."

"I'm just checking the news. I don't want to walk into the lion's den like I don't have a clue what's going on, Mike."

"That's exactly the way Skeeter and the crew want you, babe," Mike said, grabbing the machine from my hands and slapping the cover closed. "They need to talk to you before your facts are conflated with all the crap that's floating around on the Internet. You be straight with them and they'll be straight with you."

"I saw the headline," I said, smiling up at Mike. "At least give me credit for that."

"For what?"

"OPERATION DEADFALL. The *Times* headline," I said. That was as far as I'd been able to read. "That's what the task force is naming the investigation."

"Credit?" Mike said, looking at me as though I'd lost it. "You must be out of your mind. You think that's a compliment?"

"It's what I told Stern and Tinsley. That the DA and I went down together, totally entangled in each other."

Mike sat down beside me on the bed, stroking my damp hair away from my face.

"It's a double entendre, Coop," Mike said. "Or maybe you just didn't know that."

"What is?" I asked. "I don't know what you're talking about."

"You're the one that suggested to Jaxon Stern that Battaglia's life ended in a deadfall?"

"Don't look so sad about it, Mike—it just means—"

"I'll tell you what it means, Madam Prosecutor," Mike said, standing up and shaking his head at me. "It's not just an entanglement. It's a term used in hunting, okay? When someone sets up a trap, kid, to catch a large animal—a really valuable kind of prey."

"You're thinking the district attorney was the prey? Is that what you're telling me?" I stood too, and took the lapel of Mike's jacket in my hand, so he would look at me.

"The animal gets lured to the trap by some kind of bait," he went on, "and then it's crushed to death by a heavy weight—or in this case, by a couple of pieces of lead."

"No, no, no," I said, pushing back, away from Mike. "That's not what I meant at all."

"The working theory—the word on the street, in Jaxon Stern–speak—is that you set the man up," Mike said. "That Paul Battaglia was the prey, and that you were the bait, Coop. That you were the deadfall."

# SIX

"Have a seat, Alexandra," Prescott said after shaking my hand.

"Thank you," I said, sweeping the conference room with my eyes to check out the members of the task force team.

One Saint Andrews Plaza, the federal prosecutor's office, was only a stone's throw from the criminal courthouse where the DA's offices were, but it was like another world. We city workers were sprawled all over the grim WPA-designed building and our overflow was housed across the street, in other dreary government buildings. The feds, who numbered only a fraction of our size, had more modern digs, as well as all the assets that the US government could place at their disposal.

"You met Jaxon Stern and Kate Tinsley earlier this morning," Prescott said, guiding me to a seat at the end of the long table.

They each forced a smile, but I glared back at them and didn't comment.

"Why don't we go around the table so you can introduce yourselves to Ms. Cooper?" Prescott suggested. "Just for the record, Alexandra and I have never worked together, and we haven't socialized in—what? Seven or eight years?"

I nodded. "And that was only because I was a friend of Skeeter's then wife. There's really no other personal connection between us."

I didn't want him to recuse himself from the case. He had a reputation for being fair, which was better than I might end up with if I made a stink about our relationship, which was nonexistent since he'd been dumped by my classmate for a hedge fund guy she represented.

"In fact, it's been so long that Alexandra knows me by my nickname," he said, laughing as he did, then addressing me again. "It's James now. James Prescott. No more Skeeter."

"I'll try," I said. "Old habits die hard, James." And if he screwed with me like the cops had done, he'd be Skeeter every time I opened my mouth.

There was a junior assistant US attorney from Prescott's criminal division, two paralegals, and two FBI agents—both men—whose names were Bart Fisher and Tom Frist.

"How are you feeling today?" Prescott asked.

"I'm feeling about the same as I did when Paul Battaglia collapsed in my arms."

The onlookers were the most earnest group of investigators I'd ever seen—except for Stern. He was slouching in his chair and appeared to be doodling on a pad, while the others were leaning in, staring at me, as though I were an extraterrestrial just set down in their midst.

"And how was that, exactly?" Prescott said.

I spoke slowly, pausing for seconds between each word. "Despondent. Terrified. Confused. Frightened. Heartbroken—"

"Heartbroken? Really? Because you and Battaglia were so close?"

"Because we had once been so close, James. Because this was a man I'd revered when I started practicing law. Because he had treated me like his daughter. Because he—"

"I understand, Alexandra," Prescott said, holding up his hand to stop me. "We can come back to that. Did you get any sleep after you left the morgue?"

"Yes, thank you. Three or four hours."

"And something to eat?"

"I had a muffin on my way down in the car," I said. "Am I being recorded, James?"

I didn't care what name he wanted me to use in addressing him. It was better than the detective's insistence that we stay at a formal arm's length when we talked at the ME's office.

"No. No, you're not."

"Not yet anyway," I said.

"I'd like to explain our process to you, before I ask you any more questions," Prescott said.

"That's fine. I have some questions for you, also."

"All right. Why don't you go first?"

"Are you going to be in charge, James?" I asked. "Is it your investigation?"

"Yes. Yes, it is."

"Because of the perceived conflict of interest with our own office—and with the NYPD?"

"That's part of it, Alexandra."

"There's more?"

"We had several matters that we were working in tandem with your office. We usually do, as you know," Prescott said.

"May I ask the nature of those cases?"

Prescott hesitated for a moment, before he figured he could give me the information in a generic way. "You probably know some of your colleagues were cross-designated to work with my staff."

"I do." I had been cross-designated, too, from time to time, to allow me to practice in federal court, when sex-trafficking cases had required the efforts of local prosecutors.

"Then you know the kind of matters I mean," Prescott said. "The breakup of international drug cartels, the occasional money laundering by foreign banks, seizures of illegal ivory sold by antique dealers in the city, the importation of contraband weapons. Those sorts of things."

"Specifics, James," I said. "Can you give me more specifics?"

"No. Not yet, anyway."

"You're working on this yourself?" I asked. "At least, with me?"

"For the time being," Prescott said. "For now."

"What does that mean?" Until I was cleared, or until I was up to my eyeballs in mud?

"Next question."

"What do you know about the shooting so far?" I asked. "What kind of gun? How many guys in the car? Did you get any images of the car from surveillance cameras?"

My eyes darted from Prescott to the agents to the AUSAs, but no one even blinked.

"We haven't made any of that information public yet," Prescott said.

"I'm not the damn public," I said, trying to rein in my temper. "I was one of Battaglia's most loyal soldiers. I was his confidante."

"More important to us, Alexandra, is that you were an eyewitness to this," Prescott said. "All the rest will fall into place. May we get started, or do you have any other questions?"

"What's the point? You're not giving me an inch."

"Shall we, then?" Prescott said, leaning over the table and picking up his pen.

"This is the way you do your investigations?" I asked, making a sweeping motion around the room. "A gaggle of your buddies?"

"Excuse me?"

"I'll talk to you and one of your deputies, James, but I'm not singing for all the boys."

I leaned back in my chair and steepled my fingers.

"Look, Alexandra," Prescott said, "we've got a long road ahead of us. I have no idea where this shooting is going to take us. The more hands, the better. The more agents I bring in—"

"The more agents you bring in, the more leaks I can expect,

James. Is that what you were going to tell me?" I said. "Because I learned that a long time ago. Your people leak like they're on their way to the ocean floor on the *Titanic*."

Prescott exuded cool. If he was bothered by my attitude, he didn't show it.

"Bart," he said to the younger of the two FBI agents, "you stay with me. The rest of you all have business to get on with."

There was a low rumble as chairs were pushed back and the crew picked up briefcases and muttered comments as they readied themselves to leave the room.

"One more thing, Chief," Jaxon Stern said to Prescott.

"What is it?" Prescott asked.

"I want Ms. Cooper's cell phone," the detective said. "We've got the tech unit waiting to download all the emails and texts, check the outgoing and incoming calls."

None of the men on the team moved.

Of course they would interrogate my phone. I should have thought to look at it on my way downtown, but I was too out of sorts to think of random communications of the past week.

As I leaned over to dig around in my tote to find it, I tried to remember the office drivel I had gossiped about recently with my buddies in the unit. For once I was grateful that Mike didn't commit personal intimacies to digital forms.

The men and Tinsley—all standing around me with Prescott sitting directly across—watched while I unpacked my wallet and sunglasses, my credit card holder and my assortment of pens and small change.

"I don't have my phone," I said, sinking back into my seat. "I just realized that I don't have it here."

"Dump out your bag, Ms. Cooper," Stern said.

I laughed to myself. I had said that, to those witnesses whom I had caught in a lie, so many times my colleagues made fun of it.

The bag dump had often revealed items of evidence that my com-plainants wanted to hide—a slip of paper with the accused's phone number, suggesting they had arranged a way to get in touch; con-doms she had taken along for the date; even a handgun, once, that a young woman carried to secure her demand for money after the sexual encounter.

"You dump it, Detective. That will give you more pleasure than it gives me," I said.

Stern took my tote by the handles and turned it over on top of the conference table. Lipstick cases and mascara and a shopping list and more coins that rolled off onto the floor. But there was no phone.

Jaxon Stern threw my empty bag down. "She must have given it to Chapman, Chief."

"Did you, Alexandra? Does Mike Chapman have it?"

I shook my head. "No, he doesn't."

"Help me, will you? Where is your phone?"

I was playing for time. I didn't want Stern to get his hands on my device before I checked it myself.

"Will you let me see it before you take it to TARU?" I asked. The Technical Assistance Response Unit would know more about me than I knew about myself once they downloaded all the infor-mation on my smartphone.

"You'd better get your head around the fact that you're not running this case, Alexandra," Prescott said. "Give it up."

I thought back to last evening. I had dressed for the Costume Institute gala at the home of my friend Joan Stafford's mother. I had borrowed one of Joan's gowns and her mother's pearl necklace.

"On the way to the Met," I said, "from a friend's apartment on the Upper East Side, I dropped off my things with my doorman."

"What things?" Prescott asked.

"My cell phone," I said. "My ski jacket and my apartment keys."

"I don't believe it," Stern said.

"All I needed for the party was my ID to get inside the museum, and a twenty-dollar bill for my carfare home." I directed my words to James Prescott. "I wasn't expecting a murder. I wasn't planning a call to 911."

"You didn't stop on your way in this morning to pick up the phone?"

I met Prescott's expression of disbelief with a defiant stare. "I made an unexpected detour to the morgue, James. I had a really rough go with a hard-ass detective who seems to want to see me in handcuffs and leg restraints."

"Don't exaggerate—"

"So when I reached my home I was pretty much shattered. I wasn't thinking about making any calls or catching up on my correspondence."

"Then how did you get into your apartment?" he asked, thinking he had nailed the "gotcha" question.

"Mike," I said, remembering that he had opened the door, letting go of my shoulder to get out his key. "Mike Chapman has a key."

Jaxon Stern snickered.

"And this morning?" Prescott asked.

"I—I showered and dressed and didn't even stop to think about it," I said. "I picked up my tote and just assumed my phone was in there."

"I'm on it, Chief," Stern said. "I'll get it from the day doorman now."

"Be sure you take a subpoena, Detective," I said. "Vinny wouldn't give you anything I left with him otherwise."

"You think you tip that good, Ms. Cooper?" Stern said. "He'll give it up to me."

"Look, Alexandra," Prescott said. "I haven't opened a grand jury investigation yet. I haven't had a minute to do it. So I can't issue a subpoena, and you know that."

"I'm counting on it, James," I said. "I want my phone, too."

"Call your doorman," he said, offering his phone to me.

"Sorry. His number's with the contacts in my phone, which I don't seem to have," I said, holding my hands up in the air. "I can't recall what it is offhand. Anyway, I don't know what has you so anxious to get hold of my emails and messages. I've been on a leave of absence for weeks. I'm not exactly loaded up with breaking cases and top secret information."

James Prescott stood and pointed at Jaxon Stern. "Go get her phone, Detective. If the doorman gives you any problem, dial me up."

"You know, Skeeter," I said, "leopards really don't ever change their spots, do you?"

He looked over my head and spoke to the AUSA who'd be working with him. "Get into the grand jury before they break for lunch and open a matter."

"United States against—?" the young lawyer asked, looking blankly at me.

"No subject," Prescott said. "We don't have a perp yet, obviously. Just title it 'Investigation into the death of Paul Battaglia.'"

I faked a sigh of relief. "Must be my lucky day, guys. I'm not yet the perp."

James Prescott wasn't amused. "We've got the district attorney's phone, Alexandra."

Sure they did. That would have been in his pocket. "I understand."

"I'm just trying to find out why he called you three times on his way to meet with you," Prescott said. "On his way to his death."

# SEVEN

"Again?" I asked.

The scene on the front steps of the Met, from the moment I walked out the door until Battaglia was hit, had lasted less than three minutes. Maybe two. James Prescott had taken me through it five times already, breaking each moment into longer and longer pieces.

"Did you see anyone else on the steps?"

"No."

"Were you aware of the traffic going by on Fifth Avenue?"

"No."

"What color was the car?"

"I don't know."

"Think harder," Prescott said. "You must have noticed it."

"I didn't."

"But you saw an arm extend out of the window?"

"I think so," I said. "I mean, I assume that's what it was. It was all so dark."

"There are streetlights on Fifth Avenue, Alexandra," Prescott said. "And the steps of the Met are illuminated too."

"Then I was just tired, okay? I had no reason to be on the lookout for anything."

They were dizzying rounds of questions, but my answers didn't offer any more clarity—to James Prescott or to me.

"Let's move on to some of the cases you've been handling," he said.

"They were reassigned during my leave."

"Start before your kidnapping. That was only a few weeks ago," Prescott said. "We may find something relevant there."

"Do you mind if we take a break?" I asked.

"Certainly," Prescott said. "I'll get my secretary to walk you to the restroom."

"I don't have a phone, James. Remember? I don't have a Dick Tracy watch with a walkie-talkie radio built into the wristband so I can send out a rescue signal," I said. "Or is it my escape you're worried about?"

Prescott had perfected the art of ignoring my jabs in the short time we'd been together. "Bart, you want to get Ella to escort Alexandra to the ladies' room?"

"Will do," Agent Fisher said, stepping out of the room.

James and I were silent at first.

"Look," I said, "if it's not online already, the *Post* will have every fact I need to know by the time you and I have finished this standoff."

He looked to the open door, walked over, and shut it.

"Between you and me?" he asked.

"Yes."

"That obviously means Mike Chapman, too, doesn't it?"

"It does," I said.

"Okay, Alexandra. So, the car was stolen, as you've probably figured."

"Yeah. You've found it?"

"You bet," Prescott said. "They abandoned it six blocks away. Stole it in Harlem, on a side street without a camera. They probably weren't inside the car for more than ten minutes."

"Wiped clean?"

"These are professionals, Alexandra."

"I don't know what their experience is as car thieves," I said, "but the guy with his arm out the window was clearly a sharp-shooter."

"The Fifth Avenue camera closest to the Met got an image. Both men wore ski masks and gloves. The photos are being enlarged but they're pretty worthless."

"What do you know about the gun?" I asked.

"Start with the bullets," he said. "Twenty-two caliber. We'll know more about the weapon once the photo is enhanced. Stern thinks it's a Ruger, a really reliable gun. With a suppressor."

There must have been a silencer, but the shots had sounded like cannon fire to me.

"His bodyguard, James. Who was driving him last night?" I asked. The DA had an NYPD detective assigned 24/7. "Where was he when Battaglia was coming up the steps?"

"Parked opposite the museum, just off Fifth Avenue," Prescott said. "The car was pointed eastbound. The DA had told the guy to wait there, that he just needed five minutes with you."

"But the shots?"

"He heard them. Jumped out of the car and ran up to do what he could for your boss," he said. "Don't you remember seeing him?"

"Actually," I said, "I don't."

I didn't remember much beyond the fact of the dead man pinning me against the museum steps.

Bart Fisher knocked on the door before he opened it. "Ms. Cooper, this is Ella."

I stood up and walked over to her. "Hi, I'm Alex Cooper. We've spoken on the phone several times."

"Yes," she said. She flashed the first genuine smile I'd seen in hours.

"You're my keeper?" I asked.

"Well, I—" she said, looking at Prescott.

"That's okay. I just need to freshen up," I said.

We walked down the hall together and Ella let me go into the bathroom by myself. Once done, I ran cold water into the sink and splashed it on my face, two or three times.

Then I spread my legs and stood back from the tiled wall, pressing my arms against it to brace myself, as though stretching before a run. Everything ached—my limbs and my back and my eyes and most of all my brain. But this was only the beginning, and I knew that.

Ella walked me back to the conference room and I took my seat.

"Have you talked to Amy Battaglia?" I asked, as Prescott and Fisher sat back down.

"Briefly," he said.

"Mike said she's got it in for me."

Prescott didn't respond.

"You're not swayed by that nonsense, are you?" I asked.

He grimaced.

"I noticed Paul wasn't wearing his wedding ring," I said.

"Noticed when?"

"In the morgue. Before Amy got there," I said. "You better check into what was going on between them."

"Please, Alexandra, that doesn't become you."

"Paul liked me. He didn't like or trust that many people, but he used to like me a lot," I said. "You want to talk about friction? There were days he hated you. We all knew that."

"You're in the gutter with this kind of talk," he said, blowing me off with a wave of his hand. "There's always tension between a federal prosecutor and the DA."

That fact was true. Battaglia hated the jurisdictional confines of his territory—the island of Manhattan. He had overreached his hand to pull in fraud cases involving foreign banks that had branches in the city or corporate tax evaders who shipped million-dollar paintings from an address in New York to a second home, only to return the art to their apartments. He had feuded publicly with every United States attorney, fighting for the same high-profile cases, since Rudy Giuliani had grandstanded by locking up Wall Street executives on the courthouse steps.

"He hated your political ambition," I said to Prescott. "Hated it."

Agent Fisher seemed to be twitching as I took the US attorney on.

"C'mon, Alexandra. Let it alone."

"He's probably rolling over in his refrigerated box right now to think that you're the one who is going to be handling his murder investigation," I said, getting myself more wound up by the minute. "He wanted to be a US senator more than he wanted to breathe fresh air, and here *you* are, positioning yourself for the big run in two years."

"Are you done?" Prescott asked.

"He hated you for that, too. For stepping on his prosecutorial toes with your pre-indictment press conferences and for thinking you could elbow your way into Congress."

Prescott stood up again. "Anytime you're ready to go forward, Alexandra, though I have to compliment you on deflecting the subject so handily," he said. "It was *you* Paul was hustling to confront on the steps of the Met, not I."

"Who said anything about a confrontation?" I asked.

"Detective Stern said your last conversation with Paul didn't go all that well."

"There's a light-year between that fact and the idea that I lured the man to his death."

"So talk to me about what cases he was interested in, Alexandra," James said, leaning in toward me as he took his seat again. "Calm yourself down. Give me some direction here."

My stomach was roiling. No matter where my thoughts headed, there was nothing calming on any front.

"I can't think of anything helpful right now," I said. "Nothing comes to mind."

"You've sent a lot of scum to prison," he said. "You and Paul both made enemies easily."

"Most of my offenders are lone wolves. They're rapists, James. They usually operate solo."

"But they still hold grudges."

"Yes, and the office has just been through a thorough search of everyone I've convicted or busted or even annoyed in the last decade," I said. "My—my kidnapping had the DA, my SVU legal team, the whole detective division, and the commissioner himself going over my entire body of work."

"What did you learn?" he asked, with that earnest look on his face.

"Me? I'm the one who was out of the loop. Five days with my captors," I said. "Ask Catherine Dashfer, who took over for me. Ask Pat McKinney, the chief of the trial division. I was missing in action."

"Ultimately, the abduction wasn't about you, Alex," Prescott said. "Am I right?"

I swallowed hard. "Dead right. Not about me and not about Paul Battaglia."

"So, this case that just—well, just unraveled at the Met last night, is the suspect on the loose a problem?" Prescott was making his list on a legal pad.

"Most fugitives are, don't you think?"

"I meant for Paul," Prescott said. "There was an international angle to the murder, wasn't there?"

"Global," I said. "The dead man's company was trying to get into every fashion market in the world."

"And you knew about that case, even though you were officially on leave?" he asked.

"Yes, and Battaglia was peeved about my involvement," I said. "But I can't think of anything in the entire matter that put him at risk."

"Then we should talk about the Reverend Shipley," Prescott said, after twenty minutes of pounding me about the Wolf Savage murder.

"Hal Shipley?" I said. "He's a total fraud."

"What kind of relationship did he have with the district attorney?"

"A very complicated one."

"Detective Stern said you worked on a murder case recently that involved a vic who used to work for Shipley's community action network."

"What about it?" I asked.

"I need to know more."

"You tell me why you never prosecuted Reverend Hal for federal tax evasion, and maybe it will jog my memory."

James Prescott rubbed his hands together. "So this is the way it's going to be, Alexandra?"

"I don't know who to trust in this—or don't you get that yet?" I said, trying to keep my voice from wavering. I had been as wimpy and spineless as a jellyfish in the days following the release from my captors. Now I felt as though some of my vertebrae were regenerating.

"I don't know who has my back in all this."

"Give me the tools I need—the information I need—to get there," he said.

"I promise to work on that," I said. "Can we call it a day? I've got to get to the store to buy a new cell phone, unless you let me—"

"You'll need a new phone," Prescott said. "No question about that."

"I hear you. And I'd like to get some rest before I go to the wake tonight."

"Wake?"

"I know you're a 24/7 kind of guy, James," I said, "but I'd like to put in an appearance at Paul's wake."

Prescott shook his head. "There's not going to be a wake, Alexandra. And the funeral service is going to be private, with a memorial several months from now."

"I can't believe Amy isn't having a service," I said, half laughing at the thought that Paul Battaglia would be deprived of the public expressions of his importance by the famous and well-to-do. "I'd bet he's written his own eulogy, and it's just short of Caesar's in lavishing praise."

"Amy can't have a service now," James Prescott said. "Not even by invitation only. Imagine what an embarrassment it would be down the line if the killer turned out to have been seated in the front row."

# EIGHT

"How are you feeling now, Alexandra?" Prescott said as he reentered the room.

It was after five o'clock in the afternoon. The United States attorney for the Southern District of New York had tried to play me like I was an unwitting witness he could break simply by isolating me from my world, my friends, and my family for half a day.

"You do this well, James," I said. "You do this so much better than I do."

I knew the drill. I had practiced it on lying perps and predators many times. First an hour of questions about the facts. Then expand the picture to motives and opportunities. That had been the piece about Savage and Shipley and public enemies. After that, leave the poor slob in an empty room with no phone, no iPad, no way to communicate with anyone. A cup of vanilla yogurt and a bottle of water. Station a cop or agent at the door to heighten the feeling that the next stop might be an empty cell.

I was beyond exhaustion. My head was resting on my folded arms on the long table. I picked it up at the sound of Prescott's voice.

"Ready for waterboarding, if that's what's next," I said.

"Diana," Prescott said, sitting next to me, so close I could smell his bad breath.

"What?" I asked.

"Talk to me about Diana," he said. "Tell me who she is."

He had my attention now. I put my hand on my hip and arched

my back in a late-afternoon stretch. I repeated the woman's name out loud, three or four times.

"Diana who?" I asked.

"No, no, no, Alexandra," Prescott said, wagging his finger at me like it was the tail of a dog. "You're supposed to tell *me*."

"There's a woman named Diana in Special Narcotics," I said. "There's a paralegal in the hiring office, too."

Prescott was writing on his pad. "Last names?"

I told him.

"What's your connection to each of them?"

"None. Zero. Zilch," I said. "We've got five hundred lawyers and a support staff twice that size."

"But you don't know these two?"

"No. I mean only to say hello to. And I didn't know the Princess of Wales, either."

"Who, then?" he asked, frowning at me.

"Who, then, what?"

"Stop playing games with me, Alexandra," he said. "Have you had a victim named Diana?"

"Ever?"

"Ever or lately. Take your pick."

"I can't think of a single one," I said, putting my elbows on the table and my head in my hands. "Call Catherine, like I told you. She'll put the name in the computer system and all the Dianas who've been to our office or made a police report will pop right up."

"Think harder," Prescott said, blasting his foul breath at me. "I'm giving you a chance to help yourself, Alexandra. I'm throwing you a lifeline here."

"Screw your lifeline," I said. "I didn't do anything wrong."

"You've got five minutes alone with me to rattle this around in your brain."

"Then what? Off to Guantánamo?"

"Why do you insist on making a joke about this?" Prescott asked.

"Because that's what I do when I get scared," I said, as much as I hated to admit to him that his isolation technique was working on me. "I suppose Diana has something to do with the district attorney."

"Keep going."

"I'm supposed to know about their relationship?"

"Do you?" he asked.

"Does it have to do with the fact that he wasn't wearing his wedding ring?" I asked. "Diana's the mistress, right?"

Prescott threw his pen on the table. "Are you telling me or asking me?"

"I don't know, James. I'm in the dark."

"A few hours ago you said you were his confidante."

"I was. Used to be. Past tense."

He stood up and grabbed his pad. "I'll be back shortly. If you think of something you'd like to tell me—without the cops or agents in here—just alert the guy outside the door."

I walked over to the window and looked out at the dusky sky. I didn't know a headache could hurt so much, be so blinding.

I sat on the foot-wide windowsill and wrapped my arms around my knees. It was at least ten minutes before Prescott returned, this time with Jaxon Stern and Kate Tinsley.

"Back to the table, please," Prescott said.

I went to my hard wooden chair and seated myself.

"We've got something we'd like you to listen to," he said.

Detective Stern had a small digital recorder. He placed it on the table.

"I got your phone from your buddy Vinny," Stern said. "You might want to increase your tip come Christmas, Ms. Cooper. He gave it right up."

"I'll double down on him, but with a reminder about not being so trusting next time someone comes along and wants my belongings."

"TARU has the phone," Stern said to Prescott, "but they downloaded the voice messages for you."

I pulled my chair in. TARU detectives had edited in the times of the calls.

"*Eight oh two p.m.*," the NYPD tech guru said. Then the DA's voice. "*Alex? It's Paul. Sorry to disturb you at dinnertime but there's some urgency to this. Call me on my cell as soon as you pick this up.*"

"*Eight twenty-two p.m.*" A new voice. "*Alex, it's me.*" It was my friend Joan Stafford. "*I can't believe my mother loaned you her pearls. She really does like you more than she likes me. Have fun at Dendur.*"

"*Nine thirty-six p.m.*" Paul Battaglia again. "*Where the hell are you? You've picked a bad time to play hard to get, Alex. You have exactly what I need and you know it. You want me to come to you? I may just do that.*"

If you were buying into the deadfall theory, then you would think I had heard this message during the course of the evening. You'd think I was a siren, luring the district attorney toward the rocks.

"I don't know what he's talking about," I said. I spoke too quickly and too soon. "You know I didn't have my phone with me. I didn't know Paul was looking for me."

Prescott stopped the audio. "You could have picked them up remotely, Alexandra."

"Wouldn't TARU know that?" I asked Stern, looking to him for backup in my desperation. "They'd be able to tell that the messages had never been played before they got the phone this afternoon, wouldn't they?"

Stern's gaze was glacial. He didn't bother to respond.

Prescott pressed the Start button.

"*Ten fourteen p.m.*" Static on the line. Maybe an overseas call.

*"Alex? I'm just checking in to see how you're doing, baby. Call us tomorrow, will you?"*

I bit down on my lip. My mother, from my parents' home in the Caribbean. The only person in the world who could still call me "baby." They'd been thunderstruck by my kidnapping and rarely went two days now without wanting to hear my voice.

That message summoned up every emotion in me that could possibly interfere with my focus. I needed to shake it off as fast as possible.

*"Ten twenty-three p.m."* This would likely be Battaglia's third call. I held on to the arms of the chair as though I was flying through turbulence. *"Jesus Christ, Alex. I've got the ten-o'clock news on, ready to turn out the lights for the night, and I can see you're in the middle of that goddamn mess at the museum. You don't listen to anything I tell you to do—not even the fact that you were instructed to keep your nose out of investigations."*

Battaglia must have stopped to turn up the volume on his television, because the background noise got louder and he paused before going on.

*"I'll meet you, Alex. Don't you dare leave the museum before I get there. You and our mutual friend think you're having a private get-together? Think again. I need to know everything you found out about Diana. There are lives on the line, Alex. Human lives."*

Prescott's eyes were boring a hole through my face.

Battaglia started up again. *"Diana is none of your business. Got that, dammit? Got that?"*

The call ended abruptly. Battaglia still had a landline and he slammed the mouthpiece into the receiver when he was done.

"I'm going to ask you again, Alexandra," Prescott said, clicking the Stop button. "Who is Diana?"

I was white-knuckled, clutching the arms of the chair.

"Did you hear Paul? Did you hear him demand that you tell him what you know about Diana?"

"How many times are you going to ask me?" I said. "The answer will always be the same. That's exactly what I would have said to the district attorney if I'd had my phone in my hand when he called."

"Were you at the Met for business, Alexandra?"

I couldn't think of how to answer the question.

"Yes or no? Simple enough."

"Not officially. I wasn't there as an assistant district attorney," I said.

"Because Battaglia put you on leave, am I right?"

I nodded.

"But you decided to go rogue at some point and work on a murder case," Prescott said. "That's why the DA was so surprised to turn on the news and see you in the middle of a crime scene. Because you put yourself on the very notorious murder case of Wolf Savage."

"It wasn't notorious when I was asked to help out with it."

"Asked by Paul Battaglia?" he said.

I shook my head. "No."

"By whom, then?"

"The daughter of the deceased," I said. "She was a childhood friend."

Prescott kept coming at me, turning the screws, not giving me a second between questions.

"Diana?" he asked. "Is her name Diana?"

"No, it's not."

"Is she the mutual friend that Paul was talking about?"

I took a deep breath.

"Wolf Savage's daughter? No. Of course not," I said, more as a reminder to myself than an answer to Prescott. "Paul never met her. She was just an acquaintance of mine, from childhood."

"Who, then?" he asked. "Mike Chapman?"

"Mike was there. So was Mercer Wallace," I said. "So were lots of cops and ex-cops the DA knows who work for Citadel Security. I wouldn't think any of them was the mutual friend Paul was referring to."

Mutual friend, I said to myself over again, mentally scanning the rows of guests who had been part of the social setting at the Temple of Dendur. I couldn't think of one.

"Surely the list of attendees is in today's paper," I said. "If you let me look through the names, maybe I'll think of someone who fits that description. A mutual friend of ours, I mean."

"Do that on your own time," Prescott said. "Whose lives were on the line, Alexandra?"

"I—I didn't think anyone was in danger," I said. "I—we had just broken a case, and the killer—uh—one of the killers was in custody."

"That's a tell, Chief," Detective Stern said. "You get close to a nerve and Cooper starts with that stammering bullshit."

Prescott didn't say a word.

"She knows something she's not saying," Stern said.

"Paul Battaglia's life was obviously in danger," Prescott said. "You must have known that."

"I'm done, James," I said. "I'm all out of gas. You want something from me that I just don't have to give you. Had I known the DA's life was at risk while I was in the company of the best homicide detective you'll ever meet, the man would still be alive. We'd never have let Battaglia get in the crosshairs of a killer."

Prescott didn't try to stop me when I got to my feet.

"I'm tired of being badgered all night and day. I'm so out of here now," I said. "Let me know when you have something constructive for me to do."

"You want me to call Chapman for you?" Prescott said. "I assume he's downstairs, waiting to take you home."

"I'll buy a MetroCard, thanks." I just wanted to sprint out the door and away from the building, before Prescott changed his mind and held me overnight as a material witness.

"Your assignment," James said, "is Diana. Work that name every which way you can, through every source you have. And figure out the mutual friend."

"I'm sure Battaglia had plenty of contacts at the gala," I said, "but very f-f-few people we both knew. I—I can bet you money on that. I—I'm quite sure."

This time I couldn't control the stammer. Now I actually had an idea of who Battaglia might have freaked out about when he spotted the man on the evening news at the Met—at the same event as me. It must have been George Kwan, a witness in the Savage murder case—and whose home Mike and I had spotted Battaglia leaving a few days before his death.

Kwan wasn't my friend. I met him briefly in the course of the Savage case interviews, but it was just like Battaglia to use sarcasm to score a dig at me.

I wanted to tell Prescott that Kwan was in fact a friend of Battaglia's. I wanted to tell him the truth about the last time I saw the district attorney. But I just couldn't bring myself to admit that I had lied to Jaxon Stern.

# NINE

"I want to walk," I said.

"Get in the car."

"I need fresh air, Mike."

"I've waited for you all day," he said, jogging to overtake my long, angry stride.

"That's so sweet," I said.

"Say it like you mean it, kid."

I stopped in my tracks. "I really do mean it. And I apologize."

"My car's behind the courthouse."

"I'll take the train uptown and meet you there," I said. "I really need to blow off steam."

"The last time you were on the subway, Coop, they were still using tokens," Mike said. "Anyone tell you they're no good anymore?"

"Okay, okay, okay. Take me home. Please," I said, reaching for his hand. "And thank you for waiting. It was a gruesome day."

We had outlasted the paparazzi and the newshounds. City workers leaving their offices at the end of another day brushed past us on the sidewalk.

"Who questioned you today?" I asked.

"Save the conversation for the car."

"Don't make me paranoid," I said, glancing around. "Do you think—?"

"It wouldn't surprise me if they put an agent on you," Mike said. "Tail you for a while."

"How about if I become a recluse?" I asked.

Mike unlocked the beat-up black department car and I got inside.

"My kind of girl. Maybe you'll use your stay-at home time to learn how to cook," he said, closing the door, then going around and sliding in behind the wheel. "Talk to me, Coop. Tell me what Prescott did to you."

I leaned back against the headrest and took Mike through the lowlights of the day as he headed for the uptown FDR Drive and my apartment.

"Who do you know named Diana?" I asked as we neared home.

"Diana who?"

"You must have a Diana in your inventory, Mike," I said. "Apparently that's who Battaglia was charging up the steps to talk to me about."

"Yeah," he said. "My mother's butcher's wife. Diana Della Veccia DiVencenzo. Two hundred eighty pounds, with a mustache heavier than my five-o'clock shadow. I doubt she's been doing much the DA was interested in, except slicing bologna."

"They played my voice mails back to me at the end of the day," I said. "I'd forgotten that I'd walked right past the night doorman when we got home in the middle of the night and didn't think to pick up my phone and stuff."

"So Prescott has your cell?"

"TARU's already downloaded everything. My texts, my emails," I said, "and the three messages Battaglia left for me last night."

"You didn't bring your phone to the museum?" Mike asked.

"I didn't think I'd need it," I said. "Who interviewed you? Jaxon Stern?"

"Nope. They didn't want it to be cop on cop," Mike said. "It was one of the feebs—Tom Frist—with another of Prescott's assistants."

"Any surprises?"

"Pretty straightforward. Hell, the shooting was over in a flash," he said. "They were way more into you."

"Great," I said, rubbing my eyes.

"You and me. You and the Reverend Shipley. You and why you stuck your nose in the Savage investigation," he said. "Mostly you and Battaglia."

"What did you tell them about us?" I said as Mike backed into a tight parking space.

"Us?" Mike said. "None of their business."

"Not *us*. About the DA and me. That us."

"That things had turned. That he was treating you badly, in a way he had never done before."

"Why in the world did you go there?" I asked. "They'll think I murdered him."

"Not after I got done."

"Why's that?"

"Because you wouldn't have ended it so fast," Mike said. "You would have made his death slow and painful, torturing him every step of the way."

I got out of the car and slammed the door.

"Don't give me your back 'cause I said that, Coop," he said. "That's your nature."

"Sorry," I said. "Did they ask you about George Kwan?"

"Nope."

"On the last call Battaglia made to me, he was talking about me seeing our 'mutual friend,'" I said. "I can't figure out who the hell he was talking about. Then I sort of wondered if he meant George Kwan."

"Kwan's not your friend."

"You know the way Battaglia could get a dig in. Who else was at the museum—besides you and Mercer and some ex-cop security guys—besides Kwan?"

"So you 'fessed up about seeing the DA at Kwan's house?"

"Tomorrow," I said. "Or next time I'm down there. There was so much else going on that this just came to me on my way down from Prescott's office."

Now I was lying to Mike, too. I didn't want to be weaving a tangled web, but I was doing just that.

The doorman on the afternoon shift greeted us as we entered the lobby and passed him to go to the elevator.

"Ms. Cooper," he said.

"Yes?"

"I just let Detective Wallace go upstairs with three of your friends from the office," he said. "The detective told me you were expecting them."

I looked quizzically at Mike, who waved to the doorman and thanked him.

"You thought this was a good idea?" I asked Mike.

"You're not the only one in mourning, blondie," he said. "Ever think of it that way? All your pals have taken a huge hit. Battaglia's murder has rocked the office."

We got on the elevator and Mike hit twenty.

I don't think I'd ever been as self-centered as I had been for the last twenty hours. I hadn't even thought of the turmoil Battaglia's death had caused to all the people who worked in the office of the New York County district attorney. They were public servants, loyal to their leader to a fault, and so steeped in integrity that these circumstances would shake each of them to the core.

The door was unlocked. Mercer and my three closest friends from the office—Catherine, Nan, and Marisa—were in the den, watching television. The only sound from the room was the voice of the local NBC news anchor repeating the headline story of Battaglia's death.

Nan Toth noticed Mike and me walk in and reached me first.

We put our arms around each other in a tight embrace. I'm not sure whether any words would have come to me at that moment, but we had such a close friendship that we didn't need to speak.

"Take some deep breaths, Alex," Nan said.

I tried to shake off the jittery way I felt. "Glad you're all here."

"You've been to hell and back," Marisa said. "Don't say another word."

"Should I ask how the office was today? How you are?"

"I'd say it was like a morgue," Catherine offered, "but that's below the belt."

"I'll pour you a drink," Nan said.

"She's not drinking," Mike said. "No Scotch."

Mercer was fixing cocktails for each of them—and a martini for Mike.

"He's kidding," I said. "Plenty of ice for me, too."

"You're on the wagon, Coop."

I laughed at Mike. "Since when?"

"Since right now. You've never needed to be more sober than you do right now, till the US attorney gets off your ass."

"Here's the national news," Mercer said, clicking on the remote to raise the volume. "How Battaglia loved being the lead on that."

So true. He played his media connections to the max. He called in stories to the *Times* editorial staff and the network news outlets, whether a white-collar crime indictment or the murder of a mogul.

"Good evening," the anchor said. "From Manhattan, where a city is still in shock over last night's assassination of the longtime, popular district attorney on the front steps of the Metropolitan Museum of Art."

An old campaign photograph of Paul Battaglia filled the screen, with the oversize bolded letters *DA* above his face—and in similar typeface below, the letters *DOA*.

"He'd be calling up to scream at the producer right now if he could," I said, holding my thumb and forefinger together in a signal to Mercer to pour me a short drink. "He hated that photo. It was the campaign poster for his losing Senate bid."

"He truly hated losing," Marisa said. "Anything."

Mercer shook his head. He wasn't bartending for me tonight.

Everyone waited for a commercial break to fire questions.

"Coop's been in the hot seat all day," Mike said, handing me a glass of sparkling water. "Your turn. What's the buzz in the office?"

They were humoring me, all three of them. They were sticking to the story that there hadn't been much gossip today that had involved my relationship with Battaglia. Neither Mike nor I believed it.

BREAKING NEWS. The flashing red headline was the lead as the anchor picked up the story.

"This just in. A man walking his dog on Fifth Avenue at the time of last night's shooting of DA Paul Battaglia captured a photo on his cell phone camera. A warning to our viewers—this is an extremely graphic image."

A grainy shot—taken across the street from the museum steps—flashed on the screen. I looked up, then covered my eyes with my hand.

"The man in the dark suit, with a gaping wound to the back of his head, is the late Paul Battaglia," the anchor said. "You can see that his body is being held by a person—a young woman, actually—who seems to be sitting on the museum steps. They are literally knotted in each other. That person beneath him is one of his top assistants, Special Victims Unit Chief Alexandra Cooper. It's Ms. Cooper who has the DA in a death grip."

# TEN

"Now they've ratcheted up the language to a death grip," I said, sinking into the sofa and turning to Mike. "Why didn't you tell me there was a photograph?"

"I didn't know there was one," he said. "Mercer's checking."

The story went on to cover the arc of Battaglia's life. The six of us in my den knew it far better than the newsmen did.

Mercer finished the call and stowed the phone in his blazer pocket. "I just spoke to Vickee, who got the word from the press office. The only NYPD shots were taken by the Crime Scene Unit, and they're not released to the public. They didn't see this one until just this minute."

"So this dog-walking asshole just sold his snapshots to the media. Witness to an assassination and he shutterbugs it onto the nightly news instead of calling 911," Mike said.

"He's about to get a knock on his door," Mercer said. "Homicide wants his photos."

"Count on it, Coop," Mike said. "You'll be cover girl on the morning's *Post*."

This was the new normal. I had prosecuted a murder case a few years back, and after the verdict, we learned that a friend of the perp's had taken a video of him, mocking the death of his victim and strangling a doll to show how he had killed his girlfriend. She didn't give the evidence to law enforcement, but chose instead to sell it to a tabloid reality show for twenty-five thousand dollars. The dog walker had done the same.

"How many pooch paraders you think were out there last night?" Mike said. "Somebody must have seen something."

"The task force is using all our NYPD manpower to do a canvass tonight to find them," Mercer said. "Dogs and drunks and anyone else out for a stroll."

"What else is the task force doing, besides making my life miserable?" I said.

"Lose that, Coop," Mike said. "*Your* life is not the issue here."

"Collateral damage," I said. "Is that all I am?"

"All you want to be is the mattress the body fell on," he said. "Back off. The less you make of this, the better you'll come out of it."

"I hate to agree with Mike," Nan said, refilling her wineglass. "Ever. But the best thing for you would be to normalize. Think about being back at work and getting into a rhythm again."

I couldn't even concentrate on a good book these last few weeks. How could I be an advocate for a rape victim or cross-examine a defendant with a felony conviction at stake?

"It's a thought," I said, giving my friends a wan smile.

How was I going to face hundreds of lawyers—my colleagues and literal partners in crime—who would only want to know why their boss was rushing to a clandestine meeting with me?

I was beginning to feel claustrophobic in my own home, with my best friends. I was sweating, though the evening was cool and crisp.

I powered through the rest of the news, then went into the bathroom to shower. I put one of Mike's button-down shirts over a pair of leggings and came back to find Nan setting the dining room table. She had ordered a couple of pizzas and some salad.

"Pony up the money, ladies and gent," Mike said. The jingle announcing Final Jeopardy! had begun to play. It was rare for Mike ever to miss a bet on the weeknight quiz show's big question—whether at a bar or death scene or squad room.

Mercer, Mike, and I had a long tradition of making this twenty-dollar wager. Mercer—son of a Delta mechanic who had grown up with world maps on every wall of his room—was a maven on geography; Mike knew more about military history—he had been fascinated with it since childhood and studied it at Fordham—than anyone I'd ever met; and I was a student of English literature—a devotee of romantic poetry and dense Victorian novels.

"Let's go, Coop," Mike said, yanking on my wet hair. "Get back in the game."

"Soon," I said. "Not tonight."

"The Final Jeopardy! category is: OSCAR WINNERS," Alex Trebek said. "OSCAR WINNERS."

All three contestants smiled and started to write their bets on the electronic boards in front of them.

"Everybody plays," Mike said. He sat on the sofa and pulled me onto his lap.

Movies and Motown were the two categories that he, Mercer, and I went overboard on. The stakes got higher because we each thought we knew so much.

"Show me Mr. Green," Mike said to our friends, holding out his hand for their money. "Double or nothing."

My girls went to their bags to take out some twenties. They were doing it to pull me into the spirit of the moment. I didn't move.

Trebek read aloud as the answer was revealed: THRICE NOMINATED AS BEST ACTOR, HE SUPPORTED HIMSELF WHEN BROKE BY HUSTLING CHESS PLAYERS IN NEW YORK CITY PARKS AND ARCADES.

The *Jeopardy!* music ticked away as the on-air players wrote out their questions.

"We're in this to win, Coop." Mike put his arms around me and nuzzled my neck. "What's your best guess, Catherine?"

"Who was Paul Newman?" she asked.

"I'm in on that," Marisa said.

"So wrong," Mike said, reaching forward to snag their four bills from the coffee table. "He played Fast Eddie in *The Hustler*, but he wasn't one. And nominated ten times. Popcorn and salad dressing, ladies. You are so wrong."

Then he pointed at Nan.

"Daniel Day-Lewis?" she asked.

"You don't even deserve to be in our league," Mike said. "He's a Brit."

He reached for her money, too.

"What you got, big guy?" Mike said to Mercer.

"I'm going Nicholson. Who is Jack Nicholson?" Mercer said.

Before the winning question was offered by Trebek, Mike swept all the cash off the table. "Tell them, Coop."

I shrugged. "Don't know."

"You really know how to disappoint me, babe," he said. "You need to lighten up. Who was Humphrey Bogart?"

"That's right," Trebek said to the second contestant. "As a struggling young actor, Humphrey Bogart used to play for a dollar a match at New York's famed Coney Island."

Mike muted the sound. "Those scenes in *Casablanca* with Bogie playing chess? They were all his idea."

"You just bought us some serious pizza," Mercer said to Mike, getting up to answer the intercom from the front door announcing the dinner delivery. "A mind is a terrible thing to waste, Chapman."

We were moving to the dinner table, with each of my friends working hard to find neutral topics to discuss.

"Tell you what," Mike said. "If you shut down the Dewar's, I'll spot you one glass of wine. How's that for a compromise?"

"I'll take that deal," I said. "White. Really cold."

Catherine's cell phone rang and she looked at me before answering. We both had the same thought, that it was a detective calling about a new case. A call that would have come to me had I not been on leave. She must have known that it pained me to be professionally crippled by my own victimization.

She turned her back to me and answered the phone, then just as quickly faced me again when the speaker announced himself to her.

"Yes, Governor," she said. "This is Catherine."

What the hell was he calling *her* about?

"Actually, I'm with Alex right now," Catherine said. "I'm about to have dinner with her."

The governor had been a prosecutor when I joined Battaglia's staff. I had worked with him on a number of matters and he had been like a mentor to me.

"No, sir," Catherine said. "The task force has her phone—just a routine part of their investigation."

I was waving my arms over my head, telling Catherine I didn't want to speak with him tonight.

"Of course you can, sir. I'll just pass her my phone."

I took a deep breath and put Catherine's phone to my ear. "Hello, Governor," I said. "Thanks for calling."

We chatted for a minute or two, exchanging remembrances of Paul Battaglia and expressing our sorrow to each other. He told me how sorry he was that I was exposed to this violence, and in such a public setting.

Nan and Mercer were plating the pizza. I figured the governor was done.

"I wanted you to hear this straight from me, Alex," he said. "I'm likely to give an interview tomorrow or Thursday."

"What's that?" I asked. What else could possibly impact me now?

"I'm not sure if you know any of the politics that apply in this situation," he said.

"I don't."

Battaglia's campaign slogan had repeatedly been YOU CAN'T PLAY POLITICS WITH PEOPLE'S LIVES, though he had become a master at doing just that throughout his career. I despised the part of the job that sucked any of us line prosecutors into the mix.

"The election for DA is next fall. November," the governor said.

I knew that. Battaglia had already been off and running, thirteen months ahead.

"It's my responsibility, Alex, to appoint an interim district attorney for Manhattan," he said. "And I'll have to do it within the next six weeks."

I hadn't given a thought to that. It hadn't yet sunk in that Battaglia's death left this critically important office without a leader.

"You know I'm very fond of you, Alex. You know how much respect I have for your work, for how you've helped with the legislative reform I've sponsored in your field since the start of my first term."

I grabbed the back of a chair, pulled it out, and sat down. The room was spinning. I didn't need the governor to thrust me further into the spotlight right now by flattering me with a job I'd never wanted—a job I certainly couldn't handle at the moment.

"But, sir—" I said, scripting a polite way to refuse him.

"I wanted to tell you myself that despite my personal feelings, I can't see any way to put your name up with the other nominees I'm considering," the governor said.

"I'm sorry," I said, putting my elbows on the table. "I'm not sure I heard you correctly. Did you say you *won't* consider me to replace Battaglia?"

If I was truly relieved not to be a candidate, then why was my first reaction to the governor's news to feel crushed? Why did it seem like another weight had been tossed around my neck?

"It's not just your kidnapping and the fact that you're on a forced leave of absence now, Alex," he said. "But Commissioner

Scully suggested there's the potential for scandal in the aftermath of the DA's murder. That you're totally tangled up in his death."

"I understand, Governor," I said, practically whispering into the phone. "I understand completely."

"You're out of the running, Alex. I wanted to be the one to tell you that I had to take your name off the list."

# ELEVEN

I was awake before Mike. I went to the door and picked up the newspapers.

*New York Post* headline writers are brilliant at what they do, and often made me smile.

But not today.

## DEAD MAN STALKING

The lede was plastered above the photograph of my fatal embrace with Paul Battaglia. It went on to entice the reader with a story questioning why the DA set out for a midnight assignation with one of his assistants—a single woman who was in the company of another man.

I was on my third cup of coffee when Mike joined me in the kitchen.

I tossed the paper across the room like it was a Frisbee.

"Do you think it can get any worse?" I asked. "Now they've got the idea the DA was stalking me."

"Hey—the man was only human."

"Sort of a delicate balance, don't you think? My friends tell me that going back to work will be good for me, but I know the office will just be a hotbed of petty rumors—personal and political."

"Give it a week to calm down," Mike said.

"How about we go up to the Vineyard and hibernate till then?"

I had an old farmhouse in Chilmark, on the quiet end of my

favorite island. It was late October—after the season—so we could be there, out of harm's way and out of the spotlight. It had always been my haven when the pressures of the job or the mayhem I often created in my personal life threatened to overtake me.

"When James Prescott clears you to leave town, I'll FedEx you up there for an overnight delivery," Mike said. "Lobster from Larsen's, fried clams from the Bite, chowder at the Galley."

"Home," I said. "It's not the food. It's just home."

"We'll get there. I promise you that."

"So what's the plan?" I asked. "What am I supposed to do today?"

"No instructions from Prescott?"

"Not yet."

"I took the rest of the week off," Mike said. "That way we can hang together."

I walked over and kissed him on the top of his head. "I like that."

"Let's get a new routine going. We can go for a run in the park, or work out at the gym," he said. "Lunch at the Beach Café. Go to the store and get a new phone."

"I'm sort of liking it without one," I said. "I don't have to talk to anyone I don't want to, and the reporters can't find me."

I opened my iPad and showed Mike the 237 pieces of new mail in my inbox.

"My friends can find me through you or Catherine. I like it better this way," I said, scrolling through the latest batch of twelve that had just loaded.

"Remember the task force dudes are reading all your mail, too, from your phone."

"I'm keenly aware of that, Detective. The less communicating I do for the time being, the safer I feel," I said. "And the crazier it will make the team that's monitoring me, waiting for word from Diana."

I clicked and opened a few more emails. Lifelong friends and former colleagues were checking in, while every reporter who'd ever gotten my email address from the press office was writing to ask for an exclusive.

"Joan Stafford wants to know if she should come up from DC and stay with me," I said. "That one came in yesterday. This morning she wants to know why I was trysting with Battaglia."

"That's what friends are for, Coop. The *Post* is Joan's Bible."

"Remind me to call her from your cell when we get back from the run," I said. "Whoops. Here's one from Prescott's secretary, Ella. 'Mr. Prescott wants to know your new cell number. He'd like to get in touch with you.'"

"Perfect reason not to invest in a new phone," Mike said. "Let's get some fresh air."

I flapped the lid of the case over my iPad screen without answering Ella. Let them figure out how to talk to me.

We dressed for a run and went downstairs to the lobby. Vinny was standing in front of the door when it opened.

"I saw the elevator coming down from twenty and I figured it might be you, Ms. Cooper," he said. "There's a pack of photographers at each end of the driveway. You might want to slip out through the basement."

I gave him a thumbs-up and hit the *B* button. There was no one waiting for me at the back door, so Mike and I broke into a jog and headed for Central Park.

It felt good to do something that required no thought, no emotion. I wanted to get back in shape. Plus, both running and my Saturday morning ballet class traditionally helped relieve my stress and keep me on an even keel.

We did the mile and a half around the decommissioned reservoir and loped back on the sidewalk.

When we paused for the traffic light at the corner of Park Avenue, Mike checked the messages on his cell phone.

"One from Mercer," Mike said. "He'll meet us at your place. And two from Prescott."

"Only two?"

"Yeah. Both today. First he wants to know whether I'm with you, and the next is asking if you can call him on my phone," Mike said. "The second one is more of a demand than a question."

"I don't usually like playing hard to get," I said, sprinting across Park when the light changed, "but under the circumstances, it's a delight."

We went back into my building the same way we had exited. Mercer was waiting for us in my apartment.

"Did you take the week off, too?" I asked.

"No," he said. "I asked to be put on the task force to work on the murder, but Prescott refuses because he claims I'll just pass all the info they gather along to you. So I'm making myself useful by picking up cases—and, yes, gathering intel to pass along to you."

I went to the fridge to get bottles of water, then flopped in an armchair in my living room, in between Mercer and Mike.

"So what have you got?" I asked.

"If you don't like the twists and turns so far, you really won't be too pleased with the latest," Mercer said. "Vickee got called into work early this morning by DCPI."

The deputy commissioner of public information was one of the most powerful people within the NYPD. He was responsible for every piece of official news that was released concerning the work of the thirty-five thousand police officers in the city, with a department that was sitting on a five-billion-dollar budget. His team had to decide when a pattern of crimes was designated as the work of a serial killer—not too soon so as to falsely alarm the citizenry, but in time to protect them when needed. He had to consider the effect of every statement issued by Commissioner Scully as well as the mayor and the five DAs—one in each borough of the city. It was intensely high-pressure work, and Vickee Eaton had to help make those decisions, those close calls, every day she was on the job.

"But Logan—?" I asked.

"He's fine," Mercer said. "Fever's gone—you know the way kids are—and he's back in school."

"What's Vickee got?" Mike asked.

"DCPI is trying to put out ground fires, rumors that are spreading throughout the media," Mercer said.

"About what?" I asked.

"You know that every assassination, every scandal, every event that people don't understand, breeds conspiracy theories," he said. "MLK, JFK, UFOs crashing in Roswell, and NASA faking the moon landing."

"Princess Diana killed by British Special Forces and that sort of crap," I said. "There's that name again."

"She's not playing in this one," Mercer said. "Not yet, anyway."

"What one?" I asked. "What are they saying I did now?"

"You're out of the bull's-eye for the moment, but what do you remember about Scalia's death?"

"Supreme Court Justice Antonin Scalia?" I said, puzzled by the mention of a name that was entirely extraneous to last night's events. "That Scalia?"

"Exactly."

Mike and Mercer both looked at me for an answer. "He died in February 2016. I think he was almost eighty years old, and he was at some ranch in Texas," I said.

"Not a ranch," Mercer said. "More like a luxury hunting resort."

"That's right. Hunting. Last thing I would have guessed about the man—being a big-game hunter," I said. "I want to say he had refused his normal security detail, right?"

"Yeah," Mercer said. "US Marshals guard the Supremes, but Scalia went to Texas without protection."

Paul Battaglia had ordered his bodyguard to wait in the car. Was I supposed to be drawing similarities between them on that basis alone?

"What did Scalia die of?" Mike asked.

"Natural causes," I said. "He must have had a heart attack. Went to dinner at the ranch but never woke up the next morning."

"Some conspiracy theorists claim the justice was murdered," Mercer said.

"But why?" I asked. "I get the no-marshals bit."

"And no medical examiner either. No autopsy was performed, even though Scalia was alone when he died—and there was a pillow found on his face."

"On his face?" I said. "That's crazy."

"Well, it's probably crazy and it's certainly Texas for you," Mercer said. "A local justice of the peace got the news by phone, and she made the decision that there wouldn't have to be an autopsy."

"His family was okay with that?" Mike asked.

"Seemed to be very okay with it," Mercer said. "They had his body cremated, so even when the conspiracy stories first made the rounds, there was nothing to be done to confirm the manner of death."

"No one checked for petechial hemorrhaging in his eyes?" I said, referring to one of the hallmarks of an asphyxia death. "No mention of an odor on his breath for signs of possible poisoning?"

"None of the above."

"Why was Scalia there in the first place?" Mike asked.

"Way to go, Mike," Mercer said, pointing his finger at his friend. "What do you know about the Venerable Order of Saint Hubertus?"

"The what of who?"

"Saint Hubertus," Mercer said. "Either of you ever hear of him?"

We both shook our heads.

"Vickee's been doing the research on it."

"What's the connection?" I said.

Mercer held out his arm to me, palm outward, telling me to wait. "Hubert was the patron saint of hunters—archers, trappers, fur hunters. When the Hapsburgs ruled the Austro-Hungarian Empire, Count Anton von Sporck—"

"Spock?" Mike said.

"Sporck," Mercer repeated. "Von Sporck."

"No matter. The Trekkies will buy right into this conspiracy."

"Sporck gathered the greatest noblemen—hunters, of course— of the seventeenth century," Mercer said, reading from his notepad. "Created this kind of knighthood of the rich and famous, related to hunting wild animals."

"Three hundred plus years ago, and it's still a thriving order?" I asked.

"Yeah," Mercer said. "It was put on a temporary hold by Hitler, because the group didn't allow any Nazis in."

"Those bastards weren't exactly hunting wild animals," Mike said. "But the order is alive and well today? And Antonin Scalia was a member?"

"Member or guest," Mercer said. "Valerie's got to nail that down before Commissioner Scully gets his public grilling from the hungry media. This much is clear: Justice Scalia died at Cibolo Creek Ranch. Thirty thousand acres of a private hunting preserve— stocked with deer and elk, buffalo and mountain lions. A really secretive fraternity of men with a boatload of expensive guns at their disposal."

"I think the plot's about to thicken," Mike said.

"Paul Battaglia," Mercer said, "was a member of the Order of Saint Hubertus."

"That's not possible," I said, pressing my fingers against the crown of my head, which felt like it was about to split in two. "He was such an activist about gun control. He's on—he was on the board of the Wildlife Conservation Society. There's no way he would hunt and kill wild animals."

"I'm telling you, Alex," Mercer said. "You want to hear conspiracy chatter? The network has one assassination for sure, out in plain sight, with you as an unimpeachable witness. Maybe Scalia makes two."

"It just can't be," I said. "What's the link, besides this Saint Hubertus nonsense?"

"You won't think it's nonsense at all when I tell you that Paul Battaglia was at Cibolo Creek the night Justice Scalia died."

# TWELVE

"I'm just *not* buying into any conspiracy theories," I said. "We've got to make sense of Battaglia's murder before we do anything else. His politics were totally different from Scalia's."

"We've still got to find out why the DA was at Cibolo Creek," Mercer said.

"Sure we do," I said. "There may be a common thread here—I mean, I know that they were acquaintances, through the law, but let's not jump in bed with the conspiracy faction."

The three of us were sitting at a round table in the corner at the Beach Café on Second Avenue. It had been my favorite neighborhood joint since I'd moved into my apartment, and Dave, the owner, treated us with kid gloves. They served the best burgers in the city, but somehow the idea of animal hunting had steered me to a really good salad for my lunch.

"Wet work," Mike said. "I bet that's the angle the media bites at when they find out."

"No question," Mercer agreed.

"'Wet work' is a covert ops term for an assassination, Coop," Mike said. "You know, spilling blood."

"I'm all too familiar with the term." I put down my fork. My flashbacks were all about spilled blood. "They can run with some bullshit theory all they want, but we need to separate that crap from the truth."

"Professional killers," Mercer said. "For certain, whoever shot Battaglia was an expert. That's a more important connection to a game preserve in Texas—the sharpshooters the DA would have come in contact with."

"How did Vickee find out that Battaglia was a member of Saint Hubertus?" I asked.

"It came in on the TIPS hotline," Mercer said.

"An anonymous caller, then," I said.

"So far, but they're trying to up the amount of the reward to get more specifics."

"Did he tell us how we can confirm about Battaglia?"

"It's a she, Alex," Mercer said. "The caller is a she."

"Interesting," I said. "Are there any women in the order?"

"No, ma'am," Mercer said.

"Did you hear the man say it's a knighthood, Coop? A secret fraternity?"

"Things change," I said.

"Vickee has a hunch," Mercer said.

"Tell me it was a hooker," Mike said, sinking his teeth into a cheeseburger piled high with onions and pickles. "Every hunter needs a hooker."

"I hope Vickee has a better guess than that," I said.

"The caller made a reference to taking Battaglia to the ranch," Mercer continued. "Now, you can drive into that place. It's a very long ride—actually miles and miles. But there's a private jet landing strip, too, and a helicopter pad."

"So we're looking at a flight attendant on some NetJets thing that Battaglia might have used, out of Teterboro or Westchester," Mike said.

I took the bottle of ketchup and covered his fries till they were lost beneath a damp mound of red mush. "She might have been the pilot, Detective. Like I said, things change."

"The woman who called also said that photographs exist," Mercer went on. "That every time these men get together, they take a formal photograph of the group before the new investitures."

"Did she have one?" Mike asked.

"No, but we found an old one online."

"With Battaglia?" I asked.

"No such luck," Mercer said, reaching for his iPad and Googling the Saint Hubertus name. "No Battaglia and no Scalia. But the shot is five years old."

He turned the machine around so that Mike and I could view the image. My jaw dropped.

The photograph had been taken in Madrid, in front of El Escorial, the royal palace of the king of Spain.

"Grown men playing dress-up!" I said, in utter disbelief of the picture before us.

"The order is run by former King Juan Carlos of Spain," Mercer said. "He's the old guy in the middle of the front row. The others next to him are grand masters."

"They call them that? Grand masters?" I asked. "All they're missing are white hoods."

Each of the men was dressed in a charcoal-gray suit and tie, but over their clothing, each wore a full-length cape. The material appeared to be a dark green velvet—forest green, as a designer might have dubbed it, or even more appropriately, hunter green. The capes were flung back on one side so that they draped over the right shoulder of every knight, exposing a bright red silk lining.

"What the hell was a justice of the Supreme Court doing with these clowns?" Mike asked. "And how could the DA keep this a secret?"

On the chest of each man's cape, large and bold, was an insignia the size of a dessert plate. Against a background of embroidered gold thread was a dark green cross.

"Can you enlarge it?" I asked. "Can you read the motto sewn into the insignia?"

Mercer clicked on the screen.

"Damn it," I said. "Latin gets me every time."

I relied on Mike and his parochial school education, but even as he squinted, it appeared to be too difficult for him.

"Looks like *Deum diligite animalia diligentes*," Mike said. "But I have no idea what it means."

"You're still sure about dead men not biting, aren't you?" I asked, raising my eyebrows. "I mean, we're going into Battaglia's secret territory now, and he wouldn't take kindly to that."

Mercer was checking the Hubertus motto online. "That translates to 'Honor God by honoring his creatures.' Sound about right, Mike?"

"That may be the meaning of the words, Mercer," he said, "but it feels more like these assholes are honoring God's creatures by blowing their brains out."

# THIRTEEN

"It doesn't fit," I said. "You'll never convince me that Paul Battaglia is part of this group."

I was having another cup of coffee.

"Stubborn doesn't always work for you," Mike said.

"Two years ago, he was honored by Animals Without Borders, an offshoot of the great Wildlife Conservation Society," I said. "Man of the year and all that goes with it. The whole executive staff had to fill seats at the black-tie dinner."

"Maybe they made a mistake," Mike said. "Maybe Battaglia left his green robe at home in the bathroom."

"What does the society do?" Mercer asked.

"Wonderful work," I said. "Everywhere on the planet. They save endangered species all over the world. They keep places wild and free, when they can. They're about conserving animal populations, not killing them."

"Why did they honor Battaglia?" Mike said.

"He launched a really clever investigation in the White Collar Crimes Unit," I said, referring to the prosecutors who handled commercial litigation and racketeering. Special Victims was part of the Trial Division, the group that specialized in violent street crime. "That's why I don't know all the details. But it grew out of the Lacey Act."

"What's that about?" Mercer asked. "A new conservation law?"

"It dates from 1900, actually," I said. "A congressional act, designed more than a century ago because so many game species here at home were threatened with extinction. The laws have been updated and modified scores of times, to try to shut down international suppliers who find such a huge market in this country."

"What made the DA a hero?" Mike asked.

"Operation Crash," I said.

"Crash?"

"A herd of rhinos is called a crash," I said. "Like a murder of crows."

I was actually thinking of a murder of a prosecutor when that phrase came to mind.

"Some of the government agencies were working with US attorneys across the country to investigate the black market trade in rhino horns and other protected species," I said.

"What's the deal with rhino horns?" Mike asked.

"They're a big deal in many of the Asian nations," I said. "Vietnam, for instance. As a medicinal cure-all and as an aphrodisiac. A three-kilogram horn is worth three hundred thousand dollars. They're more valuable per ounce than diamonds—or cocaine."

"We don't have rhinos here," Mike said.

"Of course not," I said. "But they're protected by our laws as well as by international laws, because of the potential for smugglers."

"How did Battaglia get into the act?" Mike asked.

"There's a guy in Texas who used some day laborers to buy a couple of horns at an Austin auction house. Then he came here to sell them for a quarter of a million dollars," I said. "It was Battaglia who ran the sting."

Mike was eating a slice of apple pie. "But it's a federal law that was violated, right?"

"Well done, Detective," I said. "But James Prescott was too busy with Wall Street predators to worry about a crash of rhinos. He told the Department of Justice honchos that he couldn't spare the manpower for undercovers to sit in a hotel room waiting for a bunch of bad guys to show up with the horns."

"So Paul Battaglia jumped right on it," Mike said.

"Sure he did."

"The crime was federal," Mercer said. "So how did the local DA prosecute it?"

"Same way as always," I said, "by being creative. I think he nailed them for presenting fraudulent bills of sale and forged documents, all well within his jurisdictional limits. Paul did the legwork himself and stood on the podium at the presser with the two big rhino horns—quite a sight—and when the spotlight went off, he quietly turned over the underlying Lacey Act violations to Prescott to carry over the finish line."

"Ouch," Mike said. "That must have been a sticky day between the two of them."

"One of many," I said. "I bet Prescott goes berserk when this Hubertus stuff hits the airwaves. He's likely to be so tempted to point out Battaglia's hypocrisy."

Reporters would quickly uncover the animus that had surfaced during·Operation Crash, when Battaglia presented himself as a wildlife champion and pointed the finger at Prescott, who hadn't gotten off the mark on the issue. Now, the worm seemed to have turned, and the press would be trying every which way to find out about the Saint Hubertus lifestyle.

"First the tabloids will try to put the district attorney in a green velvet robe," I said, "and then they'll drill down on Prescott."

"What's to find?" Mercer asked.

"I told you he was a southerner. A good ole boy from Middleburg, Virginia," I said. "If I remember correctly, Skeeter specialized in game birds—pheasants, quail, partridges. And occasionally rode to the hounds for foxes."

Mike's phone rang. "Chapman here."

The caller spoke to him.

"Hey, Vinny. What's up?" Mike said. "You're right, she left home an hour ago. I'll give him a call. Thanks."

"Vinny, the doorman? What did he want?"

"The US attorney sent two agents to your apartment to fetch you," Mike said.

"Unfetchable. That's what I am."

"Why don't you step outside for a few minutes," Mike said.

"Why?"

"That way when I call Prescott back, I can tell him we're not together right now," Mike said. "I can tell him I'm not really sure where you are."

Mercer nodded at me. He and I got up and strolled out the door, leaving Mike with the bill and a chance to get to James Prescott.

We were standing on Second Avenue, next to the new subway entrance that had finally opened. I put on my sunglasses to avoid the glare of the one P.M. brightness.

"What's the sport in shooting living things?" Mercer asked. "I've never understood it."

"Neither do I."

Mike followed us out a few minutes later. "Prescott's getting steamed up, Coop."

"What now?"

"I told him we ran together this morning—just in case anyone spotted us in the park—but I couldn't be sure where you were right now."

"You're living dangerously, Detective."

"He wants me to find you and take you to buy a phone," Mike said. "And he wants me to tell you to call him, when I see you."

"Mission accomplished," I said. "You've done your bit."

"And he wants you to be in his office first thing tomorrow morning."

Mike offered me his phone.

I shook my head. "I'll be sure to tell him I got the message to call, but I've got other things to do first."

"Like what?" Mike asked.

"Prescott told me yesterday that I had an assignment, actually. He told me I had to figure out two things—who Diana is, and which person was the mutual friend of Battaglia's and mine who was at the Met Monday night."

"So?"

"I say we start with the WCS. I say we jump all over this Saint Hubertus mystery before I meet with Prescott tomorrow, so I go in ahead of the game."

"Wildlife Conservation Society," Mike said. "That's WCS?"

"Yes," I said. "Where's your car?"

"Exactly where we left it last night. Do they have an office here?"

"Sure they do," I said. "When's the last time you went to the zoo?"

"Zoo?" Mike asked.

"That's the local home of the WCS," I said, starting into the crosswalk when the light changed. "The Bronx Zoo, gentlemen. We're going ape."

# FOURTEEN

"Why do we have to go overseas?" Mike asked as he showed his laminated NYPD pass going through the tollbooth on the Triborough Bridge, over the Hell Gate waterway.

"Because the Wildlife Conservation Society is headquartered at the Bronx Zoo," I said. "They work alongside Animals Without Borders—the one that honored Battaglia—because that group doesn't have an office in New York."

"Good idea," Mercer said.

"Go to the source," I added. "Isn't that always the best way to get reliable information?"

"Yeah," Mercer agreed with me. "It beats a website. Maybe people in that organization can reconcile something like the DA's membership in a hunt club with his conservation concerns."

"What's wrong with the zoo in Central Park?" Mike asked.

"It's not the real deal," I said. "That's mostly a children's zoo."

"It was good enough for you the first time you wanted to spend the night with me," Mike said. "On the roof of the Arsenal."

We had been working a murder of a girl in the park's rowboat lake. The rooftop of the Arsenal, overlooking the tiny zoo, had been magical—the backdrop for the dramatic change in my relationship with Mike.

"I'm not complaining about it. Not that night, anyway," I said. "It's just that it's only six acres within a huge park, versus the two hundred sixty-five acres in the Bronx. And it's a menagerie. It's not where the conservation efforts are centered."

"A menagerie?"

"That's what the Central Park Zoo was called when it was founded," I said. "Eighteen fifty-nine. It was only for the exhibition of animals."

"We heard all this when we were scouring the park on the Bethesda angel murder," Mercer said. "The zoo wasn't even designed as part of the park."

"Yes," I said. "At least two of us were listening. People just started donating exotic animals that they brought back from trips out west or abroad. Everything from swans and snakes to bear cubs."

"Then all those fancy buildings went up along Fifth Avenue— Vanderbilts and Astors and Fricks and Mellons," Mercer said. "Millionaire's Row."

"And the rich folk who moved uptown didn't like the smell of the animals all that much," I said. "So the creatures went from being housed in open enclosures to having some structures built to keep them off the city streets. But the real plan called for a zoological park—like the great ones of Europe. The only place left to build it, in the city, was in the wilderness."

Mercer laughed. "I guess that's what the Bronx was, back in 1900. Wilderness."

"Did you come here to the zoo a lot growing up?" Mike asked.

"Tons."

I had been raised in a suburb north of the city—in Harrison, a small village that was part of Westchester County. My parents, whom I adored, moved there after my father and his partner—both physicians—invented a plastic device that was used worldwide in most cardiac valve replacement surgery, even to this day. The small piece of tubing—the Cooper-Hoffman valve—funded educations for my two brothers and for me—first at Wellesley College, then at the University of Virginia School of Law.

"Me too," Mercer said. "I took the subway here every chance I got. What was your favorite thing to see?"

We were driving on the Deegan Expressway, getting off at the exit near Yankee Stadium to wind across Fordham Road, past the bodegas and restaurants that specialized in chimichangas and burritos, in a neighborhood that was home to Jewish immigrants a century ago.

"Gorillas," I said. "The great apes. They seem so intelligent and, well—almost human. I could watch them all day. And you?"

"Elephants," Mercer said. "I've always loved those beasts. I hated to lose the Ringling Brothers circus, but how I despised the way those gentle giants were treated."

"Me, I'm a lions and tigers guy," Mike said. "I used to have all these fantasies about going to live in the jungle."

"How Tarzan of you," I said. "I never knew."

"But without Jane. No use for her."

"So glad you outgrew that phase."

"I'm working on it," Mike said. "Did you know tiger stripes are like fingerprints?"

"No."

"No two are alike. Each set of stripes is unique."

"I had no idea."

I needed a day like this. I felt like I was playing hooky with my two best friends from school, going to the coolest playground in the city of New York.

"Book of common knowledge," Mike said. "Kind of stuff you should know."

For the last couple of weeks, I had desperately wanted to regain my stability but had continued to struggle with my post-kidnapping PTSD.

I'd always liked to settle down with a drink in the evening. But I had treated my taste for alcohol like an addiction lately. I despised the fog it created in my brain late at night, and hated, too, the way the hangovers compelled me to stay in bed the morning after.

"Did you hear me, Coop?" Mike said.

"Sorry. I've been daydreaming."

"I asked if you've thought this outing through."

"Not entirely."

"I like that," Mike said, looking at me in his rearview mirror. I was stretched out across the backseat. "It's totally in character with the old you."

I wanted to be that me again badly. I had been drawn into the Wolf Savage investigation in the most unlikely way, but it had jolted me back into doing what I did best.

Paul Battaglia deserved a better ending than he got. We had been at sixes and sevens for months now, and he had long ago compromised my once-idealistic view of his integrity. But he had helped shape me into the prosecutor I was today, and the two best detectives I knew—Mike and Mercer—should not have been side-lined from solving the mystery of his murder.

"I want us to break this case," I said.

"How's that going to happen?" Mercer asked. "The old combo-platter solution? Intel from Vickee, surfing the Internet, and a whole lot of ESP?"

"Look, guys," I said, sitting up and leaning forward, "there's nobody who knows more about this situation than we do, is there?"

"You positioned yourself well for that one, Coop," Mike said. "Between a rock and a hard place, for sure."

"I clearly wasn't the target, because the shooter was such a marksman that if he'd intended to kill both Battaglia and me—or just me—he'd have taken another shot. Another perfect shot."

"Fair enough."

"So I'm the key witness. The man was coming to see me," I said. "And I'm supposed to know why that is."

"But you don't," Mike said.

"But they *think* I do, so I figure I'm actually likely to know before they find out. I mean, that's what they assigned me to do. We'll have to break it before the task force does, is all."

"Is she making sense yet, Mercer?" Mike asked.

"Slow and steady wins the race. She'll get there."

Few people knew Battaglia as well as I did—the good, the bad, and the ugly. A dozen years by his side, handling his most sensitive cases and representing him in the community whenever he wanted to duck an appearance or not take the heat for a criminal justice situation.

"I was there for the Wildlife Conservation dinner," I said. "I did the research for his remarks and helped write his acceptance speech."

My English lit major at Wellesley had put me squarely in the DA's sights whenever he needed a ghost for his scripted public remarks.

"I've known Prescott for years," I said. "I've got a Skeeter-meter that lets me read him, courtesy of his ex-wife, and anticipate most of his moves."

"All good, Coop," Mike said. "But Mercer's right; we can't just fly blind."

"I have no intention of doing that," I said. "My brain is getting back in gear, okay?"

"Sure—but—?"

"How many people has Battaglia prosecuted—well, overseen the prosecutions of—in the last three decades?" I asked.

"Hundreds of thousands," Mike said, easing the car off Southern Boulevard and into the parking lot at the zoo.

"Most of them misdemeanors," I said. "Low-level crimes."

"Sure, but thousands of felonies every year, too."

"Not a Pablo Escobar among them," I said. "No big cartel hot-shot, killing off the narcos and cops and district attorneys, simply because the city's Special Narcotics prosecutor handles all of those matters. Took them away from our office. From Battaglia."

"True."

"So follow my thinking for a minute, guys."

Mike turned off the motor and both men turned in their seats to look at me.

"Here's what we've got," I said, ticking off a list on my fingers. "The Saint Hubertus Club. A Supreme Court justice who dies under somewhat suspicious circumstances. The district attorney—man of the year of Animals Without Borders."

"Operation Crash," Mike said, "and the friction between US Attorney James Prescott and District Attorney Paul Battaglia. That's your excuse for going off the reservation to play Sherlock with us."

"That's if you really think I'm going to need an excuse, Detective," I said. "Because at some point the man of the year switches uniforms and shows up at a Saint Hubertus retreat. A private hunting preserve. A meeting so secretive that no one even spills the beans that Battaglia was there—except for an anonymous caller."

"Lord, make his companion be a hooker," Mike said. "It'll be the perfect case."

"Fast-forward to the middle of his displeasure with me," I said. "Last week, showing up for a face-off, backing me away from the Savage case. And then going ballistic—"

"Bad choice of words," Mercer said.

"Stalking me, if you think that's any more suitable language, to the Met Museum to confront me about having something to do with a friend of his who was also there," I said. "Are you following my theme? Is it any surprise that what brings the great man down is a sharpshooter? A professional hunter of some sort who tracked a moving target and nailed it. That, I would suggest to you, has nothing to do with any disgruntled felon Battaglia has ever prosecuted."

Mercer cocked his head and nodded, putting the pieces together.

"Don't forget Diana," Mike said.

"Oh, I haven't let that one slip, Detective. Skeeter Prescott charged me with figuring out who she is," I said, "and he's the last guy I want to let down."

Mike squinted and looked at me, clearly puzzled. "You got Diana?"

"I think I do, gentlemen," I said, sitting back on the rear seat. "Goddess of the hunt, guys. Roman mythology. Diana was goddess of the hunt—and wild animals."

"Now all we have to do"—Mike nodded as he spoke—"is figure out what human form this goddess takes."

# FIFTEEN

"Do you remember meeting any of these fellows back in the day?" Mercer asked.

The three of us were standing in front of the magnificent Rainey gates—the bronze sculptures, oxidized now so that their patina was the same shade of green as the Statue of Liberty, that have been the iconic images of the entrance to the Bronx Zoo since the 1930s.

"I do," I said. "Isn't that Sultan the lion, posing on top of the arches?"

"My department," Mike said. "A Barbary lion—a gift to the zoo just after 1900."

"What are Barbary lions?" I asked.

"The largest in the subspecies," Mike said. "North African. They were massive beasts, with really plush manes. They're the lions that were brought to Rome to fight the gladiators in the Colosseum."

"Of course you would know that," I said.

"There was also a menagerie at the Tower of London," Mike said. "They've actually dug up remains of Barbary lions at the tower going way back before Sultan took up residence here. Big, bold creatures, but extinct now."

"That's the fate of too many of these animals," Mercer said.

The sculptor had captured the mane brilliantly—with layers and layers of waves worked into the bronze material.

I walked beneath the gated archway—under the white-tailed deer and great hornbill, the penguin and pelican, the baboon and flamingo and trio of bears. All of them seemed to be resting on the shell of Buster, a three-hundred-year-old Galapagos tortoise. The handsome animals had drawn me into the zoo for as many years back as I could remember.

"You know they posed for the sculptor?" Mike said.

"C'mon."

"No kidding, Coop. Each of these animals was taken into one of the cages for his sitting. And Rainey was a big-game hunter," he said. "He captured and brought some of the earliest animal specimens back here from Africa."

"Wait a minute," I said. "You remember this from childhood?"

"He's cheating," Mercer said, slapping Mike on the back.

"Where are we, Coop?" Mike asked.

"How stupid of me," I said. "This is the Fordham Road entrance to the zoo."

Mike had gone to Fordham University, which was a stone's throw away.

"It wasn't that long ago that I could tell you the name of every animal in the whole place," he said. "What they ate for breakfast and dinner, and what time they got fed. When I didn't have the cash to dine out with my dates—no trust fund like you, kid—I'd bring my ladies here, for a hot dog and some peanuts."

"I bet it worked every time," I said.

"Pretty much so, as long as I stayed out of the reptile house," Mike said. "There's something about slithering pythons and constrictors. I used to think they'd make the broads want to wrap themselves around me once we got back to the dorm, but they were simply repulsive cold-blooded vipers. A total buzzkill."

"So you're going to be our guide at the zoo," I said, stepping off the walkway as a group of schoolkids ran past me. "I may never get another phone. If you keep me by your side day and night, I won't need one."

"You and I would last side by side for about forty-eight hours. Then all your usual control-freak habits would kick in and I'd be out on the street, trolling for homicides."

"You know where we're going, Alex?" Mercer asked.

"I don't remember my way around, but the woman who helped me with the information for Battaglia's speech, when he was honored, was from the Development Office of the WCS—which lent a hand to Animals Without Borders," I said. "I had to call her a good bit to get the facts right."

"You remember her name?" he asked.

I laughed. "It's in my contacts. On my phone," I said. "It's Deirdre—Deirdre something."

Mercer dialed 411 and asked for the Bronx Zoological Society. It was no longer conservation-speak to call these places "zoos." When information put him through to the switchboard, he asked the operator for the Development Office, passing the phone to me.

"Deirdre, please," I said, and waited for the call to transfer. "Hello, Deirdre? This is Alex Cooper."

"Who?"

"Alex Cooper. We've never met, but we've had a few conversations. I'm the prosecutor who worked with you on the fund-raising dinner honoring Paul Battaglia in—"

"Oh, of course," she said. "I'm so sorry for your loss—and for your, well, your own terrible—what can I say—your experience."

"Thank you for your condolences," I said. "In fact, I'm calling about the district attorney."

"Really?" Deirdre asked. "Is there something I can help you with?"

"There is, actually," I said. "Just unofficially. I mean, I'm not asking as a prosecutor. There won't be a memorial service for the district attorney for weeks, maybe months. But I thought it would bring such a personal element to the event if I could start to organize some of the speakers around the things he cared about most. Maybe bring in some of the people from your world that we don't even know about."

"To contribute to our fund in his honor?"

That, too, I thought, although it hadn't been on my mind. Most of the staff would donate to our favorite advocacy group—Safe Horizon—in his memory, but this would be a fine tribute and a cause we could all respect. "Certainly."

"That's so generous of you," Deirdre said. "I'd need to pull my files, of course. When would you like to talk?"

"Meet. I'd like to meet with you."

"That's fine. Why don't you give me some dates that suit you?"

"How would this afternoon work?"

Deirdre chuckled. "I like fund-raisers with a sense of urgency. But we're up in the Bronx, you know? It's not like I'm around the corner."

"Yes, that's what reminded me of you," I said. "Coincidentally, I'm just a few blocks away, at Fordham, with a couple of my friends."

"Fordham?"

"Yes—um—we were, uh, exploring the chapel there as a possible site for the service. You know it has those gorgeous windows that were made in France, intended for the original Saint Patrick's Cathedral."

"Oh."

"You're trying too hard," Mike whispered to me. "Relax."

"So we're only ten minutes away," I said.

"It's two now," Deirdre said, "and I have a meeting in fifteen minutes. Why don't you come over at three, and I'll get you started. Would that work?"

"Sure. Sure it will."

"Very good. Come in at the Fordham Road entrance—the Rainey gates—and head up, well, do you know where Astor Court is?" she asked.

"Astor Court?" I repeated the name aloud, shrugging my shoulders.

Mike nodded and gave me a thumbs-up.

"Yes," I said. "I do."

"Head for that and then just ask one of the guards for the Heads and Horns building. I'm on the second floor," Deirdre said. "Room 206."

"Thank you. We'll see you soon."

I handed the phone back to Mercer. "So now we're the memorial committee?" Mercer asked.

"I've been told not to mope around feeling sorry for myself," I said. "What a good thing to involve myself in, to honor the late district attorney. Didn't I make it clear that I'm not doing anything official?"

"James Prescott will have your head," Mercer said.

"Heads and Horns it is," I said. "You know where that building is, Mike?"

"Follow me," he said. "You know how this place—I mean the zoo—was founded, don't you?"

"Not a clue."

"European royalty had its Saint Hubertus Society, as we found out, but America had a Boone and Crockett Club."

"Daniel Boone?" I asked. "King of the Wild Frontier?"

"Those are the guys," Mike said.

We were walking along a broad path, beautifully landscaped, and circling a tall stone fountain that was adorned with mythical creatures of all sorts. We continued on up the steps, stopping in front of the original buildings that had housed the first animals ever brought to the zoo.

"What do Boone and Crockett have to do with this?" Mercer asked.

"So far as I can remember," I said, thinking back to my brothers' fascination with their coonskin caps and all things related to Crockett, "those two managed to shoot and kill and skin and trap just about every critter that crossed their paths. Not very conservation-minded."

"Nobody was," Mike said, "when this country was growing westward. Nobody saw any need to be."

"Crockett would be one of your heroes because he was in the Tennessee militia," Mercer said, "and he died fighting Santa Anna and the Mexicans at the Alamo."

"That would be right. So Teddy Roosevelt and his friends created something called the Boone and Crockett Club in the 1880s. No green robes. No white hoods," Mike said. "They were early crusaders for saving wildlife."

"I don't get it," I said. "TR was a big-game hunter. He was slaughtering animals everywhere he went. I've seen photographs of him on these testosterone-filled trips with the guys standing next to dead elephants and zebras in Africa, elk and buffalo in the Dakotas. Don't tell me this club was about conservation."

"Teddy knew better than anyone that these animals were doomed to extinction unless there were ways to save them."

"Yeah," I said. "Don't shoot them. That's one way."

"I'm telling you, Coop, TR introduced legislation to stop deer hunting in New York, and this club dedicated itself to creating the zoological park. This park."

"Why here?" Mercer asked. "Was this part of the Bronx really that wild?"

"Totally unkempt," Mike said. "They've got loads of pictures of it over at the university. It was like a jungle of trees and weeds, a few huge bogs, a deadly sewer stream that flowed through it, and not a drop of drinking water anywhere on these two hundred sixty acres. What they created here is nothing short of miraculous."

The pavement was redbrick, and the staircase led up to an enormous building with a great dome on top of it.

"Recognize that architecture? This is the Elephant House—and it was modeled on one of the great creations of the Columbian Exposition," Mike said. "Chicago, 1893."

"I don't know much about the exposition except for the devil in the White City," I said, thinking of the extraordinary story of the serial killer who murdered dozens of women during its run, "but the building is pretty spectacular."

We walked through the arch under the dome—which was lined with Guastavino tiles, just like the magnificent ghost station in the subway below city hall and over the whispering corner in Grand Central Terminal.

"Can you imagine elephants penned up in buildings like this?" Mercer asked. "African elephants on one side and Asians on the other, with a small caged area outside where they could walk for a few hours a day."

"What's the difference between African and Asian elephants?" I asked.

"Pretty much two things," Mercer said. "The Africans tend to be larger than their counterparts. They also have larger ears, which are sort of shaped like the continent itself."

"This whole place was obviously built before the idea of designing spaces that resemble the natural habitats of the animals came to be," Mike said. "You could go a little stir-crazy inside an old brick building if you were used to the freedom of the jungle."

"That's what happened to the zoo's very first elephant," Mercer said, obviously recalling his youthful obsession with the large gray beasts. "He was caught in the wild, in Assam. The zookeepers here were hoping to tame the big guy, but docile wasn't in the stars for Gunda. He injured so many of the staff that he wound up in shackles."

"Leg shackles?" I asked.

"Yes, chained down by all fours," Mercer said. "But he still raged and charged at everyone who came near him, till they finally put him down."

"With an elephant gun, no doubt," Mike said.

"I thought zoos were such happy places," I said.

"Better when we were kids than way back then," Mercer said, patting me on the head.

"Straight forward to Heads and Horns," Mike said. "At the far end of Astor Court, to your right."

"What was that named for?" I asked. "Heads and Horns."

"The first director of this facility," Mike said, "was a man named William Hornaday."

"He was a zoologist?"

"Not exactly, Coop. He was a taxidermist."

"What? The guy stuffed dead animals?"

"That's what he did," Mike said.

"Why did they let him run a zoo, full of live ones?" I asked. "That makes no sense."

"Listen to me, kid. Before 1900, it was pretty damn rare to find a man who made a distinction between killing for sport—like the great white hunters—and killing for scientific study, for education," Mike said. "Hornaday made it his goal to preserve the animals of North America. He was really the forefather of this conservation movement."

"But in the meantime," I said, speeding up my gait, "he built a museum full of stuffed heads."

"That's what people who couldn't go on safari with Teddy wanted to see, Coop. Rhinos and elephants and giraffes—on the wall from floor to ceiling."

"Breaks my heart," I said. "What's the reason to shoot a giraffe, just to hang its beautiful long neck on the wall? They're not predators."

"Different times," Mike said. "All the animals in the dioramas at the Museum of Natural History were shot specifically for the purpose of displaying them, to educate people who'd never otherwise see them."

"Different moral compass." I loved that museum—I think everyone did. Re-creations of animal life created in the 1940s. Real skin and actual bones underneath, stuffed with papier-mâché to make the creatures come to life.

"In the middle of the room here at Heads and Horns was a pair of the largest elephant tusks in the world," Mike said, "each one more than twelve feet long."

"Blood ivory," I said. "Then and now."

"You don't have to run, kid. This whole museum was dismantled fifty years ago. That moment of trophy heads and horns has passed. I studied it while I was at Fordham. I've only seen pictures," Mike said. "The old building just holds administrative offices now."

There were sea lions at play in the large pool beyond the original Primate House. It was so refreshing to see living things in spaces that resembled their native homes, instead of hearing these tales of cement captivity from Mike. Schoolkids surrounded the wrought iron fence, fixated on the barking creatures that climbed up to bask in the October sunlight before diving back into the chilly water.

Almost everything that used to be a brick-and-mortar enclosure seemed to have been repurposed for some other space—a cafeteria that had been the Lion House, once filled with majestic royal palms that fronted the cages that held pacing beasts, and an education facility in the former Antelope House.

Rhinos, horns intact, grazed behind the buildings off to our right, and peacocks seemed to have no confines at all, strutting on the footpaths as though they owned the property.

"We're still early," Mike said, pulling out his phone. "I'd better check in with the US attorney before he implodes."

I sat down on a bench, watching the endless march of visitors, most adults with maps in hand and kids running ahead to find their favorite animals.

"Is this Ella?" he asked. "It's Mike Chapman for Mr. Prescott."

I threw back my head to catch some of the rays while Mike waited.

"Good afternoon, sir."

Mike started to listen—and then held the phone away from his ear so that I could hear James shouting at him.

"I'm actually not working this week, sir," Mike said. "I'm not required to keep my phone on, so you really don't have to yell at me for not returning your calls."

Then a pause while Prescott spoke.

"Yes, I had lunch with Alexandra today and, yes, I gave her your message," he said. "She didn't much feel like calling you, but I expect she'll be in your office tomorrow. She intends to give you her complete cooperation."

I couldn't make out the words James was speaking, but I could hear the tone of his voice.

"Alexandra was pulling a Garbo, sir," Mike said. "No? Not a movie guy, are you, then?"

Prescott's volume increased.

"It means she wanted to be alone," Mike said. "And frankly, she's on a leave of absence, so it's not really any of your business."

Another question.

"I didn't say that, sir. I didn't say I don't know where she is, because you never asked me that. If I'm not mistaken, Mr. Prescott, Alexandra is visiting relatives in the Bronx."

A short burst this time.

"You may not have known she had relatives there, but I think we pretty much all do. It's a generational thing," Mike said, before shutting off his phone.

I got up to high-five my lover. "Well done," I said, kissing him on each cheek.

"I couldn't help myself, Coop. I'm staring at the sign that says Primate House. These creatures are Prescott's missing links, too, no matter how he wound up in horse country."

Mercer had backed off in the other direction, probably to check in with Vickee and to call his lieutenant, who was clearly giving him a break for the afternoon.

When he returned, he had a grim expression on his face.

"All quiet on Vickee's end," Mercer said. "They can't confirm the fact that Battaglia was actually in Texas the night Justice Scalia died, so that buys DCPI at least another day with the media."

Unlike the tabloids, the mainstream media required two sources to go with a story. Thankfully, they were short one on the Saint Hubertus angle.

"And no new clues on the assassins," Mercer said, "so the Police Foundation has upped the reward money to two hundred fifty thousand dollars."

"Life is cheap. I'd have thought the Manhattan DA was worth way more than that," Mike said. "I guess he was past his sell-by date at this point."

"What's the bad news?" I asked.

"The lieutenant asked me to tell you that this didn't come from him," Mercer said.

"Deal."

"You're not wrong about Detective Stern wanting to put the screws to you, Alex," Mercer said.

"What now?" I asked, tensing up at the mention of his name. "What did I do to ask for that?"

"You just did your job," he said. "But it turns out that the guy you convicted of drugging and raping that grad student eighteen months ago—you know the case I mean?"

"Yes, he doped her with roofies, then practically drowned her in his bathtub trying to wake her up. Threatened her not to call the police, because he had connections at the precinct."

"That perp's connection is none other than Jaxon Stern," Mercer said. "He's married to Stern's sister."

"So what?" I said. "The guy I convicted is a total asshole."

"Yeah, but Detective I-Am-Internal-Affairs actually bailed him out when the arrest happened. He almost lost his chance to go from IAB to Homicide. So now Jaxon not only got a serious dressing down, but he's stuck with supporting his sister and her kids. The man would like nothing better than to see you go down in flames."

# SIXTEEN

"Hello, I'm Deirdre Wright."

"I'm Alex," I said, introducing her to Mike and Mercer. "It's very nice to meet you in person."

"Likewise, although I wish it were under different circumstances."

"So do we all."

She ushered us into Room 206 and we each grabbed a seat around the small table in the middle of the room. Over Deirdre's shoulder, I could see the bright plumage of a variety of birds, flying high in the giant aviary across from the rear of the building.

"Just to be clear," I said, repeating what I had told her on the phone, "I have nothing to do with the investigation into Paul Battaglia's death."

"I understand that," Deirdre said. "The newspaper stories say you're on leave, and beside that, I can't imagine any reason the murder case would reach into the WCS or the zoo. I appreciate that you're thinking of us for the bigger picture."

We were good. No matter what came after this, Deirdre Wright could truthfully say that I had not represented to her that I was working with the feds on the DA's shooting.

"Happy to," I said.

She glanced at my companions, showing she was not to be trifled with. "Are you all on leave?"

"Just keeping an eye on Ms. Cooper," Mike said, running his fingers through his thick dark hair and giving Deirdre his classic

Chapman grin. "We work with her, and since she and I were both eyewitnesses to the shooting, we're laying low for the week. Mercer's our bodyguard."

Deirdre responded to the word "bodyguard" by sitting up straight and losing her smile. I had the feeling that when people looked at me now and knew who I was, they would see the words DEATH GRIP written across my forehead in scarlet letters.

"Did you have a chance to work with Paul Battaglia when you helped Animals Without Borders organize the dinner in his honor?" I asked.

Deirdre had her hand on a small stack of folders, color-coded and tabbed by subject.

"I only met the DA twice," she said. "If you've ever planned one of these charity dinners—or been honored at one—you sort of know the drill."

"Start from scratch," Mike said. "I'm a novice."

She pulled out the red folder from the bottom of the pile. "First, the executive committee of their board comes up with some nominees for the annual award. That happens about a week after the annual dinner is over."

"You plunge right into the next year?" Mike asked.

"Yes," Deirdre said. "You can't imagine how much planning one of these events takes—from selecting the venue, choosing a date that works for everyone involved, finding an honoree acceptable to the committee, growing the guest list, collecting the money, and choosing a speaker who can keep a crowd awake and not walking out the door before the coffee is served. We all take a week off—I'm the liaison between the two groups—then we dive right in all over again."

"Was Battaglia the unanimous choice of the committee when he was honored—what was it—two years ago?" I asked.

Deirdre opened the red folder, then looked up at me. "Do you really need this kind of detail to plan a memorial?"

"She can't help herself sometimes," Mike said, leaning forward with clasped hands on the table, trying to bond with Deirdre—loosen her up a bit. "It's the investigative gene in her DNA. Kind of drives Mercer and me crazy, too."

Deirdre responded to him and returned the smile with a wide one of her own.

"We're trying to distract her for a few days," Mike went on, as though I wasn't in the room. "Hey, if she thinks she can solve the murder case at the same time as she can do good for her old boss, what's the harm? There are snakes around every corner, out on the street and right here inside your park. We like to cut Coop some slack."

"No harm at all," Deirdre said. Now she was looking at me more like I was a mental patient than a killer.

She flipped through a sheaf of papers. "They've got a really tough board. Not just smart and rich and prestigious, but men and women who take wildlife conservation more seriously than anything else. Sure they're patrons of the arts and they're captains of industry, but this zoological park—and do not, Alex, whenever it is that you make your remarks, refer to it as a 'zoo,' okay?—this zoological park is the center of their universe. It drives all their efforts worldwide to save species and to save wild places."

"Why can't you call it a zoo?" Mercer asked.

"From the time this place was founded," Deirdre said, "the word 'zoo' was frowned upon. It referred to small places—like our Central Park facility—where animals are kept in cages and not allowed to roam free."

"But at first, even here—" Mike started to say.

"Yes, but that was never the plan for these two hundred sixty acres," she replied. "It was always to be a place where animals could roam freely, with a habitat re-created to resemble the homes they were taken from. A park—which sounded far more dignified to our founders than a zoo. It has only reached this great level of sophistication with modern technology. If you haven't visited the park lately, I'm going to insist that you take a tour."

"We'd love to do that," I said. I reached to the center of the table and grabbed a pad and pencil. "Thanks, too, for reminding me about the importance of the wordage. You held me to it—not referring to this place as a zoo—in Battaglia's dinner speech, and I would have forgotten how important it is by this point in time."

I jotted down the words "zoological park," as Deirdre watched me write. I wanted her to know I was on target, concentrating on a memorial tribute, not searching for clues. She seemed to appreciate my expression of gratitude.

"So what you asked was whether Mr. Battaglia was the board's unanimous choice," Deirdre said. "I'd prefer you keep what I'm about to tell you just between us, as background."

"Of course we will."

"He was not." Deirdre looked at her notes and laughed. "Not even close."

Mike looked at me and my eyes opened wide. Was it possible someone knew, two years ago, of Battaglia's association with a private big-game hunting preserve?

"Someone objected to Battaglia because they didn't think he was sincere when he did the work on Operation Crash?" I asked.

"Oh, no," Deirdre said. "That's the case that had most of the board in his corner. From the perspective of our work, it was a unique and powerful piece of public service. I'm skimming my notes and I see there were complaints about making a politician the honoree. You know, there are people who didn't vote for Paul Battaglia."

"Not many," Mike said. "Eight terms, and most of the time no one ran against him."

Deirdre turned a page. "Then there's the problem—voiced by many—that when you honor a public servant, you can't raise nearly as much money as you can with a corporate leader."

"That's certainly true," I said. The staff prosecutors didn't make enough money to chip in for fifty-thousand-dollar tables or bid on twenty-five-thousand-dollar auction items. It always worked better to bestow the award on the CEO of a Fortune 500 company and let his underlings fill the ballroom with equally wealthy syco-phants or rivals.

"But, just so I don't head off in the wrong direction when I'm writing this," I said, "there was nothing in your vetting that turned up opposition material to Battaglia on the wildlife issue itself?"

"Of course not," Deirdre said.

"Like if the man was off herding elk into his garage and shoot-ing them," Mike said, "you would have known about it?"

Deirdre thought he was funny. "You're kidding, right?"

"Isn't that what it's like to be on a shooting preserve? Someone rounds up all the animals and you just take pot shots at them, for sport?"

"That's my view of it," Deirdre said, shaking her head. "This spring, a group imported ninety kangaroos and released them into the wild in Wyoming."

"Kangaroos?" I asked.

"Yes. The climate resembles that in Australia, and, well, hunt-ers will love the novelty of killing those creatures, I'm sure."

"It's shocking."

"There's even a preserve in Texas where the guests shoot at wild boar from a helicopter," Deirdre said. "I don't know where the word 'sportsmanship' fits into that scenario."

The idea sickened me, but the mention of Texas perked me up.

"Texas? Are you talking about the ranch—the preserve—where Justice Scalia died?" I asked. "Do you know anything about Saint Hubertus?"

"Hey, I'm just development," Deirdre said. "I don't know a thing about that organization except that the honorable justice would not have been on our short list of honorees."

"Diana," I said, hungry for a positive answer. "Is there a hunt club named after the Roman goddess?"

"Not that I know of, but most of these societies are so secretive, Alex—by plan—that it's really rare to hear anything about them," Deirdre said. "Texas is full of these twenty-thousand-acre preserves in hill country."

"What's that about?" Mercer asked. "Deer? Buffalo? Game birds?"

"Oh, no. The owners of some of these properties have been importing exotic hoofstock from Africa for years: oryx and ibex, wildebeests, gazelles—even zebra."

"To be hunted and killed? Why would anyone find pleasure in killing a zebra?" I asked. "Is it legal?"

"Some of the imports are sanctioned, but certainly not endangered or threatened species," Deirdre said. "Take the dama gazelle, which may be the most graceful animal on earth. It's from the Sahara, but it's critically endangered."

"Why so?" Mercer asked.

"Overhunted, of course, and also because its habitat is shrinking. Society keeps encroaching on its land," Deirdre said. "But go online, Mercer. Google 'Texas and hunting preserves.' You'll get dozens of options popping up, offering you packages of game to shoot. Animals of your choosing. Somehow these gorgeous creatures—dama gazelles—have been brought into North America, some of them for captive breeding programs and others smuggled, just for the purpose of providing target practice for some rich sportsman."

"I assume Mr. Battaglia was keenly interested in all this," I said, trying to find a way back to my mission.

Deirdre Wright pursed her lips. "Not so much, frankly."

"Sorry to hear that."

"Like I said, I met with the DA twice before we honored him. The first time was in his office, when I explained to him the setup for the evening, talked about the run of show and what we expected his remarks to cover, and asked for his guest list."

"His guest list?" Mike said. "I thought it was your party."

"This is how charity dinners go, Mike," Deirdre said. "We've got a list of all our donors, and, yes, most of our loyal and regular high rollers will pay the money and come to the annual dinner. But the way an organization grows is by bringing in an honoree who has a pretty big following himself."

"So Paul Battaglia's campaign contributions," Mike said. "Eight terms' worth of them."

"That was the idea that won over the recalcitrant board members," she said, removing a green folder from the pile and waving it at us. "The color of money."

"But in the end he wouldn't play; is that what you're telling me?"

"Some people are like that," Deirdre said. "They make promises to us so we give them the award—which comes with a lot of media attention, all over the world, and introduces the honoree to many of our folks he doesn't know."

"Let me guess," I said. "Paul Battaglia gave you a rousing 'yes' when he was asked to accept the honor but got too busy with his work and major cases when time came to lean on him for the list."

"Let's just say it was a short list." Deirdre winked at me. "You do know him well."

"I assume that what you like is for the man of the year to turn his Rolodex over to you," I said.

"Ideally. But that didn't happen."

I was itching to get my fingers inside Deirdre's green folder and scan the names—her list and Battaglia's designated hitters.

"Did you get to meet Amy Battaglia?" I asked.

"The DA's wife?" Deirdre asked. "Only to shake hands at the dinner."

That left another door open for me. "If I could have a copy of the lists, I can probably come up with names to add for invites to the memorial," I said. "If Mrs. B didn't cross into this part of the DA's interests, she'll probably neglect to include them."

"Interesting idea. I mean, I know my boss would certainly like to be included," Deirdre said, though I noted her hesitation, "and maybe some of the board members of Animals Without Borders. But I—well, I'd have my head handed to me if I made a copy of this list for you."

"What if I stayed right here," I said, forcing a smile, "and just scanned the names on both lists? It could be so helpful to the family."

"It's hard to say no to that, isn't it?" she said.

Deirdre Wright played her fingers on the green folder like it was a piano.

"Why don't I turn my back for a moment, and you take a look at the names, if you think it will provide some comfort for the family," she said. "I'll try and engage Mike and Mercer to come back to the park."

She stood up and walked to the window, leaving the file with me.

"I could make this really worthwhile for you," Mike said, stepping in beside Deirdre. "Don't get fooled by the fact that Alex is a public servant. She's also a trustifarian."

"A what?"

"She's got a trust fund," Mike said, "and she's crazy about animals. The wilder the better."

Deirdre was amused. And distracted.

I was scrolling down the abbreviated list of names that Battaglia had given to AWB. There were few surprises on the first page—relatives and friends, partners at major law firms, prosperous members of the defense bar, guys he golfed with and summered with in East Hampton. I recognized names of prominent men and women who'd been similarly honored by the American Museum of Natural History or the Frick or other cultural institutes, for whom this contribution would have been payback.

"You bought a ticket to the dinner," Deirdre said to me. "You were there."

"A ticket?" Mike said. "She could have bought a table. She could have bought six or eight tables."

I let him babble on while I read on. I expected that he'd have me signed up as a supporter before we left the grounds today.

"The Reverend Shipley was a contributor?" I asked Deirdre.

She answered without turning her head. "Not a chance. The Reverend Hal is a freeloader. All the time," she said. "Battaglia specifically requested we put Hal at his table."

I didn't remember that, but the dinner was more than a year before the reverend and I had our dustup over his attempt to interfere in a case Mike and I were working on. I thought of him then as a community pariah—morally bankrupt and totally corrupt—but I had never figured his tentacles reached into Paul Battaglia's pockets.

"We do a lot of outreach in Harlem," Deirdre said, "with our educational programs for kids and our teach-ins here at the park. So we get great support from most of the Harlem leaders, but nothing at all from Hal Shipley."

"The rev's got no redeeming social value," Mike said.

While Deirdre was pointing out something through the window, I scribbled down some of the names that were less familiar to me. Tonight I could cross-check them against the fashion gala guest list that was published in yesterday's papers, in case my hunch about George Kwan was incorrect.

"We do," she was saying in answer to questions Mike and Mercer had asked. "We get more than three million visitors a year. We've got four thousand animals who live here with us, representing six hundred fifty different species."

"That must make you the largest metropolitan zoo in the country," Mercer said.

"It does."

"I see that Wolf Savage was one of your big donors," I said. "Not to the Battaglia evening, but in general, even sending in a check for that event."

"Yes, we were so saddened by Mr. Savage's death," Deirdre said. "He was such a philanthropic man. I hope the family—the corporation—keeps it up."

"That would be wonderful." It was premature for me to suggest that I could put in a word with Savage's daughter. If this turned out to be an avenue of interest, there would be plenty of time for me to do that.

"It was such a perfect fit," she said. "You know his company was named WolfWear."

"Yes."

"Well, of course you know that," Deirdre said, turning back to me. "So he made it his personal interest to help save the Mongolian gray wolf. He liked the symbolism of it."

"Tell me about the animal," I said. I was stretching to make connections now—some of them doubtless inconsequential, but sooner or later we were bound to hit pay dirt.

"The gray wolf?" she asked. "Sure. It's the largest canid in Asia."

"Canid?" Mike asked.

"Dogs, wolves, jackals—they're all in the *Canid* genus. The gray wolves are slender and long-limbed, but very powerful."

"And endangered because they're hunted?" he said.

"That, and because in Asia, where they live, they're used a lot as an ingredient in traditional medicine," Deirdre said. "They're killed for their brains."

"Brains?" Mike asked.

"Yes, wolves are key figures in Mongolian culture. They're believed to have been the ancestors of Genghis Khan."

"Ah," Mike said. "The Supreme Conqueror."

"So their brains are said to have great healing powers."

"So does Preparation H," Mike said, "but there's nothing on earth I'd shoot to get my hands on some of it."

Deirdre chuckled. "Neither would Mr. Savage. He even staged one of his Fashion Week shows in the Central Park Zoo. The models actually walked with the baby goats and the potbellied pigs and the petting zoo animals. It was a huge hit."

"I'll bet it was," Mike said.

Now I was trying to make links between the WCS donors and the Wolf Savage gala on Monday night. The names on Deirdre's list might be more important than I could factor in at the moment. Surely, some of the wildlife donors would have respected Wolf's work in this field. And maybe one of them was recognized by Battaglia—at the Met, on the late news, before he headed out to meet me in such a rush.

I flipped over the three pages of personal donors and went on to those tabbed as corporate sponsors. There was a single name that jumped out at me.

KWAN ENTERPRISES was listed in all caps and bold ink as both a Platinum Supporter of Animals Without Borders and the underwriter of the dinner honoring the district attorney.

I played it as casually as I could, hoping Mike wouldn't pile in when he heard the name.

"Kwan Enterprises," I said. "That sounds so familiar. What can you tell me about them?"

"All I know is that they're an international business of some kind. They've got big money and they give it freely to good causes, like WCS and AWB."

"The man in charge of the company," I said, "is George Kwan, if I have my information right."

"I think you do. That's the name I recognize, the signature on the checks."

"Tell me what you know about him," I said. "Tell me how he's involved with your organization."

"There's nothing to tell," Deirdre said. "Kwan is kind of a mystery to us."

"How do you mean?"

"George Kwan doesn't participate in any of our events," she said. "I'm not sure he's in the States very often, because he has businesses all over the world. But if my boss asks him for money, George Kwan sends a check."

"What does he get in return?" I asked.

Deirdre looked puzzled. "Same as all our other donors, Alex. He gets free admission to the park, tickets to our lectures, newsletters about our research, and all that sort of thing."

"No special access?"

"There's no such thing."

"Then why did you say he's mysterious?" I asked.

"Because most people who give us gobs of money make demands," Deirdre said. "They want to give parties here at the park, free admission for all their friends, and behind-the-scenes access to our animal keepers and feeding pens. They want their kids to ride on the Bug Carousel and eat breakfast with the gorillas."

"But George Kwan wants nothing?"

Deirdre Wright lifted her hands and threw back her head, as if searching in the air for an answer. "Can you believe that perhaps he just has a good heart and believes in our cause?"

"That could be, but—"

"Mr. Kwan is Chinese," Deirdre said, "and dozens of the animals in that country are facing extinction. Red pandas and white-cheeked gibbons, Siberian tigers and snow leopards. I could give you a list of fifty more."

"So you don't think Kwan is taking their brains," Mike said, "at the same time he's doling out dollars to you?"

"I seriously doubt that, Mike," she said.

"Then why do you consider him so mysterious?" I asked.

"We'd like to meet him, is all. We'd like to get to know Mr. Kwan."

"So you can dig a little deeper in his pockets?" Mercer asked.

"You nailed me," she said. "I'm really good at that. It's just that since he came to us several years ago, he's been more elusive than the yeti."

"George Kwan," Mike said. "Man of mystery, Coop."

Deirdre smiled again. "That's why we think he might just be an apparition, Mike," she said. "It's our nickname for him—we call him the ghost."

# SEVENTEEN

"Why did you get off the drive here?" I asked. "Aren't we going to midtown for dinner?"

"I think it's a good time to go ghost busting, Coop."

Mike had taken the Seventy-First Street exit of the FDR Drive, turning north on First Avenue to wind his way through the East Seventies.

"George Kwan?" I said. "We can't do that now."

"Just a drop-in," Mike said. "You can't get the man out of your head. If he had something to do with Battaglia's murder, let's get on his ass right away."

"I need to prep for this. For an interview."

"No, you don't."

"He might be a suspect in a homicide. I can't just shoot from the hip."

"Just because you don't have hips?" Mike asked. "Sure you can. Leave your OCD list making behind."

"Calm down, both of you," Mercer said. "Let's all get on the same page. What even makes you think he's at home?"

"Nothing. I've got no reason at all. But what have we got to lose by trying?"

I leaned back against the rear seat to puzzle it out. "We might scare him off by going in too early. Unprepared."

"You're the only one who's unprepared," Mike said. "You think I get to a crime scene, find a body chopped to bits and some mope holding the machete, and I get to go back to the office and make a neat list of questions to ask him?"

"This is no street mope. He's a really smart businessman. He's—"

"You've cross-examined monsters, Coop. You've stood nose to nose with some of the worst human beings on the planet. Time for you to strap on some balls again, babe."

Mercer laughed along with Mike—of course—and I just bit my lip.

"What's the approach?" Mercer asked.

"Coop and I can go to the door," Mike said. "I've got a legit reason to talk to Kwan."

"Remind me what that would be," I said.

"The man knew Battaglia, right?"

"Check."

"The man knew Wolf Savage and was actually a business rival of his."

"Check."

"Kwan possibly saw some of our encounter with Savage's killers at the museum."

"Okay. Check."

"We don't know what time he walked down the steps of the Met to leave," Mike said, "so what's to say he doesn't have information—normal witness information—about either Battaglia's unfortunate and untimely end or the fugitive in the Savage murder?"

"So this is a routine homicide investigation interview," I said.

"Sounds right to me," Mercer chimed in. "Just don't set off any alarm buttons in case Coop's sniffer is on the right track."

"I don't piss everybody off, pal. I'm very selective in my approach."

By the time we reached the block on East Seventy-Eighth Street where George Kwan's town house was located, it was almost six o'clock in the evening.

Mike parked the car and we left Mercer in it to walk up the steps of the building and ring the bell.

When the door was opened, behind the handsome wrought iron gates, I assumed it was one of Kwan's bodyguards who asked what our business was.

"To see Mr. Kwan," Mike said.

It wasn't the bodyguard who answered. It was George Kwan himself.

"About what?" Kwan asked, his bodyguard right behind him, adjusting a camel hair overcoat on the businessman's shoulders. They seemed to be about to leave the house.

"A few questions," Mike said, holding up his gold shield. "This is Ms. Cooper, and I'm Detective Chapman. Homicide. We met at the offices of the Savage family early last week."

"Yes, I remember that."

"May we come in?" Mike said, his hand on the door, ready to push it back.

"I'm on my way out, as you can see," Kwan said. "A dinner engagement."

"Surely you can spare us a couple of minutes. You don't look like the early-bird-special type, Mr. Kwan."

The bodyguard held the door firmly in place by the large brass handle.

"We can talk on the way to my car," Kwan said, waving the bodyguard to follow him out.

"It's murder," Mike said. "It deserves a sit-down, don't you think?"

"You've wrapped up that mess around Wolf Savage, haven't you?" Kwan asked.

No one moved—neither in nor out.

"Mr. Kwan," I said. "If you would just give us fifteen minutes.

You were at the gala on Monday night, and we have some questions about what you saw there and what time you left."

"My condolences, Ms. Cooper. Perhaps this is about the district attorney's death, and not Wolf Savage after all?"

"We're still missing one perp in the Savage case," Mike said. "I was hoping you could help us with that. You knew most of the people in that family business."

"I'm glad to answer your questions. You have my numbers," Kwan said. "Just call for an appointment. Your timing tonight is most inconvenient."

Kwan was taller than Mike, and leaner, too. He had an elegant air about him and was trying to be cooperative even though we had ambushed him.

He angled his body and walked between Mike and me, through the gates and down the steps. When he reached the sidewalk, he stopped and waited for us to descend.

"There's some urgency to finding the fugitive who was part of Wolf Savage's murder," I said. "The sooner you can sit down with us, the faster we can get moving."

"I understand, Ms. Cooper."

"And since you mentioned the death of Paul Battaglia, we'd like to ask you some things about that, too."

"Shocking. Completely shocking, for you, I'm sure—and for this city," Kwan said. "You know I left the museum only an hour or so before Battaglia was shot."

I appreciated his candor. Kwan looked me in the eye and didn't blink when talking about the dead DA.

"Then it must have hit you very hard, too," I said. "I know you were friends."

"Friends? Me," he asked, "and Paul Battaglia?"

"Yes."

"I'd hardly call it that, Ms. Cooper. We were acquaintances." Kwan lifted his arm, pulled back the sleeve of his coat, and looked at his watch. "I really have to be going, if you don't mind."

The bodyguard opened the rear passenger door of the navy-blue Bentley. Kwan ducked his head and stepped into it.

"That's so odd," I said. "Battaglia described your relationship so differently to me."

Kwan put his window down. "What was that?"

"He was so grateful for your support in the Animals Without Borders fund-raiser that honored him," I said. "I know, because I worked on the event with him."

"One of my own causes, Ms. Cooper. The world would be a much sorrier place without all the Asian and African species that are so threatened," he said, smiling at me. "On the edge of extinction."

"I must be wrong," I said, mustering all the false humility that I could. "I just remember that Battaglia spoke about you on much more familiar terms."

Kwan shook his head as he pressed the button to raise the window.

"Two years ago, at the time of that dinner?" he said, pausing it halfway up. "I hardly knew him."

"Much more recently than that."

Kwan seemed interested now. "Really? When was that? I mean, the last time you spoke with him about me?"

"On Monday. On the day he died," I said. "On the day he was assassinated at the museum."

"I can't think of any reason he would have done so," Kwan said.

The tinted window closed and the dark car drove off down the street.

# EIGHTEEN

"The usual for Mercer and me," Mike said, "and a Shirley Temple for the broad."

We were in the cozy bar at Aretsky's Patroon, the upscale restaurant on East Forty-Sixth Street, catching the Final Jeopardy! question on the small TV mounted on a corner wall, before going to our table to wait for Vickee.

"Tonight's category is AVIAN FEATS," Trebek said. "All about our winged friends."

One contestant smiled and two others looked puzzled as they decided how much of their winnings they'd bet on the birds.

"Stake me to the twenty, will you, Coop?" Mike said.

"When's payday?" I asked, nipping an olive from his vodka martini.

"Friday," he said. "I'm good for it."

Mercer and I put our money on the bar. We made small talk with the bartender, whom I hadn't seen in weeks, waiting for the answer to be posted.

"SATELLITES CAPTURED IMAGES OF THIS BIRD STAYING ALOFT— WITHOUT TOUCHING DOWN—FOR TWO MONTHS."

As the lilting theme song played in the background and the on-air contestants wrote out their questions, Mike pointed at me.

"I have no idea," I said. "I pass."

"Take a guess."

"I don't know. What is the bald eagle?"

"Bad guess, Coop, really bad. But a raptor kind of suits you, kid," Mike said. "How about you, m' man?"

"I'm going with vulture," Mercer said. "What's a turkey vulture?"

"Getting warmer, Mercer. Also a raptor, but rides thermals, huge wingspan."

"No bird can go without touching down for two months," I said.

"Once again, you would be wrong, Ms. Cooper," Mike said, taking Mercer's money and mine off the bar. "The video is streaming live on the Discovery site. You gotta see it."

"What is—?" I asked.

"The frigate bird," Mike said, just before Trebek confirmed his question was correct. "Rides the wind like a roller coaster. Glides forty miles without flapping its wings."

I got off the barstool and walked toward the dining room. "Why in the world would you know that?"

"Because they were named for fast warships, Coop," Mike said. "Frigates were built for speed and maneuverability."

"Warships. Of course you'd know."

Mike and Mercer followed me to our regular booth in the front corner at Aretsky's Patroon, our destination whenever they wanted the best New York strip steak and I had a craving for Dover sole.

"Are you sure, Alexandra? *C'est vrai?*" Stephane asked, looking incredulous as he seated us and heard Mike order me a Diet Coke. "*Pas de* Dewar's?"

I adored the maître d' and his divine accent. I could almost forget there was any violent crime in the city when I was nestled into the padded leather banquette and coddled by Stephane, even though it was a bad sign when the waitstaff could anticipate my every cocktail.

"I feel like nursing a glass of a full-bodied red wine," I said. "Would you pick one for me?"

"*Bien sûr,*" Stephane said.

Mike, Mercer, and I were joined ten minutes later by Vickee, who squeezed my hand across the table when she sat down.

"The commissioner sends regards," she said to me.

"You told him we'd be having dinner together?"

"I think Scully knows our friendship is—well, thicker than blood, to be blunt about it," Vickee said. "He actually wants me to hang out with you. He thinks you'll be candid with me—that I have a lighter touch than the US attorney. Maybe something we all talk about will get you thinking."

"I'm not holding anything back, Vickee," I said. "I want this thing solved."

"Scully knows that. Everyone does."

"What's come in?" I asked. "What does he expect us to talk about?"

"Back down, Coop," Mike said.

"You know how it goes," Vickee said. "Once we offer money to the public, the TIPS hotline lights up like a Christmas tree. We've got three officers screening the calls."

"Anything real?"

"Two residents of Fifth Avenue co-ops who were stargazing on Monday night saw the whole thing," she said, sipping from a glass of sparkling water.

"What's the whole thing?" I asked, practically hoisting myself on the table.

"I'm sorry, Alex. I'm joking, of course. One of the callers can describe Mike to a tee—she must have had binoculars trained on him," Vickee said. "She's not sure what he did, but she thinks he's guilty."

"I'm always guilty of something," Mike said.

"The other?" I asked.

"The second tipster is sure it was one of the fashionistas, waiting till after the gala. Mike's accuser was anonymous, but this one gave her name and everything. She's convinced there's so much jealousy in that industry that it had to be another designer, who mistook Battaglia for a rival."

"And me?" I asked. "It could have been *me* who was killed."

"That lady looking out her window probably pegged you for Anna Wintour, Coop," Mike said. "The devil wore my blazer over her shoulders."

"No doubt," I said, relaxing against the cushioned seat. "Wintour was there too. Let's ask Stephane to find us a newspaper so I can go over the names when I get home."

"Has Scully told James Prescott that Paul Battaglia may have been at the Texas shooting preserve the night Justice Scalia died?" Mike asked.

"This morning," Vickee said. "Prescott and the commissioner are going to meet for an hour every day. Prescott promised to put all his cards on the table, and to keep all the info he gets from us as need-to-know."

The tension between the NYPD and the feds was real. There was no way Scully could withhold critical information—verified or not—from the US attorney. But once it went from top dog to top dog, there would be hell to pay if anyone on Prescott's end leaked it.

"Did Prescott have any reaction?" I asked. "Was he as surprised as we were?"

"Kept his poker face on for the commissioner. It didn't seem to set off any fresh leads," Vickee said. Then she opened her tote. "Here's the official list, from Citadel Security, of the gala attendees. Scully wants you to study it and make any connections you can."

Stephane returned with our drinks and took our orders. Two black-and-blue strip steaks, two grilled soles for Vickee and me, along with sides of onion rings and crispy Brussels sprouts. I was beginning to feel hungry for the first time in days. I wanted to regain some of my strength.

Vickee waited till we four were alone. "I've got nothing for you on the perp front. TARU has blown up stills of the shooter and the driver. Every identification expert we have, every facial recognition tool, is being used."

"But—?" Mike said.

"Nothing of value. Hoods and masks. They both had sunglasses on and the shooter only took them off in front of the museum, to aim his gun and fire. Brown eyes, that's all we know. Nothing else distinctive about their eyes or lips."

"Clothing?" Mercer asked. "Confirmation on the gun?"

"You guys were right about the weapon. Twenty-two-caliber Ruger," she said. "Clothes? The shooter had a long-sleeved black tee or turtleneck and some kind of thin gloves on his hands. They were both in all black."

"Sounds like they weren't looking to make mistakes," Mercer said.

"And so far as the task force can determine, they didn't make any," Vickee said.

"Race?" Mike asked. "Do we know anything about the race of these men?"

"We aren't even sure they're both men," she said.

I put my head in my hands, elbows on the table. I was playing back the moments of the shooting, from the time I saw the DA trotting up the museum steps to approach me.

"I just put a call in to Lieutenant Peterson," Mike said, rubbing my back. "He'll tell Scully tonight. We just stopped at George Kwan's house, 'cause Coop can't get this Kwan guy out of her head, just so Scully knows."

"How'd that go?" Vickee asked. "Did you talk to him?"

"Front step flyby. I used the ruse that we had to tie up some loose ends on the Savage investigation, since we've got one suspect in the wind."

"Get anything?"

"Besides an invitation to return another time?" Mike said. "We were doing fine till Coop kind of lit a fire under his tail."

I picked my head up from the table. "I gave him something to think about, didn't I? If I didn't hit a nerve, then no harm, no foul."

"And if you did," Mike said, "he'll be on a not-so-slow boat to China."

"Who had the idea to just wing it?" I asked.

"Look, why don't we change the subject," Mike said, obviously aware that he was losing me to darker thoughts.

"One more thing," Vickee said. "From the commissioner. It ties in to what you're talking about."

I looked up.

"Vickee," Mike said in his sternest voice. "This is something you think you have to do right now?"

"Let me just put it on the table," she said.

"I'm ready," I said.

"So we've had a team of cops going through the news footage from Monday night's gala—the hours before the shooting."

Nothing unusual in that.

"The planners had some of the biggest names from the fashion world there to honor Wolf Savage, and they had the most gorgeous venue in Manhattan—the Temple of Dendur—as a backdrop."

I closed my eyes and called up the spectacular setting—before the Savage melee and before the bloodshed.

"All the local news outlets covered it, and all of them ran video in the eleven-o'clock hour," Vickee said. "CBS, NBC, ABC, Fox 5, NY1, WPIX."

I knew there had been cameras everywhere. But they had been focused on the fashion, not the felons. I hadn't paid them any attention.

"That must have been what Battaglia saw," Mike said. "Something—someone on the news that drove him to head off to the Met."

"But he'd never have made me," I said. "I was wearing that dress I borrowed from Joan, with a dark wig and makeup that I never use."

"Stevie Wonder would have known it was you, Coop," Mike said. "You looked ridiculous, but you looked like you, even in that awful getup."

"We got television outtakes, too, Alex," Vickee said. "Film that was shot but never aired."

"How did you ever get outtakes?" I asked. "The networks never give them up. I've subpoenaed them in cases and always meet with a brick wall."

"This is an assassination, Coop," Mike said. "This is the murder of an elected official. Nobody's going to stonewall the US attorney about video feed from a fashion show, for Christ's sakes."

I hadn't touched the glass of wine yet, but I was ready for a large gulp.

"We were watching the clips this afternoon, Alex," Vickee said to me. "You're in several of them, actually, as you walked around the room, during the prelude to the show on the runway, as the guests were being seated."

"I know what you're going to tell me," I said. "I'd been drinking before the show. I had a cocktail with Joan's mother after I got dressed at her apartment, and then some of the champagne that they were passing out at the party in Dendur."

I had probably been a bit reckless, because I thought no one there would know who I was. I was going cold turkey with my Scotch intake. If there was something to embarrass me on the tapes, I was changing my behavior faster than a lightning strike.

"Do you remember talking to anyone?"

"To anyone?" I said. I was getting as defensive with my dear friend Vickee as I'd been with Prescott. "I'm sure I was perfectly sociable. I greeted lots of people."

"You heard Mike mention Anna Wintour," Vickee said.

"Yes."

"Do you remember seeing her there?"

"Of course I do," I said. "She had the best seat in the house. Fifty-yard line, front row."

"Did you talk to her?" Vickee asked.

"That would be crazy," I said, snapping at Vickee and pulling my hand away from Mike. "I don't know Anna Wintour."

"You were circling the room," Vickee said. "Remember that?"

"Sure. Sure I do."

"When you reached the point where Wintour was sitting, you stopped," Vickee said. "You stopped cold in your tracks."

"I did?"

Vickee looked at Mike. She seemed unhappy to be pressing me, but he nodded at her, and so she went on.

"You leaned in to say something to someone, didn't you?"

"You must know," I said. "You were watching outtakes."

"Well, it's just that most of the cameras were focused on Anna Wintour before the show started," Vickee said, offering me a warm smile. "You happened to be in a lot of those shots, and this one got airtime. Do you know what I'm talking about?"

"Go for it, Vickee," I said. All I recalled was swallowed in a haze.

"There was a man sitting next to Wintour. You leaned over and it looks like your lips were moving, Alex. You spoke to one of them," Vickee said. "Did you know the man?"

I bit my lip and stared at Stephane's face—over Vickee's back—as he prepared a Caesar salad from scratch for diners at the next table.

I must have noticed who had the seat next to Anna Wintour on Monday night. It was prime real estate at the show. But I couldn't call it up for the life of me.

"I must have said 'excuse me' as I passed by," I said. "Maybe I stepped on her foot."

Vickee glanced at Mike again, then at me. "You were behind them, Alex—nowhere near their feet. You leaned over to say something to one of them."

She was trying to feed me the information, but I wasn't picking up any of the signals.

"I wish I could help you," I said. "All of you. I mean, it would help me, too, if I knew what made Battaglia leave home and come after me."

Vickee reached into her tote again. She pulled out an eight-by-ten photograph, then reached across the table, moved my plate, and placed it in front of me.

"That's a still of the camera shot," she said. "See yourself?"

"I do."

"See the man next to Anna Wintour?" Vickee asked. "Do you know who he is?"

I grabbed the edge of the photo. "I know it looks like I'm saying something to one of them, but I couldn't have been. I had no reason to."

"What's his name, Alex?" she asked. "Who is he?"

"That's Kwan," I said to her. "That's the man we've been telling you about just now. It looks like I'm talking to George Kwan."

# NINETEEN

"What the fuck?" Mike said. "Why were you talking to Kwan? You didn't tell me anything about that. And he just played dumb on me, too. What the fuck's been going on?"

"You're all just pounding on me," I said, pushing against Mike's shoulder to urge him to stand up. I was between Mike and Mercer on the circular banquette and I wanted them to release me. "Let me get up, will you, please?"

"Stay calm and let's just figure this out," Mercer said. "Sit tight."

"You tell me you want the old me back," I said. "That I've been wimpy and whiny and soaking myself in alcohol since I was kidnapped."

"But it will take—" Vickee tried to placate me but I didn't give her the chance.

"The bad news is—I'm back. Okay with that? *I am back*," I said. "I am so ripped about the way I'm being treated by Prescott and Detective Stern and now—now by my best friends. And you, Detective Chapman, can take that glass of Montepulciano and suck on it yourself. I am angry beyond your imagining and about to explode. But I am very much back, so be careful what you wish for."

My three friends were silent for a few moments.

"What's the good news?" Mike asked.

"Let me out of this booth and I'll tell you."

"Spit it out, 'cause I'm not moving."

My head was spinning.

Mike looked away from me to Vickee. "So why did Scully give

you the green light to talk to Coop about this? It seems like it would have been the perfect fodder for Prescott to go at her with tomorrow morning. Did he give the task force the same tapes?"

"Yes, Prescott's got it all too. But frankly, since this snippet already aired on the news, as opposed to being buried in outtakes, the commissioner figured Alex or you might have seen it," Vickee said. "Or at least been alerted to it by her team in the unit."

The DA's press office taped local news stories all day and evening. It had been a long tradition, yielding the occasional bit of luck when an eyewitness to a crime talked to a reporter instead of a cop, or a defense attorney stood on the courthouse steps, announcing the names of his witnesses for the next day at trial. Any prosecutor could walk into the pressroom and play back clips that might be of interest.

"Nobody called me," I said. "This is the first time I'm seeing the photo."

"Better here than in front of James Prescott," Mercer said. "You can think it through now."

"There's nothing to think through. I don't need excuses."

"Look, babe," Mike said. "Mercer and I know you met George Kwan in the Savage offices, at WolfWear. And I was with you when your boss walked out his front door the next afternoon. What I don't understand is why you would have said anything to him at the gala."

"I didn't," I said. "I swear to you I didn't."

"The footage from which that still was made was taken before all the ruckus began," she said. "Are you sure you remember?"

Mike slid the glass of Montepulciano out of my reach.

"I'd never have done that. Talk to him, I mean."

"You've got all night to figure it out, Coop," Mike said. "'Cause your man Skeeter will be ready to rip you a new body part if you hold out on him."

I was already in the hole with Prescott. Now I had a logical way in to address my omission of Kwan's name earlier in the week. The photograph reminded me about my sighting of Battaglia at his home. But it also muddied the waters in my own mind.

"Slow down," Vickee said. "What made the three of you detour to Kwan's house tonight?"

"This afternoon, Deirdre Wright—my contact in the Development Office at the Bronx Zoo—said Kwan was a big donor."

"So she knows him?" Vickee said.

"No, she's never met him. She called Kwan a man of mystery," I said. "She thinks of him as an apparition—a ghost. That creeped me out."

"It's funny how that got me thinking on the ride back to Manhattan," Mike said, "although we're all too young to know about this, but the idea of an Asian ghost—who might be a bad guy—made me think of one of my old man's biggest cases."

"First of all, you're on your way to political incorrectness," I said.

"Nothing new under the sun," Mercer said.

"Why Asian ghosts would be different from any other phantoms isn't clear," I said, chewing on a piece of baguette Stephane had brought with our drinks. "And two, the last time you channeled one of your dad's cases, it almost turned out to be the end of me. It's a noble attempt at distracting me, I'll give you that."

Mike's father, Brian, had been one of the most decorated detectives in the NYPD. His unique combination of intelligence, skill, and great instincts had solved more homicides than an entire squad of officers could do in a year. Something in his DNA had been passed along to his son.

"I'm thinking ghost. Chinese ghost," Mike said. "Chinatown. Ghost Shadows. Ring a bell?"

"Not even a whisper of a chime," I said. "Educate me."

"The Ghost Shadows was a gang that terrorized Chinatown for a decade, up through the early 1990s."

"Our Chinatown?" I asked.

The DA's office fronted on Centre Street, but the back door—once known as the notorious Five Points, made famous by its killer gangs of New York—had been Chinatown for more than a century, with the largest concentration of Asians living together in the Western Hemisphere.

"What was their business?" Mercer asked.

"It was a criminal empire," Mike said. "As diverse as crime could be, the Ghost Shadows got into it. Extortion, gambling, and racketeering. There was a time not so long ago when they owned the streets in that 'hood."

"How?"

"Because gambling has always been a problem in the Chinese community. It's a big part of their culture, as is not trusting banks with their money," Mike said. "Fact. Not a slur."

"I remember the first time I ever handled a robbery on Pell Street," Mercer said. "The guy's mattress had been ripped to shreds because that's where a lot of the older immigrants kept their money."

"Exactly," Mike said. "And all the young gangstas had guns, which they stashed in those metal mailboxes in the lobbies of the tenement buildings they were robbing. It was almost impossible to catch them carrying heat."

"There was enough money in gambling?" Vickee asked.

"Betting parlors on Mott Street and Baxter and Division?" Mike said. "They were all illegal. The locals played for tens of thousands of dollars—dominoes, thirteen-card poker, even mahjongg. The Ghost Shadows offered them protection from the police—at the cost of about twenty thousand a week back then, so it was real money—and then roughed them up when they didn't make payments."

"Murdered them," I said, "if your father was involved."

"Yeah. Roughing up in the first degree," Mike said. "There was a five-year period in the eighties when there was a trail of thirty rival gang members and a handful of bystanders killed. They had a hand in everything that happened in and around Canal Street."

Mercer snapped his fingers and pointed at Mike. "You started thinking of Kwan because basically what he was trying to do to the late Wolf Savage was extortion. Big-time extortion."

"You know, it's one of those weird word-association things," Mike said. "Why does Kwan's name keep coming up in this case?"

I stopped chewing.

"He and his brothers have turned a respectable generations-old family business into a shady global operation. What once was export-import generations ago is now this concept of the Kwans finding the cheapest labor, much of it in Asia and India, to steal production away from many of the high-end fashion houses. They go low-scale and increase the risks for half the people who work for them, in places that have no regulations on the working conditions of the labor force. The Kwans were pushing hard to drive the Savages out of contention—so, yes, extortion was part of it," Mike went on. "Then, why is George Kwan cozy enough with Battaglia that the DA goes to the guy's town house—which is guarded like a fortress—in the middle of the afternoon?"

"And why does Battaglia lose his marbles when he thinks he sees me talking to Kwan at the museum?" I said.

"Then we get the tip about Battaglia and the Order of Saint Hubertus," Mike continued, making connections, "that led to Alex remembering the DA being honored at the Animals Without Borders dinner."

"Which Kwan Enterprises also supported," Mercer said. "So Deirdre mentions the man's name, and calls him a ghost—"

"And all I can think of is the bad old days in Chinatown, wondering whether any of the gang leaders my father locked up— like Wing Yeung Kwan—were the ancestor ghost shadows of our man George."

"Any sign that he's into the gambling business?" Mercer asked.

"The Chinese gambling industry was shut down when the big casinos were opened in Connecticut by Native Americans," Mike said. "But the minute Deirdre Wright said the word 'ghost' in describing George Kwan, I started thinking of the Chinese and criminal enterprise. The Ghost Shadows actually went international."

"From Canal Street?" Mercer said.

"The last murder rap my father nailed against them was for fleecing investors for millions of dollars in a phony international bullion-trading company," Mike said. "The head of the enterprise set up a bogus firm in Hong Kong to do business in Chinatown as the Evergreen Bullion Company—to buy and sell gold on the open market. Instead, it was all phony trades, fake confirmation slips, and a huge commission for trading."

"I bet all the investors were immigrants—from his own country," Mercer said.

"Yup. That's why most of them wouldn't go to the police, because so many were here illegally," Mike said. "The Ghost Shadows were extremely opportunistic. When they saw a way to make money, they jumped on it. My father handled the murders that happened when the Green Dragons tried to get a cut of the business."

He paused and looked at Mercer.

"Sort of reminds me of what I know about Kwan Enterprises," Mike went on, "sensing a weakness in the fashion industry and filling the gap with a dangerously cheap overseas operation."

Mike stopped talking when the waiters came to the table with our dinners.

"That's a bit of a reach," I said.

"We've got nothing at the moment. I'll give you that. That's when I start stretching for ideas," Mike said. "Why didn't your boss tell you he had a relationship with the man when Kwan surfaced in the Wolf Savage investigation?"

"Obviously, I can't answer that. I wasn't supposed to be working on the case," I said. "I don't know if word ever got to him, before the case was solved—just an hour before Battaglia was killed—that we met Kwan the week before."

"How did Kwan figure in that one?" Vickee asked. "Tell me more about his business."

"Kwan Enterprises is an investment holding company that's headquartered in Hong Kong, just like the phony bullion business was." I sat quietly, letting Mike tell the backstory. "For several generations, it was a trading company, concentrating on the export of porcelain and jade and silk, until the UN imposed a trade embargo on China."

"Got that," Vickee said.

"Then, according to my research about the family last week," Mike added, "almost everyone in the Asian export business stepped over the line into smuggling a century ago."

"Smuggling their goods?"

"Sure. These operations had been around for decades before that in the nineteenth century, and suddenly the US government banned a lot of the products being imported. Many of the Chinese resorted to smuggling, as a way for their businesses to survive."

"That's what Kwan Enterprises did?" Vickee asked.

"While a lot of Asian companies buckled and went under, the Kwans were more nimble," Mike said. "They got involved in some illegal export work, but then shifted their interest to the apparel industry, outsourcing the production of goods to the cheapest labor markets around the world."

"They're a trading group," Vickee said. "That's not criminal."

"It's ugly, though," Mike said. "It's a lot like slave labor."

Vickee responded to those last two words. "That's different."

"Think Bangladesh or some remote part of China," he said. "Unsafe facilities. Places where buildings collapse on workers, or they get trapped by fires, or child labor is used. That's Kwan Enterprises."

"I've got the image," she said. "So how do you know the DA had something to do with him?"

"We didn't," Mike said. "We chanced on Kwan when we crashed a business meeting at the offices of Wolf Savage's company. So Coop and I decided to follow him to his town house on East Seventy-Eighth Street, in the middle of the afternoon."

"Did he meet with you then?" Vickee asked. "Did you talk to him?"

"No," Mike said. "I tried to get in the house, but his security guards wouldn't let me. So I got back into the car with Coop."

"You couldn't get past security either?" Vickee asked, turning to me.

"I'm the one who wasn't supposed to be there," I said, giving her a sheepish grin. "And lucky for me I didn't try to take on the guards when Mike was turned away, because the person who emerged from the town house was none other than Paul Battaglia."

Vickee put down her fork. "Strange bedfellows, especially in the middle of the Savage homicide investigation."

"You bet," I said.

"And Battaglia never told you or Mike about his relationship to Kwan," she asked her husband, "even though he knew you were working the case?"

"Not a word," Mercer said.

"So what if the guy—what if Kwan Enterprises is into some other kind of illegal operation?" Mike said.

"Like what?" I asked. "What made you think of that today,

besides the word-association stuff, at the zoo—the zoological park—of all places?"

"What Deirdre said about traditional medicine and how many of the Asians don't even care about killing their own endangered species to get the ingredients," Mike said. "I can't put my finger on it, but the late district attorney, if it's true he was at the hunting preserve where Scalia died, and the ghostlike Mr. Kwan, who doesn't put any stock in the lives of the humans who work for him, seem out of place in the world of animal conservation."

"Did you bring any of that up to Kwan tonight?" Vickee asked. "Did he react to it?"

"I couldn't read him," Mike said, shaking his head back and forth. "He's totally without emotion on the surface. Oozes confidence, but he didn't convince me that anything he said—about his relationship with Battaglia or his interest in wildlife—was sincere."

Vickee turned her head to me. "How about your impression?"

"Pretty much the same," I said. "Kwan managed to express how important the conservation issue is, but both he and the DA really seem like misfits in that world," I said, "especially if you get confirmation on Battaglia and the Saint Hubertus story."

"I would have pressed him more on the animal stuff," Mike said, "but I didn't want to make my interest too obvious, since he wasn't giving us a minute more. He practically slammed the door in Coop's face as it was."

"What does tomorrow look like?" Vickee asked.

"I start the day with Prescott," I said.

"I'm going to take you home so you can get your ducks in a row for that one," Mike said, ordering a round of decafs for the table. "I'll go down to his office with you."

"He's not going to let you in, Mike. He'll make you sit and wait downstairs again."

"You did that to me for ten years, kid. I can take a few hours more."

"How about you?" Vickee asked Mercer.

"I'll go to the squad for the morning. Make an appearance. See if anything needs doing."

"I think we take Deirdre Wright up on her offer to have someone on staff give us a tour of the entire park tomorrow afternoon," I said. "Tell us about the animals—where they come from and how they live. Which ones are endangered and which ones interest smugglers."

"You're back into the idea of smuggling, then?" Vickee said.

"That doesn't mean it's the Kwans," I said. "But the rhino horns and other contraband certainly don't get here legally. Someone has to have the means to transport them to this country."

"That zoo is still two hundred sixty acres of wilderness in the middle of a big city," Mike said. "If it's part of the backdrop for the death of the district attorney, then we have to figure out why."

# TWENTY

"I won't answer another question with Detective Stern in the room," I said.

James Prescott was standing face-to-face with me. Jaxon Stern was sitting near the door. It was nine thirty Thursday morning, and I wasn't in the mood to be intimidated.

"We're a team, Alex," Prescott said. "What you tell me, you tell all of us."

"Let me repeat, in case you didn't understand me. Detective Stern leaves the room—maybe he can keep Mike Chapman company downstairs in the library—or I leave the room."

"I remember that streak from your younger days," Prescott said. "Irascible, some called it. Others had stronger words, with less pleasant connotations."

"Fortunately, it's part of my nature that hasn't changed over the years. It's a trait I practice and polish all the time, because it's served me so well in the face of adversity," I said. "Stern goes or I go."

"Detective Stern is here because I need him to run your piece of the case. You're here," Prescott said, turning to his desk and reaching for a piece of paper, "because I had a chance to open this matter before the grand jury yesterday and I came out with a subpoena for your appearance to testify before them."

I took the paper from him. A prosecutor doesn't need a perp in custody to start a grand jury proceeding. He just needs evidence of the commission of a crime, and the fact that he wants to dig further to investigate it. Prescott certainly had that.

"Looks like I have to come back in a week," I said, looking at the date on the document. "That works just fine for me."

I turned to leave the room.

"You know I can't put you in cold, Alex," Prescott said. "You know I've got to prepare you beforehand. I have to know what you're going to say. That's what today is for—and the next several days."

"You'll have to take your chances on this one," I said. "You'll just have to trust me, the way you used to do."

"You know I trust you."

"Jaxon goes."

Stern got to his feet when I used his first name.

I turned to look at him. "James and I have been close for so long that I just feel it's time for you and I to be on a first-name basis, too—much as you don't like that."

"Suit yourself," Stern said.

"After all, you're so far up and inside all my business—or haven't you told that to the US attorney yet?" I asked.

Stern didn't flinch.

"You never met each other until the night before last," Prescott said. "You don't know each other. I went to great lengths to find a homicide detective who hadn't worked with you, Alex, so we don't get burned by a defense attorney once we have a case to mount. We're all in your business now, and we've got every right to be."

"I wouldn't care if Jaxon had just been tough on me the other night because he imagined I'd be uncooperative before he actually met me or he tagged me as a coconspirator in Battaglia's assassination," I said. "But that isn't the case."

"That's his style," Prescott said.

"Tell him, Jaxon," I said.

"We've never met," Detective Stern said.

"Did you know I prosecuted the detective's brother-in-law?" I asked Prescott. "Convicted his ass of rape in the first degree—for drugging and molesting a Columbia grad student?"

Prescott looked quizzically at Stern, who was stone-faced.

"Jaxon came to the arraignment himself and posted bail, 'cause the perp used every ounce of the influence he counted on his brother-in-law to bring to bear, once the cuffs were tightened around his wrists."

The detective was looking right through me.

"Jaxon asked the SVU detectives to charge the case as a misdemeanor so his brother-in-law could make bail, and when they refused to do that, he had his sister call in anonymous complaints against them to the CCRB."

"Any of this true?" Prescott asked the detective.

"Your team leader here was almost flopped to a foot patrol in Bed-Stuy for trying to pull strings and get the case fixed, instead of upgraded to the Homicide Squad," I said. "Somebody in the chain of command was watching out for him. He tends to step out of line, James."

"My sister never made any such calls," Stern said.

I didn't know at the time who had made them, but I bet we could prove it now, with phone records and email traces.

"But your brother-in-law was the prisoner?" Prescott asked. "It actually was one of Alexandra's cases?"

"I had no idea who the prosecutor was, sir," Stern said. "I only went to the arraignment because my sister begged me to. I did it for her, sir, and for her kids. But I never showed up at any trial."

"You can hold to your affirmative action stance, James," I said, "or you can excuse the detective and I'll answer your questions, but Jaxon Stern and I are not going to fly in the same airspace any longer."

I could see James Prescott weighing his political future. I could count the seconds as he looked at each of us.

"Why don't you excuse yourself for a while, Detective?" Prescott said to Jaxon Stern. "I'd like to talk reason to Alexandra so we can move on and solve this damn case."

Prescott was in my corner on this one, maybe thinking I still had a future if I came out of this investigation unscathed. I guessed the news that I would not be on the governor's short list to be the interim DA hadn't yet reached the street.

# TWENTY-ONE

"Thanks, James," I said. "You can't begin to imagine how it unhinged me when I put Stern together with the case I handled last year. It made his animosity toward me crystal clear."

Prescott was seated at his desk. He stood a Redweld on its side and lifted the flap. The label facing me had my name on it, typed in all caps. It was already a pretty thick folder.

"I heard he was tough, but I don't believe there was any conflict involved," Prescott said. "It just seems to be the man's style."

"You're not taking him off the case, after what I just told you?"

"Try to remember you're not in charge, Alexandra."

"I'm fine with that. You feds have a way of screwing up all on your own," I said, keeping my composure. "We run a much cleaner operation. If any cop dared to undermine a case one of my guys was working on—"

"I heard you the first time," Prescott said. "We have a lot of work to do before you testify and I'd like to get started."

"Is there anything new you'd like to tell me about?" I asked.

"Nothing breaking our way yet," he said, removing a stack of photographs from the folder and placing it in front of him.

It wasn't hard to guess what the pictures were. I settled back in my chair.

"That's bound to change, sooner rather than later," I said.

"I did get some material from Commissioner Scully yesterday afternoon that I'd like to start with," he said.

They were the still shots from the fashion show Monday

evening—the ones Vickee had brought to dinner last night. Everyone involved—including me—was trying to figure why Battaglia made a mad dash to the museum, and they were hoping a replay would offer the missing clue.

I had wanted Jaxon Stern off my ass for more than one reason. This was my opportunity to set the record straight.

"Before you do that," I said, "I've been in such a—well, such a state of confusion—and I was so crushed by Stern's manner the other night—that I'm not sure I got all the facts out in order."

"Really? I think of you as so compulsive about the way you organize yourself."

"I'm sure he got it all down," I said, "but you have to understand the trauma to me of witnessing Paul Battaglia's death, of having him collapse onto me—and I'm not sure Stern had an ounce of the empathy the situation required."

Prescott listened without responding.

"I just want to be sure it's all clear," I said. "The questioning started just a couple of hours after the murder."

"What do you think Stern missed?" Prescott asked.

"You can appreciate that I didn't know where he was coming from when he started the interview with such antagonism," I said.

"Go on."

"I know I was running on fumes then. You must realize that, don't you?"

"Give me an example, Alexandra."

"I'm sort of fuzzy on whether or not I talked about the day Battaglia showed up at my apartment," I said, wearing my most earnest expression. "He actually crossed paths with me on the street, on my way home."

"We have that," Prescott said. "I'll get back to it when I reach that point in the prep."

"Good," I said. "Then I wasn't as addled as I feared."

"Let's get on with it."

"I must have talked about the Reverend Hal, didn't I? Hal Shipley, and his curious influence on Battaglia?" I asked. "I mean, I'd been keeping that pretty close to the vest, which is the way the DA wanted me to play it—"

"You told Stern and Tinsley about Shipley," Prescott said, interrupting me. "When I'm ready for more detail on that issue, I'll come back to it."

"Sure. I understand."

I needed to put George Kwan's name on the table before Prescott did. I had to have a reason for not disclosing his meeting with Paul Battaglia to Detective Stern when he had me jumping all over the place at the morgue interrogation.

"I guess they made notes of my last sighting of the district attorney, too," I said.

Prescott flipped the pages of notes that must have been the first night's interview of me by Stern.

"Near your apartment," he said, nodding as he looked for the reference.

"No, no. Those were two separate occasions," I said, as evenly as I could, shaking a finger at him.

Prescott studied what I assumed were the lines Stern had written when he questioned me.

"Explain that," he said.

"Like I told the detectives, I was walking down East Seventieth Street, coming from the Met, I think, when I heard Battaglia's bodyguard—"

"Not that one," he said. He was getting short with me. "There was a later time?"

"Yes, like I told the detectives, a day or so after that, Mike Chapman and I were on our way to interview a witness in the Wolf Savage case," I said.

Prescott was flipping the pages back and forth, looking for this notation—in vain.

"Which witness?" he asked.

"A man named Kwan. George Kwan."

Prescott wouldn't give me the satisfaction of looking up, but he stopped flipping pages. I couldn't tell whether he would challenge my recollections.

"You recognize his name?" I asked.

"Go on, Alexandra. Just go on."

"We had met Kwan at the Savage offices and wanted to ask him some more questions—apart from the family. So Mike and I went to the town house, on East Seventy-Eighth Street, I think it was."

Now I knew he was bluffing, pretending to be following along with me on Stern's notes by running his forefinger across the page.

"Yes?" he asked. "And you got in?"

"No, no. It's just like I told Stern and Tinsley," I said, with a wan smile. "At least I'm pretty sure I did."

An omission in Stern's notes didn't trouble me. I had proven his reason to trash me by citing the case I had tried, and Prescott had signed on to that.

Tinsley was another matter. But she hadn't taken notes. She had simply observed our interplay, so her memory of the three A.M. interrogation was as fallible as my own.

"The security guard refused to admit Mike to Kwan's home. His home is the enterprise office too," I said. "But it's not this guy Kwan who's important, of course. The issue was about Paul. It was the last time I saw Paul."

"When?" Prescott asked, tipping his empty hand by looking up at me. "What was? On the street near your home?"

"No," I said. "Like I told them the other night, Mike got back into his car and we were pulling out of the block, a bit frustrated that we hadn't gotten a chance to get in and meet with Mr. Kwan."

"And?"

"I looked up and saw one of the security men step out, so I told Mike to stop the car, figuring we might be able to get inside," I said. "But that's when the district attorney came through the front door. The last time I saw Paul Battaglia—before he was shot—he was leaving the home of a man named George Kwan."

# TWENTY-TWO

"You got out of the car to talk to Battaglia, I assume," Prescott said.

He was scrambling to make sense of this piece of news, which was under his nose for the first time. I felt a huge sense of relief having unpacked the heavy piece of baggage—a link between Kwan and the dead DA—and doing so before it was Prescott who brought up the name George Kwan.

"Actually, Mike had already turned the corner, and that gave me a second to catch myself from jumping out to approach Paul, since he was already urging me to keep out of the case."

Prescott looked as though he was trying to see through a very dark cloud that had just descended in front of his face.

"This factoid isn't in the notes, Alexandra," he said.

"It's not a factoid," I said. "It's a fact. It happened. You can ask Mike about it too."

Prescott looked for another Redweld labeled CHAPMAN.

"I mean, that's assuming Stern asked him that question about having seen Battaglia, James. After all, Stern's just out of Internal Affairs. He's not exactly a crack homicide detective, but that's the choice you made when you put him on this case."

He rifled through it, but it was much thinner than my folder— and of course, no one had any reason to ask Mike about the last time *he* saw the DA.

"It seems like I took you away from where you wanted to go with me this morning," I said. "I'm happy to carry on."

"Alexandra, have you got that new phone number for me yet?" Prescott asked.

"I'm enjoying the radio silence. It's good for my mental health."

"Being available to me would be even better for you."

Prescott tossed the Chapman folder to the side of his desk and picked up the stack of photographs again.

"Do you believe in coincidence, Alexandra?" he asked, eyeing me like the enemy.

"No, I don't."

"Neither do I," he said. "I've got to hand it to you. Somehow, you got out ahead of me on this one."

"I don't know what you mean."

"George Kwan," he said, sifting through the photographs to pull one out from the bottom of the pile. "He was on my list of things—of people—to talk to you about today, and yet here you go, bringing up his name before I can get the first question in."

"Now, that's really uncanny," I said.

Prescott slapped the photograph—the same one Vickee had shown us last night—in front of me on his desk and turned it around so it faced me.

"I understand that's you in some kind of disguise, is it not?"

"An outfit, James. Not a disguise. A vintage dress designed by the man being honored at the Met gala."

"You've seen the photograph already, haven't you?" he asked.

"Last night, yes," I said. "Commissioner Scully sent me a set of the shots that were downloaded from the television feed."

"That wasn't coincidence, either," he said. "More like convenience, wasn't it?"

"Scully's not a 'gotcha' kind of guy, James. The video was already public record," I said. "He had a pretty good idea that the image was familiar to me."

"So you're telling me between Monday night of the murder

and last evening, you'd already seen this image?" Prescott asked, pushing the full-color image closer to me. "Do me the favor of looking at the picture, Alexandra, and not at my forehead."

I held up the photograph. "I lived that moment, James. I was there, can't you tell?"

"Fetching, weren't you?" he said, with arrogant sneer. "And that's Anna Wintour?"

"Sure thing."

"And obviously—now that you've just refreshed my recollection of what you claim to have told Detective Stern—you know the man seated next to her, too."

I ignored his use of the word "claim."

"I don't *know* him, James," I said. "I'd met him once before Monday night."

"George Kwan."

"Exactly."

"And you stopped to talk to him," Prescott said.

"It certainly looks like I did," I said.

"What did you say?" The US attorney asked.

"To Kwan? Nothing at all."

"This is a photograph, Alexandra. It doesn't lie."

I had stayed up most of the night, since leaving Patroon, struggling to recall what had actually happened in this moment, captured on film.

"It's the money shot in this case," Prescott said. "It's what propelled Paul Battaglia out of his lair to come at you."

"Then he was a fool to put himself at risk over something that never happened."

"Something else, perhaps, that you neglected to tell Jaxon Stern?"

I stood up and put the photograph between us on James Prescott's desk.

"Do you know how I described to Vickee Eaton where Ms.

Wintour was sitting?" I asked. "I told her it was on the fifty-yard line. Best seat in the house, front row and right in the middle of the runway."

"Obviously," he said.

"Where was the photographer who shot the roll of tape standing, do you think, from looking at this shot?"

"I'd have to call it the end zone," Prescott said, "using your lingo. Right between the goalposts."

"Fair to say he was at an angle from the prime seats, right? You get Wintour and Kwan in profile, and you get me almost face-forward into the camera, because I was leaning over, looking that way, between the uprights," I said. "That's how Battaglia made me—that's the moment he recognized my face."

"So now tell me what it is you muttered to Kwan," Prescott said, not giving me an inch.

"You think I muttered? Or do you think I asked him what Battaglia was doing at his house the other day?" I said. "Really, what are the bets, James? Who's got the over-under that I was luring Paul Battaglia out to a meet by whispering in George Kwan's ear?"

Prescott just stared.

"Not to prove that Mike Chapman is ten times the investigator Jaxon Stern pretends to be," I said, "but Mike had the idea to take me down to One PP this morning, on our way here."

One Police Plaza—NYPD headquarters—was adjacent to the US Attorney's Office for the Southern District.

"We spent thirty-six minutes going through the tapes that aired on the local news channels Monday night," I said. "And lucky for me, one of the cameramen actually set up directly across the way from Ms. Wintour—behind the last row of seats on the opposite side's fifty-yard line. One photographer—that's all it takes—

was more interested in Wintour's reaction to the runway show than in the models vamping on the catwalk."

Prescott had picked up a yellow pencil and was holding it with both hands.

"Would you like to know what that tape showed, Skeeter? Because it seems your team stopped searching after they found the one shot they thought nails me as a conspirator," I said. "Because contrary to this optical illusion you're banking on to skewer me, I never had the reason or the opportunity to speak with Mr. Kwan."

"What then?"

"I was all over the Savage investigation, because the dead man's daughter, Lily, grew up with me," I said. "She called me when his body was found. When everyone else—Battaglia included—believed Savage was a suicide. When everyone else was ready to shut the case down and bury the man without an autopsy."

"So Lone Ranger of you, Alexandra," Prescott said. "Along with Tonto, of course, always faithful to you."

I reached for my iPad and opened the photograph app. "Here's a screenshot I took just an hour ago," I said. "It's a better angle, don't you think?"

I handed the device to Prescott, who put his thumb and forefinger on the photo to enlarge it.

"Can you see all the players?" I asked.

He wouldn't answer. He just shifted the image from larger to smaller and back again.

"That guy sitting next to George Kwan, on his other side—the one who looks like Oddjob," I said. The muscled Asian man with the stone-faced expression was a body double for a character in a Bond movie. "The one that has 'killer' written all over him. He's one of Kwan's bodyguards, but you couldn't see him in the photos you were working from, because of the angle."

"Next to him is my childhood swim-team pal," I said. "Wolf Savage's daughter, Lily. You can't see her in your set of photographs, can you? She just moved into that seat beyond Oddjob from the back row, seconds before I went by."

"You're telling me that's the person you leaned in to talk to?" Prescott said, his voice lowered a notch. He seemed almost disappointed by the visual proof that I wasn't in cahoots with Kwan. "This woman? This—this Lily? You actually remember that encounter, despite your—shall we call it your state of shock?"

"Frankly, James, I didn't remember at all until I saw the tape at headquarters this morning. I was blank on the whole thing— alcohol, shock, exhaustion—that part of the evening was all a total blank to me," I said. "Then this popped up on the screen this morning. Full-frontal image, with no dead angles to skew the view."

"You were talking to Lily," Prescott said, all hostility drained from his voice. "Why?"

"She was the only person in that row I knew, James. Nothing else makes sense. She had talked to me backstage and started to ask me, earlier in the night, if I thought we were close to catching her father's killers."

"What did you tell her?"

"I didn't answer her. I cut her off, actually, because there were too many people around to bring up that subject, and I was trying to keep a very low profile," I said. "Lily was standing up, looking for her husband, when she saw me walking by, as this photo shows. She waved—she waved repeatedly to me—and so I stopped."

"She asked you something, didn't she?" Prescott said.

I shook my head. "Lily told me something," I said. "She told me that the DA—that Battaglia—had just texted her. That he told her he wanted her to come to his office the next day."

"Did you answer her?" he asked.

I didn't speak to Prescott. I took the photograph of Lily and me and held it up in front of his face.

"What did you say to her, Alexandra?"

"Go to the videotape, James. You can read my lips," I said. "You can read my lips for yourself, on the outtakes from Channel 5."

Prescott put down the pencil and banged his clenched fist on the desk. "What the hell did you tell your friend Lily about Battaglia's invitation?"

"'Don't go,' is what I said to her. Just two words, behind George Kwan's back. 'Don't go.'"

# TWENTY-THREE

"When does he want you back?" Mike asked.

We had grabbed lunch in the federal courthouse cafeteria and were finishing up, shortly after one P.M.

"Tomorrow afternoon," I said. "We'll be going over my phone records, emails, and texts, if you want to talk about painful."

"Too much gossip with your buddies," Mike said.

"That's only because I haven't had any business to discuss while I was on leave," I said, scraping my tray and following Mike out the door. "No worries. It's not like I've been talking about the size of your—"

"My appetite?" he said, reaching back to tousle my hair as he interrupted me. "Talk all you want. Any surprises you should be prepared for? You or I, that is?"

"No old lovers, if that's what you mean," I said. "Joan's latest manuscript, Nina's kid, manicures and pedicures, hair color. It'll sound like a broken record."

"You were doing plenty of e-chatting and texting about the Wolf Savage investigation," Mike said. "That will give them some fodder."

"I went rogue and you came along with me," I said. "Old news."

"They must have all of Battaglia's communications by now, too," Mike said. "They'll wonder why the text to Lily didn't show up as outgoing on his phone. They must have run all of Monday's numbers on his devices by now."

"When he was communicating from home," I said, "he often used his wife's phone. No point to that, really, but whichever device was closer to where he was sitting. I'd better tell Prescott to get Amy's records, too, or he'll challenge me about that text."

"Lily can back you up."

"Yeah. That's true." I hadn't heard from Lily since the takedown of her father's killers at the Met. But then, without a phone, it was hard to know whether she or anyone else was trying to call me.

"Did you tell Prescott we're going to the Bronx Zoo now?" Mike asked.

"I didn't see the need. He's been briefed on everything we know, including the possibility that Battaglia was at the hunting preserve the night Justice Scalia died, but he never went near that subject with me."

"Okay."

"Besides that," I said, "James is still refusing to take Jaxon Stern off the case. He ended by telling me that he thinks the solution to this whole thing—Battaglia's murder—is within my grasp, if I can just clear all the emotion out of my head."

"What kind of bullshit is that?" Mike asked. "He thinks you're holding something out on him?"

"Must be, and he's also convinced I could read Battaglia because I knew him so well," I said. "Surely I can sort out why he was coming to talk to me with such urgency."

"In that case, you need to be thinking how to solve this 24/7, just like the man told you to do," Mike said.

"What if Battaglia's first calls to me were about Lily?" I asked. "Maybe when she responded to his invitation to come to the office, she told him I was there with her at the Met and told her to say no?"

"Would she have done that?"

"Who knows?" I said. "It would have made the old guy really mad if she did."

"What now?"

"Weren't we going back to the Bronx this afternoon? For that tour at the zoo?"

"The zoological park," Mike said. "You still think there's some link there to Battaglia's death?"

"We've got nothing but our guts to go on," I said. "And I had such a good time yesterday. So humor me, will you?"

"Every now and then you get a good hunch, kid. Mercer's at the squad, having a quiet day," Mike said, handing me his phone. "He'll shoot across the bridge and meet us there if you give him a call."

I reached Mercer as we got in the car and headed to the FDR to drive uptown and cross over into the Bronx. I called Deirdre Wright and asked if she could set us up with a guide in half an hour. The more exotic, the more endangered, the more valuable the animal—those were the ones we wanted to see.

"How's your head?" Mike asked, keeping his eyes on the road.

"By the time I was finished this morning, I felt like it was going to split in half."

"You made me a promise, Coop, just days before the murder," he said. "You told me you were ready to start going to talk to Dr. Ricky."

"I know I did." I slinked down in the car seat and rested my head against the window. "I saw her twice, but I didn't feel any better at the end of the session."

When I was kidnapped, the chief of detectives made Mike sit down with a shrink—a brilliant psychiatrist whose job it was to get inside his brain to help the commissioner and the hostage negotiation squad try to assess how I might react to the stresses of my abduction. Mike kicked and screamed at the idea of it, but came away with boundless respect for Ricky Friedman and urged me to see her to try to deal with the flashbacks from my kidnapping.

"Twice?" Mike said. "You didn't even give her the chance to get through your thick skull. She's not about making you feel better. It's not like an appointment at a day spa."

"Dr. Ricky was pushing me too hard," I said. "Too fast."

"Do you want me to call her and see if she'll squeeze you in?" he asked.

"I was almost ready to do that again myself," I said.

This was a punishing position for me to be in: a witness to the assassination of a professional mentor and good friend of a dozen years, as well as a survivor of an abduction that had taken five days—and countless sleepless nights—out of my life. I was finding ways to cope with the latter—none of them good for me—but the former still registered as shattering.

"I feel a 'but' coming on," Mike said.

"A big 'but,'" I said. "James doesn't want me getting what he calls brain-teased by a shrink. He doesn't want my recollections—such as they are—to be tinkered with by analysis and psychobabble. He figures I'll eventually be the centerpiece of a trial, and he wants my mind in pristine condition."

"Then he should have put your head in a bubble when you were twelve years old," Mike said. "You've seen as much bad shit as anyone I know."

"He's counting on that," I said. "He wants to control me, and I get that. He's giving me enough rope to either lead him and the task force in the right direction, or better still, to hang myself in the process."

"I don't give a damn what *he* wants," Mike said. "I'm talking about what *you* need."

I reached over and took Mike's right hand off the steering wheel. "I've got that."

"All the more reason you need a good shrink, kid," he said, withdrawing his hand from mine.

Mercer was waiting for us in the parking lot when we reached the Bronx Zoo. He walked to the car and opened my door. "Good afternoon to you both. Who showed up today, James Prescott or his Skeeter alter ego?"

"Both were in the house," I said, stepping out. "I am so grateful to Vickee—to the commissioner—for sending over the photographs, and to Mike for taking me to view all the tapes this morning. What's happening at the SVU?"

"Low numbers, Alex. Crime stats continue to stay down," he said. "One date rape after an office party at an ad firm, but the vic went right to Catherine. Skipped the 911 call completely. I'm cool to hang with you two unless she calls me in."

"Good."

"The whole team at One PP thinks Prescott's got something in his mind that he's not willing to let them in on," Mercer said. "Some far-ranging international target that Battaglia must have tried to cross him up on."

"Dancing in the dark," Mike said. "DA gets assassinated and his archrival can't bring himself to get in the sandbox and play nice with everyone else."

"Vickee did have this, though," Mercer said, reaching into his jacket pocket and coming out with a Xerox copy of an old newspaper clipping. "Seems this William Hornaday fellow—the taxidermist who was the zoo's first director?"

"Yes," I said, as we walked toward Astor Court on our way to the Development Office, "the guy Deirdre talked about yesterday."

"He put Vickee's great-grandmother out of business," Mercer said, handing me the paper.

The 1916 *New York Tribune* didn't have quite the headline writers that the *Post* can brag about, but it wasn't bad for an old-time news desk: HARLEM HATTERY CLOSED BY HORNADAY.

I looked at it and laughed.

"Old granny Eaton had one of the first black-owned businesses in Harlem," Mercer said. "We didn't know her, of course, but we've heard plenty of stories about Leola's Plumes."

There was a picture of the handsome woman in front of her plume shop, wearing a grand hat with several long feathers pointing back from the brim over her shoulder.

Mike was trying to read along with me, but I was moving too fast. "What'd he do to her?"

"The style of the day, according to my wife," Mercer said, "involved feathers on the fanciest hats. The bigger the better. Peacock, ostrich, birds of paradise. But this Hornaday dude wrote a clause into the Tariff Act of 1913 that forbade the importation of wild-bird plumage for millinery purposes. Border guards actually seized shipments of feathers, if you can believe it—especially from Australia and the South Seas islands, where these tropical birds flourished."

"Poor Leola," I said.

"Then the Audubon Society piled on," Mercer said. "They argued that American boys would be shooting domestic birds to fill the gap. Ducks, geese, pheasants. You get the picture."

"What happened to Leola?" I asked.

"She moved on to beaded gowns. Nobody to bust her bubble with beads."

In a minute, we spotted Deirdre in front of the old Heads and Horns building, talking with another young woman. When we reached them, the introductions began.

"I'm tied up in meetings all afternoon," Deirdre said. "But you have a much better guide in Hillary Hawes. She's been a zookeeper with us for eight years, so she's the one to ask about the animals."

Deirdre turned to go back into the building, then stopped and looked at me. "I've got a feeling that there's something you're not telling me," she said. "A reason you're here that isn't just about a memorial service."

"To tell you the truth, Deirdre, I can't quite explain it all myself," I said, letting down my guard. "But it's an instinct I've got, and I think I owe it to Paul Battaglia to follow through with what my gut is saying. I owe it to you to tell you—as soon as I know."

"Well," she said, loosening up with the hint of a smile, "the tours are free."

I knew what she was thinking. She didn't want me to bring any of my bad karma into her animal safe haven. I had that same concern.

"Where would you like to start?" Hillary asked Mike.

"You'll have to tell us," he said. "It's been too long."

"Hop on," she said, pointing to her six-seater golf cart. "I'll give you some highlights and you tell me when to slow down and dig deeper."

"Sounds fair," Mike said, sitting in the front beside her.

Mercer and I took the middle row.

"I've got an obvious place to go," she said. "Deirdre told me you're interested in endangered species."

"Thanks."

"Have either of you guys been to that little building?"

"Not I," Mike said.

"No," Mercer added. "Why?"

"As you can see from the architecture, it's one of the original campus buildings," Hillary said.

It was a small structure, handsomely designed, like a nineteenth-century office building.

"It's a police precinct," she said.

"C'mon," Mike said, pointing at the building with a laugh. "There's no precinct at the zoo. There's no zoo patrol."

"We have our own security," she said, "but this is actually a substation of the Forty-Eighth Precinct."

"No way," Mike said, "with real live cops?"

"Not many of them. You'll see a cop on a scooter from time to time, especially in the summer. They're just assigned during the day, in case a child gets separated from a parent, or someone drops a handbag in the African Plains."

"Kind of suits me perfectly," he said.

"No homicides here," Hillary said.

"In this Bronx wilderness?" Mercer asked. "No murders?"

"Let's just say we've had some maulings over the decades. People who wound up on the wrong side of the enclosure, but it's their own fault," Hillary said. "There was actually a teenager who came here in the 1920s, after her debutante party. She and her friends slipped in, pretty intoxicated, and she started dancing with a polar bear."

"Unhappy ending?" he asked.

"She left the zoo short one arm, as the story goes," she said. "And you probably read about the guy who jumped off the monorail a few years ago."

"Yeah," Mike said. "And some tigers tried to gnaw on him."

"They didn't get much," Hillary said, "but he came out fine. Although nobody has a clue why he did it."

"Those were trespassers," Mike said. "The animals couldn't have been guilty."

"They weren't," she said. "Never a homicide here, Mike. So you just stay where you are."

Hillary drove the cart past the Children's Zoo and around the Bug Carousel, and stopped beyond the Butterfly Garden. I could see how easy it would be to lose ourselves in the beauty of the wildlife while tackling a more serious task.

She parked and we got off to follow her, through a short tunnel that brought us out—according to the signage—in the Congo Gorilla Forest.

"I remember a day when all the great apes were in the Primate House," Mike said. "Cement walls and iron bars. Kind of the Attica of the animal world."

"Before my time," Hillary said. "But that has all changed. We've got acres and acres here, and of course these glass enclosures are a lot more civilized, aren't they?"

"Who are we looking at?" Mercer asked.

"That's Ernie," she said.

"Big boy," Mike said, getting up close to the glass.

"Thirty-five years old, and he weighs around five hundred pounds."

"He's a silverback gorilla," Mercer said, "isn't he?"

"Yes, the adult males grow that distinctive silver stripe down the center of their backs."

"Born in the Congo?" I asked.

"Actually not," Hillary said. "In Cleveland, like most other gorillas in our zoo populations throughout the country—Cleveland's got a great gorilla-breeding program—though both Ernie's parents were captured in the wild."

"Hey, he survived Cleveland," Mike said, watching as a baby gorilla swung from a viny branch and jumped onto his back. "Must be a tough guy. And none of the other gorillas in sight look anywhere near his size."

"That's because they're all female or his kids," Hillary said. "It's his harem. Ernie's the alpha dog in this group, and you can't have two males around the same troop of females—not here, and not in the wild."

"He doesn't mind that little guy jumping onto his back?" Mike asked.

"Ernie loves his babies," she said. "Gorillas are very social animals."

"What does he eat to get that big?"

"Gorillas are herbivores, Mike," Hillary said. "They mostly eat plants."

Mike kept walking through the exhibit, watching the gorillas interact. "I guess that's why there are no leaves left on the trees."

"The keepers feed them leaves every day," Hillary said, laughing at Mike. "That particular tree isn't real."

"What do you mean?" he said, staring into the enclosure at the fallen tree trunk as close to his nose as the piece of glass between them would allow.

"We've got a workshop on-site where environmental objects are simulated."

"You're telling me that's fake?" Mike asked. "That huge tree trunk and all those vines the baby gorillas are swinging on?"

"Completely man-made," Hillary said. "This exhibit is indoors and outdoors, as you can see, and covers more than six acres, one acre of which is this particular enclosure."

"Time changes everything," Mike said. "Now it's the humans who are penned in and the gorillas roam free."

"That's the plan. You won't see any bars in our park. There's this glass wall to keep the animals in," Hillary said, "but mostly they're separated from other species—and us—by ravines and streams and artificial cliffs, and fences around the perimeters."

We continued on our way on the wooden path, through the exhibit.

"Tell me about the trees," Mike said.

"One of our best features," Hillary said. "About half of the trees in the exhibit—and all of the green plants—are real. The others are fakes, but require painstaking work to be able to fool you."

"It did the job. That trunk was about seven feet in diameter."

"There's an entire tree crew in our shop," she explained. "The foreman starts by making a scale model out of clay. That's then built up and out—full size—with heavy steel pipes to create the trunk itself, and a very lightweight steel—something that can be bent and shaped—to make the limbs. The form is finished with a sort of mesh skin that they stretch over the tree trunk and then spray with an epoxy resin."

"Tricked me for sure," Mike said.

I wanted to find out if we were on a fool's errand or had some purpose here.

"So what are the biggest dangers for these magnificent creatures, back in the Congo?" I asked.

"Three things, primarily," Hillary said. "They live in a part of the world that's been savaged by civil wars, so gorillas have been caught in the cross fire for decades. Then there's the destruction of their habitat, as people encroach on the places where they've lived—the heavily forested parts of the Congo."

She paused to watch a couple of Ernie's kids playing with each other—a primate hide-and-seek around the giant enclosure.

"The third reason for the decline in population is poaching, of course," she said. "There are probably fewer than nine hundred mountain gorillas left—they're really facing extinction, as well as all the other subspecies. So you combine humans, habitat, and throw in that they also get snared in traps that are intended for other animals, like antelope, bongos, and kobs. That's one of the reasons we work so hard on breeding efforts in zoological parks like this one."

The poaching interested me. I hadn't thought gorillas were hunted like rhinos but I was obviously wrong. "Poached for what?"

Hillary looked at me, as though to gauge my reaction. "For their meat, Alex. For bushmeat."

"*Bushmeat?*" I asked. "Who would eat that?"

"You'd be surprised. There are a lot of locals in the Congo—men who work in the tantalite mines or loggers, and they can't find much else in the forest to keep them going."

"So they shoot gorillas?"

"Yes. They get about six dollars for a piece of meat the size of Mercer's hand."

It didn't sound like the kind of poaching that supported an international cartel. I looked at these intelligent primates, who seemed to be mimicking our behavior so closely, and swallowed hard in disgust at the thought of harming them.

Mike picked up the thread. "We know a lot of the animals have uses in traditional medicines," he said. "Is the gorilla one of them?"

"Occasionally," Hillary said.

"Like an ingredient in Asian healing recipes?" he asked, going to the same continent I was thinking about.

"No. The Asians don't seem to be interested in gorillas, thankfully."

There goes that connection, I thought.

"Who, then?" Mercer said.

"It's pretty much a local tradition," she said. "Many of the Congolese feed gorilla meat to young boys in the belief it will make them grow strong or give them courage."

Somehow, I couldn't see Paul Battaglia risking his life for bushmeat.

"No international angle to gorillas?" I asked.

Hillary Hawes shook her head. "But I can show you plenty of that, if you're looking for risky business," she said, winding us along the path and back toward her cart.

"What do you mean?" I said.

"We haven't discussed trafficking yet."

"Wild animals?" Mike said. "Trafficked? You mean they're smuggled out of Africa and shipped abroad?"

"We can try to stop the slaughter," Hillary said, "but as long as there is a demand for products, the animals—and their most valuable parts—will be trafficked around the world. That's where the big money is—and that's what traffickers think is worth killing for."

# TWENTY-FOUR

"Talk to us about trafficking," I said.

Hillary sat behind the wheel of the cart and started to drive. "I'm a keeper, you understand. I care for the animals here. I'll certainly tell you what I know, and Deirdre can also point you in the right direction."

"What's here?" Mike asked. "What's in this zoo that's endangered and trafficked?"

"Where do you want to start?" she said, trying to deal with Mike's attitude as the sightseeing tour changed to a more intense form of conversation. "I don't know where you want me to go."

"Just drive," he said. "Take us to see things you know about."

"I can do that, but I meant information. What are you looking for?"

"Years ago," I said, trying to stay loose and easy with Hillary, "there was a Supreme Court decision on pornography that resulted in a justice writing one of the most famous lines in that institution's history. He couldn't define the materials that fit the definition of hard-core pornography, but Justice Stewart famously said, 'I know it when I see it.'"

"I guess I can guide you that far," Hillary said, stepping on the accelerator. "Do you know about pangolins?"

"Did you say 'penguins'?" Mercer asked.

"No, pangolins. They're the most trafficked mammals in the world."

"I've never heard of them," I said.

"Most Americans haven't, but they're incredibly valuable," Hillary said. "Think of them as small anteaters, covered with scales. Four species live in sub-Saharan Africa, and four in Asia."

"What are they trafficked for?"

"Again, for their meat. But unlike gorillas, the pangolins are considered a delicacy, so they're in much greater demand beyond Africa than bushmeat is," she said. "And then there are the pangolin's scales."

"Literally, the scales that cover them?" I said.

"Yes. The scales are made of keratin," she said, "which is the same substance as our fingernails. But the Asians think it cures a variety of ailments—so they roast the scales or boil them in oil, then serve them up. It's traditional Chinese medicine."

"Got it. All about Asia," Mike said. I could see the imaginary wheels turning in his mind as he registered the Chinese association. "Where to now?"

"I'm getting wilder," Hillary said. She juiced the cart and sped on the roadway—dodging school groups, parents, strollers, and tourists to get to the entrance to the monorail, which was literally called a Ride on the Wild Side.

She skipped past the waiting crowd of visitors—everyone from ticket takers to security seemed to know her—and took us to the front of the line.

"Best way to show you the most animals is this way—from above—over the Asian wildlife preserve. You'll see everything, pick out what you want to know more about, and I'll answer all your questions, if I can."

One of the trains was pulling out of the station as we climbed the stairs to get to it.

"Don't worry," Hillary said. "We usually run three or four of these a day—nine cars per train—so there'll be another one along in ten or twelve minutes. It's only a twenty-minute ride. You're lucky, because even though the park is open all winter, this ride shuts down at the end of this month."

"Why's that?" Mike asked.

"Not all of the animals can survive outside all winter," she said. "You can't quite spot them from the air, but behind each of these areas, there are corrals where they get fed and spend the night. They're sheltered when they need to be. That's where their food is kept, too—apples and fruit and greens. All in the corrals."

"What happened to the Skyfari?" Mike said.

"I remember that," I said. "Trams like ski gondolas that carried us over the African plains. I was always terrified—when the high winds started to blow—that I'd wind up as lunch for one of the lions."

"Another one of your misplaced fears, Coop," Mike said.

"They're out of service these last few years," Hillary said. "Too many mechanical problems, and everyone loves the monorail even more."

We had our own private monorail trip, high above the wide-open spaces that were home to an astounding variety of species. As promised, none were penned or restricted to small places. Each looked to be quite at home, and if there were fences around them, they were quite invisible to us.

Hillary provided the commentary as we cruised slowly on our trek. The rail car was open, too, so I asked Mike for his phone and started to photograph the animals. Mercer was writing down the details.

"The first thing you see below us are deer and antelope," she said. "This part of the park encompasses more than thirty acres, so the designers were really able to re-create the habitats of their homes."

"It looks like there are horses grazing with the deer," Mercer said.

"There are. Mongolian wild horses. Stockier animals than the horses you know, with a short mane that looks like a Mohawk cut," Hillary said.

"They're so beautiful," I said.

"They were believed to be extinct in the wild," she said. "Then they were reintroduced a few years ago, and while endangered—though not from poaching—they seem to be coming back."

Hillary directed the driver to stop anytime we came close to an animal we hadn't seen before. There were gaurs—the world's largest wild cattle—capable of killing lions because of their great size and fierce horns; several markhors—goats that were the national animal of Pakistan, with long, thick hair and fabulous antlers that curled up over their heads like corkscrews on steroids; Himalayan tahrs—ungulates that were somehow distantly related to wild goats; and hog deer, indigenous to different parts of Southeast Asia.

"Why are they called hog deer?" Mercer asked.

"Because they move like pigs—they're shorter than the deer we know—and they actually put their heads down the way pigs do when they're on the run," Hillary said.

"Endangered?" I asked.

"Some of the species are, and some are doing okay—in India and Nepal and Bhutan," she said. "But if you Google one of those Texas hunting preserves, they're really a trophy animal down there, brought in to be bred in captivity—just to be hunted."

Texas again. Another wild animal smuggled in for the sport of it.

"Can you please bring this train to a stop?" Mercer asked. He was leaning forward with his arms on the edge of the railing. He had spotted his favorite beasts—the elephants that were below us. I could see three of them, one of whom was rolling in the mud while the other two seemed not to care about our arrival.

"These were always the animals I came to see years ago," he said. "But they, too, used to live behind bars back then."

"We actually abandoned our elephant program more than a decade ago," Hillary said, "in favor of devoting our resources to elephants in the wild."

"But these elephants?" Mercer asked.

"You probably know that lady in the mud," she said, smiling at Mercer. "Her name is Happy, and she's about forty-five years old. I suspect you saw her when you were here as a kid."

"Happy and Grumpy, if I'm not mistaken," Mercer said. "Seven elephants from Thailand—babies when they were captured, if I remember right, and all of them named for Snow White's dwarfs."

"Exactly."

"One of those things that sticks with you from childhood."

"Well, it just seemed right to keep the three elephants who'd spent all their lives here with us till the end," Hillary said. "They can live to be sixty or so. Fortunately, the circuses have stopped using them—the training always seemed to be so cruel—and now most zoos have given them up, too."

"How come these three don't have tusks?" Mike asked.

"That's one of the differences between Asian and African elephants," she said. "The African elephants, male and female, all have tusks. But only some of the Asian males have tusks and about half of the Asian females have short tusks. Tushes, actually, is what they're called. Sort of like stunted tusks."

"And endangered of course," I said. "The Africans."

"Critically so," she responded. "Three-quarters of Africa's forest elephants have been killed in the last dozen years. Thousands and thousands and thousands of them, in forests and on the savannas, too."

We were silent.

"For their tusks," I said.

"Pure human greed," Hillary said. "It's not the animals that are trafficked, as you know. They're just slaughtered and their carcasses left to rot. Ninety-six elephants a day—that's how many are being killed. Just for the trade in ivory."

"Shot?" Mike asked. "Are most of them shot?"

"The poachers will get them any which way they can," she said. "In villages where people can't afford guns—in a country like Malawi—they literally inject chemicals into things the elephants eat, like pumpkins, and poison them to death. Or they ensnare them in wire traps."

"What about the good people?" Mercer asked. "The locals who sign up to be wildlife rangers, to protect the animals?"

"Here's what happens, Mercer. The poachers who are funded— some by rebel groups and some by businessmen—sneak into a wildlife preserve. First they kill the elephants and take the ivory," Hillary explained, talking with both hands. "Then they spread poison on the carcasses to kill vultures attracted to the dead animals."

"Otherwise the rangers might show up to stop them from stealing the tusks," Mercer said.

"Dead-on," she said. "By the time the rangers arrive, there's no reason to stop the bad guys from killing them, too. The ivory is way too valuable."

"So it's the local governments who pay for rangers," I said.

"Yes, and also with some of the funding from the WCS and AWB, and other conservation groups like them."

"But that hasn't done much to shut it down," I said.

Hillary Hawes sat up and looked at me, realizing I missed her whole point. "It's not a local problem, Alex. It's a worldwide criminal enterprise."

I apologized to her for my insensitivity, for my misunderstanding.

"I thought the United States had adopted an ivory ban in 2016," I said. "I thought our government had shut down the trade in it, and that in order to sell any ivory one had to be able to prove that the object—like a musical instrument—had been made before 1976, or that the antique pieces had been in this country for one hundred years."

"That's a start," Hillary said. "But it's a bit naïve to think they've shut things down."

"Didn't the Chinese announce that they were going to do the same kind of thing? Ban all commerce in ivory, that is," Mercer said. "By the end of this year, I think."

"I'm guessing it's lip service, if it's even to be believed," Hillary said. "They're supposed to shut the trade down in phases, but something like fifty to seventy percent of all smuggled elephant ivory winds up in China—where there are still collectors and scores of master carvers."

"I guess I've had my head in the sand," I said. "I don't understand how these treasures—whether elephant tusks or pangolin scales or rhino horns—get from the heart of Africa to America . . . or to China, for that matter. There are oceans between them, and laws now, that make it a pretty dangerous game."

"It's not too hard to get," Hillary said, snapping at me.

"Well, you've given us the image of the impoverished Congolese miner who's trying to keep himself alive in the forest by eating bushmeat, or a poacher from a small village putting poison in a pumpkin. What's behind this? I think we all get a sense that it's pretty big, but no idea of how it works."

"What do you know about human trafficking?" Hillary asked.

"There's nothing Coop *doesn't* know," Mike said. "That's her territory."

"Well, then, it's just like trafficking in humans," she said, "or in heroin. It's organized crime that moves the goods. They get them past government agencies that are weak or corrupt—or both—and they go to sell them in whatever places yield the highest profits."

"What kind of profit?" Mercer asked.

"A large elephant, with tusks that weigh two hundred fifty pounds each," Hillary said, driving home her point with a terribly sad image, "figure he's worth three hundred fifty thousand dollars dead, for the tusks that get to market."

"That's a fortune," Mike said.

"If perspective helps," she said, "the rangers make about eight dollars a day. They risk their lives for that."

I was racing away from what my own narrow focus had been—small bundles of rhino horns like Battaglia had intercepted in Operation Crash, which were brought across the border by a loose cohort of amateurs—and thinking instead about the financial opportunities this bloody business offered its takers.

"Humans, heroin, and wildlife," I said. "Trafficked globally by a large organization."

"I can see just where you're going with this, Coop."

"And I'll bet that Paul Battaglia got there first."

# TWENTY-FIVE

"The Baboon Café," Mike said.

"I'm not in the mood for jokes."

"That's what it's called, Coop. Let's sit down, have a coffee, put our next steps together."

We walked past Tiger Mountain, where the six Siberian cats were taking in the afternoon sun.

Again, no bars. They were enclosed behind a two-inch-thick glass wall, encircling three acres that—according to the signs—was their own personal habitat.

"You're not wearing Calvin Klein's perfume, are you?" Mike asked. "Obsession."

"Strictly Chanel, as you ought to know by now."

"One of the things I remember from hanging out with these guys when I was in college is that when the keepers wanted to attract them back to the corrals to groom or feed them, they'd douse rags in Obsession."

"What was it about that particular perfume?"

"The musk in the scent mixed with vanilla and some of the other ingredients."

"A good reminder to stick to my floral notes," I said, sitting down at a table, waiting as Mercer went to get three coffees.

Mike turned on his phone and held it to his ear to pick up his messages, listening for three or four minutes before relaying the ones that were meant for me.

"Absence is making their hearts grow fonder," Mike said.

"Whose?"

"A whole list of people jamming up my phone. You need to call your mother tonight. She won't be happy until she hears your voice," he said. "Catherine checked in on behalf of all the girls at the office. Everybody's coping. The place is wild with rumors about who'll replace the DA, and half the line assistants are sure it's going to be you."

"They'll be disappointed, won't they?"

"She didn't say they *want* you to be the boss of them, kid. Just that the gov is going to lean on you."

I put my elbows on the table and rested my face in my hands. "And I'd say that there's more than a reasonable doubt about that verdict, Mike. Wouldn't you?"

"Hope springs eternal, Coop. I think the governor is kind of sweet on you."

"Who else?"

"Laura."

Laura Wilkie had been my secretary—an executive assistant, really—for a very long time.

"I've got to call her. I think she's the most loyal person on the planet," I said, lifting my head. "What now?"

"Laura rambled off a list of names of callers. You can play it back yourself to see who you want to talk to," Mike said. "And she's messengering up a stack of mail and some packages that have come to the office."

"Packages? What kind of packages?"

"She didn't open any. That can be your bedtime project," he said.

Mercer set the steaming-hot cups down in front of us.

"Who would be sending me things to the office?"

"If you get any pumpkins, Coop, I'd suggest you don't eat them."

"My canines aren't all that valuable."

"But your brain is," Mike said. "Traffickers could crush it to bits and feed it to baby girls. Traditional medicine. Make them snarky and acid tongued, fond of ballet, with deep knowledge of Victorian English lit and romantic poetry, a strong sense of justice, refined taste in wine and a particular amber-colored alcohol—"

"Don't forget the courage," Mercer said. "Give her cred for that."

"Snarky brave girls," Mike said. "I like that. An entire subspecies of Coopsters."

"I'm craving their company," I said. "You haven't mentioned media calls."

"That's because Laura's required to pass them all on to the press office—there are tons of them—and not to tell you who they are."

"I'm fine with that," I said. "Let's think about the late DA and the subject of wildlife trafficking."

"Ready," Mercer said.

"Go back to Operation Crash. Battaglia jumped in—for the press attention and acclaim it got him—when James Prescott turned his back on the rhino-horn smuggling. How deep do you think this goes?"

"Wasn't Battaglia one of the early proponents of RICO laws, back when he was a rookie prosecutor?" Mercer asked.

The Racketeer Influenced and Corrupt Organizations Act—a set of laws promulgated in the 1970s under President Nixon—was meant to be a powerful tool targeting groups of criminals, so that when a low-level thug was arrested and charged, the government could also nab the leaders of the faction, the ones who were usually insulated.

"Yes," I said. "That's why he knew how to step all over Prescott about rhinos with such ease."

"So now that the ivory ban is in force," Mike said, "you think he found a way to keep himself in this effort?"

"If the target was big enough," I said. "I mean, not just some day laborers hauling horns across the border and up to a Manhattan hotel room. Really big."

"Like organized crime," Mike said. "Like global."

"There's been a movement to extend RICO to state laws," I said. "It would be so like Battaglia to push it to the limit—nab some humongous international cartel—to prove the need to do that."

"Think of it," Mike said. "The appointment of a citywide Special Narcotics prosecutor has stripped him of the power to go after drug dealers who bring large quantities of the stuff in from overseas, so he doesn't get any of the headlines that he loved so much—none of the big nabs."

"You're so right. We took the lead on human trafficking with our Hell Gate case," I said, "but as soon as Prescott woke up to the political potential on that issue, he slipped that subject away from Battaglia, too."

"You'd think the old man was still planning a Senate run," Mercer said. "Almost eighty, and boots on, ready to rumble."

"No term limits on pushing for his star-power position in the Fraternal Order of DAs in the Afterlife," I said. "He's always wanted to be the emperor. If not here, maybe at heaven's gate."

"So think like Battaglia, Coop," Mike said. "What would he have done?"

I was twisting and turning to come up with his interior mind-set. There was a point in time when I would have arrived at the goal before Battaglia did.

"Did Deirdre Wright give you the name of an expert to talk to?" Mercer asked. "From Animals Without Borders, I mean. Not in development, but someone with field experience and knowledge."

I nodded.

"Why don't you give him a call?"

I was headed out of the café to the exit. "Because I'd just rather show up at his doorstep. Give him no time to plan a strategy. No time to reach out to a supervisor," I said. "I want the unedited version. I want to know how tusks get from Africa to China, and why our government wants its fingers in the pie."

# TWENTY-SIX

"I'm Detective Mercer Wallace."

The man who had buzzed us into a brownstone on West Ninety-Fourth Street was staring at the blue-and-gold badge that Mercer presented to him. Since Mike had taken some days off and I was on official leave, Mercer offered to be the legit NYPD representative, leaving out the fact that his command assignment was sexual assault.

"How do you do?" the bespectacled man said, holding out his hand. "Is there a problem of some kind?"

"No, sir," Mercer said. "But we'd like some help from you. We have some pretty urgent questions about trafficking. Wildlife trafficking."

The stenciled black-ink letters on the glass door had Liebman's name written under the initials of the organization. He ushered us into a cramped room and we each took a seat, barely able to see Liebman over the stacks of papers on his desk.

"I'm Mike Chapman. Also a detective."

"And I'm Alex Cooper. I'm a p—"

"I know who you are, young lady," Liebman said. "I read the newspapers."

Liebman's title was president of AWB's Africa Program. A quick Google check on our way back to Manhattan confirmed that he had a PhD in biology from Yale, working at the intersection of science and conservation policy before overseeing AWB's portfolio of programs across forty countries in Asia, Africa, and the

Americas for the last two decades. There was a hint of an accent in his voice—maybe South African, but I couldn't be sure.

"Does this unexpected mission have something to do with the district attorney's death?" he asked.

"It might," I said. "We're all still in the dark."

"You're working on the case, Ms. Cooper? I would have thought you'd be kept at arm's length, being a witness and all that."

"I am at arm's length," I said. "And we're certainly not running the investigation. Both Mike and I are witnesses, as you probably noted from the news."

"What, then?" Liebman asked, picking up a carved stone paperweight—shaped like a penguin—and rolling it between the fingers of both hands like Captain Queeg's steel balls.

"It's kind of an all-hands-on-deck thing," Mike said.

Mercer put his arm out in front of Mike's chest, suggesting he lean back. "Better if I explain."

"Do try," Liebman said, looking from face to face to face as though it would help him understand the disarray in our approach.

"There's a task force handling this case, as the papers have reported," Mercer said. "I've got a piece of that work, and we're looking for your guidance."

Liebman kept rolling the penguin, which was upside down in his hands.

"I have to tell you that Alex Cooper knew her boss as well as anyone in his professional life," Mercer said. "She studied his connection to your organization and the great work it does."

Liebman looked at me and bowed his head.

"We'd like you to tell us more about the trafficking of animals from the wild," Mercer said. "We think there may be a connection to something Paul Battaglia was working on."

"I imagine you have colleagues who would know about that," Liebman said.

"I'm really of the view that my boss stumbled onto something," I said. "That he crossed paths, perhaps, into a territory where he didn't belong—wrong place, wrong time—rather than that he was deep into a case."

It was difficult—maybe impossible—to explain to an outsider how secretive the district attorney could be, how he didn't trust people, even his closest aides, for fear that they would leak word of a matter that would be picked up by another jurisdiction. Most of all, it was hard to explain how he hated James Prescott and feared the feds would steal his thunder once again by running off with one of his projects. The older Battaglia got, the more selfish he grew to be about grooming a successor, the more he wanted the glory to reflect entirely on his own individual brilliance.

"What territory would that be?" Liebman asked, replacing the penguin on top of some pamphlets and reaching for a wooden object, also carved, in the form of a monkey.

"Trafficking, like Mercer just told you. If we're right—if this is an area that the task force needs to explore—we'll pass the information on to those prosecutors and detectives as soon as we leave here."

"The focus of the investigation, as of now," Mercer said, "has been on old cases, on criminals the district attorney has prosecuted, on grudges from his past. But the three of us think we shouldn't overlook his interest in wildlife conservation, and the fact of how dangerous your work really is."

I wanted to ask Dr. Liebman what he thought about American hunting preserves, but he hadn't seemed to warm to us yet.

"Is it legislation that's needed?" I asked.

"There are laws, Ms. Cooper," he said. "Years ago, something called CITES was established. It's the Convention on International Trade in Endangered Species. By now there are scores of countries signed on, at least to talk the talk."

"Then is it enforcement?"

Liebman was holding the small monkey figurine between his thumb and forefinger. "In many places it is indeed a lack of strong enforcement efforts," he said, "but at the heart of it all is the need to stop the demand for the products. As long as people want the animal parts—rarely the animals themselves, Detective Wallace— as long as there is a demand for the parts, the slaughter and the trafficking will go on."

"So, the ivory markets," Mercer said, "and the traditional medicines."

"Have you explored the cyberworld?" Liebman asked.

"I hadn't thought about that," I said.

Some of my colleagues were experts on cybercrimes, including the most sophisticated areas of encryption—areas in which Google and Apple spent fortunes trying to deny government agencies like ours the right to break the codes to investigate cases. Maybe Battaglia was working with guys in that bureau who ought to be brought into the investigation.

"This black market thrives on the Internet," he said. "You ignore it at your peril."

"Talk to us about ivory," Mercer said. "About elephant tusks."

"Everyone's favorite subject, Detective," Liebman said. "You're thinking too common, really."

"How does the ivory get out of a small village in Africa?" Mercer said. "I understand that there's a poacher and then a middleman."

"It has become far more difficult," he said. "The Wildlife Conservation Society, for example, uses dogs at some of the larger airports. South Sudan, for example, and Entebbe. In Mozambique and Kenya."

"Dogs?"

"Yes, Mr. Wallace. They're trained to sniff ivory—and pangolin scales and the like—by the same people who train dogs to sniff for land mines and explosives in combat zones."

"How well does it work?" I asked.

Liebman reached to a bookcase shelf behind him and produced a small photograph in a frame. The picture was of a springer spaniel with floppy ears, playing with a toy while standing beside a small pile of ivory tusks.

"They've only been in operation since last year," he said, "but so far they've been a great success. Four to six busts a month, which results in seizures worth millions of dollars."

"That's good news," Mike said.

"Yes, although it has pushed the traffickers in another direction," Liebman said. "One that is much harder to control."

"What's that?" I asked.

"The illegal trade has shifted its modus operandi to moving cargo by boats instead of planes," he said. "The entire eastern coastline of Africa—and its ports—now houses the points of departure for rhino horns and ivory tusks and all else. The massive ports—like Mombasa—are far larger and much harder to patrol than the airports. A handful of spaniels can't get the job done."

"So ships?" Mike said. "Not planes."

"Container ships."

"Carrying what?"

"Meant to be carrying cargo of all kinds, across the Indian Ocean," Liebman said, "to Asia."

"Then the ivory, or whatever, is buried in the cargo."

"The ivory, Detective Chapman, is packed in with the heroin, which is why wildlife trafficking has become such an integral part of organized crime operations," Liebman said. "We've all been drawn into the heart of darkness—into Africa's heroin highway."

# TWENTY-SEVEN

"Heroin and Africa?" Mike asked. "That doesn't make sense. That's not where the dope comes from."

"Perfect sense, actually," Liebman said. "With all the conflict surrounding Afghanistan—the source location you're thinking of—the preferred route for getting pure heroin to Europe, and even to America, is through East Africa."

"Really?"

"We've learned, at our organization, that more than seventy thousand kilograms a year are smuggled through that region—the southern route, as it's now known," he said. "The drug lords capitalize on nonexistent security in many of the poorest regions on the African continent, and on porous borders through the countries there as well."

"What about at sea?" I asked. "What happens when these shipments are intercepted?"

"Nothing at all," Liebman said, replacing the photograph and picking up the carved monkey again. "Seizures at an airport can be prosecuted, as you know. But when the maritime patrols intercept drugs or even arms in international waters, they can't even detain the smugglers."

"What do they do to them?"

"Simply dump the contraband at sea, Ms. Cooper, and let the criminals sail away."

"That's insane," I said.

"We know that," Liebman said. "It's part of a treaty signed by thirty countries in Africa, Europe, and Asia."

Liebman stood up and walked to the office door. Attached to the back of it—facing us—was a map of the Eastern Hemisphere.

With his long, thin finger, Dr. Liebman traced a line from Mombasa across the Indian Ocean. His first stop was the Arabian Peninsula. He jabbed Dubai with his forefinger.

"It all depends on demand, like I say. The crown prince of Dubai likes to post photos of himself on Instagram, holding his pet lion."

"Pet?" I asked.

"Exotic pets are a huge status symbol in the Emirates, Ms. Cooper. A rare white lion—the kind the prince favors—might set him back one hundred thousand dollars," Liebman said. "It's the favorite trading place for cheetahs, too."

"The Egyptian pharaohs kept cheetahs as pets," Mike said. "Makes me crazy to think of the fastest land animal on earth kept on a leash."

"Oh, they're driven around in Bentley convertibles or on the front of a speedboat, too," Liebman said sarcastically. "Not a bad life, unless you understand that their habitat loss has nearly driven them to extinction."

"How do they get to the boats?" I asked.

"They're smuggled through the war zones of Somalia across the sea to Yemen—where cheetahs are the least of anyone's problems— and on to the oil-rich countries of the UAE, for a king's ransom."

"The animal that needs space to run," Mike said, "winds up in a cage in a royal palace."

"So I must ask you," Liebman said, "did Paul Battaglia have enemies in any of the Arabian countries?"

"Big-time," Mike said. "What was the bank, Coop?"

"BCCA," I said. "I'm sure you read about it last year. Battaglia prosecuted the men who ran the Bank of Commerce and Credit of

Arabia. Major jail sentences and a hundred forty million dollars in restitution."

The tabloids had a ball with the case. They came up with an alternate explanation for the lettered acronym: the Bank of Crooks and Criminals of Arabia. When James Prescott had been too slow to move on the international banking scheme, Battaglia had clawed back jurisdiction by virtue of a handful of transactions that had occurred in Manhattan. It had ratcheted up the tension between the two prosecutors so badly that they didn't speak for weeks.

"That's one place you should look, then," Liebman said. "If the district attorney uncovered any of the wildlife-smuggling schemes in the bank records of the oil royals, that might have put him deeper into the quicksand."

Mercer and I exchanged glances. We might be able to narrow the focus on a suspect, but the wide reach of the manner of the crime was beginning to seem overwhelming.

Stuart Liebman was as droll as he was brilliant. He moved his finger out of the Red Sea, around the peninsula, and over to India.

"Then there's walking gold, as we call it," he said. "Did your office have any ongoing investigations in India?"

"Not for lack of trying," I said. "But the US attorney got the jump on the most recent one. The biggest that I can think of."

"What's that?" Mike asked.

"Cybercrimes. Child porn," I said. "The cops brought the matter to me."

"At the same time," Mercer said, "as the FBI put it on Prescott's desk."

"Because of the strength of their tech industry," I said, "the Indians have developed very robust cyberlaws, much like our own. The FBI was working with the Indian government on a huge hacking case. Password hacking, actually. And it led to a massive child porn operation out of Delhi, linked to Thailand."

"Did you try to keep the investigation for Battaglia? For your unit?" Mike asked me.

"Yes."

"But the feds raked it in?"

"You bet. They had much greater resources available to deal with witnesses abroad," I said. "Unlike the banking improprieties, which are mostly paper chases."

"Did Battaglia go batshit when Prescott took it over?" Mike asked.

"He didn't seem to care at all," I said. "He was distracted by something at the time. He just told me to let it go."

"Really uncharacteristic of him, wasn't it?"

"This Prescott fellow you keep mentioning," Liebman said. "Do you trust him?"

I didn't have a ready answer. I had never questioned his integrity before.

"He's straight," I said, speaking softly. "I've known him a long time. He's a true public servant. I trust James Prescott."

"Very well, then," Liebman said.

"What's walking gold?" Mike asked.

"Tigers, Detective. Tigers are being slaughtered across India," he said. "For their skin and for their bones. And none of that is the work of small-town poachers."

"All organized gangs?" Mercer said.

"Yes, the same kind of syndicate that's wiping out elephants and rhinos in Africa."

"Shooting tigers, too," Mike said.

"They're not shot," Liebman said. "You can't sell those pelts if they've got bullet holes in them, can you?"

"How, then?"

"Jaw traps, Detective. Large iron contraptions about a foot in diameter—rusty, most of them—with serrated teeth, anchored to the ground by a thick chain."

I winced at the thought.

"There are more than a dozen tiger reserves—protected areas—in Central India, but the syndicates get into them and secure the jaw traps, usually near watering holes. Once the trap clamps down in the tiger's mouth, it's far too powerful for the animal to escape. Best to do it when the moon is full," Liebman went on, "so that there's no need of flashlights to give the traffickers away in the dark of night."

"And the dead tigers?" I asked.

"It's like a surgical strike, Ms. Cooper. The gang surrounds the dead animal and can have all the parts ready to go within a couple of hours," he said. "And it's usually the women who carry off the skin and the bones, because they're far less likely to be searched."

"The skins are purely decorative," I said. "And Americans buy as many of them as anyone else in the world, am I right?"

"You are. Luxury ornamentation."

"And the bones?"

"They're smuggled almost exclusively to China," he said.

There it was again. There was that country in which the trafficking seemed to be centered, no matter how many detours along the Red Sea and Indian Ocean.

"Traditional medicine?" I asked.

"Tiger bone wine, Ms. Cooper. A very traditional, very expensive tonic believed to impart the tiger's great strength and vigor to all who drink it," Liebman said. "It's not medicine at all. It's centuries of superstition."

Superstition, I thought. All of these species—and so many others—killed because of human ignorance, for beliefs in magical fixes and supernatural protections.

Mercer knew trade routes from the collection of maps that his father had given him all throughout his youth. He stood up next to Stuart Liebman and studied the world chart.

"Get us to China," he said. "It's still a long way off."

Liebman threaded his finger from the ocean past the Bay of Bengal, between Malaysia and Indonesia, and brought it to a rest on the southern tip of Vietnam.

"Did Battaglia have any business here?"

"In Vietnam?" I said. "Not that I know of."

"Well, it's the weakest link on the path to China," Liebman said. "You can bring your goods in anywhere along the Vietnamese coastline, because what the smugglers are searching out is the easiest place to make the border crossing."

"And it's well-known for that purpose?" Mercer asked.

"Completely. It's a place right here in North Vietnam," he said, putting his fingertip on the spot. "Called Mong Cai City."

Mercer leaned in to see it.

"Why?" he asked. "What's there?"

"More corrupt government officials than you can count on all your collective fingers and toes run Mong Cai," Liebman said. "Gambling casinos create a great diversion, as do all the tourists and shoppers looking for counterfeit goods. They keep the border guards wide-eyed and hungry for bribes of every kind. Most smugglers can slip across into China—into Dongxing City—as though the bridges had been greased with oil to ease them over. If there's one arrest for every three hundred attempts to get across the border, I'd be surprised."

"So the traffickers go where the government is most corrupt and least regulated—" Mercer said.

"And where the profit margins are the greatest," Liebman said. "For every kind of wildlife that's traded, getting to China is the goal. That's where the stakes are highest."

"Organized crime," Mercer said as he sat down and shrugged his shoulders. "Heroin and wild animals. I'd never have linked them together."

"Surely the district attorney knew of syndicates linked to Asia," Liebman said.

"We'll look into it," I said. "We'll tell the feds what you've told us, of course."

"Keep your eye on this James Prescott fellow," Liebman said, going back to his desk, picking up his stone penguin, and starting to stroke its back again. "I doubt I've told you anything he doesn't already know. I suspect he's way out ahead of you on this."

# TWENTY-EIGHT

"I have no idea what Liebman meant by that statement about Prescott," I said to Mike.

The three of us were sitting in the basement office of Giuliano, the owner of my favorite Italian restaurant, Primola. He always let us go downstairs to watch the Final Jeopardy! question before we sat at our table for dinner.

"How did it make you feel, Coop?"

"Queasy."

"Enough to spoil your appetite?"

"You know what I mean," I said. "Of course the feds have their fingers in every kind of trafficking operation worldwide. And they all network with each other through the Department of Justice, so whether Prescott himself is ahead of us on any of this, he'll certainly know which other US attorneys—San Fran, Los Angeles, Miami—whether any of them were going down this path. But Prescott isn't about to tell us anything, including what he and Battaglia crossed swords about."

"Liebman also said the name Diana meant nothing to him," Mercer said. "No help there."

"He didn't react at all when I asked him about that," I said. "There wasn't a glimmer of recognition."

"What do you tell Prescott tomorrow?" Mercer asked.

"Everything we just heard. I have no choice in this."

The category was revealed on the big board. "MONUMENT

MEN," Trebek said, reading the words aloud. "How do you feel about MONUMENT MEN tonight?"

The three contestants smiled at Trebek. One nodded as they all began to write their wagers on their electronic tablets.

"I'm feeling good about it," Mike said.

"That's just because so many monuments are dedicated to war heroes," I said, reluctantly slapping my twenty-dollar bill on Giuliano's desk. "Twenty-two historical statues in Central Park and not one is a woman."

"You don't count Alice in Wonderland?" Mike said.

"I rest my case," I said. "What if James Prescott is messed up in some kind of corrupt trafficking scandal? What if he shouldn't be handling this investigation?"

"None of that old paranoia, Coop. I'm going to let you have some tiger tonic tonight just to shore up your strength."

Trebek stood back and the Final Jeopardy! answer was displayed: "STONE CARVER LUIGI DEL BIANCO SCULPTED A PRESIDENTIAL EYE WITH WEDGE-SHAPED GRANITE STONES TO REFLECT THE LIGHT ON THIS FAMED MONUMENT, SO THAT IT CAN BE SEEN FROM MILES AWAY."

"Give me a break," Mike said. "Trick question, actually. I got it."

"You go," Mercer said.

"What is the Washington Monument?"

"I was short on laughs today," I said. "But you just saved me. That's an obelisk, as you well know, and there's no carving of the president's face on it."

"Yeah, but it's got those holes on top with blinking lights," he said. "Like devil's eyes. Eyes you can see for miles."

"I'm going with Lincoln," Mercer said. "What's the Lincoln Memorial?"

"Right president," I said, sweeping up the money with my

right hand. "Right president but wrong location. What is Mount Rushmore?"

"Stop, thief!" Mike said. "You're just going by Hitchcock. *North by Northwest.*"

"That Rushmore was made on a movie set," I said. "The real one has Del Bianco's great touch. I've been there, babe. He highlighted Lincoln's pupils and he fixed the huge crack in Jefferson's lip by patching it. Now, feed me."

Trebek had confirmed the same answer, without my longer explanation.

We went upstairs and Dominick led us to our usual table in the front corner, between the window and the door.

"Your usual, *signorina*?" Dominick asked.

"No, thanks. Just a glass of Pinot Grigio," I said.

Mike and Mercer ordered their drinks and we nibbled on lightly fried zucchini strips while we waited for our main courses.

"I want to try to diagram this tomorrow," I said.

"How do you mean?"

"Like we did in middle school, Mike. Mercer can lay out maps and draw lines between places abroad and Manhattan and the Texas hunting preserves," I said. "You and I can make a list of the characters and see who cross-connects with whom. Then I'd really like to meet with a couple of the guys who worked on Operation Crash for Battaglia. See what they know about smuggling and the angle of it that involves animal parts imported in the same shipments as drugs. They're both in private practice now."

Dominick came back with our dinners. Mike changed the subject to football, to get our heads out of the case while we ate.

"Are you able to sleep okay?" Mercer asked, watching me yawn at him across the table.

"Not yet."

"You look worn-out, Alex," he said. "Sleep will come in time."

"Let's get going," Mike said, pulling out my chair. He signaled to Dominick to put the dinner bill on my tab.

Mercer hugged me and walked up Second Avenue toward his car. Mike and I turned the corner onto Sixty-Fourth Street, headed east, to get to his.

He opened the door to the passenger side and waited until I belted myself in.

Then he crossed in front of the car, stopped at the curb to kick his tire. He knelt down and I lost sight of him. He stood up and kicked the tire again.

I opened my door and got out. "What's up?"

"A flat," he said, planting his hands on his hips and staring at the wheel. "I've got a fucking flat tire."

"What's the problem? Let's change it."

"It's a department car, Coop, from the Homicide Squad. There's no spare in it."

He turned away from me and took out his phone.

"You calling Mercer?" I asked. "He can't be too far."

Mike nodded.

"I'll go back to Primola and wait."

"No, you won't," Mike said, holding out his arm to tell me to stop.

"I won't drink," I said, walking to his side to reach up and kiss him on the tip of his nose. "I promise you."

"Get back in the car, Coop. You'll stay with me."

"Lightning doesn't strike twice," I said.

I knew he was thinking of my abduction. I knew he was thinking that I had mistakenly gotten into a black car that I thought was my Uber after walking out of Primola—just like we did minutes earlier.

"Listen to me, kid," Mike said. "Get back in the car."

I let him lead me into the street as he reached Mercer. "Yo, pal. You got a spare? My tire's flat out of air."

A kid on a bike with a food delivery bag hanging from his handlebars whizzed past me, so close that he practically ran over my toes. He had no headlight and I hadn't seen him in the dark.

"Careful," I said to Mike. "There's another kid coming. Don't open the door."

The second bicyclist had no light either. He was wearing a dark hoodie and bearing down on us like he had a train to catch.

Mike stepped from behind me and slammed me against the side of his car. That's when I saw the biker slow down just as he passed us. He pulled something out of his pocket, lit it, and tossed it on the hood of the old Crown Vic.

The windshield exploded as a fireball ignited the car's interior, showering glass fragments all over us. A searing blast of hot air raced up my back, as though a torch had been held against it. We fell to the ground together, Mike scrambling to roll me away from the car, then dropping his body on top of mine as a taxi came to a screeching halt just inches from our heads.

# TWENTY-NINE

"You knew something was going to happen, didn't you?" I asked Mike.

He was sitting on a gurney in a hallway outside the ER at New York–Presbyterian Hospital.

"Not then. Not tonight," he said. "You think I would have told you to stay there with me?"

I had no injuries. Two of the nurses had used tweezers to pick tiny pieces of glass out of my hair. They had looked me over for cuts and bruises—head to toe—but I had nothing more than a scraped knee and shattered nerves, once again.

"But you knew."

Mike had several small shards of glass that had stuck into his scalp and neck, and scraped-off skin on the palms of his hands. One of the nurses—the fiancée of a cop Mike knew—had extracted them and cleansed the open wounds. We were waiting for her to give him a tetanus shot before being discharged.

"Here's what I knew," he said, brushing my hand away from his hair. "You were at the Metropolitan Museum of Art Monday night, solving a murder case, when you had no business being there."

"Fact."

"Paul Battaglia spotted you on the evening news."

"Fact."

"Which means that a boatload of other people saw you there too."

"But they don't know me," I said. "The thousands of viewers in the tristate area had no idea who I was."

"Lucky for that," Mike said. "Battaglia makes a beeline for the

Met, late at night, and someone actually followed him there, thinking it was a fine place to make a statement and end his life."

"Fact."

"Which means that the killer or killers had been tailing him—who knows for how long—in order to take their shots on such short notice."

"Good point."

"Battaglia ran up the steps—facing you," Mike said. "He called out your name, said a few words. And you responded."

"Yes, but all I said was that I would *not* talk to him."

"But the killers—and whoever was running them—couldn't hear the back-and-forth. They don't know what either of you said."

"Oh. You're right."

"You're quick, Coop. I like that about you."

"I'm not operating on all cylinders. Get that?"

"Loud and clear," Mike said. "And Battaglia called you several times throughout the evening on Monday, because he was agitated about something."

"Yeah, but I didn't pick up. I didn't have my phone."

"I didn't even know that," Mike said, "so for sure no one else did. The killers might have figured you summoned him to come meet you."

"Deadfall," I said, climbing up to sit on the gurney opposite Mike's in the wide hallway at the ER entrance. "I had no idea I was so irresistible till this happened."

"They kill the district attorney, and then they're in the wind. Came out of nowhere and disappeared—so it seems—without a trace."

"Fact."

"You can bank on the point they had no idea who Battaglia was going to meet when he trotted up the museum steps."

"Probably so," I said, wagging my head from side to side. "Fair enough."

"That's what saved your life Monday night."

I looked over at Mike. "What do you mean?"

"Battaglia was silenced for a reason, kid. We're not sure what reason, yet—and I don't know what kind of progress Prescott has made," Mike said, rubbing his forehead, "but whoever killed the district attorney now wants *you* dead, too."

"I don't believe that," I said, ignoring the chills that flashed up and down my spine.

"Fact, as you would say."

"If someone wanted to kill me, that was the perfect moment."

"Not if they didn't realize who you were," Mike said. "The shooters were just the operatives acting for whoever wanted Battaglia dead. Then the smoke cleared and whoever ordered the hit realized the DA was on his way to see you—to talk to you."

"But I don't know what he wanted to talk about," I said. "I still haven't been able to figure out who Diana is and why that was on Paul's agenda."

"Not even the good guys believe that, Coop. Not even the task force."

"That doesn't prove anything. Nobody seemed particularly worried about me after I left the morgue, did they?" I asked. "They all left me to my own devices."

Mike was feeling the top of his head, as though he still had glass splinters.

I slid off the gurney and started pacing. "Prescott didn't make an issue of relocating me. He didn't think I was in danger or he would have told me," I said. "The commissioner would have insisted on a detail to bodyguard me."

Mike didn't pick up his head.

Suddenly, it dawned on me. "Something you want to tell me, Detective?" I asked.

"What?"

"You haven't taken days off at all," I said. "You've been assigned to me 24/7, haven't you? No wonder you're still driving around in a department car."

"Somebody had to do it. You think I want anyone else keeping watch on your bedroom?" Mike said, pulling on the arm of my sweater, trying to loosen me up.

"Why didn't you let me know, at least?"

"It didn't make any difference, Coop. You had Mercer and me with you all the time."

"Really, Mike," I said. "Now you're getting paid to sleep with me?"

"Sometimes that's a thankless job, kid," he said, flashing his best grin.

"Is that why you didn't make love to me?"

"You must be fucking nuts," Mike said, lifting both arms in the air. "A few days ago, I was three feet away from a man who had his brains blown out. I know how that impacted you, but may I remind you it was not high on my list of sexual stimulants either. I've been no more interested in thinking of making love than I expect you are."

"It just would have been nice if you'd tried," I said, forcing a smile. "I always like it when you try."

"Is that your way of apologizing to me?"

"I think it helps me to know when my life is in danger," I said. "I dodged two bullets Monday night. I thought the worst was over."

I heard Keith Scully's footsteps before he turned the corner and came into sight—the sharp-paced, firm march of a marine who never relaxed his bearing. Three men were in formation close behind him.

"Are you okay, Alex?" the commissioner said, placing a strong hand on my elbow. "You've had a helluva week."

"I'm fine, thanks. It was shocking and frightening, but a more pleasant result than Monday's experience," I said. "It's Mike who took the hit."

"How's your thick head, Chapman?" Scully asked as they shook hands.

"Aerated, Commissioner," Mike said. "That can only help the gray matter to breathe some fresh air."

"Crime Scene's going over your car," he said. "It appears to have been a Molotov cocktail. Really primitive. The lab will analyze it but it's probably just some gas in a soda bottle."

"It did the job," Mike said. "It was a scorcher."

"Mercer told me what you saw," the commissioner said to me. "Would you mind repeating it?"

One of the detectives stepped forward to take notes.

"The first kid practically nailed me when I went to get back in the car," I said.

"First kid?" Scully asked. "Mercer didn't tell me that there was more than one."

"Two," I said. "Maybe I didn't get a chance to tell Mercer. Anyway, I think the first one was delivering food. At least I saw a bag dangling from the handlebars."

"Chinese? Italian? American?"

"The food?" I asked. "I couldn't see the writing on the bag."

"Not the food," he said. "The kid."

"I didn't get a good look. He was coming at me too fast," I said. "It was all I could do to flatten myself against the side of the car."

"You didn't flatten yourself," Mike said. "I'm the one who pushed you when I saw the second biker coming our way."

Keith Scully looked at me as though I'd just committed perjury. "Which is it, Alex?"

"Why bother asking me?" I said.

"Did you hit your head on the pavement or something?"

"Not hard enough to put me out of my misery, apparently," I said. "Did you think that I was likely to be the target of a killer this time, Keith?"

"You thought Battaglia's assassin was done?" the commissioner said.

I clapped both hands to my ears. "We're all answering one another's questions with questions."

"Can you describe the first biker?"

"He had no headlights on the bike and no reflectors on his clothes. He was all in black with a hoodie pulled down on his forehead. Dark-skinned, I know, because I saw his forearms. He had gloves on his hands, but his sweatshirt sleeves were pushed up."

"Age?" the commissioner asked.

"A kid. I thought he was a kid. A teenager, maybe."

"And the second one?"

"Same," I said. "Young, dark skin. I couldn't make out any facial characteristics, and he was also wearing a hoodie."

Scully seemed to think I was useless, so he turned to Mike. "What's your guess? Were they together? One to throw you off, make you unsteady, while the other tossed the cocktail?"

"Probably so," Mike said. "They were only seconds apart from each other when they rode by. Seconds, not even a minute."

"Amateurs, hired by a pro," the commissioner said.

"You have ideas?" Mike asked.

"Yes, Chapman. Three other incendiary cocktails went off like this around town within the last hour. There's already a bunch of Facebook posts claiming that radicals were randomly blowing up cars to protest the jailing of one of the sheiks who was convicted in federal court by Prescott last week."

"Then these radicals should have lit a fire under Skeeter's ass," I said. "Not mine."

"All the episodes had two bike riders?" Mike asked.

"Yes," Scully said. "Tailing each other by seconds."

"Injuries?"

"None, except for you. All the other cars were unoccupied, and no one was around them."

"Like you say, Commissioner, amateurs hired by a pro," Mike said. "Poor man's grenades, to make the whole thing look like a bunch of disenfranchised street kids in action, rather than a targeted attack."

"No sign of any of the pairs of bicyclists in the aftermath of each explosion," Scully said. "I'm sure my guys will find abandoned bikes before morning. Gloved hands, so no prints. The bastards will slip out of the hoodies and split up, and be on their way back to Throgs Neck or Gravesend."

"So if someone's out to kill me, why didn't he—or they—just send sharpshooters, like they did for Battaglia?" I asked.

"Not that tonight's attacks are subtle, Alex," the commissioner said, putting his arm around my shoulders, "but they create the illusion that this coincidence—"

"Coincidence?" I said.

"That's how it will appear to the public, as happenstance. When they read the news of tonight's four blasts—since we have no intention of releasing the information that you and Mike were close enough to the car to have been blown to bits—it will appear to be in no way connected to Battaglia's death."

"But it's a police car," I said. "You won't fool anyone."

"The car was unmarked," Scully said, "and there isn't enough of it left for people to know what it used to be."

"The plates? The license plates can be traced."

"Mercer had those removed while the vehicle was still smoking."

Battaglia's dangerous world was closing in around me. I took a few deep breaths and tried to think clearly.

"So these kids just get lucky? They happen to come along when Mike and Mercer and I leave the restaurant and part ways, heading for our cars?" I said. "Mike always swears there are no coincidences in policing."

"There aren't," he said.

"If I hadn't stepped out of the car to see what you were looking at," I said, letting all of this sink in, "I'd have lit up the night sky, along with all the empty cardboard coffee cups that you litter your car with."

"Fact," Mike said. "That's a fact."

"So I'm just supposed to believe these thugs had the good fortune to come along at the moment they did, capitalizing on the fact of your flat tire?"

"The truth of it is, Coop, that those bikers were waiting for us since I parked the car and we went into Primola," Mike said. "They had you in their sights. Me too, I guess."

"And the flat tire is the coincidence they needed. The one that defies your theory," I said.

"Not on your life, Coop," Mike said. "It's the bad guys who made the tire flat while you were chowing down on your pasta primavera."

"They what?" I looked from Mike's face to Keith Scully.

"That tire was slashed by a knife, babe. Intentionally maimed. My car couldn't have rolled to the next corner, there were so many cuts in the rubber," Mike said. "And I'm the fool who insisted you stay by my side."

# THIRTY

"Things have changed, Alex," the commissioner said. "So my setup has to change too."

"I get that."

"It's all moved so much faster than we expected, and it was never my plan to put you in harm's way."

Keith Scully had walked me away from Mike, into a corner of the hallway.

"You didn't do that," I said, although now I kept rethinking why I had been left so exposed in the days since Battaglia's murder.

"I have to move you out of the city," Scully said. "There's no way to ensure your safety here."

"I'll go to Martha's Vineyard," I said, anxiously looking over his shoulder at the nurse who was waiting for Mike to roll up his shirtsleeve for his injection. "We're good there."

"I can't let you go to your own home. That wouldn't be smart."

"But with Mike—"

"Not with Mike," Scully said. "I've got to do something about him, too."

My heart was racing and my head pounding. "Together, though, right? He and I will be together?"

"For tonight, yes."

"Look, Commissioner," I said. "I'll do anything you want me to do, as long as you don't cut me off from the people I need."

"The first thing you're going to do for me is call your parents," he said. "They're in the Caribbean?"

"Yes." They had retired there several years ago, and now I was especially glad they were on an island at a distant remove from my work.

"Reassure them that you're fine and that I just need to send you underground for a few days."

"I don't have a phone," I said, pointing at the nurse with the needle. "I need Mike."

"Use mine," Scully said, pulling it out of the breast pocket of his suit.

"They'll freak out if that's the message," I said, trying to think of something else to say to my family.

"Suit yourself. I'll get on the phone with them myself if that helps."

"It won't. It might even make matters worse."

Once a marine, always a marine. Scully's armor didn't crack. "Then you'll call Catherine Dashfer. Tell her the same thing," he said. "Need-to-know basis only, among your office buddies, but assure her that you're fine. Tell her the explosions scared you."

This was going in a dark direction. Whatever the newly improvised plan was, I knew I wasn't going to like it.

Mike was walking toward us, rolling down his sleeve and buttoning his shirt at the wrist. He stopped three feet away and just stared at Scully and me.

"Where are we going, Commissioner?" I asked.

I'd known Keith Scully for so long, before he had rocketed to the top of the department, that I usually called him by his first name. When he went into full commando mode, I used his title.

He reached for my arm again, but I pulled back.

"Three Sisters Hospital, in Westchester," he said. "Just for a night or two."

"A psych ward? A psych ward run by nuns?" I said, putting my finger between my teeth to stop myself from screaming at the police commissioner. "It's not *me* who's crazy this time."

"It's not about crazy, Alex. It's about safe."

"I've been there, Commissioner," I said, practically foaming at the mouth. "We had to put one of my witnesses in Three Sisters when she had a breakdown. It's a nuthouse, with padded walls and wrist restraints."

"I'm not committing you, Alex," Scully said, laughing at me. "I should have made that clear."

"Make it clear to my family and friends, then, will you?" I asked. "When people find out about this—when some rag reporter figures out that's where you've warehoused me for the weekend and the story goes viral—the lede in the papers will be that I've lost it."

"If you calm down and let me finish, Alex—"

"Finish what?" I asked, motioning to Mike. "You've got to hear this, Mike. The commissioner thinks I should be at Three Sisters. He thinks—"

Scully lifted his hand like it was a stop sign and Mike didn't move.

"The plan is, Alex, that an hour from now—after you've settled down and had a chance to make your calls—you'll leave this hospital."

"With Mike, right?" I said, my eyes darting back and forth between Scully's face and Mike's.

"Yes, with Mike."

I inhaled and exhaled slowly. "Okay. What else?"

"There'll be a van waiting outside the hospital, by the driveway on Seventieth Street."

"The rear door," I said.

"Yes," Scully said. "You'll be wheeled out on a gurney and—"

"I'm fine, Keith. I really am." He was my friend at this moment, not the commissioner. I knew he'd respond to me if I leaned on our old relationship. "No gurney."

"I know you're fine, Alex. I counted on that," he said.

This time he took hold of me by both arms and stopped my fidgeting with his tight grip.

"What then?"

"You'll be on a gurney, wheeled out to the van," Scully said. "It's the medical examiner's morgue van, Alex."

I shuddered and twitched, but Scully kept his hands on me.

"I don't want people to think you're crazy, Alex. I want them to think you're dead."

# THIRTY-ONE

"What does one wear to one's own autopsy?" I asked. "Are they letting me keep my clothes on for the ride downtown?"

Mike and I were sitting in an empty hospital administration office about one hundred yards down the hallway from the ER.

"You're doing well, kid. You took it like a champ."

"Remind me what choice I had," I said.

We had made the calls to my parents, both brothers, Catherine—and I threw in my two best friends, Joan and Nina, as well. No details offered.

"Vickee's meeting Mercer at your apartment," Mike said. "She'll pack up what you need for the next few days."

"How about your stuff?"

"They'll get that, too."

"I'm not going out in a body bag," I said. "I can't cope with that."

"Scully knows. You'll be under a sheet."

"Is there press outside?" I asked.

"I'm not sure, but with the commissioner's car here, I'm guessing he wants someone to notice."

It was almost one in the morning when Scully came inside to tell me that an unidentified woman had expired just minutes earlier.

"That's me? Unidentified?"

"For the time being," Scully said. "The story we're giving out is that an unidentified woman—burned beyond recognition—was collateral damage in the Upper East Side explosion. Possibly homeless, because she was in the middle of the street. Not inside the car."

"A bag lady, Coop. Suits you to a tee."

"That way," Scully said, "we can vamp about how long it's going to take to get a match to her DNA if she's not known to us."

"But the bad guys," I said. "What will they think?"

The police commissioner hesitated. "They might hope you're the dead woman, or they might think the bikers screwed up. If it keeps them from looking for you for a few days, I'll breathe more easily."

"So will I."

"Take off your shoes, Alex," Scully said. "I'll have the nurses put them in a bag. The shoe shapes would be obvious under the sheet. And when I leave the room, strip down to your underwear, okay?"

"But there's a sheet," I said. "Isn't that enough?"

"There'll be two sheets, in fact, just to be safe. You'll just need to hold your breath for thirty seconds while they roll the gurney out to the van."

"Promise me one thing," I said. "Tell me it's not the van they transported the district attorney in, is it?"

"Get real, Coop," Mike said. "What's the difference?"

"It spooks me."

"I'll be with you," he said.

"That spooks me, too."

"Thanks for all this, Alex," Scully said. "You'll be in good hands, and by the time you're back at home, I'll get a department phone for you. I don't care that Prescott wants you to go shopping at your local AT&T store. I need to get you something that can't be traced and that only comes directly to me. Just give me a few days."

The only thing missing from his farewell remarks was a "semper fi." He turned away and closed the door behind him.

A few minutes later, after knocking, two morgue attendants wheeled in the ME's gurney. They left the room while I stripped down to my bra and panties. I climbed on and lay down, letting

Mike drape my body with two white sheets. They were stamped in green ink with the words PROPERTY OF THE NYC MEDICAL EXAMINER on the border.

"Are you going to be okay when I cover your face?" Mike asked. He was stroking my hair and bent over to kiss me on the forehead.

I bit my lip and nodded. He kissed me on the mouth and I responded, clutching at his hand. Then he broke away and pulled the sheets up over my face and head.

The morgue attendants came back in and told me to brace myself for the short ride on the gurney. They led me out of the room and down the hallway. I was breathing normally, but careful not to move.

The double outer doors swung open automatically. Several nurses flanked us—at least, I assumed they did because I heard Mike and the attendants thank them as I felt a blast of cold air when we left the hospital corridor.

"Run silent, run deep," Mike said. I knew he was referring to one of his favorite World War II movies. I was supposed to be the American sub turning off its engines to pass beneath the Japanese warship. No sound, no movement, no sign of life.

I could hear Keith Scully's voice, maybe fifty feet away. He must have been talking to reporters.

There was a short passage from the hospital exit to the van. My ride stopped abruptly as the two men opened the rear doors of the morgue vehicle. They each took a side of the metal bed and lifted it, collapsing the base, which held the wheels, and shoving the entire contraption—with me aboard—into the van.

"You're good, babe," Mike said. "Stay down."

He hoisted himself up and one of the men slammed the doors. There were no windows on the side panels, of course, so it seemed doubly dark inside.

Mike waited until we moved out of the driveway and up the short block, turning south on York Avenue to ride downtown to the morgue, before he lifted the sheets.

"You can open your eyes now," Mike said.

"I really don't want to."

There were too many ghosts who had taken this bumpy ride. I had no desire to check out my grim surroundings.

"What did Scully say?" I asked.

"Nothing more than he told you," Mike said. "He was just creating a diversion to keep the press with him while we slipped you out."

"No photographers?" I asked.

"A couple. I saw some flashes go off, but they were at long distance."

It took only eight or nine minutes to get to the morgue. There was a long bay large enough to accommodate the vans. I could feel the motion as the driver made a U-turn and backed us in, then down the slight incline that led right to the doors of the basement morgue, while Mike covered my head again—just to be safe.

I was unloaded as quickly as I had been loaded. Doors slammed behind us and I figured we were in the private space that was reserved for the recently dead.

Mike lifted the sheets from my face and put my clothes on the table next to the gurney.

"Turn off the Stryker saw," he said, smoothing out my hair while he had a conversation with an imaginary pathologist. "Looks like I've got a live one."

# THIRTY-TWO

"What happens now?" I asked.

We were back in the ME's conference room, where Jaxon Stern had first interrogated me less than four days earlier. It was three A.M. and I was slumped across the table, my head resting on my arms, too tired to think straight. A suitcase with my clothes and toiletries was in the corner. Vickee had delivered it to the local precinct, as the commissioner had directed, and a uniformed cop brought it here.

"You leave for Three Sisters," Mike said. "Scully just wants to give it enough time to make sure any reporters who might have followed the van down here have left."

"Is Mercer taking us?"

"Nope. Too obvious," Mike said. "There'd be no reason for him to come to the morgue."

"Who?"

"Lieutenant Peterson," Mike said. "Ray lives in Westchester County. It makes sense for him to stop by here to check on the body of a Manhattan North homicide victim before he heads for home."

Ray Peterson was one of my heroes. A smart, steady, old-fashioned detective who had long ago earned his grade as lieutenant by combining his experience and intelligence with cutting-edge technology to run the best homicide squad in the country.

"When do we go?"

"Soon, Coop, very soon," Mike said. "One more thing, kid, and I don't want any theatrics on account of it, okay?"

"I feel it coming," I said, without even picking up my head. "I'm going solo."

"That's the spirit."

"To a nuthouse," I said. "To a nunnery."

"Good for all that ails you, as my mother would say."

"Who's going to be there for me?" I asked.

"Jimmy North," Mike said, referring to one of my favorite young guys on the squad. "And Kate. Kate Tinsley."

I opened my eyes and glared at Mike, but didn't pick my head up. It seemed too heavy to lift.

"She's got a pipeline to Jaxon Stern," I said. "I don't like that."

"We're doing it Scully's way," Mike said. "He thinks it would send some kind of signal if I disappeared at the same time you did. He wants me in the city and at work."

"Kate? How about her?"

"I told the commissioner about Jaxon Stern and what his problem is," Mike said. "Kate didn't do you any harm, kid, and Scully really needs to keep one of his people in the mix. Someone who's been in on all the task force meetings since the first night."

"I'm too whipped to fight my own battles," I said, pulling myself up and shaking my head to wake myself up. "How are we going to stay in touch?"

"There are real phones at Three Sisters," Mike said. "I can call you in your room. Three or four days; that's all it's going to be."

Ray Peterson knocked on the door before he walked in. He slapped Mike on the back and clasped both his hands over mine.

"You hanging in, Alex?" he asked.

I nodded. "Thanks, Loo."

"Glad to have your company going home," he said. "Chapman

tell you we think it's best if you lie down on the backseat for the ride? I've got a pillow and a blanket, so maybe you can nap on the way."

"Good to go," I said. "Want to give us a minute?"

Mike was lacking the gene for empathy, but I had known that for more than a decade. "No long good-byes, Coop," he said, wrapping his arm around me and leading me out of the room.

"I'll back my SUV into the bay," the lieutenant said. "You can tuck Alex in. Looks pretty quiet outside."

I crawled onto the rear seat a few minutes later and curled up for the forty-five-minute ride. Somehow, the motion of the car helped knock me out and I dozed for the last half of the journey. Peterson had to wake me up when we reached the psychiatric hospital—founded in the 1960s by three nuns who worked with emotionally disturbed patients.

Sister Louise ran the facility. She was out on the lawn in front of the main building by the time I was awake. It was pitch-black but I could make out the large yellow neo-Victorian house that I had visited years earlier, which I remembered as set on a beautifully landscaped hilltop that looked more like a Swiss canton than a piece of suburban New York.

She welcomed me warmly and offered me food, which I refused, before walking us across the lawn to one of the outbuildings. It was a two-bedroom cottage, which had been set up for my arrival. Both detectives—Kate Tinsley and Jimmy North—were waiting for me in the living room.

I greeted the team, thanked Peterson for the ride and for carrying my luggage, and asked what my instructions were. I watched Sister Louise as she walked down the steps of my temporary shelter, turning to say good night, her face framed by her white coif under the dark head veil that blended in with the color of the sky.

"Sleep, Alex," the lieutenant said. "Nobody needs you in the morning. James Prescott's been told you can't come in. No more than that at the moment. This will be the first time you can catch up on your sleep all week."

"This is a psych ward, Loo," I said. "If you can find someone on staff to dispense a sleeping pill, I might be able to take your advice. Otherwise, I'm fresh out of pleasant dreams."

"I'll ask. There are a couple of docs in residence," he said. "That phone next to your bed is for incoming only. Don't you give the number out to anyone, okay? If you need someone or something, let Tinsley or North make the call. They'll take turns sleeping— twelve hours on, twelve off. Something like that. You understand they'll get you whatever you need."

"I do."

"You're safe here, Alex. Give in to that."

"Thanks, Loo. I intend on trying."

I readied myself for bed, showering and changing into my pajamas and robe. There was no minibar or television, and no lock on my bedroom door, but there were no straitjackets or restraints either. Peterson had come back with a Lunesta. I took it from him, along with a bottle of water, swallowing it and climbing under the covers.

I slept until eleven o'clock Friday morning, feeling halfway human when I awakened. North was asleep in one of the twin beds in the other room. Tinsley called the main house to ask for some coffee, cereal, and fruit to be sent over to me.

I showered again and put on clean clothes, then ate my breakfast when it arrived.

"What's the news from headquarters?" I asked.

"The explosions made all the papers—at least, online," Tinsley said. "No mention of you, just Scully saying that the ME would be trying to identify the remains of the homeless woman."

"Would you mind calling Mike for me?"

"Not at all." She dialed the number and handed me the phone, but it went right to voice mail after one ring.

I left Mike a message and gave back the phone.

"How about a walk?" Tinsley said. "You'll go stir-crazy if you don't get out, and Sister Louise said there are pretty nice hiking trails."

It looked like a beautiful fall day, so I threw on a sweater and we left the cottage for a brisk walk in the woods.

Prescott's assistant was my first caller. He reached Tinsley while we were on a path that circled a small pond on the property. Since Scully wouldn't give out my location, they decided to postpone my meeting until Monday morning, when they hoped to be able to get to me. I liked being lost in the woods, even if I did have keepers to monitor my activities.

We were back in the cottage by two. The detectives switched duties—Tinsley going inside to rest—and I was glad for the chance to talk with Jimmy, whom I trusted and liked.

It was after four when Mike called for the first time. The phone rang next to my bed, and I went in the room to answer it, closing the door behind me.

"Hey," he said. "All good?"

"Too much time to think," I said. "That's never good when what I'm thinking about is murder."

"Missing me?"

"Sister Louise does empathy a lot better than you do, Detective," I said. "You calling because you woke up without me today?"

"I'm calling to tell you what a good nose you have."

"For what?"

"Snooping," Mike said. "Instincts. Sense of smell."

"Better than a springer spaniel?" I asked, sitting down on the bed.

"More like a grizzly, kid. They can sniff out an elk carcass that's underwater from six miles away."

"What'd I do to earn your praise?"

"For starters, you kept your cool last night on Sixty-Fourth Street, when my car got singed."

"Thanks."

"And for another, you may have hit the jackpot on your theory about Battaglia and the animals."

"What is it?" I asked.

"Sanitation found an abandoned bicycle this morning."

"That must happen ten times a day, Mike."

"A racer. An expensive ten-speed that looks brand-new," he said. "On East Sixty-Fifth Street, just off Lexington Avenue, in an alleyway."

That was only around the corner and a few blocks from where the explosion had been.

"Does the lab have the bike?" I asked.

"Yeah. Going over it for prints and any kind of trace evidence. Clothing fibers, glass fragments, oil."

"Near Lex," I said. "Interesting location. Have they checked video for the subway entrance at Lex and Sixty-Eighth after nine in the evening?"

"The last twelve hours the tech guys, supplemented by an FBI unit, have been checking street surveillance videos enough to blind them. They were on it full-time since Monday night's shooting. This latest focus is for the explosions," Mike said. "But it's not the Lexington Avenue line that may have captured our Molotov man."

"Somewhere else?"

"Yes. There's a video of a young guy stripping off a hoodie and trashing it in a can on Fifth Avenue," Mike said. "Fifth and Sixty-Fifth Street, before he started to run."

"Run where?" I asked. "There's a stop for the Q train, and I think the N, a block south of there."

"Across Fifth Avenue," Mike said. "But this clown wasn't headed for the subway. He ran right down the path that leads into the zoo. The Central Park Zoo."

# THIRTY-THREE

"How about if Kate and Jimmy drive me down to the city?" I said, pacing the small cottage bedroom.

"Don't need you yet," Mike said. "I've been to the zoo."

"Did this guy actually get inside?" I asked. "I mean, it's not open at night."

"Seems like you're not the only one with keepers, Ms. Cooper. He works there."

"You've ID'd him? That's fantastic."

"I have a name and a bogus address at the moment. I've only been on this for half an hour."

"Tell me," I said. "Is he Asian?"

"Profiling is bad for you, Coop. His name is Henry Dibaba," Mike said. "His parents emigrated from Kenya thirty years ago. He's twenty-two. No worries, he's a citizen."

"What does he do at the zoo?" I asked.

"Night shift. Henry works eight P.M. to eight A.M. He called in that he'd be late last night—which fits our time frame—and he was gone, as expected, by the time I got the heads-up a while ago about his premiere on the CCTV street scenes."

"You like him as our bomber?"

"Too early to tell," Mike said. "I couldn't ID either of them. You think you can?"

"No way. But there should be more video from other avenues in that grid, don't you think?"

"I do. These tech analysts are working as fast as they can."

"Last night," I asked, "how many people were on staff at the Central Park Zoo?"

"Just a handful. There are two guys who work security—one of them let Henry in at that gate when he arrived. The rest are animal keepers and feeders."

"Only two security at night?"

"Don't forget," Mike said. "This little zoo is inside Central Park. So you've got an entire police precinct—not a miniature substation like in the Bronx—surrounding it, protecting it. It's not hundreds of acres of wilderness in the Bronx, like the big one is. That's so much harder to patrol."

"Understood," I said. "But both are run by the Wildlife Conservation Society?"

"They are," Mike said. "And the connection proved helpful to me."

"How?"

"So Henry is a feeder. He's in charge of midnight snacks for the snow leopards."

"Love those cats."

"But he's not your kind of guy," Mike said. "His passion is snakes, the bigger the better."

"Spare me," I said.

"Henry likes feeding rats to the blood pythons and tree boas. Keeps him busy at night. He's a herpetologist at heart."

"Oh, Henry! How I hate snakes."

"So he used to live with his parents in Brooklyn," Mike said. "Moved out last year to a girlfriend's house, but she said he split from her a couple of months back. She said Henry took his favorite gopher snake with him when he left, so she's pretty sure he's done with her."

"The zoo doesn't have a more current address?"

"Nothing. Henry shows up for work on time—usually—and

does the deed. Some people don't mind handling live rats, and others can deal with slimy serpents. But very few folk like to do both. In fact, Henry used to work at the Bronx Zoo but requested a transfer to Central Park."

"Recently?" I asked.

"Two months ago."

"Did you run a rap sheet?"

"Yeah, the snake's got a couple of assaults, Coop. One attempt at strangulation and—"

"No games. Henry Dibaba, not the serpent," I said. "I'll pull a better escape from this place than Houdini unless you keep me in the loop."

"Henry's got two collars," Mike said. "Both in the Bronx. Low-level felony for a controlled substance, pleaded down to a misdemeanor and fine because it was his first arrest."

"What drug?"

"Patience, kid. One PP is pulling up the records now."

"What's his other arrest?"

"Henry took one of his snakes for a ride on the C train," Mike said. "Just a harassment of some kind. The lady sitting next to him fainted when the snake poked his head out of a Barnes and Noble book bag. But it's opened a new vista for the US attorney."

"How?"

"Prescott has subpoenaed a list of all the employees at Wildlife Conservation—both zoos and the society's staff—and Animals Without Borders," Mike said. "We'll be running record checks on everyone. Amazing what the feds can do that we can't. They're also going to put all the names into passport control. See who's been traveling where. Even if we can only find some of the low-level runners this way, they can eventually lead us to the head of the enterprise."

"That's a needle in quite a big haystack," I said. "People like

Deirdre Wright and Stuart Liebman—a lot of the other employees, too—have to go abroad."

"No harm in knowing who's dancing with the animals, and who shouldn't be."

I had walked back and forth so many times I was leaving footprints in the carpet.

"Why can't you come up here for dinner, Mike?" I asked, feeling restless and removed from my routine.

"I'm short one department car, Coop, until the lieutenant replaces it. Remember that?"

"Mine's in the garage."

"Against the rules. You just hunker down and listen to Kate and Jimmy," Mike said. "I'll call you later."

At five o'clock, Sister Louise came over with a man she introduced as a staff physician. He took my blood pressure, asked me five innocuous questions about my mental health, offered to listen to me if I wanted to vent, and doled out a single sleeping pill to get me through the night.

As in most institutions, the dinner plan included an early meal. Three of the nuns walked over with trays—some unidentifiable fish covered in a thick white sauce, an underdone baked potato, and a soft roll with margarine on the side. I probably wasn't the only patient on a bland diet—I think that's all the kitchen had in its repertoire.

Jimmy and Kate were both hanging out with me for the evening, doing all they could to pretend it was not an assignment. One of them occasionally went outside to check the perimeter of the building and walk down the main driveway, following the six-o'clock curfew, to make sure there were no unwelcome visitors making their way onto the property.

The cottage was way too small for three of us to have a comfortable evening with no TV to divert us. I made as much small talk as I could and was grateful that Vickee had packed a volume of Conan Doyle stories that she found next to my bed. There was nothing like Holmes to get me out of a funk.

Mike called at ten. He was in Queens, having dinner with Vickee and Mercer. I envied him the normalcy of life in the home of our dearest friends. I didn't know the Final Jeopardy! question he answered for me—no surprise—since the category was physics. I said good night to him, then to the detectives, before washing up and getting in bed to read.

I took my pill—my sleeping draught, as Conan Doyle would have it—and before Watson could engage me in the tale of the creeping man, I fell asleep.

"Alex?"

I heard my name and sat up in bed, glad that I had left a light on in the bathroom. The small clock next to my bed showed that it was 2:53 A.M.

"Sorry," Kate Tinsley said. "I knocked but you didn't hear me."

"What is it?" The drug had worked. My sense of alarm had been dulled but I was unnerved enough by Kate's voice to try to shake off the sleep.

"It's James Prescott, Alex," Tinsley said. "Put on your robe and come into the living room."

"He's called?"

"No, Alex. He's here."

I reached for the phone next to my bed. I was frightened by this unexpected nocturnal visit from the US attorney, and I wanted to talk to Mike.

"Prescott's not on the phone, Alex. He's right here."

"I heard that," I said, snapping at her, remembering that my landline didn't make outgoing calls. "I'd like to use your phone."

She was next to my bed, holding out my robe. "I'm afraid you'll have to wait."

I slipped it on and tied the belt, fumbling with it because my hands were shaking. "What's wrong? What's going on?"

"I have no idea," Tinsley said.

I walked into the living room. James Prescott was flanked by two men—the agents Bart Fisher and Tom Frist, whom I had met in his office the first day. They were each dressed in jeans and outdoor jackets—country gentlemen ready for a hike in the woods.

"I'm sorry to wake you, Alex, but it's all good."

I cocked my head and looked at him. Good for whom? I wondered.

"It's the middle of the night," I said. "You should have called."

"I texted Kate. I told her to let you sleep until we arrived," Prescott said. "You gave us a good lead, whether you realized it or not."

Kate Tinsley was standing in the doorway to my bedroom, and Jimmy North in the doorway to the second bedroom. Prescott and crew were between me and the cottage door. I felt as though the room was closing in on me.

I didn't remember giving Prescott any lead.

"I'll bite."

"It was your suggestion to get Amy Battaglia's phone, to look for texts," Prescott said. "Mike passed along the word that the DA often used her phone when he was at home, picked it up if it was close by."

I felt queasy. I had put them into the private space of the DA's wife, giving her even more reason to hate me.

"What's good about that?" I asked.

"Battaglia's text to Lily—your school friend—was there, like you thought."

"Any mention of me?" I asked, swallowing hard.

"Yes. Lily replied to Battaglia," Prescott said. "She told him that you advised her not to meet with him."

It was no wonder, then, that Battaglia's first two phone messages to me had an urgency to them. They were probably motivated by Lily's mention of me in her text. That urgency had turned to anger by the last call, when the news clip placed me at the Met— not only with Lily, but with George Kwan. The combination of players must have caused the DA to go ballistic.

"The more important thing is that we've found Diana," Prescott said. "The guys at TARU going over the phone records with Mrs. B's luds and muds identified Diana."

"That's amazing." I said, trying to shake off the effects of the sleeping pill. "Who is she?"

"Goddess of the hunt," he said.

"I guessed that much myself," I said, picking up the collar of my robe and holding it tightly against my chest. "I hope you can do better."

"That's the 'who' part of it," Prescott said. "Diana's also the name of a private club—like Saint Hubertus. A billionaire boys' club for big-game hunters."

"Paul Battaglia?" I asked.

"Amy called him two weekends ago, while he was holed up with his buddies at a game preserve. The number of the place shows up on her outgoing calls four times in three days. All she knows about it is that he went out there to meet with someone about a case."

James Prescott had my complete attention.

"Battaglia and four others, as well as their host, were on the ranch together," Prescott said. "It didn't make the national news because the dead man wasn't a Supreme Court justice, so the local paper just notes that one of them perished in a hunting accident."

"Six people on a weekend trip, and one died?" I said.

"Yes, he was shot in the chest—friendly fire—by one of his companions," Prescott said.

"The local sheriff must have deemed it an accident," I said, noting the irony of that fact, like the Scalia death. "Private preserve of the rich and famous, right? Kind of a Dick Cheney moment, planting birdshot in the aorta of a crony."

"No autopsy. No official inquiry," Prescott said. "You're right. Only this time it was an arrow straight to the heart, and not birdshot."

"That takes real skill," I said, shaking my head. "Shooting someone with a bow and arrow, I mean. Texas again?"

"No. This time, Montana."

"So of those six worshippers of the goddess Diana who started the weekend together, one didn't even make it off the preserve, and Paul Battaglia raises the death toll to two. Slim odds—two bull's-eyes out of six," I said. "I hope the other four have invested in bullet-proof vests."

# THIRTY-FOUR

"Put some clothes on, Alexandra," Prescott said. "I'd like you to come with us."

"Let me call Mike," I said, standing my ground.

"There'll be time for that later. Just get dressed."

"Where are we going? It's the middle of the night."

"It's okay, Alex," Jimmy North said. "I'll come with you."

"Where?"

I had done a complete three-sixty in my bare feet, trying to figure out who knew what, and why I was the last to be told.

"Livingston, Montana," Prescott said.

"When do the covered wagons pull out?" I said. "You must be kidding me."

"That's where the game preserve is. Big Sky country."

"Take Jaxon Stern. He's got more wild cowboy in him than I do."

"I'm taking you, Alexandra. There's a Challenger waiting for us at Westchester County Airport. Wheels up as soon as we get there," he said. "We should be at Mission Field in Livingston in five hours. You're the one I need."

"A Challenger?" I said. "Really? You feds live the life. I have to go through hoops to get office permission to take Amtrak to DC."

"I'll explain, but you have to get a move on."

"And now you need me, James? That's rich," I said. "There's something about this that doesn't smell right."

I crossed my arms and waited for more of an explanation.

"The people we have to talk to are in Montana, Alexandra," Prescott said. "I can't cherry-pick among them from long distance. I can't try to figure out in the next hour who might have something to tell us and then realize I had the wrong witness. We have a unique opportunity to get to the site before anyone finds out what we're up to. By the beginning of the week, word will be on the street. Someone will leak it."

"You're right about that. You ought to go. Especially since Amy Battaglia told you the DA was out there working on a case."

"Hear me out," Prescott said. "TARU moved as fast as they could on Mrs. Battaglia's phone. The calls and texts on her device from the night of the murder were what made that assignment so urgent. Then they put her device aside until yesterday afternoon—which is when they went back to see what else was in her messages and hit this news."

"Run with it, James."

"We've got the member who brought Battaglia there as a guest," Prescott said, "willing to take us to Livingston on the private plane, get the hunting guide to talk to us, dig down and find names of all the members—as well as any connections to the Order of Saint Hubertus."

"No one will notice you touch down on the small-town tarmac in his jet?"

"They come and go all the time—hunters, fly-fishermen, movie star ranch owners. That's the preferred mode of transportation for this crowd."

"Who is he?" I asked. "Who's Battaglia's friend? Why didn't you tell me that first?"

"You come with me now and I'll introduce you."

"Do *not* play games with me, Skeeter," I said, wagging a finger at him. "I've known that side of you for a very long time, and I don't like it."

I turned my back on the US attorney.

"Just step out of my way, Detective Tinsley," I said, "so I can sleep off this intrusion."

"Twenty-four hours and we're back here, Alexandra," Prescott said.

I was eyeball to eyeball with Kate Tinsley, who didn't budge.

"What I'm about to tell you stays in this room," Prescott said, talking to Tinsley and North, as well as to me. "The name of Battaglia's host."

I gave Prescott the courtesy of facing him. I was pretty sure I knew everyone on the DA's Rolodex, so curiosity got the better of me.

"Chidra Persaud," he said.

"Chidra?" I said, repeating the first name. "That's a woman's name."

"Yes," Prescott said. "Do you know her?"

"I've never heard of her, never heard Battaglia mention her," I said. "What's she doing at a billionaire boys' club?"

"She seems to have been the only woman playing in the sandbox with the big boys."

"Who is she?" I asked.

"One of India's most successful young entrepreneurs," Prescott said. "Raised there and educated at Oxford. Eight years ago, she created a start-up that makes high-end clothing gear for sportswomen—safari to kitesurfing. Her company's called Tiger Tail."

"Very high-end indeed," I said. "I've seen her khakis at Bergdorf's and Barneys. Classy stuff, quite overpriced. How old is she?"

"Forty-one," he said. "Just a couple of years older than you are."

I hated to tip my hand, but now I was intrigued.

"What's her connection to Battaglia?"

"I don't have the entire picture yet," Prescott said. "I just learned about her at ten o'clock last evening, when TARU found cross-calls with her number on Amy Battaglia's phone."

"Where was she?" I asked.

"She's got a penthouse in Tribeca."

"So she lives here?"

I was untying the knot on my robe. I was going along for the ride, despite my desire not to give in to Prescott's tactics.

"Chidra Persaud, according to the team, has two homes in India, a flat in London, a house on Nantucket, and a ranch in Mc-Leod, Montana."

"Battaglia," I said. "She must have told you something about him."

"Persaud told me she was introduced to him just recently," Prescott said. "She wanted help with a business problem she was having."

"What kind of problem?"

"Ask her yourself, Alexandra. I haven't had time to download her information. Don't hold us up."

Kate Tinsley stepped aside. I went into the bathroom to brush my teeth. Things were moving too fast for me now. I looked through the bag Vickee had packed for me and put on a pair of jeans and a navy-blue turtleneck sweater.

I grabbed a handful of toiletries and my ID and reentered the living room.

"Who's coming with me?" I asked.

"Fisher and Frist," Prescott said. "You've met them."

"I want a cop. I want someone from the NYPD," I said, pointing at Jimmy North.

"City cops don't have any jurisdiction there, Alexandra," he said, motioning me to follow him.

"Neither did Battaglia," I said, knowing that he must have been stepping on the toes of the feds when he made the trip to Montana. "Neither do I."

"But you're useful," he said, trying to be humorous. "You knew Battaglia so well, and you've got a jump on the conservation piece of this, on the exotic-animal angle."

"We fly out now," I said, "and come back when?"

"I expect we can get this all done today."

I picked up a couple of bottles of water from the coffee table. Prescott turned to one of the agents behind him, asking him to pull the car up in front of the cottage.

"Does Ms. Persaud hunt?" I asked, pulling on my jacket.

"It's in the blood, I think. Her grandfather was a guide for tiger hunts in India," Prescott said. "Led Queen Elizabeth and Prince Philip on one during their visit in the sixties, when they were the guests of the maharaja of Jaipur. Persaud's father was also in that business, so she grew up with a rifle in her hands, my short Google search suggests."

I saw headlights go on at the bottom of the driveway.

"I guess with tigers facing extinction at home, Ms. Persaud had nowhere to go but out west," I said. "After all, our bison are bouncing back, I hear. And they're bigger than tigers, so harder for her to miss."

"Keep your temper under wraps for twenty-four hours, if you can. Your tongue, too," Prescott said. "Let's see where she leads us."

"Am I warm, James? Were they shooting buffalo? Maybe Wyoming kangaroos crossed over the state line?"

"Not even close, Alexandra."

"Clue me in," I said, as the car pulled up to the door.

"They were hunting for sheep—"

"Sheep? For Christ's sakes," I said, interrupting Prescott. "Cats and dogs will be next."

"Not domestic animals. Not that kind of sheep."

"Like that makes it better?" I asked.

"Rocky Mountain bighorns," Prescott said. "Chidra Persaud calls it the ultimate pursuit."

# THIRTY-FIVE

"Good morning. I'm Chidra Persaud."

The brown-skinned woman with luminous dark eyes and long straight hair got up from the leather seat—one of a dozen on the plane—to greet me when I boarded. She was dressed in a blazer and tan pants—from her own fashion line, I assumed. Her foundation and blush had been applied flawlessly.

It was four A.M. when we boarded the sleek jet. I looked like I was a runaway from a psych facility—no makeup, snarled hair, sloppy clothes—stopped in my tracks by a cover girl from the latest issue of *Town & Country*.

"Alex Cooper."

"Why don't you sit across from me?" she said. "May I call you Alex?"

"Sure."

"And call me Chidra," she said. "Do you mind riding backwards?"

The ivory leather cushions were so plush I didn't think I'd notice which direction we were headed. "It's business, Chidra. I'll be wherever you want me to be."

"Thank you," she said. "James, why don't you sit there?"

Persaud pointed at the other backward-facing seat across the way. It was such a narrow space that one could hardly call it an aisle.

"Is it all right if the agents ride behind us, with my assistant?"

"That's fine," Prescott said.

We were three in the four front seats, and Persaud's assistant—a young man—was in the grouping behind her back, with Fisher and Frist.

The copilot stepped in from the cockpit to give the instructions to belt up and tell us the travel time. There was an attendant—a young Indian woman in traditional dress—who asked if we wanted coffee before takeoff. I wasn't ready for my three cups of black joe quite yet.

I had called Mike from the car, using James Prescott's phone. He was as startled by the situation as I was, and didn't like being excluded from the field trip.

The copilot pulled up the steps and secured the cabin door. As soon as he did, the pilot steered the plane onto the short runway.

"How long had you known Paul Battaglia?" I asked.

Chidra put her finger to her lips, as though to shush me. "Let's wait till we're airborne. I can't hear you over the sound of the engines."

She exuded confidence. Charm, too, but mostly she had a presence that suggested a woman who was supremely sure of herself.

The plane lifted off—seemingly without effort. A few lights dotted the suburbs of northern Westchester and Connecticut as we banked and turned left over Long Island Sound, on our way across the middle of the country. But mostly, it was dark below and above us, whatever stars there were occluded by a gray haze.

"You asked me something?" Persaud said, when we leveled off at altitude.

"I'm interested in how long you knew Paul Battaglia, and how you met him."

"I've been aware of him for a very long time," she said. "Through his work. Of course I'd shaken his hand at benefits and fund-raisers and the like, but he wouldn't have remembered that."

It was a stock answer people gave all the time. I had expected better from her.

"He actually had an eye for beautiful women, Chidra. I'm sure you would have caught his attention."

Now I was wondering about the fact that Battaglia hadn't been wearing a wedding ring the night he was killed. Chidra Persaud was practically half the DA's age—but she was entirely his type. She didn't wear a wedding ring either.

She readily accepted the compliment. "I didn't meet him for-mally until six months ago, in the early spring," she said. "Through my lawyer, actually. I believe he's a former colleague of yours."

"Who would that be?"

"Charles. Charles Swenson," she said.

"Good man," Prescott said, accepting a glass of orange juice from the attendant.

I didn't know Swenson well. He'd been an early disciple of Paul Battaglia but left the office long before I'd joined the staff. He was a well-respected member of the white-collar-crime defense bar, who did most of his work in federal court.

"Swenson helps you with your business dealings?" I asked.

"My company has lawyers in-house, Alex. Charles helps me when problems bubble up from time to time."

I didn't like weasel words. I preferred straightforward responses.

"Were there bubbles lately, or something more tangible than that?" I asked. "Did the matter involve my office?"

"Yes, it was the reason Charles introduced me to Paul Battaglia."

"Legal problems, is that what you mean?"

"Yes."

"Of what nature?" I asked.

"As you would imagine, it's quite difficult to manage all the aspects of an international business," Persaud said. "Most of our clothing is made in India, where I own several factories."

"Based there because of the cheap labor?" I asked, taking a stab at her—which I knew was unnecessary the moment the words came out of my mouth. I'd had a short, intense lesson in the global fashion world working on Wolf Savage's death. It might prove useful today, but I didn't need to step on her already.

"No, Alex," Persaud said. "Because India is my home, where I started the company. Because I wanted to employ people in areas of my country where industry is scarce."

"It must be very hard to oversee things with all the travel you do," Prescott said, unlatching the lock that held his seat in takeoff and landing position, swiveling it to face us.

"That's necessary, of course," she said. "I'm the face of the company, which is—as you certainly know, Alex—rare for a woman at this level of enterprise."

"Very impressive," I said. "And then, you take time off for pleasure, like these hunting trips."

"They relax me. I need some release from the intensity of my work, just as I assume you do," Persaud said. "I grew up with a Holland & Holland as my closest friend."

She must have noticed my puzzlement. I didn't know what Holland & Holland was.

"The world's best gunmaker," she said. "By appointment to Her Majesty, the Queen, and many royals before her. The first accessory I remember owning—long before jewelry and fancy shoes—is a .375 H & H Magnum, but I'll get to that."

"Go on," I said.

"We're growing so fast—in Asia, on the Arabian Peninsula, in Europe, and here in America—that I've tried to staff up my executive wing so I can have men and women all over the world who are capable of covering my back, capable of thinking for me, capable of earning my trust."

I had forty lawyers in my unit, who stood to profit only by

doing justice. I understood the qualities Chidra Persaud was seeking in professional colleagues.

"What legal problems have you encountered?"

She waited for the attendant to lift our trays and set our places with china and silverware, in anticipation of the breakfast service, before she spoke.

"The British have a very complicated tax structure," Persaud said, "especially for a foreigner doing business there. Charles Swenson says we'll come out of this fine, but it's important you know that my company is being investigated there, in the UK."

"On tax issues?"

"There's an allegation of fraud, actually," she said, adding two sugars to the coffee that had been placed in front of her. "Corporate tax fraud."

"Here, also?" I asked, glancing at James before speaking again to her. "I'm surprised you two haven't met before."

"Charles Swenson has guided my hand for years, in all sorts of legal matters," Persaud said, managing a smile at each of us. "None of them setting us on the wrong side of the law."

I started sipping my first cup of coffee as soon as it was set down on my tray.

"I met with him seven or eight months ago, in New York, at the suggestion of my legal team in London, to make sure he knew what was going on."

"Tax matters," I said, "would be something for James's office to deal with."

"Oh, no," Persaud said. "I'm not facing any charges, any investigations in this country. In fact, I wanted Charles to know that I thought Tiger Tail had been targeted by thieves—that we were losing vast amounts of product between our factories and the shipments that arrived in our foreign markets. That's far more important to me than bogus tax issues."

"Ah, so you think you've been the *victim* of a crime," I said, hoping my facetious tone wasn't clear to her.

"Precisely that, on a very large scale. The shippers we've been dealing with or some mob operation unloading our product at the docks, from container ships," she said. "I can't put my finger on where the problem is yet, but I'm sure trained investigators can help."

Our breakfast plates were served. Smoked salmon with capers, fresh cream, and toast points. It was better than starting my day at Three Sisters.

"I guess what surprises me," I said, trying to infuse my voice with some sincerity, "is that on both ends of your issues—taxes and possible theft by your cohorts—well, they seem to fall exactly into the purview of the United States attorney. Don't you think these were matters for your office, James? Not for ours?"

He was chewing on a large chunk of salmon when I turned to him. I appreciated how difficult it was to criticize one's hostess while cruising in her jet at thirty-six thousand feet and nibbling on her well-catered snacks.

"But Swenson said you had no comparable tax problems here?" Prescott asked her.

"So far as he could tell," Persaud said. "That's correct."

"How about Chidra's victimization, too?" I said to Prescott. "Not my bailiwick, of course, but the long arm of the law reaches so much further with federal powers than what we've got. Wouldn't you think?"

James was washing down his meal with some freshly squeezed orange juice. "It depends on so many factors, and Battaglia was very creative that way, as you know."

I was sure James Prescott could read this situation exactly as I did. It was as blatantly transparent as a pane of glass. Charles Swenson, sensing some tax liability in his client's case, had gone for the preemptive strike. Make Chidra Persaud a victim of a crime before she's outed in England—and perhaps in the United States—as a perp. Wrap her in the respectable embrace of Paul Battaglia, who was Swenson's longtime friend, in the office where Swenson could help control the narrative.

"I hate to suggest this in front of Chidra," I said to Prescott, "but since all cards need to be on the table at this point, I guess it also makes sense for Swenson to walk it into our office, knowing how Battaglia would enjoy sticking a shiv in your back, too, if he could make a case for her."

Prescott blushed and looked at Chidra to see if she seemed to get what I was saying. But she was stone-faced, checking her iPad for mail as we bickered.

"Don't speak ill of the dead," Prescott said to me.

"That's not speaking ill at all. Battaglia prided himself on being able to do that to you," I said. "He'd rather like knowing I could say it to your face."

A second round of coffee was offered.

"What trading company do you use for getting your company's goods to market?" I asked Persaud.

"Different ones in different parts of the world."

"Did Battaglia assign someone—a lawyer from our Frauds Bureau—to work on your case? Were you interviewed by one of my colleagues?"

"I'm scheduled for an interview in December," Persaud said.

"He let it go until then?"

"My fault entirely," she said, making eye contact again. "He tried to have me sit down with someone, but I was abroad through most of the last few months. I spent a lot of time at home in India, and some in London. I didn't get the meeting done."

I guessed there was no urgency to Chidra's claims of foul play. Swenson had set her up for exactly the reasons I suspected.

"Charles will know the name of the young prosecutor I'm supposed to meet with," she added. "I neglected to add him to my contacts."

"Thanks," I said. "I can call Charles tomorrow."

"I have some questions, too," Prescott said.

"If I may finish with a few," I continued, leaning in toward Persaud. "Do you know a man named George Kwan?"

Chidra Persaud's brow furrowed. "I know his name. I'm aware of his business holdings," she said. "Kwan Enterprises, isn't it? But I've never met the man."

"Do you use his company—his trading company—for any of your shipping or marketing needs?"

"No. No, I've never had dealings with him," she said. "I know at one time his associates in the London office were pressuring me to use their services, to hire them to ship our products, but we never did."

"Did Kwan's people—his associates—ever tell you about his interest in wildlife conservation?"

"Maybe so," Persaud said. "But so do lots of people I meet."

"Did you and Paul Battaglia ever discuss Mr. Kwan?" I asked.

The furrow deepened. "No. Not that I remember."

"Think hard," I said. "That sounds like exactly the kind of connection the DA would like to know about."

"For any particular reason?" she asked.

"My boss is dead, Chidra," I said. "Murdered. And no one—so far as James and I can tell—no one in Paul's professional world knew anything about this piece of his life. This interest in hunting wild animals."

"But you knew he was interested in wildlife conservation too, didn't you?" she asked. "You knew he'd won a major award for a case he handled. Operation Crash, I think it was named."

"Conserving the endangered species and killing them as well,"

I said. "Seems pretty oxymoronic to me. I can't manage to reconcile the two."

"I'll help you with that," she said. "You'll see."

"Didn't you meet George Kwan at the Metropolitan Museum on Monday night?" I asked. "Weren't you at the gala that honored Wolf Savage?"

"Don't mistake me for stupid, Alex."

"That's the last thing I would do."

"You planted the fact of my presence in your question," she said. "Did you think I'd walk into that trap?"

I sat back. "I apologize to you. I thought there was a good chance you would have attended, owning an international sportswear company of your own."

"Tiger Tail has a royal warrant in the UK, Alex," she said. "Do you know what that means?"

"I don't."

"It's granted to tradespeople by the queen, allowing us to advertise that we supply our goods to the royal family," Persaud said. "Wolf Savage created a fine business thirty years ago, but it's a bit dated—and very much in trouble, in terms of financial stability. I didn't want to be seen at his show, to be mixed up in his branding."

"George Kwan was there Monday night. He was trying to buy a piece of the Savage business," I said. "I was thinking, if you'd been at the Met, you might have met him."

"Apology accepted," she said with a nod and a smile.

"Of course, that's where Paul went when he left his home so abruptly," I said, ready to take my chance with Chidra. "I understand now that you didn't attend, but it had crossed my mind for a minute that maybe it was *you* Paul saw on the late news—that maybe he rushed out to meet you to discuss something of importance to you both, or just to rendezvous."

Chidra Persaud was not amused. "I Googled you on my way to

the airport, Alex. One might say the same of you, isn't that true? That Paul Battaglia had some professional matter of great urgency to discuss at that late hour on Monday—or could it have been personal?"

There was daylight outside the window now. We were somewhere over one of the Great Lakes, with hours of flying still to go.

"It must have been about a case," I said, "about a crime or an investigation I knew nothing of. But no, we didn't have that kind of personal relationship."

"Don't be afraid to ask the direct question, Alex."

"What would that be?" I said.

"Paul Battaglia and I didn't have 'that kind of personal relationship' either. I think those were your words."

"It wouldn't have been out of the question," I said. I hadn't meant the idea as an insult. "I know his taste."

"You certainly don't know mine."

"That's true, Chidra," I said, aware that I had crossed another line. "I'd never heard of you until James showed up at three this morning."

"I'm in a long-term relationship, and I'm monogamous, if that's where you were going."

"I didn't mean to pry," I said. "It might well have been relevant if things were otherwise."

Chidra Persaud summoned the attendant to clear our tables.

"I'm gay, Alex. Paul Battaglia didn't get it at first," she said. "But I made it clear to him. My partner lives in London, if that's of any concern."

"Thanks for your candor," I said.

I felt like I'd been beating into the wind. I knew it was time to change course, to turn my sails in another direction.

"I'm sure James told you that I know nothing about hunting," I said.

"Apparently you managed to put Battaglia together with the Order of Saint Hubertus, didn't you?" Persaud said.

"I had some help. But that's an all-male society, isn't it?"

"For centuries. Yes, it is."

"I'm told you were the only woman on the hunt out here two weeks ago, when Battaglia was present," I said.

"I was."

"So this club—is it called Diana?" I asked. "This club obviously admits women."

"It does," she said. "Someday you'll have to tell me how you came to know about us. Or maybe it was James who made the discovery?"

"Will James and I be able to get a list of members?"

Chidra Persaud shrugged. "I suppose we can ask Charles Swenson. There are rules, you know, and one mustn't violate them."

"Was Battaglia a member?" I asked.

"He'd been accepted," she said. "He would have been inducted at our next meeting, early next year. I guess there's no need for secrecy now that he's dead."

"Accepted by whom?"

"That's part of the point, Alex," Persaud said. "The rest of the committee—the other members—need to be consulted before I give you their names."

I turned to James Prescott. "Have you explained to Chidra that you're able to subpoena whatever information you need? That you've opened this matter before a grand jury?"

"Before I got on this plane, Alex," Persaud said, flipping her tray closed, "Charles Swenson assured me he'd be talking to James, laying out the ground rules for my cooperation. The club is headquartered in the UK. I'm not sure an American subpoena will stretch that far."

What the hell good was it to take this trip with Chidra

Persaud? Ground rules—for what? James Prescott knew something he hadn't yet confided to me. Amy Battaglia had told him that the reason for her husband's trip involved a case he was working on. James must now have an idea what that case was. I was right not to trust him entirely.

"Tell me, James," I said, "is this a wild-goose chase of some sort?"

"Keep your cool, Alex," he said.

"What the hell is this about? What does all of this have to do with Battaglia's murder?" I asked. "What did the DA think I possibly knew about Diana, and more to the point—what did *he* know?"

"For one thing, Alex, Paul Battaglia knew that Diana is *me*," Chidra Persaud said. "That I am Diana. What I'm not sure about is whether he was ready for anyone else to know that, too."

# THIRTY-SIX

I reset my watch when we landed on Mission Field in Livingston, Montana. It was still only 6:37 A.M. local time.

A silver GMC Sierra was waiting at the end of the airstrip, and a black government car had been rustled up from some local agency. The pickup was driven by Chidra Persaud's caretaker. She got in the front seat and left the rear for Prescott and me. Her assistant rode with the two agents in the other car.

James had asked more questions throughout the flight than I did. On the personal side, we learned that Diana's ties to the British royals had started in early childhood, connected to their seasonal visits because of her grandfather's legendary prowess as a hunting guide for the rich.

A lesser royal—an earl from Devonshire—had nicknamed the young Chidra "Diana" when he saw her kill a tiger that was mauling a villager with a single shot. She was thereafter invited to accompany the earl's hunting party, which previously had been all adults, year after year. It was eventually that Englishman who sponsored the young woman for her education in London and at Oxford, and who gave her the seed money to start her company.

"Where are we going?" I asked. "To your ranch?"

"No," Persaud said. "I thought you wanted to see the preserve the club uses, the one where Battaglia stayed two weeks ago."

"We do," James said. "Also the site where one of your hunters was killed. You said a couple of the men would talk to us but wouldn't leave Montana to do it."

"We're going to the mountain," she said. "Literally, I guess I'm bringing Muhammad to the mountain, since they wouldn't go to you. Bowing to the inevitable, as I was taught that expression to mean."

The landscape in the valley was spectacular. I had never seen such vast wide-open spaces, with a richness and variance of topography. There were acres of land, green with grasses or alfalfa—kept colorful by irrigation—and there were huge patches of brown earth. All around were mountains, the northern end of the Absaroka Range, which were capped in snow and made a dazzling backdrop for our vista.

Along the way we saw herds of pronghorn antelope grazing by the side of the road, and every now and then a couple of deer would dart across the highway.

The driver went off-road at one point and began to wind around a hill on a dirt path that didn't look as though it could handle traffic coming from the opposite direction.

"The location isn't marked?" I asked.

"That's the way we like it around here," Persaud said.

"Do you own the land?"

"I do. It's about seven hundred acres, some of it on the Yellowstone River. It backs onto a national forest, so there can't be any development in the future," she said. "Hunters like remote. And we like privacy."

"This isn't your home?" I asked.

"No, no. McLeod's about ninety minutes away. My partner doesn't like to hunt, nor does she enjoy the company of strangers."

When the pickup finally came to a stop, near the top of the mountain, James and I stepped out to stretch.

"That's the main lodge," Persaud said.

Straight ahead of us was a modern-day log cabin. It was enormous—probably eight thousand square feet—built on prime hilltop.

She walked toward it, looking back, expecting us to follow.

"You're welcome to freshen up," she said. "There are four bedrooms down that hallway, all for guests. Mine is to the left. I'll be right back and then we can get started."

The front of the lodge—a long wall of timber interrupted by a front door and several small windows—had been deceptive. The living areas, I saw once we were inside, faced out over the valley and nearby mountains through a wall of glass. There was nothing to disturb the view out over the river and for as far as one could see.

The interior looked as though Ralph Lauren had curated the space himself. There were stone fireplaces at each end of the room, and sofas covered in subtle plaids placed at regular intervals. The sconces on the wall were gaslights, and the folk-art antiques that sat on tables or stood against the wainscoting were perfect accents.

There were no stuffed heads and horns—to my delight—although there was an array of vintage hunting rifles hung on the walls that might have chilled even Boone and Crockett.

I went to one of the guest rooms to freshen up. There was nothing personal in any of them, but enough decorative art to keep a warm feeling in the house—collections of old game boards, vintage bottles from local dairy farms, egg crates and cartons that added a cozy, local touch to the tastefully done lodge.

There was a telephone on the night table. I picked it up and waited for a dial tone. When I heard it, I dialed Catherine Dashfer's cell.

"Alex? Are you okay?" she said. "Dead or alive? I hope you're not calling me from the other side."

"Think Mark Twain," I said. "Rumors of my death were greatly exaggerated. Please tell me there wasn't an obit."

"Nope. Just that people who know you might have leaped to the wrong conclusion," Catherine said. "I was hoping you'd left me those sapphire earrings. Otherwise, I'm glad you're not blown to bits."

"They're yours. Any time you want them," I said.

"I was told not to try to reach you," she said. "We all were."

"You couldn't, and you shouldn't. Who's your best buddy in the Frauds Bureau?" I asked.

"Mimi Hershenson."

"Do you trust her?"

"She's solid. We went to law school together."

"Call her. Try the computer case file system first, but I doubt it's in there. Make a call and see who was assigned to work with Battaglia on an investigation involving a company called Tiger Tail, owned by Chidra Persaud, that came in sometime earlier this year," I said. "When you get the name, call and give it to Mike."

"When am I going to see you?" she asked.

"Next week. They can't keep me cooped up much longer," I said. "Gotta go. Thanks for this."

I pressed the buttons down and waited for a dial tone again. I called Mike but was sent right to voice mail.

"Miss you. Flight was fine. Weird dynamic among the people— look up the name Chidra Persaud as soon as you can, and run a background check on her. She's Diana—I'm not kidding. Goddess of the hunt—just ask her, especially about the goddess part," I said. "Her club is based—I guess incorporated—in the UK, so dig for that, too, if you can. Nothing else of value so far."

I paused. "Check in with Catherine about an investigation Battaglia was doing with this Persaud woman. I just called and asked her to snoop around the DANY white-collar crew," I said. "See if you come up with anything that corresponds on the NYPD side. And spring me from the nunnery as soon as you can. I want you, and I want to be home."

By the time I returned to the living room, Chidra Persaud had seated herself in a ladder-back chair, next to an older man who was standing sideways to her, staring out the window. He was dressed for an outdoor trek—weathered jeans, hiking boots, a flannel shirt, a beat-up jacket, and a three-day growth of beard. He had a rifle tucked comfortably under his arm, resting on his right hip.

"Alex, that was quick," Persaud said, getting to her feet. "Did you have trouble with the phone? We sometimes have issues out here in the wild."

"Phone?" I knew my voice hadn't been loud enough to carry back to this room.

She pointed to the large telephone on a desk at the end of the room, with a dozen plastic buttons on a panel. "It lights up when in use. I was afraid you needed something."

"Oh," I said, trying to act less surprised than I was. "Just checking in with my boyfriend."

My paranoia was on high alert. I didn't trust anyone.

"I'd like you to meet Karl—Karl Jansen. Karl runs the preserve for me."

We shook hands as Prescott entered the room right behind me, and Jansen offered each of us a cool "howdy."

"Before we go out and look around, I assume you want Karl to talk about what happened the weekend Paul Battaglia was here," she said.

"We do," Prescott answered. "Have a seat, Karl."

"Rather not. I'm fine standing."

So we all stood.

"How long have you known Mr. Battaglia?" I asked.

"Met him for the first time on a Saturday morning, two weeks ago, ma'am. He left on Sunday evening and I never saw him again."

"Did he stay here, at the lodge?"

"Nope. There are eight cottages on the property," Jansen said. "He had one of them, the way I understand it."

"Did you organize the hunting party?" I asked.

"No, ma'am. That would be my nephew, Frank."

"I see. Were you along for the hunt?"

"Yeah," he answered. "I was there."

"So it was you and Frank, the district attorney and Chidra," I said, "and two others."

"Excuse me," Persaud said. "Paul was my guest for the weekend, as were the other pair of hunters, whom I'd never met before."

"Never met?" I asked. "But they were your guests?"

"Yes, people pay dearly for the right to shoot here, as Karl will explain," Persaud said. "But I was not along for the hunt that day. Saturday."

"I don't understand. Then why did you arrange it for Paul?"

"I had planned to shoot with him, of course," she said. "He had a very competitive streak, as you both probably know."

Prescott smiled. "That's an understatement."

"It turns out the club member who was present, Anderson Groves—do you know him?"

"I don't," I said, as Prescott shook his head.

"It probably doesn't matter," Persaud said. "Anderson owns oil wells in Texas. He was a founding member of the Diana Hunt Club."

"Not enough endangered species for him to shoot down there?" I asked.

"They certainly don't have Rocky Mountain bighorn in south Texas. That's one of our major attractions," she said, unfazed by my snarky remarks. "Anyway, Anderson's been doing business in Dubai, and he happened to invite one of the oil royals for the weekend. I'll have the man's name for you shortly. I've just called the office out here to get all the names and dates, but they're not answering yet. Unfortunately, that gentleman—the prince from Dubai—refused to shoot with a woman—with me."

"Because his religion forbids it?" I asked.

"Perhaps that," she said. "Perhaps he just thought it was bad luck, as many people do."

"Even though you are 'the' Diana of this club?" Prescott said, sucking up in an entirely unctuous way.

Chidra Persaud waved off his concern with a good-natured laugh. "Not worth a flogging or a stoning to challenge his beliefs. I busied myself with paperwork for the day."

"Who was the sixth man in the party?" I asked. "Did Paul have a partner to shoot with?"

"He did," she said. "Another club member staying in one of the cottages on the river. He actually enjoys fly-fishing more than shooting. My manager will have all the names and contacts for us in an hour or so, as I mentioned."

"Did Paul know him?"

"Not before that morning. He's a young West Coast guy. Runs a tech start-up," Persaud said. "Paul was happy to have him along, but he seemed far more interested in getting to know the prince from Dubai."

"Your office must also have a log with contact information for all the participants."

"Oh, yes," Persaud said.

The two agents were making notes of the conversation.

"You want to see the cottage where Paul stayed?" Persaud asked.

"I do," Prescott said.

"Good. And I thought it would be useful for Karl to tell you as many specifics about the day as he can."

"Yes," Prescott said.

"In order to hunt for certain species in Montana, one has to hire an outfitter," Persaud said. "The Jansens have made their living for quite a long time that way—as outfitters—before I set up the preserve. They know many more hunters—more visitors— than I do. Isn't that right?"

Karl Jansen gave her a nod.

"Wait a minute," I said. "Does that mean that there are

hunters who come here—who come on your land to shoot—but they don't stay with you?"

"That's right," Persaud said. "But they can't do that without paying Karl or Junior—or someone with their kind of credentials."

"Why don't you tell them the rest, Karl? We all had coffee together that morning, and then I stayed behind. I think it makes sense for you to tell them the reason for the hunt, and what you saw and heard on the way."

Karl Jansen shuffled the rifle to his left side. "Hard for me to talk about, ma'am, but I'll try."

"Do your best," she said.

Someone had died that day. We might as well start with that fact.

"Six of you went out," I said. "Was it that day—or Sunday—when one of the men was killed?"

"Sunday morning," he said. "Saturday we were all just fine."

It wasn't Paul Battaglia, nor was it Karl Jansen, who was on the short end of the arrow.

"Who was the victim of the murder?" I asked.

"It wasn't no murder, lady," Jansen said, his steel-gray eyes meeting mine. "It was Frank who took the arrow. My nephew. My sister's boy."

"I'm so sorry," I said. "I had no idea."

Frank was in the family business too. An outfitter. A hunting guide. And if he had any secrets, they'd died with him two weeks ago.

"I'm sorry," Persaud said. "I should have told you that."

I thought it was bitchy of Chidra Persaud not to have given us the heads-up that it was Jansen's nephew who'd been killed, before introducing us to him.

"Who had the weapon?" I asked. I didn't know what else to call it. "Who fired?"

"The Arab. The guy they told me was a prince," Jansen said. "Never held a bow in his hand before."

"Had they fought about anything?" Prescott asked. "Had there been any disagreements the day before? Or during the evening?"

"Nothing I heard. Frank wasn't the sort of man who disagreed with anyone. He just liked to be off by himself in the woods."

"You didn't see it happen, then, did you?" I asked.

"No, ma'am. I was a ways away."

"Then how do you know it wasn't inten—?"

"Accidents happen, Ms. Cooper," Jansen said, stepping away from us, moving toward the door. "Sooner or later, everybody dies."

# THIRTY-SEVEN

"Are you warm enough, Alex?" Persaud asked.

She and Jansen were ahead of us, walking down a trail toward a row of cottages that looked like miniature versions of the main house. I was ten feet behind, with James Prescott.

"Plenty warm. Thanks for the gloves."

She turned her head and kept to the trail.

"What's our timetable here?" I asked Prescott. "There's something you haven't told me."

"I didn't have time to think about much from the moment I got the call last night about the phone records," he said. "Chidra offered to make the trip. The old guy—Jansen—has never left this corner of Montana. Refused to get on a plane and come to us. I thought he might know something."

"Is your office backing us up?"

"Background going full speed ahead on everyone," Prescott said. "Looking for links wherever we can, and we'll have the guest names in an hour or so. You heard that."

"Do you know what kind of case Battaglia thought he was building by coming out here?" I asked.

"If I did, I might not have dragged you out of bed. Let today play out and maybe we can figure what he walked into."

If Prescott knew more than he was telling me, he had buttoned it down pretty tight.

"Tell them to run Persaud's phone system from this end, too," I said. "I just made a call to Catherine—"

"Without asking me?"

"Correct," I said. "There's a master phone pad in the living room, and undoubtedly one in Chidra's bedroom or office, too. She knew I'd been on the phone in the guest room when I went in to use the bathroom. Your tech guys need to check the last few months of her records—these phones, New York, whatever else you can get."

He didn't like taking direction from me, but he had no choice. "Next time you can divert her, I'll call."

"You'll be lucky if you have any cell service out here," I said. "You might send Frist or Fisher into town."

"They're going to go over the cottage more thoroughly after she shows it to us," he said.

"That's fine."

Persaud was already in Cottage 3—there was a large black number painted on the door panel—when Prescott and I caught up to her.

"This is where Paul stayed," she said. "Quite by himself, I can assure you."

"Why can you assure us?" I said, scanning the ceiling for signs of a minicamera and ending up with eyes on the kitchen counter. "Is it because you have video surveillance mounted in each cabin? Or maybe cameras in the microwave?"

"How funny you think you can be, Alex," she said. "Look around. No one has stayed here since Paul left."

The cottage had obviously been cleaned up and turned over. Sanitized. I left it to the two agents to snoop more thoroughly than I could.

"What next?" Prescott asked.

I followed Chidra Persaud outside, where Karl Jansen had waited for us.

"We'll go on ATVs from here," she said. "So you can see what Paul was after. Maybe get a sense of what he was doing."

A pair of ATVs—two-seaters—were waiting in a garage between the fourth and fifth cottages. I climbed on to ride behind Persaud, while Prescott doubled up with Jansen.

It was a long, steep climb back past the main lodge and across the road, around and around the mountaintop till the path became so narrow that we had to get off the ATVs.

The land was barren, except for small bushes of sage and large craggy rocks, which formed the top of the peak.

Karl went off on his own, climbing higher and disappearing behind an enormous boulder, returning moments later with a younger man—about forty—who was his body double. It must have been his son.

The young one smiled more easily than his father and reached out to shake hands. "Good morning, Ms. Chidra. Welcome home."

She thanked him and introduced us to Junior, as Jansen's son was known. We expressed our condolences about his cousin, and he seemed grateful for the comments.

"Is it okay to talk here?" she whispered.

"Sure can," Junior said. "The animals are pretty far off."

Junior was holding a pair of binoculars in his hands. He raised them to his eyes and looked down and away—miles away, it seemed to me.

"Why don't you tell Alex and James what you've been up to this last month?" Persaud said. "They want to know about hunting the bighorn."

"Right, then," Junior said. "From scratch?"

I smiled at him. "From scratch."

"So, there are four primary kinds of wild sheep in North America. Here in Montana we've got the Rocky Mountain bighorn, which is where you might guess they'd be," he said. "There used to be millions of these fellows just over a century ago. Millions of them. Lewis and Clark probably saw bighorn every day of their travels through here."

"Hunted to near extinction now," I said. "And pushed out by a growing human population."

"Yes, ma'am," he said. "But then, people like Ms. Persaud, she's helping bring 'em back. They're coming back again."

"But you're hunting them," I said. "You and your father are guiding people out here for the specific purpose of putting a bullet— or an arrow—into one of these sheep to kill it."

Chidra Persaud took the binoculars from Junior's hands and put them to her eyes. She looked over the landscape below, moving the set back and forth, until she came to a stop. She passed the glasses to me.

"There," she said. "Can you see them?"

I looked through the lenses but saw nothing. I opened my eyes and looked again. "Dots in that field," I said. "All I see are shiny dots, like they're on a curved surface of some sort."

"That's it, Miss Alex," Junior said. "When you see that glow against the browned-out field, that's a bighorn. The curve is the horn itself, and for some reason, it shows up all shiny-like—the only animal I know to do that. There's a pack of them down there in the valley."

"They could be almost anything," I said, passing the glasses to Prescott.

"Not when they're curved," he said. "Not many circular-shaped horns on wild animals."

"Just how do you help save these creatures, when what you're doing is bringing people here to kill them?" I said to Persaud, looking at the rifle she was holding, which seemed to me to be a newer model than Karl Jansen had.

"By transplanting scores of them, Alex," she said.

"What do you mean by transplanting?"

"We capture them alive—tranquilize them and airlift them out in large canvas slings—and send them off to live on reservations all over Montana and the Dakotas."

"Native American reservations?" I asked.

"Yes, there are seven of them in Montana. I send forty or fifty bighorn to Rocky Boy's, up north, every year. It's the reservation of the Chippewa Cree, on the Canadian border. They're quite happy to have them."

"Why would you possibly need a high-powered rifle to take sheep alive?" I asked. "And if that's what you think hunters are doing to preserve a species—transplanting a few dozen a year—I'd be the first to say it isn't quite enough, in my humble opinion."

Junior walked away from us, back toward his perch behind the large boulders. Chidra Persaud followed, returning the binoculars to him, and we went behind her.

"Looking for others?" she asked.

"There was a group of about twenty on that ridge across the river, but I must have run them off a while ago," he said. "Sheep have really sharp senses. They spook easy."

Some days I felt like that myself.

"Are you looking for Horace?" Persaud said to him.

"Yes, ma'am," Junior said. "Saw six rams in that herd this morning. Horace—well, he just jumps out at you."

Persaud turned around to face us. "Let me tell you about Horace," she said. "Let me answer you by explaining what we're doing out here."

"All ears," Prescott said.

"Most people like you think that the great white whale of North American land mammals is whatever scares you the most—a giant black bear or a mountain lion, maybe a moose that charges when you get too close to its calves. You think those are the game that hunters want most to chase."

"But you're going to insist it's these bighorns," Prescott said. "And we want to know why."

"It's a rich man's sport, hunting bighorn. It's more expensive than you might imagine, for starters." Chidra Persaud rested her rifle against a rock formation twice her height. "Secondly, the opportunities to participate are limited, because of where the animals live. The third thing is that the hunts are extremely difficult, in such remote areas in the West that they can last as long as three weeks without snagging a trophy."

"How much does it cost for a chance to kill a Rocky Mountain bighorn?" I asked.

"We don't use the word 'kill,'" she said. "We call it harvesting."

"Nothing like a quaint euphemism," I said, "to make something sound more appealing."

Persaud powered on. "There are two ways to hunt wild sheep."

"Legally?" Prescott asked.

"Yes, of course legally," she said. "There's a lottery of sorts in Montana. I think it only costs about twenty dollars to enter, and the state raffles off a limited number of licenses—each restricted to a particular geographic area—to hunters."

"What are the odds of winning?" Prescott asked.

Persaud smiled. "Not very good, I'm afraid. Thousands and thousands of applications come in every year just for residents of the state. Not very many winners. Am I right, Karl?"

The senior Jansen confirmed her story. "I'm seventy-six years old. I've been tossing my hat in for a sheep tag since I was fourteen, and I've never gotten one."

"What's the other way to hunt—or, shall I say, harvest these creatures?" I asked.

"What do you think a big-game hunter would rather have,

Alex?" Persaud asked. "Season tickets to a box at Yankee Stadium, right over the dugout, or a chance to find a bighorn—a ram with some age on him?"

"I'd even take a box at Fenway, given that choice. But your folk think otherwise."

"Every January, in a ballroom at the Bellagio in Vegas, there's a dinner for a hundred or so people. Black tie," Persaud said, slipping her hands into her pants pockets. "It's an auction, actually, to sell four sheep tags—permits, if you will—to the highest bidders, to hunt for bighorn in Montana."

"So these beautiful creatures, with their enormous curly horns, are peacefully grazing out here on your land, while some high rollers are standing around at cocktail hour in Vegas, looking to spend money to take out the biggest and oldest in the pack," I said. "Am I close?"

"Close enough."

"And how much does a Montana ram go for?" Prescott asked.

"This year's top bidder paid over five hundred thousand dollars," Persaud said.

"Half a million dollars?" I said. "To shoot a sheep?"

"At least that. The number goes up every year," she said, "and it all goes to our conservation efforts, like I tried to explain earlier. We have teams of employees who collar every one of the animals so we can track them and check them for disease. We hire workers whose jobs are sheep-specific—care and control. We've really brought the number of bighorn sheep in this region back way up."

"So the hunter gets a tax write-off to a charitable wildlife foundation of some sort," Prescott said, "and a chance to bag the big kahuna."

"The Rocky Mountain Bighorn Foundation," she said. "That's what we fund."

"Collar or kill 'em. That's quite a contrast," I said. "Where's

Longmire when I need him? Aren't these the Absaroka Mountains?"

"Walt Longmire has Vic. He's got no use for you," Prescott said to me, before turning to Persaud. "Who won the auction this year?"

"I don't go, James. This is my backyard," she said. "I'm sure you can find the names of the top bidders online."

"What makes this kind of hunt so tough?" I said. "Those sheep in the valley look like sitting ducks down there."

The older Karl Jansen spoke up. "The big money don't buy much for an amateur hunter," he said. "Any fool can get himself a bear if he sits alongside a trout stream out here long enough. Could be half-blind and still get lucky hitting a big elk or a turkey. Hell, I could bag those from my easy chair."

"Comforting to know," I said.

"What you're looking down on is not where the bighorn spend their time," Jansen said. "Like Junior told you, that herd must have been spooked off a ridge. Maybe a helicopter or something came in real low."

"Why? Where do you usually have to go to find them?" I said.

"Follow my son," Jansen said, pointing off in the distance, to the northeast. "He'll show you why it's so difficult. Bighorn live in steep terrain, above the timberline. Places not many folks have been to or care to go. It's not like standing still behind a duck blind and shooting one out of the sky. You can stalk these sheep for weeks till you get them."

Good for the sheep, I thought.

Chidra Persaud and James Prescott disappeared out of sight, behind the tall rocks, following Junior. I didn't like that three of the people in our group of five had guns. I didn't like the idea of being one of the two who were unarmed.

Karl Jansen brought up the rear.

"Paul Battaglia made this climb?" I asked, trying to scramble over some brush that had blown onto the path.

"Slower than you," Jansen said. "With a tall walking stick. But he stayed on it most of the way."

"Pretty good for a man his age," I said. "I bet he talked a lot. I bet he asked a ton of questions."

I was interrogating a man who was parsimonious with his words.

"Did that," Jansen said.

"What kind of things?" I asked, looking over my shoulder at him.

"Keep your eyes forward, ma'am. Keep moving."

I pulled myself ahead by grabbing the bare branch of some sort of scraggly tree.

"What did Battaglia ask about?"

"Names, mostly. Wanted to know more about Miss Chidra, but that shouldn't have been any of his business."

"What other kind of names?" I said, cresting that slope, until I realized there was another crest—even higher—right around the bend.

"He asked fewer questions than you," Jansen said. "Move on. They'll be waiting for you."

We spiraled upward and onward. I finally caught up with the others, who were standing on a flat boulder, high enough over the valley to make me dizzy when I looked down.

Chidra Persaud put her fingers to her lips to signal me to be quiet, and passed me the binoculars, pointing to a craggy ledge across the river. We were on the back side of the hill that we been climbing, facing across to a low part of a mountain range instead of the valley.

I looked through the glasses but saw nothing. Rocks, dirt, cacti, and brush. Nothing moved.

I lowered them and held up my hands.

Karl Jansen came up from behind and raised the binoculars in front of me again, training them on a specific spot. The shiny objects like the ones I had seen below, earlier, came into sight. I adjusted the lenses. Now I could see a dozen or so sheep—some of which were rams, with long curly horns.

I nodded to Chidra and the others.

She walked back to me and whispered in my ear.

"Do you see the very large ram? Much bigger than the others?"

I squinted into the binoculars and fine-tuned my focus. "Yeah."

"That's Horace," Persaud said.

"What does that mean?" I asked. "Is it like you thinking you're Diana?"

Chidra Persaud bit her lip. She had obviously been brought up to be more polite than I had.

"Junior Jansen has been following Horace for five years now, all up and down these mountaintops," she said. "We figure he's close to fifteen years old."

"You can pick Horace out from the other rams, year after year?"

Persaud smiled. "It's like parental instincts, separating identical twins who would fool the rest of us, at any distance," she said. "Junior uses a hunting scope. He can recognize Horace by the details on his horns—the battle scars, if you will—from years of head butting. Horace has been broomed."

"Did you say 'groomed'?" I whispered back. "These guys get groomed before you kill them?"

I don't know why I kept my voice so low. I would have been happy for the sheep to scatter and run away; I wasn't going to let anyone shoot at a living target while I was around.

"No. It's called 'brooming,'" Persaud said. "It happens to them naturally. They lose the tips of their horns in battle. It shows that Horace is one of the old boys, king of the hill. He's a real prize."

I handed back the glasses. "Why not just transplant Horace?" I asked. "Airlift him in one of those wildlife slings and send him off to the rez. Let him out to stud, like he deserves. Seems like the right thing to do."

"You don't understand his value, Alex," she said. "If one of the Montana permit auction winners comes here to shoot, and Junior can help him get Horace—who is really a prized animal—well, that can save a lot of other sheep. It gives us half a million dollars to work with."

Naming the poor beast—identifying him and tracking him for years—made me feel even worse about the doomed Horace.

"When's the hunt?"

"It starts in another ten days," Persaud said. "November first is when the season begins. I doubt Junior will take his eyes off Horace between now and then, no matter how far that trek takes him."

"You knew that Horace would be here today?" I said.

"He likes that bluff across the way," she said. "Seems to come back to it all the time."

"Till he hears the first rifle shot," Junior said. "Then he's in the wind. So I like him to get used to the sight of me over here, with no sound at all. He's gotten to trust me after all these years. Me and Frank, we've gotten to know Horace real good."

I wanted to signal a warning to Horace. He looked so majestic, standing tall on the silent peak.

"This is the spot where the accident happened," Persaud said, breaking the spell of the moment with a reality check. "Right where I'm standing."

"You wouldn't let any of the men use their guns?" Prescott asked Karl Jansen, who had been along with Battaglia that day.

"That's right," he said. "Neither would Frank. The season hadn't opened. Wouldn't have been fair."

But any day now it would become "fair" to put one through Horace's heart.

"The other man—the Arabian fellow—thought he could get one of those rams from over here with a bow and arrow?" I asked.

"Don't know nobody except Junior and Frank who could have done that," Jansen said. "But the fool was stubborn. Frank told him it wasn't yet bow season either, but he brought the damn thing along claiming he might use it on some other animal. Then he saw Horace and just picked up the bow and aimed."

"Not at Frank, though, did he?" I said.

"Course not," the older Jansen said. "It was your boss who got mad at him."

"Battaglia?" Prescott asked. "What'd he say?"

"It wasn't anything so much as what he said. It's what he did," Jansen went on. "The DA grabbed the Arab by his arm and tried to turn him away from the herd."

"So Paul didn't want to kill animals after all," I said, triumphant about Battaglia's moral compass, but still in the dark about his reasons for trekking out here.

"Can't speak to that," Jansen said. "He didn't mean to kill Frank either, but that's where the arrow went."

"You mean, because Paul Battaglia pulled on the man's arm, that's the reason the arrow hit your nephew?" Prescott said.

"Paul must have been saving Horace," I said.

"I'd correct that, Alex," Chidra Persaud said. "The truth is that Paul was saving Horace for himself."

"What does that mean?"

"Your boss had booked a return visit here to the preserve," she said. "He was coming back on November first, for the hunt. He told me he was bringing a high roller who'd pay even more to kill the trophy ram."

"Who?" I asked. "What's the name of the man he was bringing?"

"He didn't tell me the name. He told me not to worry, that it would be worth my while," Persaud said. "That this hunter could buy Montana without blinking."

"But who—?" I said, looking at Prescott.

Chidra started to retrace her steps. "When you two figure it out, do let me know. Otherwise, I'll have two spots to fill before the season starts."

I stood at the highest point for a few minutes longer, letting Persaud and Prescott walk slowly downhill with Junior.

Karl Jansen waited beside me, taking in the view with what seemed as much appreciation as I had for it, though he had seen it thousands of times before.

"You must have been curious about who Mr. Battaglia was bringing out here for the big hunt," I said to Jansen. "That high roller must mean a lot to you—to your family."

"Money's money, Miss Alex. Didn't much matter who it was to me."

I grabbed onto the side of a boulder to steady myself as I took some baby steps down the side of the mountain. I figured I could play to his emotions.

"I bet Frank cared," I said. "I bet Frank wanted to know who was going to get Horace. He and your son have such a connection to that animal."

"Watch your footing," Jansen said. "You got to think like a billy goat when you're walking down these slopes."

"Even if Chidra wasn't along for your hunt that Saturday, I knew my boss well enough to know that he would have been bragging to you, bragging to Frank, about how he was bringing someone fancy with him when the season opened."

"Lordy, that man could brag all right," Jansen said, stopping to offer me his gnarled, weathered hand as the hill steepened. "Boasted all day about his cases and his career and his fancy friends. You got that right about him."

"I won't give you up, Mr. Jansen," I said, taking his hand and resting my other one on his shoulder. "Chidra doesn't have to know, I promise you. It would make me feel a lot better if I could know who he wanted to shoot with. It's just—well—just kind of personal for me."

"I'd help you if I could, young lady."

Jansen dropped my hand when I got level with him. He turned his back to me and kept on walking down.

"I thought I could tell his wife something that would ease her pain a bit," I said, pressing the family angle. "I was sure he'd have boasted about his hunting companion, but I guess I'm wrong."

"Like I told you, Mr. Battaglia wasn't short on bragging," Jansen said. "But all he'd tell us was that the man he wanted to bring wouldn't spook the sheep."

"That's what he said? I wonder why."

"Your boss told us he was bringing a ghost. And a ghost wouldn't spook no sheep."

# THIRTY-EIGHT

"Did you hear me, Alex?" Prescott asked me, sitting at the dining table in the lodge.

"Sorry. I spaced out. What did you say?"

I was trying to concentrate on Prescott's conversation, but my mind was on ghosts. Deirdre Wright, the development department worker at the Bronx Zoo, had called George Kwan a ghost. Mike had raised the connection between Kwan and the Asian gang that had terrorized Chinatown in the eighties—the Ghost Shadows. Why was Battaglia using that particular word to describe his hunting partner?

"That must have tortured Battaglia, is what I said," Prescott went on. "Even though Frank's death was an accident, he had to blame himself for pulling the guy's arm when he had a loaded bow in his hands."

It was almost one o'clock by the time we finished our descent and got back to the main lodge. We had finished lunch an hour later and were waiting for Chidra Persaud to sit down with us to give us information from the office at the preserve.

"You knew him better than that," I said. "Paul didn't blame himself for anything. Ever."

"I guess. Frank shouldn't have been standing where he was, the Arabian prince shouldn't have picked up a bow and arrow—"

"Horace shouldn't have been so tempting a target. Like that," I said. "But why did Chidra want to bring us out here? What does that do for her?"

James Prescott couldn't quite figure it either. "She brought us to the very spot where Frank—Jansen's nephew—was killed," he said, "and she implicated Battaglia in his death."

"Long way to come to do that," I said. "My bet is that she's trying to take your eye off the ball."

"What ball?"

"Something going on back in New York."

"Tell me what you're thinking."

Nothing that I would suggest without telling Mike first. I was thinking about ghosts, about why Paul Battaglia wouldn't have wanted the name of his hunting partner to go public yet. And I was keenly aware that if James Prescott had picked up anything on this trip, he would not have confided the fact of it to me. I did the same.

Chidra was walking back into the dining room, where we were lingering over coffee.

"I don't have everything you need, but perhaps this is a start."

She had copied several sheets of paper and given a set to each of us.

"You wanted names and addresses of guests who've stayed at the preserve," she said. "Here you go."

I skimmed the names, but nothing stood out to me.

"This is the note with Paul Battaglia's request for a cabin starting November first, for the hunt, and a reservation for an adjacent cabin for a friend he wanted to bring."

"But you haven't listed a name here," I said.

"Sorry, but he hadn't given me one yet."

"How often were you in touch with him?"

"As he needed me, Alex. I had little reason to call him," she said. "In fact, most of our contact went through Charles Swenson."

I took a last drag on my coffee cup. "Did he ever tell you that he thought his life was in danger?"

Chidra Persaud almost laughed. "Quite the opposite. Paul

Battaglia seemed to think he was immortal. Talked about things ten years out, like it was nothing. Like he could control the future for as long as he could see it."

I sat back in my chair. She had spent enough time with the man to know that about him. It was part of the syndrome that allowed him to think he'd been elected DA for life.

"If the two of you are about ready, we should get going," she said. "I've got a fresh crew at the airstrip and if we take off by three—remember, it's five in New York—you'll be home in time to sleep in your own beds."

"Ready to go," Prescott said.

We traveled back to Mission Field the same way we had arrived. As we walked to the steps of the plane, I slowed down to talk to Prescott.

"You get to sleep in your own bed," I said. "Your incentive for hurrying home, James. May I just remind you that even murderers up at Dannemora get conjugal visits?"

"No way."

"I know it doesn't happen in federal prisons, but New York State allows it."

"Seriously?" he asked.

"Clean sheets and towels. Soap. Toothpaste," I said. "In a trailer outside the prison walls, for anywhere from twelve to twenty-four hours. Oh, and the state provides condoms, too."

"What's this? A plea for Chapman?"

"Tomorrow's Sunday. If you're not going to parole me, you can at least let me have a shot at enjoying myself. The Sunday *Times* crossword puzzle and a date."

Prescott removed his phone and handed it to me.

"Thanks, James," I said, dialing Mike's number. It rang twice and Mike picked it up. "Hey. What's up?"

"Where are you?" he asked.

"Heading home."

"Anything good come out of this?" Mike said.

"I'm not quite sure, but I've got happy news for you."

"What's that?"

"Mr. Prescott has allowed me to invite you to spend the night at Three Sisters."

"Are you serious? You have a debrief for me?" Mike asked.

"Save that thought till we're alone," I said.

Prescott looked over at me. I knew I didn't want to tell Mike about the day until I was out of the presence of the US attorney. I could see Prescott didn't want me to talk to him about it at all.

"Just be sure and bring me a turkey sandwich on rye from P J Bernstein's, okay? Extra Russian dressing," I said. "We're due to land at ten fifteen, unless we get a good tailwind. See you at the airport."

"Roger that."

"You'll make me," I said. "I'm the one who smells like I've been stepping in sheep scat all day."

I handed the phone back to Prescott. "Thanks. I appreciate the gesture."

"I can't tell you not to talk to him, but I hope you let us absorb what we've got—let my guys check out these names, and maybe we'll have a team meet up at Three Sisters on Monday."

"I'm good with that," I said.

I wasn't ready to tell Prescott that I had phoned Mike earlier, to start putting facts together. Twenty-four hours would buy us both time.

"I say we get on top of all the names before we meet, and then I'll call Charles Swenson on Monday morning," Prescott said. "I want to insist on a more substantive meeting with Chidra, in case you're right on her efforts to take my eyes off the ball. I can be up to your place by nine and back in my office to take her on by one."

"Toss her in the grand jury," I said. "Get her under oath."

"Maybe."

We had stopped on the tarmac before boarding, letting Chidra and her assistant settle in while we finished talking.

"Think of it, James," I said. "Paul was killed by a sharpshooter."

He raised his head to look at me.

"Who knew, between the preserve in Texas where Scalia died and this trip—or these trips—to Montana," I said, "that he was hanging around so many people who were capable of killing with such deadly accuracy?"

"That's certainly one way to think of it," Prescott said.

"I'm telling you. You want sworn testimony from this woman," I said. "Try locking her in on Monday."

I knew we had different prosecutorial approaches, but I thought he needed to take a hard line with Chidra Persaud, sooner rather than later.

Once airborne and heading east, Prescott continued asking Chidra questions. He was getting stonewalled, most politely, on just about everything that would have been helpful to us.

When she sidestepped the subjects that were of interest to us and went on to discuss the new tariff plans, I felt myself nodding off. The attendant covered me with a cashmere blanket, and I reclined my seat and closed my eyes, telling her that I would skip the meal service.

Rough air bounced us most of the way home, so I slept in fits and starts.

We touched down at 10:05 and taxied to a stop at the private aviation section of the airport.

The attendant opened the door and lowered the steps. The two agents were first out, and I could see them shaking hands with Mike as they walked off the field onto the pathway.

I went down next, followed by Prescott. He reached the bottom and held up his hand for Chidra's assistant. Then we waited for Chidra herself to come down.

She stood in the doorway and cupped her hands over her mouth. "Give me five minutes, James. I'll pick up my things and meet you inside the terminal."

Mike had his arm around my shoulders and we were walking, against the wind, toward the door.

Prescott called my name and I turned back to see what he wanted.

"I think you're right, Alex," he said. "I'm going to tell Chidra to be in my office Monday afternoon with Swenson. There's no point giving her the chance to back out of it."

"I'm all for that."

"I might as well let her know now," he said.

I watched as the flight attendant raised the staircase and the pilots fired up the engines and started to roll to the runway.

"I think she does know already, James. I think she figured it out all by herself."

The smart-looking jet was on its way to airborne as soon as the tower gave the pilot the all clear to take off.

"Where's that plane going?" Mike asked the two men in blue overalls who must have been the ground crew.

"Gander, Newfoundland," one of them said.

"Gander," I said. "Gateway to Europe."

"She's got enough fuel to make it there—two and a half hours," the workman said. "Then refuel for the trip to London."

"Whatever we asked her," I said to Prescott, "she spooks more easily than sheep."

"I don't get it, Alex. The district attorney was going to be handling a case about supposed thieves in her company," he said. "She was Battaglia's witness, for Christ's sakes."

"You've got that wrong," I said. "Some of the haze is lifting, I think. She wasn't Battaglia's witness at all. Chidra Persaud was his snitch."

# THIRTY-NINE

I was back in my cell at Three Sisters. But at least I had Mike with me, and a thick deli sandwich, and a cooler with a chilled bottle of my favorite Chardonnay—Au Bon Climat.

Prescott had called ahead to give Tinsley and North the night off. They were instructed to return at noon on Sunday.

"What a stunt," I said. "Taking off to London without a bit of notice, and no way to stop her. She's running from Prescott—from this investigation. That much is certain."

"Wouldn't it be nice to know why?" Mike said.

I kept thinking of the playback of Battaglia's phone messages to me the night he was killed, the night he came after me on the steps of the Met. He had worked himself up over Diana—asking me what I knew about her, telling me that she was none of my business. At this moment—other than connecting that name to Chidra Persaud and a hunt club—I had no more of an idea than I had when I heard the calls in Prescott's office.

"Go back to my 'ghost' theory," I said. "If I got nothing else out of the trip, I got that by stumbling along with Karl Jansen."

"It's got possibilities," Mike said, "but Persaud dragged Prescott a long way just to see the scenery."

"And he dragged me," I said. "She wanted him out of town for a reason. Did anything at all happen yesterday that would affect the case?"

"Battaglia's murder?" Mike asked. "I haven't heard anything from anyone. I doubt it."

"Maybe Persaud wanted to defang James Prescott," I said. "Her tax investigation is going to end up in his lap—Battaglia had no business entertaining it. It's a federal case, after all. Now he'll have to recuse himself."

"So the trip could have been a total red herring," Mike said. "Pretty clever of her."

"Devious, too. But I think it was more than that."

"Why?"

"When Prescott came to Three Sisters to get me in the middle of the night, he told me that he had talked to Amy Battaglia. That she insisted the DA's trip involved a case."

"So what was Chidra snitching about?"

"I think she must have been looking for leverage against possible prosecution."

"On the theory that if she was defrauding the Brits, she was playing fast and loose with her tax issues here?" Mike asked.

"Probably so," I said. "It's entirely like Charles Swenson to have her bat her eyelashes at Battaglia and for him to bring her in as a possible victim. Make a preemptive strike."

"Swenson's close enough to Battaglia that he might have encouraged the trip to Montana," Mike said. "Who do you think Chidra was ratting out?"

"Well, there's the mystery man—the guy Battaglia was supposed to bring for the bighorn sheep hunt," I said. "And I can't stop wondering about George Kwan."

"Does Chidra know him?"

"She denied that. But she says he was trying to work some kind of merger with her business. She refused to team up with him."

"So—?"

"So maybe her 'due diligence' turned up dirt on Kwan Enterprises," I said. "Maybe that was to be her ace in the hole if Battaglia turned on her."

"Wish you had asked her more about it."

"I didn't have a clue that might be the case until she pulled that fast one at the airport and disappeared into the wild blue yonder."

"Look on the bright side. At least you got the ghost news," Mike said. "Let's see where we go with that."

"Did you and Catherine turn up anything on Tiger Tail?" I asked, biting into my sandwich.

Mike was uncorking the wine and pouring it into the plastic cups—no glass allowed in the psych ward—from my bathroom.

"All the public information is homogenized. *Wall Street Journal* profile of Persaud, lots of articles about her in the foreign press, active presence on social media. All created to enhance her image," Mike said, coming back into the room and handing me a cup.

"What about the company?"

"Don't talk with your mouth full. I can't understand you."

I swallowed hard. "Tiger Tail? How about the business side of things?"

"Almost one year ago, the British tabloids started in on her tax troubles," Mike said. "But it all simmered down within months."

"I'd love to link that to the point in time Charles Swenson brought her in to meet Battaglia."

"Good luck," he said. "Catherine came up empty."

"What do you mean?"

"She called the chief of the Frauds Bureau—Mimi Hershenson— like you asked her to, and she's got no record of Chidra Persaud— not as a witness, not as a target. Mimi's not aware of any pending appointment with the woman."

"Damn. I should have gone right to Rose Malone," I said.

Rose had been Battaglia's executive assistant for his entire tenure. She was my good friend, often alerting me—like an early warning system—to his dark moods, encouraging me to wait a day or two when I was asking for professional favors. He trusted her with every secret he had ever held close to his chest.

"That window has closed for the moment," Mike said.

"Why?"

Rose would have been as devastated as anyone in Paul Battaglia's family by his death. In my own self-involved mourning, I hadn't even called her.

"She stayed through the end of the day Thursday," Mike said. "Pretty much ripped raw. She was really helpful to Prescott and the detectives, going through Battaglia's desk—"

"An unenviable task," I said. Papers, clippings, notes, phone messages, were stacked more than a foot high in piles on his desk and on the credenza behind it. The ones on the bottom were yellowed with age—calls that had never been returned, applicants who had been pushed on the DA by some political hack to whom they were related, and stock market tips that had not been taken seriously. "But I'd like a go at his appointment book. Where's Rose now?"

"Her daughters took her away for a vacation, just to calm her down. I don't know where," Mike said, "but she'll be gone all next week. We can put in a call."

"I'll try her cell tomorrow," I said, washing the sandwich down with wine. "Does Prescott have the appointment book?"

"I can ask. What would it give you?"

"He had his own code for things—for people he liked and people he despised. Maybe Chidra Persaud is in there somewhere," I said, thinking of the black leather-bound desk diary Rose kept for the DA, an oversize volume that detailed all his meetings, in the office and out of it.

"You think Battaglia had the balls to run a witness like this himself?" Mike asked.

"I know he did," I said. "He's done it before."

"What for?"

"Whenever he thought he had something to gain by it." I was done with food, totally reinvigorated with thoughts of Paul Battaglia's penchant for secrecy. "That whole dustup with the Reverend Hal Shipley—the DA ran that by himself, just as one example. He wanted to lock in Harlem in case he ran again. He compromised himself by letting Shipley call the shots on his own investigation."

I'd had a complaint from a teenager—a statutory sex crime—in which she'd named the publicity-hungry Shipley as her seducer. Before I could make a determination about her credibility—in the end, she had none—Paul Battaglia had already assured the Reverend Shipley that he was not in danger of being charged. Shipley had bought him. Battaglia had compromised me in the letter he wrote to Shipley, and that had set us off on our final series of uncomfortable encounters.

"Did he have a code name for the rev?" Mike asked.

"Not very subtle. Slippery," I said. "He called the flimflam man Slippery, instead of Shipley."

"So—Diana?"

"I imagine it's how he referred to Chidra Persaud."

"Not subtle either," Mike said.

"Prescott must know that. It's probably why he jumped on it—on her—so quickly last night," I said. "There must be references to her in the desk diary. Prescott's coming up here to meet with me Monday morning. We can tell him to bring the diary and go through it together. I may spot some references that others who knew the DA less well might have missed."

"Say Battaglia didn't bring anyone in to work on Persaud with him; how long could he go on that way?"

"Who's to stop him?" I said. "Most of that front office is a bunch of head-bobbing yes-men. He'd milk her till he had what he wanted and then pass it on to Frauds. There would be simply no one to stop him at that point."

"What do you say about his plan to go back to Montana?"

"Persaud claims Battaglia reserved a cabin for November first," I said. "Taking a guest."

"Could be that was the climax he wanted to get to," Mike said.

"Yeah. Killing Horace," I said, going inside to shower and brush my teeth.

"You're holding out on me. Is Horace his nickname for someone?" Mike said. "One of Battaglia's put-downs?"

"It's a freaking ram," I said, undressing and willing the water to get warm. "A good-looking ole boy who's sort of king of the hunting preserve, and Battaglia was ready to blow him to oblivion with—I guess with a ghost by his side."

"A ghost with no name," Mike said. "Don't you think it's got to be George Kwan?"

"If it looks like a duck, as the saying goes. Yes, my money's on Kwan."

"There's got to be a way into this for you and me."

"Prescott will try to run it down, unless we get to it first," I said. "You can start your guys checking out who won the Montana auctions for sheep tags, just in case."

I stepped into the narrow shower and soaped up. I got out and wrapped myself in a towel, wringing the water from my hair.

"I know it was an old technique in mental hospitals to bathe patients in ice water—slow the blood flow to the brain to stop their agitation. But I'm really not enrolled here for the hydrotherapy treatment, and I'm not all that agitated at the moment," I said, coming out of the bathroom. "Warm me up, will you?"

Mike was sitting on the edge of one of the twin beds. I took the iPad out of his hands and stood between his legs, stroking his hair. He put his arms around me and squeezed tight, opening the towel to kiss me on the flat of my abdomen.

"When's the last time you slept in a bed this small?" I asked.

"Can't remember."

"Are you ready to turn out the lights?" I said. "I'm wiped."

Mike undressed and climbed in beside me. I wanted to be held and be made to feel secure. Mike did that for me. I was asleep before I could say good night to him.

When I awakened in the early morning, Mike was already up and dressed.

"Are you going to church?" I asked, knowing that on Sundays he often took his mother to mass.

"I'll take a pass. Mom will have to say a few novenas for me anyway. She might as well add missing today's mass."

"Then why are you up so early?"

"To spirit you out of here so we can get back before Tinsley and North know you went for a constitutional."

"You're springing me," I said, throwing back the covers and reaching for clean clothes. "AWOL. What a great feeling this is. A walk in the woods?"

"I was thinking more like a ride to the city," Mike said.

"Risky business," I said, lacing up the sneakers I had worn to Montana with a burst of energy I didn't know I possessed. "James Prescott won't like this one bit."

Mike must have been to the main house earlier and returned with a pot of coffee. I poured him a second cup and a first for me, while he worked his Google app.

"Did Chidra Persaud mention anything about a grand slam?" he asked.

I shook my head. "No baseball. All hunting all the time."

"I'm talking hunting."

"What's the grand slam, then?"

"There are apparently four kinds of wild sheep in North America," Mike said.

"Yeah. She told us that much."

"Your pal Horace is just one of them."

"Where are the others?"

"Desert bighorn in the Southwest," he said. "Something called Dall's in Alaska and British Columbia, and Stone's sheep in the Yukon."

"How does that connect to Chidra Persaud?" I said.

"I'm working on that," Mike said. "You were right about the state auctions for sheep tags, Coop. You led me straight to it."

"To what?"

"There's a sheep-hunting competition called the Grand Slam," Mike said. "To win, you have to bag all four species. Your ram gets weighed and measured in the judging, and they count the rings on its horns to see how old he was. High stakes, big money, real prizes."

"Spare me the part about how these sportsmen are doing so much for conservation, will you?"

"You got it," Mike said. "So four tags were auctioned in Montana this past January. I've been up half the night checking out the winners on Facebook. I think I've identified the man who Battaglia was planning to take with him to Chidra's lodge on November first. He's already bragging about it online."

"What's his name?" I said, grabbing at the corner of Mike's iPad to turn it around so that I could see the shooter for myself.

"Pedro Echevarria. Ever see him before?"

I looked at his face but didn't recognize him. "No, but he doesn't look like a ghost. Or a Ghost Shadow."

"Are you disappointed that it's not George Kwan?" Mike asked.

"Got to go where the evidence leads you," I said.

Echevarria didn't appear to be more than thirty years old. He was brown-skinned, with dark curly hair, light eyes, and a long scar that ran from his left ear down to his chin. He had posted a photo of himself kneeling behind a dead bighorn, somewhere out west, holding up its head to display his trophy.

"Born in the Bronx," Mike said. "Owns a pad in SoHo now."

"Must have made it large. Those tags cost hundreds of thousands of dollars," I said. "Add a few million for a loft in SoHo."

"Comebacks are a beautiful thing, Coop. I called in a record check an hour ago," Mike said. "Seems Pedro had a felony conviction for drugs. Glad to see he's turned his life around. Just likes to kill for sport now."

"Possession?" I asked.

"Sale," Mike said. "Sale of cocaine to an undercover. Three buys caught on tape before they locked him up."

"I'll say this is a comeback. How old is he?"

"Thirty-two. He was only eighteen when he was nailed for it. Did the minimum before he was paroled."

"How in hell does a parolee like Echevarria get the money to enter an auction where bids can run as high as half a million dollars?" I asked. "You'd think he was back in the dope-selling biz to be running in the same leagues with entrepreneurs and the oil royals."

"You've got such a suspicious mind, kid. What if I told you he's got a sponsor?" Mike said. "Maybe Pedro pulled straight, with the help of someone paying his bills."

"There's something I just love about mentoring. And I'm always so happy when the Department of Corrections actually corrects someone," I said. "It's such a rare phenomenon."

"I second the notion."

"Who's his guardian angel?"

"According to the website of the Grand Slam Club, Pedro's winning bid was underwritten by Kwan Enterprises," Mike said.

"George Kwan," I said, confident that Paul Battaglia thought what he had seen on television Monday night was me leaning in to talk to Kwan during the Met's fashion show. "We're back to him again. The apparition himself."

"Ready to ride?" Mike asked.

"Totally," I said. "Have you got wheels?"

"Yeah, the lieutenant gave me a loaner since the old one went up in flames."

"Where are we going?"

"To George Kwan's house, Coop," he said. "Only this time we're getting in."

# FORTY

"May I help you?" A petite Asian woman answered the door at the double-wide town house on East Seventy-Eighth Street. She was wearing a black maid's uniform with a white apron.

"Yes, thank you," I said. "I'm here to see Mr. Kwan."

"Too early," she said. "Mr. Kwan isn't available. No appointments on Sunday."

"He'll see me, I'm sure. Tell him my name is Alexandra Cooper. He'll remember," I said. "He just talked to me on Wednesday."

The woman tried to close the wrought iron gate but she was no match for Mike. He had been standing off to the side, to my left, when the housekeeper looked through the peephole and opened the door to me. Now he reached out his arm and forced his way in.

It was eight thirty on Sunday morning. I didn't think there was ever a time Kwan was without a bodyguard, but perhaps we had been lucky in the moment.

Mike kept going, his footsteps ringing as he charged forward on the black-and-white floor—painted like a large checkerboard—as though he knew where he was headed.

I tried to catch up to him but was brought up short by a tall man—broad shouldered and barrel-chested—who appeared in the hallway from a room on the left. He was holding a white linen napkin in one hand, as though we had interrupted his breakfast.

"Stop!" he shouted.

Mike turned and held his ground. "Don't lay a hand on her."

"Who the fuck are you?" the man said.

"Mike Chapman—NYPD. That's Alex Cooper, from the DA's office."

There was a gun holstered on the man's shoulder. I was relieved that he hadn't reached for it, and that Mike hadn't felt the need to go for his own.

"What do you want?"

"George Kwan," Mike said. "I want to talk to him."

"He's not here."

"The housekeeper told me otherwise," Mike said.

The tall man looked around for her, but she had disappeared from the hallway.

I could hear classical music playing from a speaker in a room off the hallway, close to where Mike was standing. He backed up a few steps and put his hand on the doorknob.

"Don't go in, Chapman. It's not polite," the tall man said.

"Etiquette's not my strong suit, Miss Manners," Mike said. "We won't be long."

Mike opened the door and I heard someone—presumably George Kwan—shout his guard's name: "Rudy!"

Rudy ran down the rest of the hallway but Mike was already in the room. I followed.

George Kwan was sitting at a desk, dressed in a burgundy silk jacquard smoking jacket over striped pajamas. The day's newspapers were spread out on the desktop in front of him.

"You're dismissed, Rudy," Kwan said. From the look on his face, he might have been talking about a permanent dismissal.

Kwan got to his feet and bowed his head in our direction.

"Impatient, aren't you? I told you to call for an appointment and I'd be happy to see you," he said, retying the belt on his jacket. "Now that you're in, why don't you have a seat."

I tried not to smile, remembering one of Mike's favorite

investigative tips. If you could interview a man who was still in pajamas, you had the upper hand. He would always feel somewhat naked sitting opposite his interrogators. A woman in lingerie, however, presented a more difficult challenge.

Kwan was taller than Mike, lean and fit-looking. He was in his midforties.

We sat in chairs opposite him, and he reseated himself at his desk.

"You're looking well, Ms. Cooper," he said. "There was a suggestion in one of the tabloids that you'd suffered an accident since I last saw you."

"I appreciate your concern. I'm just fine, so you might have me confused with someone else," I said. "I've been out of town for a while."

"And you, Detective Chapman," Kwan said. "Are you working overtime? Sunday morning, so early? What brings you here? The endless saga of Wolf Savage?"

Mike was right about Kwan's comfort level. He kept fussing with the lapel of his smoking jacket and adjusting the knot of his belt.

"Yeah, but the plot has kind of thickened since the other day, Mr. Kwan."

The man rested his forearms on the desk. "In what way?"

"Well, let's start with your relationship with Paul Battaglia."

"I'd hardly call it a relationship," Kwan said. "We were acquaintances, as I told you."

"Then I suppose Battaglia just stopped by to get your signature on his petition," Mike said.

"Petition? You're not making sense, Detective."

"You know," Mike said, "the way politicians go door to door, collecting signatures of registered voters to get on the ballot."

"I signed nothing."

"Of course you didn't," Mike said, leaning in the moment the fumbling started again. "I was being facetious. But we know that Paul Battaglia was here with you the week before last. Ms. Cooper and I saw him walk out your front door."

George Kwan shifted his eyes to look at me.

"We're not fucking with you, Mr. Kwan," Mike said. "Why was the district attorney paying you a visit?"

"Look, Chapman. I've got a lot on my mind. It must have been about the Savage murder. It must have been to tell me your department had identified the killer," Kwan said. "He knew my company was trying to buy a piece of Savage."

"Battaglia was swift, but he didn't have a crystal ball, Mr. Kwan. For all we knew at the time the DA left this building, *you* could have been the killer," Mike said. "We didn't have half the answers on that particular afternoon."

"Then I'm mistaken," Kwan said.

"Press the redo button and start over."

"Start where?"

"Where do you live, Mr. Kwan?" I asked. "What's your home base? Is it in China?"

"Right here, Ms. Cooper. I was born and raised in New York. This is my home."

I was surprised by that information. I knew that Kwan Enterprises was headquartered abroad. We'd learned that during the Savage investigation.

"I didn't know you were American," I said. "Perhaps it's the accent that fooled me."

"A British secondary school in Hong Kong," Kwan said. "But I lived on Pell Street, just a couple of blocks behind your office, for most of my young life."

Mike jumped on that fact. "Isn't it your father, in Hong Kong, who runs the business?"

"You've done some of your homework, Mr. Chapman, but not all."

"What did I miss?"

"My father was the black sheep of the family," Kwan said. "He ran away from home—first to Los Angeles, and then east to New York, where I was born. When I was a kid, I could stand on the fire escape of our fourth-floor walk-up on Pell; I could see Paul Battaglia's office—you know, Ms. Cooper, that huge corner office he has."

"I know it well," I said. "When were you last there?"

"You're jumping to conclusions, just like I expect you're both doing," Kwan said. "I never mentioned being *in* his office. But growing up on the mean streets of Chinatown in those days, all the parents used to point to that bay of windows and tell us the district attorney was waiting for us there. Kind of like the bogeyman in fairy tales."

"Why did they threaten you?" Mike asked. "Were you a gang kid?"

Mike was going straight for the Ghost Shadows.

"The gangs were everywhere in the 'hood," Kwan said, reaching for a cigarette. "Smoke, either of you?"

We both declined, but the cigarette holder and Dunhill lighter were two more signs of Kwan's seemingly elegant affectations.

"You either joined one by the time you were twelve, Detective, or you would likely not have survived to become an adult."

"So you did?"

"My mother wasn't Asian, Chapman. She didn't get the whole picture."

"American?"

"Latina, from Mexico. My father met her in LA," Kwan said. "What my mother didn't understand was that the gangs in Chinatown were just following the traditions of ethnic crime groups that had come before them."

Kwan inhaled, held the smoke, and blew it out slowly.

"They attacked their own before they even thought of branching out into other areas of the city, into other neighborhoods. So we were all in the danger zone—sign up to play, or become vulnerable to their reach."

"Was your father involved?" I asked.

"You can't really blame him," Kwan said. "He was trying to make his own way in a country that wasn't very friendly to immigrants who didn't speak the language."

"Friendlier than now, I'd bet," Mike said.

"I'll give you that, Detective."

"What did he do?"

George Kwan was fidgeting with his smoking jacket again, now adjusting the cuffs. "Every ethnic group had gangs that staked out their turf," he said. "That's the history of mob activity in America. During Prohibition, the Jews—like Arnold Rothstein—took over smuggling liquor all over the country."

"Narcotics too," Mike said.

"The Mafia was next to find a way to infiltrate legitimate businesses and take over control," Kwan said. "Construction, trucking, garbage."

"Before they got into narcotics," Mike said, beating the same drum.

"They denied it for a long time," Kwan said, "but then there were the Pizza Connection convictions, in the late eighties."

That Southern District trial was still the longest in federal prosecution history . . . more than a dozen mobsters found guilty of importing heroin and laundering the money to send back to Sicily, using pizza joints as fronts for trafficking around the metropolitan area.

"And Asians?" Mike asked.

"We always had the gambling dens in our own backyard,"

Kwan said. "That's how it started. Street gang against street gang, Chinese against Chinese neighbor, figuring to go mainstream with bigger cash cows someday, once they were powerful enough."

"Narcotics," Mike said, again.

"Absolutely, Detective. It was the Green Dragons first, stepping out of our world and into major crimes," Kwan said. "They'd had enough of extorting their own people—that was petty cash to them—so they went after the drug business, citywide."

There was a point in time, in the 1990s, that Chinese gangs controlled two-thirds of New York's heroin-smuggling business. Even before my prosecutorial career, the newspapers had made that fact plain.

"Was your family involved?" Mike asked.

Kwan put his head back and blew smoke in the air. "I know you'll check out everything I say, Detective—although there are probably more Kwans in the NYPD record files than there are Smiths—so, yes, some of them were involved."

Mike glanced at me.

"My father was recruited by the Green Dragons," Kwan said. "I wasn't even ten years old at the time, so I don't remember much. Except I have a pretty vivid recollection of the first time I saw him with a gun."

"I imagine that's hard to forget," I said.

"My mother left, Ms. Cooper," Kwan said. "That was devastating to me. It was more than the gun, of course; it was my father's transition to racketeering and to murder, but to me it was always symbolized by the gun."

"Where did she go?"

"I'm not sure," he said. "I only saw her once again after that day."

"When was that?" Mike asked.

"You were too young to be a cop back then, so perhaps you don't know what the situation was," Kwan said. "The only mistake an Asian gang member could make in those days was to victimize someone who wasn't one of us. To kill a Caucasian, Detective. To kill a white man."

Kwan stared at me to make sure I was listening.

"That's the only time the police ever came after any of us," he said.

Mike held his tongue. He knew his own father's integrity. He knew Kwan wasn't right.

"Your father killed someone?" I asked.

"That's unclear, Ms. Cooper," Kwan said. "He was part of a group of Green Dragons who kidnapped several rival gang members—"

"Which gang?" Mike asked.

"The Ghost Shadows, Detective, if that means anything to you."

Mike's expression didn't change.

"There was a shootout in a Chinese restaurant in Queens," Kwan said. "The Ghosts came looking for revenge, but in too public a place. They sprayed the front of the restaurant with gunfire, killing six or seven people inside. One of the dead men was simply picking up takeout for his family on a Thursday night. A white man."

"That brought the NYPD down on the Dragons and the Ghost Shadows, I guess," I said. "Did your father get caught up in the police action?"

"He didn't, Ms. Cooper," Kwan said. "But that's only because he was one of the other people left on the restaurant floor. Ko-Lin Kwan—my father—didn't get quite the investigative attention the white man's murder did, but he was every bit as dead."

# FORTY-ONE

"Both gangs tried to recruit me, even though I was so young," Kwan said. "The Green Dragons considered me family, and the Ghosts wanted me even more, so they could indoctrinate me and make me forget my past."

"You went with the Dragons, I assume," I said.

"Actually not. I was more afraid of the Ghost Shadows, because they had killed my father. I was foolish enough to think I could get inside their fold and, when I got older, pay them back for what they had done."

"Bad story. Tired plot. I think you can stream that movie right now on Netflix," Mike said.

"Who were you living with?" I asked.

"Neighbors, mostly," Kwan said. "That's when my mother reappeared, just for a day. Perhaps the happiest day of my life, but short-lived happiness it was."

"Why?" I said. "Was she hurt too?"

"No. But she had come back to send me away—far away, to China—when she got word of my father's murder," he said. "To the good relatives, as she liked to call them."

"The same day?"

"She had a fake passport made for me on Forty-Second Street—you could do that for twenty dollars back before 9/11, if you remember that. She took me to JFK in a taxi and loaded me on a flight to Hong Kong," Kwan said. "My grandfather had his driver pick me up at the airport on that end and take me to his house—more accurate to call it a mansion. It was my introduction to Kwan Enterprises."

"That must have been culture shock," Mike said.

"You cannot imagine it, Detective. The first thing my grandfather did was ground me for three months. He had me cleaned up, bought me fine clothes, taught me table manners, and had me tutored in languages—Chinese dialects, English, French, and Japanese."

"You had no problem adjusting?"

"I spent five years adjusting, Mr. Chapman, to the finest luxuries and experiences that life offered," Kwan said. "I left my youth behind. I took my grandfather's name—George—and I can't say that I never looked back, but I didn't do it very often."

Maybe Kwan had cleaned up his life. Maybe Mike was seeing ghosts where there were none. The gangs had lived out their short, violent lives in two decades. Neither one of them existed today.

"Was your father ever locked up?" Mike asked.

"I'm sure he was. There were times he'd disappear for days, and neighbors had to take me in," Kwan said, repeating his father's name and date of birth. "You'll find out more about him in police files than I know; that's for sure."

"How about you?" Mike asked.

"I was just a kid."

"Kids get locked up too."

"I guess I was just lucky, Detective. I got out of town in time."

The room looked like a museum-quality collection of antiques and stuffed heads. The mahogany paneling and shelves spoke to Kwan's wealth. The leopard-skin rugs, the taxidermied grizzly bear in one corner, and the horned creatures mounted on the walls spoke to his deadly obsession with the hunt.

"What's your mother's name?" Mike asked.

"My late mother, Mr. Chapman," Kwan said. "Her name was

Alvarez. Maria Alvarez. Now, what else do you want from this visit?"

"Where did you learn how to shoot?" Mike said.

"Long guns, Detective? In China. It's become a destination for game hunting," Kwan said, shifting positions in his chair. "My adoptive father—my grandfather, but I called him my father—insisted I learn how to shoot."

"Why's that?" Mike said. "I would have thought you'd seen enough of guns when you were a kid."

"Quite a different thing, pistols and rifles. My father took me to hunt in Mongolia," Kwan said. "By the time he sent me away to boarding school, rifle practice was a mandatory part of the curriculum."

"When you're in the States," Mike said, "when you're home, where do you hunt?"

"Back to the Paul Battaglia connection, are you?"

"Where do you hunt?"

"Anywhere I please, Mr. Chapman. I've been all over the country."

"That preserve where Justice Scalia died?" Mike asked.

"I'm not in the Order of Saint Hubertus, if that's where you're going," Kwan said. "No Asians need apply, as they used to say of the Irish. I've been other places in Texas—there are so many of them—that don't require membership."

"Have you ever hunted with Battaglia?"

"No. No, I haven't. I actually didn't believe the hunting stories were real," Kwan said. "He liked prosecuting those rhino-horn traffickers so much, I wasn't sure what he was up to with Hubertus."

"Talk to us about Chidra Persaud," Mike said.

Kwan smiled and let go of his collar. "You may think you're in a business that requires fortitude and strength, Ms. Cooper, but that Persaud is one tough broad."

"You know her?" I asked.

"Not personally, no."

"How, then?"

"One of our business partners tried to interest her in our services a year or so ago, but she wouldn't have us," Kwan said. "We threw money at her—lots of it—but we couldn't get her to engage with us."

"Did anyone from Kwan Enterprises meet with Persaud to discuss the deal?" I asked. I wanted to see how far along this proposition had gotten. So far, they both told the same story.

"Persaud came to Hong Kong. She came to look at the books. That's how I remember it."

"But you weren't around?" Maybe my due diligence theory was right. Maybe Chidra had found some evidence of criminal wrongdoing when she examined Kwan Enterprises' books—something to snitch to Battaglia about if she became the subject of an investigation.

"No, I was here at home. I would have liked to try to break her ice-maiden exterior."

"You know she has a hunting preserve in Montana?" Mike said.

"Yes. I've been told it's a first-rate place. Rocky Mountain bighorns," Kwan said, "which are the American equivalent of our Mongolian blue sheep."

My disgust about shooting sheep probably registered on my face.

"Have you been to Persaud's preserve?"

"No, I haven't."

Mike stood up, walking around his chair and picking up a leather-bound book from the edge of Kwan's desk, checking out its spine and the gilded lettering on its cover.

"What can you tell me about Pedro Echevarria?" Mike said, standing over Kwan, picking a vantage point from which to look down at him.

George Kwan picked up his monogrammed sterling case and removed another cigarette, lighting it with a slight shake of the hand.

"Good man," he said. "Excellent shot."

"I understand he won the Kwan scholarship to the big hunt at Persaud's preserve in ten days," Mike said.

"Then he's lucky, too, wouldn't you say?"

"Does he work for you, this Pedro Echevarria?"

"He does," Kwan said. "He's in charge of keeping all my hunting equipment in top shape, around the world. He often travels with me."

"Then you knew he was going to Montana on November first?" Mike went on.

"I did."

"You must have known, too, that he was going to be Paul Battaglia's partner on the hunt."

"Also that. It's actually one of the things Paul and I were talking about—now that you've reminded me—the day I missed you. The DA was hoping to get some shooting instruction from Echevarria."

"I didn't know he was a teacher," Mike said.

"You seem to know most else, Detective."

"But you weren't planning on being there, in Montana?" I asked.

"Not for that shoot, no. I expect to be in China next week."

Mike put down the book and splayed his hands on the desk, facing George Kwan.

"Ms. Cooper and I were working on something with Paul Battaglia when he was killed," Mike said. "Something so secretive that very few people knew about it—knew he was onto it."

"Surely, I wouldn't have been one of those in the know," Kwan said, crushing the cigarette in the ashtray and retying the knot on his smoking jacket.

"You want to get out of those pj's, Mr. Kwan? I always think it sounds more serious when a guy isn't talking to me in last night's rumpled bedclothes."

"Go on, Detective."

"Paul Battaglia came here to talk to you about Diana," Mike said.

Kwan's hand was on his cigarette case. He let it go, involuntary, as his fist clenched.

"I have nothing to say to you," he said. "You're wrong."

"The DA took one look at you on his television set, sitting at the Metropolitan Museum gala—and he saw Alex Cooper pass by, behind you, and speak to you—"

"That's a lie!" Kwan said, turning to me. "I never saw you there. We never talked."

He happened to be right, but that didn't stop Mike from bluffing. The photograph had worried me, too, when Prescott first showed it.

"You'll see the photo," Mike said. "Maybe you didn't recognize Ms. Cooper, but you must have heard what she said. What Battaglia sent her to tell you."

The look of panic on George Kwan's face was real. He stood up, pressing a buzzer on his desk.

"I didn't hear anything that night," Kwan said. "What was Battaglia's message to me? What are you trying to do here?"

The security guard—Rudy—had rushed into the room.

"This meeting's about to be over, Rudy," Kwan said. "I think my guests are ready to go now."

"We know that Diana is the name of a hunt club," I said. "And we know that you aren't a member."

George Kwan didn't say a word.

"And we know Paul Battaglia talked to you about Diana," I said. "He told me so himself."

Kwan spoke the next three words slowly and emphatically, separating them from each other. "He did not."

"You'd be wrong about that," I said. "I can play you a tape of our conversation."

Kwan froze momentarily. "A tape? That bastard was taping me?"

The tape I was talking about was Battaglia's last phone call to me, when he feared I had actually spoken with George Kwan at the Met. I was fine to let Kwan think otherwise.

"What is it you trade in, Mr. Kwan? I mean, besides the things printed in your advertisements?" Mike asked. "And how did you think Diana, or Chidra Persaud, could help your—shall we say 'business plan'?"

"Search all you like. We run a legitimate company," he said. "We always have."

"Were you smuggling in exotic animals from Asia, so she could stock her game preserve?"

"I want to hear the tapes," he said. "I don't even know that woman. Let me have the tapes."

"In due time," Mike said, turning his back to Kwan. "When I'm good and ready."

"Paul Battaglia was killed because someone didn't want him meddling in this world of big-game hunters and trophy animals," I said. "Someone he trusted, Mr. Kwan, betrayed him."

I knew that was the truth. I realized the DA must have found himself in a world of high stakes and endangered species, lured in by the chance to mix with an elite group of international sportsmen.

"You know exactly where I was Monday night, Ms. Cooper."

Paul Battaglia had liked the spotlight too much—more than had been good for him. Almost forty years of solving crimes and basking in the high-profile results of his young teams of lawyers had jaded him. He had risked going in on projects alone at first—like he did with the Reverend Shipley and with Operation Crash—sniffing out the illegal act with his great instinct for wrongdoing, stepping on the toes of another prosecutor whose rightful jurisdiction the matter would have been, and then turning the mess he'd stirred up over to his own faithful crew of public servants.

"I saw where you were during the show, Mr. Kwan," I said. "I have no idea what you did after you left the museum."

The security guard motioned for Mike to move out of the room.

"I don't think Paul Battaglia knew you well enough to trust you, Mr. Kwan," Mike said. "But I happen to disagree with Ms. Cooper. I don't think you have to be in so deep to betray someone, do you?"

"Battaglia didn't know me well," Kwan said, caught in the middle of that thought, "You're right about that. But I never gave him any reason not to trust me."

"We've got an eye on you, Mr. Kwan," Mike said, swiveling around to talk to the man. "And we've got a high-powered scope attached to it. Keep that in mind as you go about your day."

He saw an object on Kwan's desk and picked it up. It was a magnifying glass—a beautiful object—resting on top of the Sunday *Times*. It had brass trim and its long, carved handle was made of ivory.

"Worth killing for?" Mike asked.

"It's an antique, Detective," Kwan said, quite defensively.

"I didn't mean your ivory trinkets, Mr. Kwan," Mike said, putting down the glass. "I meant the district attorney."

"Only his killer can tell you that, Detective."

"Well, if you run into him—or her—be sure and mention that we're getting really close to bagging our prey," Mike said, walking toward the door of the dark room.

George Kwan put his hands in the pockets of his smoking jacket.

Mike wasn't quite done. "And if I'm thinking right that there's a price on Alex Cooper's head, too," he said, glancing in my direction before I interrupted him.

"Don't go there, Mike," I said. I took a deep breath. I could almost feel the flames from Friday night's Molotov cocktail licking at my neck.

"There won't be anyplace on this planet I wouldn't go," Mike said, "to put a bullet in the brain of the mastermind behind that idea."

# FORTY-TWO

"Give me a list," Mercer said.

The three of us were sitting at the back table at P J Bernstein Deli on Third Avenue, less than ten blocks from Kwan's house. Mike had stopped at a street vendor's cart to buy me a baseball cap, thinking that with the hat, my collar turned up, and shades on, some of the neighborhood regulars wouldn't make me and butt in.

"We can do this all together," I said.

It was eleven A.M. I had ordered an egg-white omelet while the guys both went for scrambled eggs and bacon.

"No, we can't, Alex. I can go to One PP," Mercer said, laughing at me, "but you're off-limits there."

"We'll eat," Mike said, "and I'll run you back up to Three Sisters."

"That's not fair," I said, peppering my omelet.

"It's safe," Mercer said. "What do you need?"

"I know the tech guys have been going over hours and hours of street surveillance," Mike said. "If Kwan's behind this, I'd start checking on whether Battaglia was being followed by someone from Kwan's team from the time he left the town house."

"That was Friday afternoon," I said. "The murder was Monday night."

"So let's assume the shooters weren't sitting near Battaglia's apartment—in plain sight of his own bodyguard—on Monday only," Mike said. "They might have figured he was tucked in for the night by that hour, and the fact that he rushed out so late could have suggested there was some urgency to his appointment."

"I get it," I said. "Whoever's behind this killing must have had a team on Battaglia—probably for days."

"Exactly. TARU needs to find street surveillance tapes from near the DA's home and play them till a week before the murder," Mike said to Mercer. "It'll take all the men they've got to free up and watch hours of this stuff. Possible tails from when he came and went from the office, coordinated with his meetings and breakfast stops—they can find them in his diary. They'll have to scan the streets from dozens of yards away."

"That might give us license plates—even faces, 'cause they wouldn't have been wearing masks until the moment of the kill."

"All on the theory that at some point, the man in charge of ordering the hit was ready to have a sharpshooter take Battaglia out—if and when that became necessary," Mercer said.

"And it seemed only to become necessary on Monday night," Mike said. "But that doesn't mean the guys tailing him—possibly gunmen—weren't in place before then. Days before then."

"TARU it is," Mercer said. He was chewing on a strip of crisp bacon. "Big job, but at least they can get started today."

"This guy, Pedro Echevarria," Mike said. "He's good with a gun. But I can't imagine anyone, especially a whiz like Kwan, would use someone as visible as Pedro to do this killing—someone who goes out in the world with Kwan, does business with him, and was even scheduled to shoot with Battaglia in Montana."

"You're probably right about that," Mercer said.

"Where do you learn to shoot around New York?" I asked.

"The NYPD range is at Rodman's Neck," Mercer said. "In the Bronx."

"Yeah, but that's the only one I know of," I said.

Cops have to go twice a year to be retrained, but civilians aren't welcome. I had been several times to observe police procedures and never saw an outsider.

Mike was on his iPad, Googling shooting ranges. "There's something called West Side Rifle and Pistol Range on Twentieth Street," he said. "Coyne Park in Yonkers. Ranges in Woodhaven and in Bay Ridge. They seem to be all over the place."

"We got some calls to make," Mercer said, jotting down the names. "Looking for—exactly what?"

"Cross-check all the names we have. See where Echevarria practices shooting, if you can find it," Mike said. "Maybe he's been giving lessons to young sharpshooters. No law against that."

"I want to check Kwan for a juvenile record," I said.

"That's hopeless," Mike said. "Even if he had one, it would be sealed by now."

"Ask Catherine to take a court order to a judge tomorrow. A friendly judge," I said to Mercer. "Let's see if there's a record first, and then get it unsealed, if there is one."

"George Kwan?" Mercer asked.

"No, no. Get Kwan's date of birth, which is in my Wolf Savage file, but run it with the name Ko-Lin Kwan—throw in a 'Junior' after the name—and an address on Pell Street."

"Ancient history," Mike said.

"History repeats itself every now and then," I said. "Humor me."

Mike was adding assignments to the task force list faster than I could think.

"That kid who dumped the bicycle and ran into the Central Park Zoo," I said.

"Henry Dibaba," Mike said. "What about him?"

"You said his narcotics arrest was made in the Bronx. Do you know where?"

Mike pointed at Mercer. "Check it out, will you? It was near the East 180th Street station. The Dyre Avenue Shuttle."

"I realize I'm never going to be Miss Subways, but I didn't even know that line existed. What's the Dyre Shuttle?"

"It's a short run that begins where the Lexington Avenue line ends," Mike said. "Just four or five stops farther east, into the Bronx."

"While you're getting us that information," I said to Mercer, "tell me where Pedro Echevarria got locked up when he was selling drugs. That's also in the Bronx, if I'm not mistaken."

"It's a big borough, Coop."

"I'm looking for a common denominator; that's all."

"For what?"

"A drug-dealing zookeeper of Nigerian parents, a sheep-hunting Hispanic with a narcotics history too, and a Chinese American importer who used to run with the Ghost Shadows."

"You'd do better looking at the United Nations than in NYPD rap sheets," Mike said.

I reached over and grabbed a couple of Mike's home fries.

"Finish that omelet, kid. I've got to get you back to the convent."

"I'd be so much more useful running down this list of things to do with Mercer than I am just sitting in my straitjacket up there."

"You keep behaving like you're the fourth sister and Prescott will parole you before too long."

We paid the bill and said good-bye to Mercer. Mike called Jimmy North to tell him that we might not make it back to Three Sisters by our noon curfew, but we were getting on the road shortly and wouldn't be too late.

The ride up the highway was restful. It was a beautiful October afternoon, sunny and mild, and the fall foliage was putting on a great show as we got north of the city. My favorite soft rock station was playing on the radio and I was as close to relaxing as I'd been in weeks. My stomach didn't start to knot up until we turned into the gates of the property at about one o'clock and I spotted Kate Tinsley's car.

Tinsley walked out to greet us. "You gave me quite a fright

until Jimmy called me with the news," she said. "I got here early but there was no sign of you."

"Don't worry," I said. "My luggage is still here. I didn't have the early-checkout option."

Mike walked me inside, while Tinsley went over to the main house to get herself some lunch.

Mike's cell rang. "Chapman," he said. Then he listened. "Let me put it on speakerphone."

He pressed the controls and held the phone in the palm of his hand.

"You wanted a denominator, Alex," Mercer said, "and I don't think it's such a common one."

"What do you mean?"

"Henry Dibaba's drug collar was right like Mike remembered. About two blocks away from the shuttle tracks, not far from the overpass of the Bronx River Parkway."

"It's pretty deserted there," Mike said. "Once you get away from the station itself—which is pretty small—you're kind of in the middle of nowhere. I think there's a rail yard where they keep old trains that are out of service."

"That's the spot," Mercer said. We had a good cell connection and I could hear him clearly. "The old NYW&B tracks."

"I've never heard of that, either," I said.

"The New York, Westchester and Boston Railroad," Mercer said. He had deep knowledge of transportation history—both from his father's interest in it and from his work at the nearby airport. "It ran from the Harlem River in the South Bronx right up to Boston. An electric commuter train."

"They went out of business in the 1930s, didn't they?" Mike said.

"Yes, but there are miles of abandoned track from here—like you mentioned—all the way up to Connecticut. Metro-North and the MTA store a lot of equipment there."

"Good place to keep a stash of drugs," I said. "An old train that isn't going anywhere. Did Dibaba have any codefendants locked up with him? Guys we can try to turn? Maybe get the address from the girlfriend he used to live with?"

"No luck on the codefendant front," Mercer said. "There actually was another perp on the scene with Dibaba—a lookout— who split when the cops charged after Dibaba. Got away clean."

"Go for the girlfriend," I said. "Take a snake with you, in case she misses Henry's."

"Here's the good news," Mercer said. "You asked me to get Pedro Echevarria's arrest record, too."

"Yes."

"It goes back ten years, Alex, but Special Narcotics busted Echevarria on a decommissioned redbird that was sitting on the tracks in the rail yard—about a quarter of a mile away from where Dibaba bit the dust a decade later."

Everybody in New York used to love redbirds—which were retired from the system in 2003, replaced by an all–stainless steel fleet. They were great-looking subway cars painted deep red, with silver roofs and black end caps—the last trains to have individual handholds overhead, instead of long bars. I remembered my first rides as a child, hanging on to my father's hand while he reached up to steady himself with the metal grabber.

"Did you hear me?" Mercer asked.

Mike moved the phone in my direction.

"I did," I said, distracted by visuals—thoughts of the handsome old redbirds left out in the elements to rot. I had driven past that huge rail yard hundreds and hundreds of times and looked down from the Bronx River Parkway as I rode over it, seeing it covered with hundreds of rusted trains. "I'm just thinking. Maybe they can do a reverse search. Check the location for the number of drug arrests, before I get my hopes too high. There must be scores of them there over the years—it's such a desolate area, especially at night."

"Good idea," Mercer said. "I'll get back to you."

Mike ended the call. "I might as well stick around till he calls. I hate leaving you without a phone."

"Just give me yours," I said, holding out my hand. "You can pick up a new one in the city."

"My incomings will make you jealous, babe."

"I hardly think so, Detective."

Mike's cell rang again. "See? It's a steady stream of callers." He winked at me and answered it. "Chapman."

Again, he listened.

"Are you sure you don't want *me*?" he said. "Okay, okay. She's right here."

This time he passed me the phone. "It's Catherine, for you."

"Like I said, Detective, you're not as universally desirable as you think." I put the phone to my ear. "Nice of you to call."

"How are you doing?" Catherine asked.

"If I wasn't crazy when I got here, I will be in another few days."

"Maybe I can get your spirit powered up."

"Try me," I said.

"Mercer called and told me you were looking for juvie records on an Asian kid named Ko-Lin Kwan," Catherine said.

"Look, I don't want to burn you, but if he's got an arrest way back when, I'd like you to make a quiet approach to the judge who likes you best, flutter your eyelashes or kick him in the balls, but I'm begging you—if something's there—to get it unsealed."

"I'm not sure I didn't like it better when you were off your game this last month, Alex. You were a lot less pushy then."

"I'm back in my badassery mode."

"You don't need to press me on this. It was easier than that."

"Done?" I asked. "You've gotten it done on a Sunday?"

"Ko-Lin Kwan would have been sealed up for eternity if he'd come to court," Catherine said, "and there aren't that many judges who like me enough to have done that kind of favor on short notice. But as it happens, Ko-Lin was arrested, thirty years ago, when he was fifteen, and he decided to jump bail instead of coming to court to face the music. Who is this guy?"

"I'll tell you tomorrow," I said. "You mean he was released at the arraignment?"

"Yeah, he was bailed out. I'll have the court papers pulled and let you know in an hour or two by whom and for how much. Suffice it to say that he jumped bail two weeks after the arrest."

"So it's still an active case?"

"Wide-open," Catherine said. "There's a bench warrant for his arrest."

"Seriously? What did he do?" I asked. I signaled to Mike to open the door. I had no plans to stay on here at my cottage in the woods. "What's the underlying felony?"

"He killed a man, Alex. Murder two," she said. "Ko-Lin Kwan stabbed a man in a robbery, on Mott Street, right behind the office."

"You're my guardian angel, Cath," I said. "Keep a copy of that warrant on your desk for Lieutenant Peterson. Speak to you later."

"What's Peterson got to do with this?" Mike asked. "And where do you think you're headed?"

"You can call Peterson and have him pick George Kwan up. We'll get him remanded without bail," I said. "Catherine found a warrant for his arrest. I think the reason young Ko-Lin fled to China all those years ago is not exactly the story he told us. It's more likely connected to the fact that he killed a man when he was fifteen years old. Get him in a cell in the squad room today and I bet he'll start talking to me about anything we want to know."

I was out the door and in the front seat of Mike's car. There was still no sign of Kate Tinsley.

"Let me tell Kate," Mike said, "so she can let Prescott know we're headed back to New York."

"Tell her nothing," I said.

Mike looked toward the main building—thinking about saying something to Kate Tinsley, I knew—but got behind the wheel instead.

"Prescott's had a week to figure this shit out, and he's nowhere at all—which may be just where he wants to be. We're taking this over from him—which would have pleased Paul Battaglia beyond imagining. This is an NYPD investigation now," I said. "Fuck the feds."

# FORTY-THREE

Peterson called back before we were halfway to the city. He had sent two detectives to the Kwan town house before we left the grounds of Three Sisters. The housekeeper let them in. There were no security guards there to stop them from gaining access this time, because George Kwan had left the house.

"Now what?" I said. "Will you take me to my apartment so we can hang out for the day? Have a little privacy?"

"That's a firm 'no can do,' Coop. Too risky that someone will find out you're there—see you coming or going."

"What's the lieutenant doing about Kwan?" I said. "How about an Amber Alert?"

"You know better," Mike said. "That's a child abduction warning system."

"So? He's wanted, and he was fifteen when he committed the crime."

"Peterson turned it over to the Warrant Squad, and he's got Port Authority Police notified at each of the airports."

"They're on it, then," I said.

Mike moved to the right lane as we approached the cloverleaf intersection of two highways just south of Scarsdale.

"Don't take me back," I said. I figured he was going to exit and make the loop to head northbound again. "It's such a gorgeous afternoon."

"Kate Tinsley's head must be spinning by now."

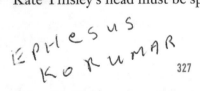

"It's only a matter of time till James Prescott calls," I said. "I love my freedom."

Mike put his turn blinker on anyway.

"Rats."

"Don't give up on me so fast, Coop."

Mike took the exit, but instead of reversing direction, he followed the large green overhead signs to the Bronx River Parkway. "How about a walk on the tracks?"

"That works for me in the daylight."

"I just want to get a sense of what the scene looks like. You game?"

"Always."

The Sunday traffic slowed us down a bit, but we passed the signs for the New York Botanical Garden and the Bronx Zoo before getting off and taking the city streets.

The residential area of the South Bronx was across the highway, leading all the way east to Long Island Sound. This part was like a vast graveyard of train cars—thousands of them—that wouldn't ever ride the rails again.

Mike drove a few blocks through deserted streets and came to a stop in front of a grand-looking building—one that looked totally out of place in this 'hood. A dozen or so people were walking in and out of it, and others were just standing beneath the entrance, which was capped by an enormous clock.

"What's wrong with this picture?" I asked. "And why are we stopping here?"

"It's the safest place around to leave a parked car, Coop. That's the station for the Dyre Avenue Shuttle I was telling you about. It's actually the old East 180th Street station, but that building was put up in the elegant old days of train travel—see the year 1912 carved into the foundation on the front?—for the NYW&B railroad that Mercer was telling you about. Got a major overhaul a few years back. It's the only part of that system that survived."

"It looks like an Italian villa," I said, "plopped down here by mistake."

There was a magnificent stone carving of a man's head, with wings that arched out over and around the giant clock.

"That would be—?" I asked.

"Mercury. The Roman god Mercury."

"Fleet-footed messenger," I said.

"God of travelers and tricksters and thieves," Mike said. "This slice of the Bronx is the perfect site for him."

"If only I could introduce him to Diana."

The clock told me that it was 2:25. We got out of the car and started to walk.

"Am I looking for anything? Anyone?"

"I'm curious," Mike said. "That's all. Two guys with drug busts right in this general area—ten years apart, but now they both show up with connections to the same case. Which seems even more significant now that we know the contraband animal parts are smuggled in as part of the drug trade. And on top of that, the rail yards back against the Bronx Zoo. I like it. I like the way it lays out for us."

"Some trainspotting, then?"

We walked away from the station and toward the acres and acres of tracks. It was clearly a maintenance area for transit departments, but nothing I could see looked like it had been maintained.

Mike was walking pretty fast. There was a chain-link fence that surrounded all the acreage of the yard. He kept pulling on sections of it, hoping to find a way to get inside. Warnings were posted everywhere—KEEP OUT; DANGER—HIGH VOLTAGE, and a few that said DON'T FEED THE CATS, but the C had been crossed out on those and graffitied over with an R.

There was no sign of life inside the fencing. No humans, but the signage made me imagine there were rats everywhere.

After seven or eight minutes, we still hadn't covered much of the territory, but Mike's banging and shaking had attracted a security guard.

"You lose something, buddy?" the guard yelled to Mike.

"Sorry. Didn't think anyone was home," Mike said, taking out his badge and showing it to the man. "NYPD."

"About what? I didn't call the precinct," the guy said, annoyed to be taken away from the sports pages of his *Daily News.*

"I know that," Mike said. "We have an old case we're working on. The DA here needs some photographs of one of the train cars—sort of from a while back. Just some interior shots to use for display."

"How long you gonna be?"

"Fifteen, twenty minutes. How's that?"

"It don't bother me. Just give a shout on your way out." The man came toward us, unlocked one of the gates to let us in, then returned to the small wooden shed from which he'd emerged.

"Will do," Mike said, calling after him.

The yard was still. Afternoon sunlight bounced off the silver surfaces of the sleeping trains as I trailed after Mike.

At one point, six or seven cars along the way, Mike dropped to the ground and spread out, full length. He stuck his head under the powerful machine, looked around, then got to his feet again and brushed off his hands.

"If you tell me what you're looking for, maybe I can help," I said.

"Nobody has to tell a real detective what to look for, Coop. You either know or you don't."

"Usually, I do."

He had picked up his pace, and I was jogging to keep up with him.

"See that car I looked under?" he asked.

I glanced back over my shoulder. "Yeah."

"Skip that model. We don't need to bother with them."

"How do I know what model it is?"

"Did you even look at it?"

"It's a subway car, Mike."

Apparently, other than the obvious exterior differences between the redbirds and the stainless steel trains that came after them, each iteration had unique features.

Fifteen cars later, tracks appeared on each side of the one we had followed in from the gate. The yard got wider and wider, with more rows of abandoned trains than I could count.

Mike dropped down again and looked under the next train. "This is what I mean."

"What?"

"This model," he said, heading for the steps to go inside it. He reached back to give me his hand for a boost up into the car. "This is what I want."

I looked around but didn't see anything worth noting.

"In the older trains, Coop, the air-conditioning units were built in under the subway car itself. It was really hard for maintenance reasons, for repairs."

"Okay."

I watched as Mike stepped up on one of the long benches along the windows of the car. Standing on his toes, he was able to grab a panel in the middle of the ceiling. He tugged at it several times, but it didn't want to budge.

Then he reached into his pocket for his Swiss Army knife and flipped open a blade, jimmying the panel open with it. The metal strip that was suspended from the ceiling—two feet long and eighteen inches wide—dropped to the floor. Dust flew out everywhere and I began to cough.

"Step back," Mike said.

"I'm okay," I said, covering my mouth with my hand. "Did you find what you're looking for?"

"In a way," he said. "This model of train is the perfect place for a dealer to keep a stash. I wasn't expecting to find a stash of heroin on my first stab. I was just hoping to see that there were train models we could identify that might be a dealer's perfect hidey-hole. A secure place to keep the drugs."

"Point taken," I said. "This kind of car is one of them, right?"

"Right. Other models have knife switches on the underbelly of the carriage, or resistor grids," Mike said. "But most of the guys I've locked up over the years prefer a location inside the train itself. They can either carry the glassines to the street or do business right inside the car—out of sight."

"That makes good sense," I said, "but they've still got to get past the guard."

He was wiping his hands on his jeans as he jumped down from the bench. "The yards cover something like thirty-forty acres, including the industrial-size maintenance shop, which has more tracks of its own," Mike said. "You figure two, maybe three guards at night, dozing in their little shacks. All a dealer needs is a wire cutter and the ability to slither through a hole in the fence."

We got off the train.

"Let's see if we can spot some gaps," he said, crossing the old tracks, stepping carefully between the ties, to get to the edge of the fencing.

Now that I knew what we were looking for, it seemed as though there was a breach in the chicken wire—some places repaired and patched over, others not—every twenty or thirty feet.

There were three kids—not more than eight or nine years old—playing around one of the old train cars not far ahead of us. When one saw us coming, he shouted to his pals and they ran to a place in the fence where the wire had been cut and bent back to create an opening low to the ground. One after the other, they crawled on their bellies till they were out on a deserted street, seemingly in the middle of nowhere, laughing at us as they made their getaway.

"Nobody would be crazy enough to leave thousands of dollars of coke or heroin out here," I said. "That's putting a lot of faith in those sleepy security guards."

"You don't know how it's done, Coop," Mike said, turning to walk back to the gate where we'd entered.

"You're right about that."

"First the dealer picks out his car—the older, the more rotted out, the less likely to ever be restored, the better. He finds the most convenient place inside to hide his wares," Mike said. "Could be in the air-conditioning pocket with the removable cover on the ceiling, could be inside the black box—if he's got an engine room. Lots of options."

"Then what?"

"Marks his turf—with some paint on the exterior, so people know who they're fooling with, or not," Mike said. "Then he sets up a security system to keep the powder safe."

"An alarm?"

"This isn't Fort Knox, Coop. No alarms," he said. "Why do you think the flamethrower on the bicycle keeps snakes?"

"Henry Dibaba? No clue."

"Snakes on a train, kid," Mike said. "Let a couple of vipers loose in your caboose, and there won't be a lot of people looking to get on board."

I shuddered at the thought of encountering a poisonous snake or constrictor in an open space, much less one coming after me down the length of a subway car.

"Guys who deal out of their homes raise pit bulls for protection. But dogs would make too much noise in an abandoned train yard."

I nodded in understanding.

"Let's get Narcotics in to do a sweep of these cars," Mike said, pulling his phone from his pocket. "Bet we'll find a whole lot of dealing goin' on out of these yards."

"I'm done for the day," I said. "No snakes for me."

"They outgrow their skins all the time. They shed them," Mike said. "I'd be happy to find some molted snakeskins and the residue of a bag of coke. Then I'd call it a day, too."

# FORTY-FOUR

It was almost four forty-five in the afternoon.

Mike and I had come back to the car an hour ago. He called Peterson and asked the lieutenant to speak directly to Commissioner Scully about getting manpower from Narcotics to sweep the train yard. There had been more than one hundred fifty arrests for drug sales—felony and misdemeanor—in the six-block radius around the East 180th Street train yards within the last year.

Everybody was moving forward now without James Prescott and the task force team.

He had left four messages on Mike's phone, but even the commissioner didn't want to split responsibility for this investigation with the US attorney.

I was in the passenger seat of Mike's car with my feet on the dashboard, watching the people come and go from the train station from time to time.

"I promised Scully I'd take you back to Three Sisters in time for dinner," Mike said.

"Push it back a bit."

Mike looked at his watch. "I'm just waiting on the Narcotics guys," he said. "Scully said all he could put together on a Sunday afternoon were two sets of partners—four guys who are familiar with this neighborhood."

"No rush."

"They should be here within the hour," Mike said. "I'd like to go through the yard with them. Hear what they think."

"I bet it's a lot dicier here when it gets dark," I said. "I wish they'd hurry up."

The character of the neighborhood was changing with the hours. The number of mothers who had emerged from the stucco train station pushing baby carriages in the early afternoon had slowed to a trickle. Older people—women and men—who came from the elevators out onto the sidewalk all seemed to get on their way more quickly.

At five twenty, two unmarked cars pulled in and parked across the street from us. Mike and I got out, crossed the street, and introduced ourselves to the four men.

"What's this about?" the senior detective asked. "I'm Skip Summers. You run into trouble today?"

"I was hoping to, to tell you the truth," Mike said. "Came up short. You guys work around here?"

"You might guess we're a little too long in the tooth to be doing undercover gigs anymore, but we run the area for the kids doing buy and busts."

"Any of you lock up a kid named Henry Dibaba earlier this year?" Mike asked.

The name wasn't familiar to them.

"What's your biggest problem in this area?" he said.

A second guy answered, obviously not happy to be pulled out on a Sunday afternoon.

"The area. That's the problem," he said. "Look around. The whole freaking area's the problem."

"Every politician in New York makes promises to clean up the South Bronx when they run for office," the senior detective said. "Then they get elected and it's still the armpit of the city. What do you want to do?"

"I'm assuming, because of the size and isolation of the rail yards—especially at night—that this is a destination point for sellers," Mike said. "Especially since the drug business was chased out of the Hunts Point Market when they gentrified that part of the Bronx."

"You could probably die of an overdose if you spent an hour sniffing your way through these tracks," Summers said. "Did you go inside the gates?"

"Yeah, the guard didn't seem to mind."

"See anything?"

The older man opened his car door and reached into the glove compartment, taking out two flashlights. His counterparts did the same, handing one of them to Mike.

"When the sun quits, you'll think you've had shades pulled over your eyes. It's one of the darkest parts of town."

"Thanks," Mike said. "We think we may be onto a big business that imports large quantities of heroin. Heroin-highway kind of operation. Afghanistan to Africa across the Indian Ocean to Asia—and then here."

"This could be your marketplace, Chapman. A lot of smack ends up right here, coming from everywhere. What was that fancy old train in France?" Summers said, sweeping his hand in front of us. "The Orient Express? Well, it's parked right here. All fourteen hundred cars of it."

"These yards are that big?" I asked.

"It goes on forever. You saw the shop, right?" Summers said. "There are twelve tracks just to hold cars that come in here for servicing to be done. For upkeep, even though it doesn't look that way."

"But those rusted old trains on the far side," I said. "They look beyond repair."

"Those are the ones on what they call storage tracks. They're not only beyond repair; they're beyond the interest of every politico in government."

"Does anyone ever take them out of storage?" I asked.

"Not a chance. The cars are picked over like they were body-part donors at the morgue."

My stomach jumped at the word "morgue." It had been less than a week since I'd stared at Paul Battaglia's corpse.

"Then there's Unionport Yard, directly adjacent to this," the detective said, pointing farther off as he talked to me. "Nineteen more tracks that occasionally hold some number 2 and number 5 trains. I mean, live ones, that get moved back out once there's a need."

"No use talking to Coop about it," Mike said. "She's allergic to subways and she doesn't do outer boroughs. She wouldn't know the 2 and 5 from the Q and N."

"I do need a translator if you're going on like this about subway numbers and rail yards," I said. I saw too many of my perps getting off at the Canal Street stop when I traveled to work that way. We were all on our way to the same courtroom, and it always made me feel too exposed.

"C'mon," Summers said. "We'll walk you through it."

He led the way to the gate, and I closed in next to Mike.

"We just came out of here," I said. "Why go back?"

"'Cause these men know the place. They can tell us where our team should focus their efforts, if I turn out to be right."

Detective Summers rattled the gate till the guard came out to open it up. We were a pack of six, walking with more purpose now, through the entrance to the vast yards.

Summers took a different route, passing the security shed to the left and cutting through the middle of the yard.

We walked past dozens of cars—tracks on each side of us that seemed to go on forever—until the maintenance shop stood in our path.

"This here is where the work gets done Monday to Friday," he said. "It's two city blocks long and half again as wide. Sort of a nine-to-five operation. In my experience, the drug dealers keep their distance from this general area, because there's too much foot traffic during the week."

Summers stood in place but made a circle, pointing at the rows of subway cars that were closest to the shop. "We've never had much action out of this area," he said, talking to his three companions. "Am I right, guys?"

They all murmured agreement with him.

We trucked on past the closed-up shop, heading farther into the yards. We were walking west, and I could see the sun starting to drop behind the city skyline. I zipped up my sweater and put my hands in the pockets of my jeans.

"Once you get another hundred yards past the shop," Summers said, "you start to hit no-man's-land."

It was clear these were much older train cars—some missing pieces of their steps, many with broken windows, all graffiti covered and looking as though time and disuse had made them obsolete.

"Tell them about that bastard your UC got here last month," Summers said to one of the others.

The war stories fed into Mike's theory. Each of the men talked as we walked, threading the tracks between cars, going toward the fences to examine places where access had been easily gained.

The undercover officers seemed to have encountered everything. Hookers who fronted for dealers, dealers who used adolescents as runners so they wouldn't do jail time if caught with the drugs, and addicts willing to pay the price to come to this desolate strip of the city to find twenty or thirty dollars' worth of what they needed to get them through the night.

"I have a kid on my team who looks one hundred percent the part," the second cop said. "One of the best I've seen in a long time. He bought from this nineteen-year-old guy from Uganda who came to work right over there, at midnight three nights a week. Lived on that decommissioned R-142 till we busted him."

"R-142?" I asked.

"Old version of some current subway cars that run on the number 5 line," he said. "Made in Japan. There's apparently no way to convert them to be functional anymore, so they're just replaced with new machines."

"This Ugandan knew he had a train that wasn't going to be touched," I said. "Is that the idea? He just made himself right at home."

"Yeah. You could consider half of this rail yard like a housing project for junkies, long as they don't come out in daylight," the cop said. "He had a sixteen-year-old girlfriend who carried the heroin in a baggie, inside her vagina."

"Your guys couldn't do a cavity search," I said, "unless they had a female officer with them."

"So she usually just dumped the shit on the street. The pair of them got away with it for weeks, 'cause our undercover was making the buys on the street, outside the fencing. By the time we closed in for the search and bust, the dope was gone."

Summers took over. "That's when we figured we had to identify and get into the right subway car. Once we found it, turns out the perp was keeping half a kilo in the control panel of the R-142, locked up tight with three padlocks. He'd hollowed the panel out and stashed his mother lode in there."

"But no snakes?" I said with a nervous laugh.

"No snakes. Just a couple of tarantulas, to keep curious folks from dipping in, if they could break the locks."

Lucky I didn't crave heroin. Snakes and spiders were two of my least favorite living creatures.

"We get the yard workers to patch up these holes as soon as

they can," the second cop said, standing next to a gap in the fence, "but the bad guys make them as fast as we get them repaired."

We were about as far away from the entrance to the yard as we could have been. It must have been close to a mile in distance.

The light was gone now, and shadows on the stainless steel train cars played tricks on my eyes. There weren't many street-lights around, but the few that turned on bounced shapes off the glass windows and silver sides of the sad old trains.

Detective Summers turned on his flashlight. Mike and the other guys followed suit. I didn't have a light, so I stayed close to Mike.

"You want a list?" Summers asked.

Mike took out his phone and opened his Word app.

"On the northern perimeter, your most likely prospects are the rows of cars on the second, third, and fourth row of tracks," Summers said. "There are dealers who squat in them, mostly at night, and all of them have weapons."

"What do you do to get them out?" I asked.

"Bronx Narcotics comes in with a SWAT team every couple of weeks, when they have manpower, but the dealers just pick an-other roost," Summers said. "They're a very transient population, as you know."

"When you have no residences in the area," the second cop added, "there aren't many neighbors to complain about a drug problem. This stuff gets pushed to the fringes of a community, and as long as the mopes stay away from the train station itself, nobody rings up the useless mayor to complain to him."

Summers was talking to Mike, listing the specifics of the trou-ble zones on three of the four corners of the train yard. If Scully agreed, he could bring uniformed men in during the day tomor-row to search the abandoned trains. The effort wouldn't be wasted, whether or not it connected to Paul Battaglia's death. It was bound to turn up a boatload of heroin and cocaine.

We doubled back toward the entrance, taking a different route. It was darker on this side of the yards, and spookier now that we were navigating entirely by flashlight.

"What's all that forest-looking stuff on the other side of the fence?" Mike asked.

He was pointing at the western perimeter of the rail yards.

"Back door of the Bronx Zoo," Summers said.

I reached for Mike's hand and aimed his flashlight that way.

"This abuts the park directly?" I asked.

"Yes, ma'am."

"Are there animals right over there?"

"No," Summers said. "No animals. It's a remote corner of the zoo—a few acres that have never been developed. Beyond the monorail, if you know where I mean."

"Yeah," Mike said. "I know exactly."

"Whenever they do fix it up," Summers said, "I hope they put the most ferocious cats they've got over here. Or make it like Jurassic Park, with raptors that can smell drug dealers. Something to scare these scumbags to another part of town."

We waved good night to the security guard who followed after us to lock up.

"Did we give you what you need to get started?" Summers asked.

"You did," Mike said. "I was hoping we'd run into a transaction."

"Come back at midnight. The whole place springs to life."

"I may just do that," Mike said. Then, talking to me, "Take you home and spin back with Jimmy North."

I shrugged. It didn't seem worth the trip.

"Mind if I keep your flashlight?" Mike asked Summers. "I'll owe you a few rounds of drinks for dragging you out."

"Glad to help," Summers said. "Going back to your car? We're parked over that way."

"I just want to walk that border along the zoo property. See where it goes."

"No problem. Safest place to be. The thought of bumping up against JungleWorld keeps the addicts away from that side of the fence."

"Thanks again," Mike said.

"In that case, Alex, why don't you take one of the high beams, too," Summers said. "It's helpful for walking in the wild up here."

"Good idea," I said.

The four men started back toward the train station, while Mike and I followed the fence as far to the west as it went, before it curved off.

The Bronx River Parkway—elevated at this point—was overhead. Traffic was whizzing by, and it was refreshing to hear the road noise after the silence of the train yard.

We walked on for fifty yards, and then fifty more.

It was all park and woodland, to be sure—remnants of what had been described a century ago as the wilderness that made Bronx County such an inviting place to create the city's wildlife zoo.

I shined my light through the mesh fencing but could see only trees and dense growth around and below it.

"Don't go so fast," I said to Mike.

"Catch up, then."

I ran to close the distance between us.

Mike was stopped at a break in the wire, too small for anyone to pass through. He pushed against it with both hands, but it didn't give.

"Is that a problem?" I asked.

"Probably not. Probably just corrosion that caused it."

He kept going, farther and farther away from the parkway underpass.

"Look, Mike, if it's the zoo you want to see, it opens at ten tomorrow."

"Almost done, Coop."

Ten feet forward and he found another hole, still too small for a human passage. I followed behind Mike and reached out my hand to touch the sharp edges of the damaged fence. It wasn't barbed wire, but it might as well have been.

I knew he wasn't turning back until he reached the far end of the zoo border.

I paused, lifted my light, and saw the outline of the monorail away in the distance. It felt good to have a familiar visual anchor on this walk.

"See this?" Mike said, and I jogged to get to his side.

"What?"

"This isn't an accident, Coop, like some of the other spots," he said, untwisting a thin metal strip that had been fastened—like a tie—to the top of a section of the wire mesh. "Someone's created an entrance here."

Mike knelt down and untied a similar strip at the bottom of the same piece of fence, and when he stood up and pushed against it, the section swung open like a small gate.

"Throw some more light on me," he said, standing just inside the opening.

We both aimed our beams inside the wooded area. There was about ten feet of low brush directly ahead, and then a mass of old growth and fallen trees.

"Higher," he said.

I directed my beam over the tall pile.

"Trees, Mike. That's all I can see up ahead. More trees."

"Be careful, Coop," he said, stepping in. "It's muddy."

"It's so close to the Bronx River," I said. "Like wetlands. No wonder they can't keep animals here, on this side of the park."

"Watch your step."

I got a few feet in, but it was like walking in quicksand. My sneakers sank in an inch or two, and I had to pull up hard to move forward.

"Forget it," I said. "You and the guys can come back in here tomorrow."

Mike had stopped at the edge of the dense mound and began to circle it. I lost sight of him when he rounded the enormous log to my right.

"The beam, kid. I need your beam."

"It's disgusting in here," I said. "I'm covered in mud up to my knees. You really want to do this now?"

"Five minutes. Just give me five minutes," he said.

Mike was shouting to me and it seemed as though he was getting farther away.

I looked over my shoulder at the opening in the fence and thought about turning back, but Mike called to me again.

"Eureka, babe," he said. "I think I've found the Holy Grail."

I sidestepped the muddiest section of the path and walked around on a bed of twigs and dead leaves, making a loud cracking noise as I plowed forward.

"Are you serious?" I called out to him.

"Better than Tut's tomb, Coop. Hurry up."

When Mike came into view, I saw that he was on one knee, dragging a handful of branches out of the way.

I stood behind him and leaned in, over his shoulder, shining my flashlight into the brush.

"Oh my God," I said, struggling to understand what I was actually looking at—all these gleaming white objects, almost glowing from within—a thick mound beneath all the brown branches. "They're tusks, aren't they? They're elephant tusks, hidden under this load of debris."

"A tangled mass of dead trees and fallen branches, hiding a stockpile of ivory—a king's ransom in blood ivory, Coop. Ready to be sold on the black market," Mike said, getting to his feet. "Ivory is the lure that can kill, kid. It makes for the perfect deadfall."

# FORTY-FIVE

"Let's go back to the car," I said. I had started to shiver—either from the idea of the magnitude of the enterprise we'd uncovered or from the night chill. "Call Peterson from there."

Mike was taking snapshots of the poached-ivory pile with his cell.

"Yeah," he said. "Let me get Mercer on it."

He speed-dialed the number and Mercer picked up right away.

"Hey. It's me," he said, turning to take my arm and walk me out of this suddenly terrifying Bronx wilderness so I didn't sink farther into the mud. "Call Peterson. Tell Vickee to get Scully on this as soon as possible. We found the perfect intersection—kind of what that Liebman guy was telling us about."

Mercer answered him but I couldn't hear that part of the conversation. I was being careful not to lose my footing on the wet ground.

"Say you're importing heroin in kilos," Mike said, "and you're bringing in illegal ivory, too. This place is the geographical center of the universe for those trades, man. Drugs in the rail yard, and ivory in the brush at a remote corner of the zoo, directly adjacent to the drug stashes. Even if someone tripped over it here, you'd think it was a hundred years of dead elephants."

Mike waited while Mercer spoke.

"Thanks. Call you from the car in five," he said, hitting the End Call button and slipping the phone in his pocket. He removed the flashlight from his pocket and we continued our way around the mound.

"You think this is Kwan?" I said.

"I do, but more important than that, it's what we've got to prove somehow," Mike said. "Let Scully claim this discovery for the department, and Prescott won't even be able to own a place on the podium."

Mike was pumped by his find, justifiably pleased by his persistence in following his gut tonight.

"Good work," I said. "Sorry I almost pulled you off it."

"Lighten up, babe. This is what I do best," Mike said. "Detect."

"I know that."

"Sherlock deduced," he said. "I detect."

"You got it from your dad," I said. "It's in your DNA."

"Meanwhile, Mercer claimed there's an APB for my arrest," Mike said, bumping his body against mine. He was almost giddy about unearthing this illegal—this hugely valuable—stockpile. "The whole NYPD is looking for some loopy cop who kidnapped a muddy blonde."

"Don't turn yourself in yet," I said, laughing with him.

"No chance."

We rounded the tall mound of trees and logs, and I heard a rustling sound on the dark path ahead of us. I stood still.

"What is it?" Mike asked. "Let's go."

"Someone's in here with us," I said, lifting my flashlight up higher.

Mike laughed again. "A loose bison, Coop? A hippo in a hurry? I'm so psyched I could take them with my bare hands."

"No moving," a man's voice said. Whoever spoke was just a few feet away from us.

Mike stepped in front of me. In the same moment, he dropped his flashlight to the ground—maybe hoping to be lost in the dark to whoever was confronting us. He reached under his jacket for his gun.

I lowered my light but didn't shut it off. I was shaking now, not just shivering, and everything seemed to be happening at once—at warp speed.

"No moving, I said," the voice repeated.

From within the shadows, I could see a figure on the path.

"Don't touch that gun, policeman," he said, with a lilting accent that was part Nigerian and part New York City street talk.

The black-skinned young man had a rifle pointed at us, and the size of it made Mike's handgun look like a toy.

"You, son," Mike said, stretching out his left arm in front of him, "you put that gun down."

"No light," he said to me. "No light, no moving."

He was shifting from one foot to the other. He looked as nervous as I felt.

I turned the beam off and lowered the flashlight to my side.

"Drop it," he said. "Drop the light."

I let it fall beside my foot.

"I know who you are, son," Mike said, playing a dangerous game of chicken with his adversary. "Your name is Henry Dibaba."

The kid seemed startled by Mike's naming him. The tip of his rifle instantly dipped toward the ground, but he raised it again.

I was startled by the connection Mike made, too—only now remembering that he had seen Dibaba on police surveillance video hours after the kid had been fleeing from our burning car. Later Mike had been given close-ups of the suspected arsonist's face in a mug shot.

"You can't shoot a cop, son," Mike said, as calmly as though he was talking to a friend. "Put that rifle down before you make a bad mistake."

"You the one making a mistake," Dibaba said. "You here. Here is the mistake."

"You have no idea why we're here, Henry, so you need to just step aside and let us out. No gunshots, no mistakes," Mike said. "Everybody goes home happy."

Dibaba lifted the rifle to his narrow shoulder. There was a scope attached to it that I could see. I also assumed there was a suppressor, to silence the terrible noise that shots would make.

"Back up," Dibaba said. "Two of you back away from here."

Then he squeezed his lips together and whistled. He whistled three times, long and loud.

Mike stepped backward, onto my toes. When he released them, I shuffled my feet to move backward too.

"You're already in trouble, Henry," Mike said. "What are you whistling for? You want help? You think someone's going to come help you?"

I didn't want Mike to keep talking. He was making the kid more jittery each time he spoke.

"No trouble," Dibaba said. "Not my trouble."

"You set my car on fire on Thursday night," Mike said. "You tried to kill me. It's all your trouble."

Dibaba held his head up and stared at Mike.

"Oh, yeah, Henry. My car, on East Sixty-Fourth Street," Mike said. "We got you on camera."

"No way," Dibaba said, a short, clipped phrase that was totally New York City.

Mike pointed over his head and Dibaba looked up. "There are cameras on streetlamps all over the city, Henry," Mike said. "You dumped the bicycle on Sixty-Fifth Street and we could see you running."

"Running where?"

Dibaba was distracted from his own rifle by Mike's words. He lowered it to his side.

"Into the zoo, Henry. The Central Park Zoo, right on Fifth Avenue."

"But how—?"

"Where you feed the animals," Mike said. "There are cameras everywhere. Even here, right outside the fence."

Dibaba whistled again, three more times. Then he turned his head to look over his shoulder, as though he expected someone to respond to his calls.

Mike was getting to the kid. He was beginning to understand that Mike was not just a stranger who had stumbled onto the stash of ivory.

"So far, Henry, you don't have a problem with me," Mike said, "or I would have been on your ass before you had a chance to point your gun."

Mike listed his parents' names and their Nigerian origins and his ex-girlfriend's name and the charge for which Henry had been arrested, right outside the rail yard.

The young man was skittish.

"Just let the two of us walk out that gate, Henry, and then I'll come back and talk to you—man-to-man. Let you know how you can make this right."

Henry's eyes darted from the large hoard of ivory tusks, aware that we had seen the treasure he must have been sent to guard, to the open gate behind his back.

"I'm going to pass through, Henry," Mike said, taking a step forward, "and you're going to let us walk out. Is that okay?"

"I heard you talk. I heard you on the phone."

I was hoping Mike didn't tell him the cavalry was coming. I was hoping that Mike didn't lay on the stuff about cops arriving to reinforce us, because I thought it would have Henry jumping out of his skin, thinking that we had already called for other police backup.

"Forget it, Henry," Mike said. "That had nothing to do with you."

The young man took a few steps closer to Mike.

I heard noise outside the gate, twenty feet or so behind where Henry Dibaba was standing. He heard it too.

A male voice called out to him in an African dialect. I guessed the cavalry was on location after all—just not our troops. The fear was paralyzing.

Dibaba turned his head again, and Mike turned his to me. "Pick up your light, Coop. Get ready to bolt."

"No talk," Dibaba said to us.

"Who you got there, Henry?" Mike said.

"Men. My men, to help me."

Men—I didn't know how many, and at least one of them was armed with a rifle—stood between us and a path back to the street.

Dibaba let one hand off his rifle, rotating his body to wave his backup in through the gate. He was speaking to him—or them—in the same dialect.

I stooped to grab my flashlight but didn't turn it on.

Mike had the three seconds he needed, too. He lunged forward, tackling the skinny kid around the hips and throwing him to the ground.

The rifle fell free—like a football jogged loose in a fumble.

Mike picked it up and stood, yelling at me to run away. I stood still, unwilling and unable to move, watching as he stomped on Dibaba's chest with his left foot, stunning the kid.

Someone outside the gate fired the first shot. It was aimed in our direction, so I turned away and headed deeper into the woods.

"Go, Coop," Mike yelled, and then I heard him discharge the rifle.

There were shouts in another language, but no screams, so I doubted he had fired at them.

I paused to look for him. He was standing over Henry, who was rolling on the ground and holding his stomach with both hands.

"This'll only hurt for a minute, kid," Mike said, cracking Henry over the head with the butt of the rifle.

Dibaba's arms fell to his sides and a rivulet of blood trickled down the side of his face.

Mike fired the rifle again—in the direction of the gate through which we had entered—but high enough not to hit anyone.

Then he ran toward me and pushed me in the small of my back.

"Make tracks, Coop. I don't know who's there with him," Mike said, "but it's time for us to make tracks."

# FORTY-SIX

"Where are we?" I asked.

We had run more than the length of a football field, bobbing and weaving around tree stumps and branches, onto higher and firmer ground than the wetlands near the entrance. It was rough going because of the uneven terrain. Twigs scratched my face and hands as I tried to swat them aside to run.

Mike hadn't let me turn on the flashlight in case any of the young men followed. He had cut an irregular path through the Bronx forest in hopes that they wouldn't be able to find us.

It was the first time we had stopped to catch our breaths.

"I can see the monorail tracks ahead. That's Wild Asia," Mike said.

"Great," I said, bending over with my hands on my knees. "I have a choice between a kid with a hunting rifle and scope—"

"I've got that gun now, Coop."

"Or a Siberian tiger," I said. "Did you kill Henry?"

"Two Tylenol and he can call a doc in the morning," Mike said, putting his forefinger to his lips to quiet me. "He's not our problem."

We listened for voices or obvious noise coming from behind us, but there was none.

"That way," Mike said in a whisper, directing me to keep going in the direction of the monorail tracks. "Get a little closer to one of the exhibits, and then I'll call 911. It will be easier for the park security to find us that way."

"Call *now*," I urged frantically.

"Park security guards aren't armed. I can't bring them into this before real cops can get here and find our position."

Of course Mike would have thought of that. There was no animal keeper or feeder who could take on the small army of drug dealers and smugglers.

He leaned his back against a thick tree and checked the rifle to see if it was loaded and how much ammunition he had. Then he reached under his jacket, into his shoulder holster, and handed me his service revolver—a powerful Glock 17.

"No, Mike," I said, recoiling at the thought of taking his weapon.

I hated guns. I hated what they did when they got in the hands of people who shouldn't ever have them. I hated how they took human lives. I hated that people used them to kill living things for sport.

He grabbed the waistband of my jeans and stuck the barrel of the gun down the front of my pants.

"You've been taught how to use it," he said, holding my face between his hands. "Remember the safety, and just hang on to it if we get separated before help comes."

I exhaled again.

Then Mike tapped my shoulder and told me to run with him. I put the flashlight—still unlit—in my left hand and kept a grip on the handle of the gun.

We were running as fast as we could go. I knew that to our right, beyond all the wooded area, was taller, thicker fencing that surrounded the entire zoological park. The Bronx River cut through the zoo—we had crossed over it on the monorail ride—so that body of water separated us from the main entrance and the office buildings, including the mini–police station house, which was not likely to have anyone on duty when the zoo was closed.

Any second now, I expected to encounter a raging beast, un-happy about the trespassers in its habitat. There weren't supposed to be any in this area, but if criminals could break in, why couldn't fierce animals break out?

When we reached the first clearing, Mike took out his phone, leaned the rifle against a dense bush, and dialed 911.

"Mike Chapman," he said, giving the operator his shield num-ber and command, but staying as calm as a pilot in heavy turbu-lence. "Ten-thirteen."

He was giving the NYPD code for "officer needs assistance."

"The zoo. Wild Asia. Somewhere on the eastern side, not far from the Bronx River Parkway."

I was looking through the forested area for signs of anyone approaching. I was chilled and nervous and as jumpy as Henry Dibaba had been.

"I didn't say 'who.' I said 'zoo.' The fucking Bronx Zoo," Mike said to the operator. "Get a car here. Police, not park security. Situation involves gunshots."

He was exasperated, and that heightened my own paranoia.

"No, lady. I didn't code 'animal down,'" Mike said, losing his patience. "The animals are fine. Shots fired. At people. We need cops stat, lady, before somebody's dead."

She was telling Mike to stay calm and remain on the phone with her.

"I can't hold on. I'm almost out of juice and I need two hands to shoot, lady. Got it?"

He ended the call and motioned to me to keep moving.

We were finally in low grass. We were clear of the thick growth and I could run faster, not as worried about tripping over branches and rocks.

I was streaking across the open space. There were some lights up ahead—probably in one of the feeding pens—and I was running toward them.

"I think I see animals, Mike," I said. "Antlers—maybe deer or gazelle."

"Just go," he said.

I knew those creatures I had seen were unlikely to harm me, and I knew they had to be separated from me by moats or twenty-foot-high glass enclosures or even electrified fences—just as they were kept apart from the Asian rhinos and the dangerous cats.

Mike had almost caught up with me. I was panting and sweating as I pulled in under the monorail tracks, resting at the edge of the lighted enclosure.

"Not there," Mike yelled at me. "Get out of the light."

But it was too late for that warning. I had made myself a target.

I heard a rifle shot explode and then a bullet crash into the concrete base of the monorail track that was just inches above my head.

# FORTY-SEVEN

Mike had returned fire in the direction the shots came from and then pulled me under the shading of the elevated tracks.

We were crouching side by side behind a concrete tower, and Mike was rubbing my back with one hand.

"We just need to buy three or four minutes, Coop. That's all the time it will take for a radio car to get here," Mike said. "These kids will run at the sound of sirens."

"Here? We just sit here in the open, because I was stupid enough to stand in the light and let them see me?"

"I want to move," Mike said. "I'm thinking it out."

"How?" I asked. "How do we move? How many of them are there?"

"Two. Maybe three," he said. "Henry's down for the count, the way I clocked him on the head. I think there's only one gun between them. Only one round of shots fired each time."

"All it takes is a single bullet," I said. I was thinking of the way Paul Battaglia had pitched forward into my arms, his brains spurting everywhere.

"You okay without your jacket?" Mike asked.

I nodded. "I'm not shivering because I'm cold."

"Take it off."

I did.

"At the count of three, I'm going to heave your jacket that way," Mike said, pointing away from us, toward the next concrete stanchion to our right. "On three, you run as fast as you can to the left, at least two towers over."

"And you?"

"Right with you," he said. "I'm just drawing fire first."

It was too still. There was no sound of police activity. I couldn't tell if the distant noise was hoofbeats or footsteps, but there were creatures on the move.

On three, Mike pushed himself to his feet and threw my jacket with an overhand pitch worthy of a stadium opening day.

I started to run and heard two gunshots, from the edge of the woods, which were volleyed in the direction opposite my destination. Behind me, following the flight path of my jacket. Mike had been right.

He overtook me and grabbed my hand, urging me to keep up with him.

We stayed under the tracks for another fifty yards, then veered off again. We zigged and zagged behind signposts that marked exhibits—which meant we were getting closer to the zoo facilities—and then past a large white board, posted with the words DO NOT ENTER.

"Here, Coop," Mike said, "Over here."

I pulled my hand back. "That way must take us to a path." I said. "That way."

"That way puts you out in the open. Don't do it."

Now we were in the brush again. Our pursuers were not. Their voices carried—it sounded like two of them—as they talked excitedly in their unfamiliar dialect.

It wasn't the place to argue. I motioned to Mike to go ahead and I followed him as closely as I could.

There was an actual trail beneath the low undergrowth. The walking was easier than I expected and we moved fast. Faster and faster.

As Mike turned a corner around a stand of trees, a small shelter—like an open-air garage—came into sight.

"What—?" I said.

There were four steel gondolas, like small versions of the ones used on ski slopes—bottoms shaped like buckets, the upper sides enclosed with mesh gratings, and rooftops also made of steel.

Mike pulled on the door of the first one and opened it. "Get in."

"It's not the monorail," I said. "No."

"Don't argue. Get in," he grabbed my arm and pulled me toward the sleeping machine.

"How do you—?"

"Skyfari, Coop. The most popular old ride at the zoo," Mike said. "A great place to score with broads when I was at Fordham."

He was trying to make light of a treacherous situation, and I was approaching the end of my emotional rope.

"Where are they?" I whispered.

"You'll know when the next bullet whizzes by," Mike said. "Get in."

"Where will it take us?"

"Up and over the river, and back to civilization," he said, holding on as I stepped into the bucket. "Just stay down, kid. Low. They can't get to you up there."

"Mike, no!" I said, as he shut the door and closed me into the caged tram. "Get in."

"I have to crank it up, babe. Turn on the switch," he said. "Then I'll jump in."

I unlatched the door and swung it open for him.

He disappeared for a few seconds, somewhere inside the structure that was the base of the two sets of trams. They didn't run on tracks like the monorail. Each car was suspended from steel ropes that rose from the base, and lurched them across the treetops and river, over the heart of the zoo. I had hated this ride as a kid—the rocking cable car, the halting motion as it was propelled forward, the fear that I would fall to the earth from a broken machine into a pit of deadly beasts.

Mike had been playing with switches and gears. I heard metal boxes banging. I was sure our adversaries heard him, too.

All of a sudden there was a great noise, as though the entire tram system had come to life again.

Our car was first in line on one set of steel ropes. I watched as the lead tram on the second set of ropes rocked in place, then rolled off the starting blocks and started its ascent—out of the garage, grunting and groaning as though it were alive, climbing up toward the sky.

I clapped my hand to my mouth. Mike must have gotten in that other one and left me behind.

I put my foot in the opening. My head wasn't clear enough to think. If his goal was to position himself to fire down on them, why had he left me alone in this godforsaken corner of the Bronx?

Shots rang out. I could hear them—three of them in a row—bouncing off the belly of the first old tram that had gone airborne across the way.

I wanted to scream Mike's name, but I knew that would call attention to the fact that I was still here—here alone.

I heard footsteps and voices now, but going away from me—following the route of the Skyfari tram. Our assailants must have been wondering, as I was, whether Mike didn't return fire because they had pierced the cab and shot him.

My hands were trembling so badly I couldn't steady myself to step down from the gondola.

I saw something move on the ground, coming toward me out of the shadows. I had my hand on the pistol grip.

It was Mike.

"Thank God," I said, letting go of the grip and stretching out my arm to try to reach him. "I thought you'd been shot up there."

"Leave you behind? Not a prayer, Coop," Mike said. "Dibaba's troops are halfway to the Himalayan Highlands by now, looking to find our bodies in that bucket and feed us to the snow leopards."

"I'm not that tasty," I said. "Our turn to ride?"

"I'm going to pull the switch to launch this tram right now," he said. "Get down on the floor. Keep that blond hair out of sight."

Mike turned to run back inside to the control panels.

I sat on the floor of the bucket and waited for him to return. He fired up the tram and the car shook beneath me, ready to take off. By the time I had scrambled to my knees, Mike was on the outside of the door, slamming it shut. He put his hand to his lips and blew me a kiss as the old cab tilted forward and rolled back, and then heaved off away from him.

I put my fingers through the holes in the mesh to pull myself up and ask what he had done.

"Stay low, Coop. I'll be there, I promise."

I ducked down, but I was feeling sick to my stomach, kneeling on the bottom of the gondola. I took Mike's gun from my waistband and placed it on the floor beside me.

The bucket rocked back and forth as it cleared the roof of its garage and rolled over the connecting joints on the first tower. It was taking me higher and higher, out into the open air with no way for me to see what was happening on the ground, swinging over the Bronx wilderness, as animals seemed to be roaring at me from below.

I heard another loud metallic noise coming from the tram base. I picked my head up, just to the rim of the wire enclosure, and looked back. Mike had launched a third tram on the adjacent track. He must have been in it.

He had set the Skyfari in motion, like a battalion of aged tanks heading off into battle.

I heard the voices from below me, two people yelling at each other, before I heard the rifle discharge. Then instantly, there was the terrible noise made by two bullets that struck my bucket and sent it rocking forward into the darkness of the night sky.

# FORTY-EIGHT

"Light, Coop!" Mike shouted. "Shine the light on the ground."

I could tell from his voice that he was in the gondola behind me, as I expected. It must have been out in the open skyway, too, creaking its way over the forest and grassy field.

I took the flashlight from my jeans pocket, switched it on, and lifted it over my head, holding the end of it with the tips of my fingers.

Mike fired at the ground—three shots in quick succession. He didn't hit his mark. No one screamed out as though injured.

I put the light down. It could only be another minute or two before we reached the Bronx River.

"Keep cool," Mike shouted to me.

The water wasn't very deep at this point in its flow from Westchester to the East River, but it was polluted and muddy—and often had a tough current, as I knew from a case at the botanical garden years earlier. Even if our pursuers could swim, it would slow them down and give us a considerable advantage, for as long as we could stay safe in our aerial cages.

The voices were below me now. I could hear two men exchanging words. They sounded agitated. I couldn't understand them, so I was agitated, too.

"The woman," one of them yelled, this time in English. "Get the woman!"

I had exposed myself by holding up the flashlight. That also made it obvious that I wasn't the one with Dibaba's gun. They must have thought I was unarmed.

"In a ball, Coop," Mike shouted. "Go fetal."

He had heard them too.

I scrunched up on the floor of the bucket. The first two shots—coming from a bit ahead of the direction in which I was moving—missed the target completely. The third one hit the roof of the gondola.

Mike must have stood and lined up his scope. He fired a shot and the men below made a lot of noise. Neither sounded injured, but he must have gotten close enough to force them on the run again.

I thought I heard a siren in the distance. I couldn't be sure whether it was on the highway outside the zoo, or inside the park property.

"Now!" a man screamed. "Shoot now."

There was the crack of a gun, way too close to me. The bucket staggered—like a drunk getting off a barstool and losing his legs beneath him. But this staggering motion came from above.

The marksman must have struck one of the steel cables holding the bucket onto the track. My car stopped abruptly and just swung back and forth in place. Now I was nauseous as well as cold, and terrifically frightened, too.

"Hold on, Coop," Mike said. "You've got three more cables holding you up, if that's what you're thinking. Just stay steady."

Before I could respond to him, he let go with three or four shots at the twosome on the ground.

I was afraid to move from my position on the floor of the bucket, afraid that by unbalancing it I would rip it free from the other cables that were holding me up, and drop to my death.

The men were laughing now, gleeful that they had crippled my carriage and had me dangling overhead. A few more well-placed shots would have me in their hands.

I sat upright, taking care not to move quickly. I needed to quell the nausea that was rising from my stomach to my throat.

"Stay still, kid. I hear sirens out there."

Mike's gondola, on the adjacent track, was just about even with mine by now. There was nothing he could do to stop it, and no way he could come to my assistance. He was about to cross over the river and leave me.

"Why can't you shoot one of them, Mike?" I said, trying to suppress my tears.

"What the hell do you think I'm trying to do?" he called out.

Now his voice was coming from the other side of my bucket. He had lapped me and was heading off into the park, going farther and farther away.

"Back at you, Coop," he said, firing off several rounds from his tram, but getting only laughter in return from the men on the ground.

I tried to swallow his words. *Back at you, Coop.* Mike had given me his Glock and now he expected me to use it.

The attackers fired twice more at the cables, and although they missed, the bucket still swung wildly.

I got on my knees, pulled on the wire mesh until I had forced an opening in one of the squares that was wide enough to hold the head of the flashlight.

I picked up the Glock and played with it for a few seconds, until it felt almost comfortable in my hands. I opened the safety.

I braced myself against the low steel wall of the bucket, brought my eyes up to the level where the mesh hit the solid metal base, turned on the flashlight, and glanced quickly at the ground beneath me.

I could make out two figures. I could see the rifle barrel sticking out in front of one of them.

I stuck the tip of the Glock through the mesh, pointed it directly downward, and fired blindly six times. Then I dropped back down onto the floor of the bucket.

One of the men started screaming immediately. It was the sound of a person in pain, not just fear.

I heard his screams for only a couple of seconds. They were drowned out by the noise of four or five sirens on the radio cars speeding into place just across the river, inside the zoo.

# FORTY-NINE

"Pick your head up, Coop," Mike said. "I'm right below you. I need to see that you're all right."

"I'm good where I am. On the floor of the bucket."

"Seasick yet?"

"Totally."

"If that's all you come out of this with, kid," Mike said, "then you're all right."

"Can't you make it stop swinging?"

"There's a mechanic on the way to guarantee safe passage."

It was about twenty minutes after I'd fired off my shots. I could hear the voices of all the cops who had responded to Mike's call, and who were gathered after several of them took the perps away. They were scouring and securing the scene as best they could in the dark.

"I hit one of the guys, didn't I?"

"You did."

"I didn't kill him, did I?"

"No, but you didn't kill any animals either. I'd call it a victory."

"What did I hit?" I asked.

"The shooter's foot. He dropped the gun and fell to the ground and was still here when we all trekked over."

"Across the river?"

"In a rubber boat, kid," Mike said. "I dinghied back to get you. I bet nobody's ever done that for you before."

Every time the wind came up, my bucket would swing uncontrollably.

"How far off the ground am I?" I asked. Mike knew how I hated heights.

"Eight, maybe ten feet."

"I can't wait much longer or I'll lose it," I said.

I sat up straighter, careful not to rock the bucket.

"We can do this," I said. "I can open the door and a bunch of you guys can help me climb down."

"I know you consider yourself a ballerina, but just sit still till they get this moving by a professional."

I thought I was graceful enough to be able to extricate myself—with Mike's help—before someone with an engineering degree was roused and reported in.

I unlatched the door and peeked out over the edge, then pulled back in immediately.

"I'll never trust you again," I said, collapsing back onto the floor. "I'm forty feet up, at least."

"At least forty," he said. "But things could be worse. You're not dangling over Tiger Mountain."

It was almost an hour before the workmen showed up. The tram was physically closer to the point of departure, so they figured how to get the bucket started again, going in reverse.

"Close your eyes," Mike called out to me, as the car started to move.

"They've been closed since I was stupid enough to look out at you."

"I'll catch you when you land, Coop. Don't kick the bucket along the way."

# FIFTY

"Everything aches," I said.

Mike had opened a can of chicken noodle soup when we reached my apartment at midnight, and it had helped settle my stomach and my nerves.

Then I took a steaming hot bath and let him wrap me in a huge towel, holding me close to him, when I finally stepped out of the tub.

"Better rub something on those scratches on your face," Mike said. "You'd think the bushes had fingernails on them, the way they scratched you."

I covered my face with lotion, hoping the aloe would calm the red marks, and I dabbed some on Mike's nose too.

Mercer and Vickee were waiting for us in the living room. They had helped themselves to drinks and mixed a vodka martini for Mike—crisp and cold—when we came out to join them. I was beyond alcohol at this point.

"Blood ivory," Mercer said. "That's the reason Paul Battaglia died."

I stretched out on the sofa, taking a cashmere throw from the back of it, covering myself to stay warm.

"Was it Kwan?" I asked. "Was it George Kwan behind the whole thing?"

"Kwan was the puppet master, Alex," Mercer said. "He was the man pulling all the strings."

"And doing it for a very long time," Vickee said, "cloaked in the respectability of his grandfather's business reputation."

"You'll have to clear it up for me," I said. "Did you get him today?"

"Nine tonight," she said. "At JFK, on his way to Hong Kong."

I put my head in my hands, shaking it from side to side as I looked down.

"How long has this been going on?" I asked.

"Kwan's not talking," Mercer said. "I'll give you the pieces we've got so far."

"Doesn't matter if he keeps mum," Mike said. "We'd only get the hard-luck story from this guy. Kid on the streets. Chinatown, Ghost Shadows. Killed a man by the time he was fifteen."

"Yeah, so his grandfather takes over back in Hong Kong. Gives George the best of everything—including his own name—educates him, and sets him up in the family business," Mercer said. "Kwan Enterprises. Legitimate—the real deal."

"But this guy was always looking to break bad," Mike said. "Am I right?"

"Right. That's why he was positioning himself to grab a piece of the Savage dynasty, when it was beginning to crumble," Mercer said. "It gave him all the global reach he needed, and he could get it done on the cheap because he already had deals going in China, India, Pakistan, and even in Africa."

"What kind of deals?" I asked.

"The family had factories in some of the cheap labor markets," Mercer said.

"I remember that, from the Savage investigation."

"Well, George folded some drug dealing into the enterprise," Mercer went on. "They were in all the right places for their legit businesses, but he saw the chance to seize on the drug connection to make an even greater fortune."

"Nothing new under the sun," I said.

"Don't give us Shakespeare in the middle of the night, babe," Mike said, stirring his drink with his finger.

"Ecclesiastes, Detective," I said. "The Old Testament. My book."

"Meaning what, in this case?"

"Kwan Enterprises has been around so long, I bet if you trace it back six or seven generations, we find George's ancestors were involved in the opium trade, just as we suspected."

"The dirty underbelly of the evolution of global trading," Mercer said.

"Scores of families made their wealth trading opium through Hong Kong in the 1800s," I said. "The Kwans, no doubt, just like the Delanos."

"Delanos?" Mike asked.

"Yes. As in Franklin Delano Roosevelt. It's what made his grandfather rich," I said. "It probably did the same for the early Kwan tradesmen. I bet it's how they built the original export-import business."

"I'm on it," Vickee said.

"How about the animals?" I asked. "Do you have any idea how that started?"

"We don't know when," Mercer said. "But it's all about supply and demand, like Deirdre Wright and Stuart Liebman both told us. The endangered species can be sold for a fortune, as we know, and the products—like horns and bones and tusks—are worth their weight in gold."

"Or blood," I said.

"Easy for Kwan," Mike said. "Same markets, same shipments as his kilos of heroin, same porous borders in countries with corrupt politicians."

I was playing back the mental tape of tonight's encounter at the zoo. "How does he enlist a small army of workers here, like Henry Dibaba?"

"First of all," Mercer said, "he can afford to pay them. There are kids like Dibaba all over this city, looking for their first dime."

"But armed with rifles?"

"Pretty unusual. They do have an instructor, though, and they've been training at a shooting range in Brooklyn."

"Tell me it's Pedro Echevarria," Mike said, high-fiving his friend. "Did I nail that one or not?"

"Indeed you did," Mercer said. "There's a whole bunch of sharpshooters in training, and I've got a good list of their names. All taking lessons from Echevarria."

"The Grand Slam sheep hunter," I said. "The man who was supposed to go shooting with Battaglia next week."

"That dude, exactly," Mercer said, giving me a thumbs-up.

"Now, how do you suppose he got mixed up with George Kwan?"

"It all came together in the record checks, once we had Kwan's birth name, today."

"How?" I asked.

"George Kwan—birth name Ko-Lin Kwan—told you his mother was Maria Alvarez," Mercer said. "A Mexican woman George's father met in LA when he emigrated here."

"Yes. She left his father because of his gang involvement."

"When his mother returned to LA," Mercer said, "she married an old friend from Mexico, whose surname is Echevarria."

It took me a few seconds to process the connection. "So Pedro is George Kwan's half brother?" I said, leaning back against the soft sofa cushion.

"He is."

"Kwan's personal sharpshooter," I said. "A blood brother, whom he could trust with every aspect of the deadly work."

Mike was up and pacing. "We've got to get our hands on Pedro. He might have been given the order to kill Battaglia," Mike said. "He certainly has the skill."

"In custody as we speak," Vickee said. "Loose hold, but we have him."

"Why?"

"Pedro Echevarria was running Henry Dibaba and the Bronx bad boys," Mercer said. "All his contacts were on Henry's phone. In fact, Pedro and his driver were in the rail yards just after you two came face-to-face with Henry."

"How'd that happen?" Mike asked.

"Because Henry had called him."

"To tell him that we had found the stockpile of ivory," I said. "That's why it took Henry a couple of minutes to come back and confront us."

"Lucky thing you two didn't try to press on and go out through that gate," Mercer said. "I don't think Pedro would have missed you, given the chance to take a few shots. He just couldn't catch up to the kids—Henry's backup duo—when they started to chase after you inside the park."

"So he's charged with—?" Mike asked.

"Possession of the ivory," Vickee said. "A federal crime. James Prescott is thrilled to have a piece of the action, you can be sure."

"But Commissioner Scully believes Pedro Echevarria was the executioner," Mercer said, getting up to come over and sit beside me. He picked up my hand and rubbed it between his two. "We've got an early match on an iris identification; that should be confirmed by morning."

"Iris? The shooter's eye?"

"TARU enhanced the video—and the eye was the only part of the killer that *is* identifiable. Vickee told us the shooter took off his sunglasses to aim at his target," Mercer said. "I think we have Battaglia's assassin."

I bit my lip, fighting back tears for the second time tonight.

"It also fits with Echevarria running the Bronx kids," Mercer said. "He's the guy Henry Dibaba reports to, and it's Dibaba who tried to kill you by firebombing Mike's car."

I nodded.

"It also fits with Battaglia's plan to go to Montana and shoot with Echevarria in November," I said. "It would give him a couple of days to get up close and personal with the man closest to Kwan. So very like Battaglia to try to wangle a way to get the inside track on someone."

"Without knowing that someone—Pedro—was able to turn on a dime and kill the DA," Mike said, "just for getting that close to the purpose behind Kwan Enterprises."

George Kwan had woven a tangled web, and Paul Battaglia had become ensnared in it. So had Chidra Persaud. So had I.

"You're safe again, Alex," Mercer said. "You know that, don't you?"

I attempted to smile, but forcing it was the best I could do.

There was so much to try to take in. This case had monstrously long tentacles that stretched from one side of the world to the other.

"Where does Chidra Persaud fit?" I asked.

"Right where you thought," Vickee said, stepping to the bar to refill her drink. "She was in tax trouble up to her ears, in England, and about to start here. She had thoroughly researched Kwan Enterprises when they made a bid for part of her business. Persaud knew enough about endangered species—and the heroin highway— that she got Kwan's dark side at once."

"So she was using Paul Battaglia to buy insurance for her own case, by snitching on George Kwan," I said. "Chidra Persaud *is* Diana, just like she claims to be. She took us to Montana so she could conflict James Prescott out of her case."

"Game well played, for the lady," Mike said. "And once George Kwan learned she was Battaglia's snitch, then the DA was a dead man. For no good reason. For money, for wealth beyond his wildest dreams. For greed."

"No wonder Chidra flew out of the country," I said. "She must have realized that she was in grave danger too."

"According to Charles Swenson," Mercer said, "you're right about that."

"Paul called me three times while I was at the Met last Monday," I said. "The first one was most certainly in response to Lily's text telling him I'd said she shouldn't sit down with him."

"Another angle," Mike said. "He probably thought Lily—Wolf Savage's daughter—had something on George Kwan. Something bad from their business dealings."

"No doubt. And once Paul thought I'd been talking to Kwan at the Met that night, he was loaded for bear," I said. "Paul was trying to run the entire case, bring it to a boil, by himself. He thought I was out of bounds, and he was ready to punish me for it."

"He was that way, Coop. You know he was."

"Vain. I do know that," I said. "So vain, so self-centered, that he was willing to die for something as foolish as protecting his turf, holding on to a case he was hoping for dear life to build because it had been such a personal effort."

"I'll finish sipping this and we'll get out of your hair," Vickee said.

"You don't know how it helps me to have you here," I said. "It's been like living in a nightmare you can't wake up from."

"Mercer will stay with you two for a while longer," she said. "My sister's watching Logan. I need to get home."

"Understood," I said, still trying to puzzle out the details. "The whole animal thing is a mystery to me. Paul's award for conservation, but his membership in Saint Hubertus, and in Persaud's club."

"Everyone at the animal foundation is sticking to the story that many of the best conservationists are hunters," Mercer said.

"I can't buy into that," I said. "It's oxymoronic."

"Yet in the case of many of these men," Mercer said, "it seems to be the truth."

"Yeah," Mike said, "it's damn near impossible to hunt extinct animals. These guys have a real incentive to save some of them."

"What becomes of all the ivory?" I asked.

"That will be up to the feds," Vickee said. "That deserted area of the zoo seems to have been the perfect place to hide the tusks. No one ever had reason to go there, and Kwan's drug dealers were able to protect it as well, from the rail yards, since the ivory had been smuggled into the country right with the drugs."

"If anyone came across the stash—well, anyone but you two," Mercer added, "it wouldn't seem totally out of place to have old elephant tusks piled up on the grounds of the Bronx Zoo."

"Where does it go now?" I asked. "Now that Kwan and his crew can't sell it off anymore?"

"In Kenya, they gather tons of poached ivory," Vickee said, "and then they set it on fire, in a huge display in the center of town. They destroy it, to prove there should be no market for it."

"Even here in New York, two years ago, they did what's called a 'crush,'" Mercer said. "The ivory was crushed, in a public place, to send the same message as when it's burned to ashes."

I closed my eyes, but all I could see when I did was the stockpile of ivory we had discovered tonight—tons of precious tusks, representing hundreds of dead elephants, loaded onto a giant mound in the Bronx wilderness. When imaginary flames started rising from the pile, licking the dark sky, I shook my head and opened my eyes, to erase the shocking visual.

"What if I hadn't gone rogue last week?" I said, sinking back against the cushions as Mike changed places with Mercer.

"No what-ifs, Coop. This is real life, not fiction," he said. "No what-ifs, no do-overs."

"If Paul hadn't seen me at the gala, he'd still be alive," I said. "Maybe I do want a drink after all."

"One and done, Mercer," Mike said. "Let her have one."

Mercer walked toward the bar in my den. I heard the ice drop into a glass.

"He was a marked man," Vickee said. "He had a giant target painted on his forehead, once George Kwan knew Battaglia had figured out his game."

"Vickee's right," Mercer said. "It was just a question of when."

"But why on *my* time?" I said. "Why did I have to be the deadfall?"

Mercer handed me the glass filled with Dewar's—a more modest pour than I'd been hammering myself with lately.

"There's no answer to that, Coop. You know that," Mike said.

Vickee was putting on her leather jacket.

"How are you getting home?" I asked.

"The commissioner gave me a driver. Scully's with you on this, Alex," she said. "Sleep in, if you can."

"I bet he'll be doing a presser as soon as they confirm Pedro Echevarria as the shooter," I said. "That, and linking Pedro to George Kwan, the global mastermind behind the murder."

"Too much drama," Mike said, clinking his glass against mine. "It's too late for that. You've got to power down."

"Scully doesn't need Alex with him for the press conference, does he?" Mercer asked Vickee, as she leaned over to give me a hug.

"Tomorrow's your day off," Vickee said to me. "You and Mike just need to chill. This week you're safe at home. No doubt the paparazzi will have you surrounded."

"I like the sound of 'safe at home,'" I said.

"It's Tuesday the commissioner wants you with him," Vickee said, kissing Mercer good night before she went to my front door.

"The debrief," I said. "I understand. I'm ready for it this time."

The Scotch tasted really fine.

"No worries about the debrief," Vickee said. "Scully wants to do a sit-down—just you and the editorial board reps of the news-papers."

"That's not happening," I said. "He can answer all the questions himself. Mike can fill him in."

"Switch gears for a minute." Vickee's eyes flashed to Mercer and Mike before she spoke to me. "The big question the reporters all have is whether you're throwing your hat in the ring."

"My hat?" I said, laughing. "What ring would that be?"

"The commissioner's already announced you're his candidate, Coop," Mike said. "The newsmen all want to know if you plan to run in the special election to be the next Manhattan DA."

"I'll need a second drink. I feel it coming," I said, taking another slug of my first one. "You've got to back them off."

"Get ready," Vickee said. "The race is on."

"I'm barely out of the woods," I said. "Literally and figuratively. All I want is my job back."

"Sleep on it," Vickee said. "There's an opening at the top."

"Can we go to the Vineyard tomorrow, Mike? Can we get away for a week or two?"

"You bet, kid. We can do anything you want."

## ACKNOWLEDGEMENTS

The spectacular Bronx Zoo – two hundred sixty-five acres of wilderness in an outer borough of New York City, conceived of more than a century ago – was a twenty-minute ride from my childhood home. I could think of no better way to spend a sunny day than to ride with family and friends down the Bronx River Parkway to learn about all the animals. It seemed cruel, even then, to see all the magnificent creatures penned in behind bars. But I was sure at that time that I'd have no other opportunity in my life to encounter an Indian elephant or a Siberian tiger, so I was grateful to have this menagerie so close to my own backyard.

Thanks to wonderful organizations like the Wildlife Conservation Society, people worldwide have been educated about better habitats for the animals that have been taken into captivity. The Bronx Zoo – still one of the most magical places on the planet – has been redesigned, like most other humane zoological parks, and the animals seem to enjoy a much better life than they did in my youth. The WCS is dedicated to saving wildlife in wild places, using science and education to fight to preserve our most beloved species facing extinction everywhere on earth.

I owe tremendous thanks to the men and women who do this work on a daily basis, making the world a much better place – and a more beautiful one. I was introduced to the WCS by my dear friends – who do so many good things for other people – Rick and Candace Beinecke. At WCS, Win Trainor became my teacher and guide, and his thoughtful reintroduction to the zoo and all its denizens was made richer by the company of Cindy Maur and Maddie Thompson. They really *do* talk to the animals.

My reading began with William Bridges' *Gathering of Animals* – a very entertaining and unconventional history of the New York Zoological Society. *The New York Times* has published fascinating articles about every aspect of animal conservation, and I leaned on its writers for a lot of my research. I owe gratitude to John Branch for his riveting piece, 'The Ultimate Pursuit in Hunting,' Dan Levin for his column on the ingredients in traditional Chinese medicine, Karl Meyer's Op-Ed on the Opium War, and so many others who provided such intelligent background about the dangers facing wildlife all over the world. Alexandra Fisher wrote about Africa's heroin highway for *The Daily Beast*; almost every responsible newspaper and magazine has covered the tragedy of elephants slaughtered for their ivory; and a single lecture by Susan Lieberman – vice president for WCS's International Policy – brought this issue to life for me with brilliant clarity.

I owe much of my understanding of the precarious world of endangered species to my beloved friend the late Howard Gilman, on whose White Oak Conservation Center board I have been privileged to serve.

As always, I thank my heroes – the women and men of the NYPD from whom I learned everything I needed to do my job with pride and dignity, and my colleagues at the New York County District Attorney's Office, and their great leader, Cyrus Vance, who do justice every day of the year.

I'm so fortunate to be published by Dutton. Stephanie Kelly has taken over the duty of editing my work, and that is a blessing and a joy. Christine Ball is top dog now, and that's pretty cool, too. Ben Sevier helped mold Coop and Chapman before moving on, and I wish him well. I've got Emily Brock, Carrie Swetonic, John Parsley, Elina Vaysbeyn, Andrea Monagle, and a battery of great players on my team. Thanks, too, to the folks at Little, Brown UK who take me around the world.

Laura Rossi Totten is the guardian angel of my social media world, and her creativity and reach stagger me.

Esther Newberg at ICM started me off in this world of books, libraries, bookstores, and writers, and she's as good as it gets. Zoe Sandler is at Esther's side at ICM, and she's great, too.

I am so fortunate to have the family and friends I do – I will lift a glass with them and to them anytime.

To Justin Feldman, Bobbie and Bones Fairstein, and Karen Cooper – you're each with me every step of the way.

And I've got Michael Goldberg, who *is* my heart, and my most loving critic, waiting to read pages at the end of every day. Life doesn't get much better than that.